I0687411

Identity Rip-off

A. J. Hall

To the ladies of J.U.L.S.
and
Book Club Members Worldwide

Acknowledgements

To my relatives and friends, thanks for your encouragement to continue this book in spite of a series of seemingly unending desktop, laptop, and printer failures that led to numerous repairs and finally a new laptop and printer. To all of you who want to write an essay, a magazine article, or a book remember that "A journey of a thousand miles begins with one step"

v

Identity Rip-off

Chapter 1

*A*ndrea re-read the Account Summary again and again, each time telling herself that this has to be some kind of sick mistake. Yet the words seemed real enough. Her name and address were in the top right corner directly under a sixteen digit account number, 951909-88-6647958-0. Andrea's face contorted as she continued to read "Mail Payment to Beneficial Finance, P.O. Box 17574, Baltimore, Maryland 21297-1574. Account Details Since Last Statement: Closing Date 06-25-2013, Payment Due Date 07-16-2013, Standard Payment 139.03, Amount past Due 690.29, Minimum payment amount 829.32."

What the Hell??? I have never set foot in Beneficial Finance or any other finance office for that matter. I deal strictly with my credit union or bank. What kind of shit is this? She asked herself quizzically before she continued reading aloud. "Your account is now seriously overdue. We expect you to pay the amount past due immediately. We may report information about your account to credit bureaus. Late payments, missed payments, or other defaults on your account may be reflected in your credit report." Oh no, if this crap gets on my credit record I'm screwed! My plans to get a

1

promotion will be screwed. If I can't handle my own affairs how can I handle other people's financial accounts?

"What is this letter referring to? I have never had one single overdue account." She wondered. Andrea had always been meticulous with her finances. She had learned money management at a very early age. Her father who was a city manager and mother a hospital administrator taught her the importance of being diligent with money.

Her temples throbbed and she continued to read. "To ensure proper and prompt credit is applied to your account, always return the top portion of your billing statement with your payment. If your name or address appears incorrect, please let us know. We take pride in addressing our customers properly. To reach a customer service specialist, please call toll free 1-877-821-2356." That's it, I'll phone them and let them know that they have reached the wrong Andrea McNair.

Not usually easy to fluster, Andrea decided to calm down, chill out and get a grip. After all, she was a high powered executive who was used to solving financial problems on an almost daily basis. She wondered why and the hell did she let this Beneficial Finance letter get her so upset. As she glanced at the Mother of Pearl dial on her Movado watch, she noted that it was too late to phone the 1-877-821-2356 customer service number. It was already 7:15 P.M and she had a dinner date. "This date may be just what the doctor ordered to get me out of the funky mood that stupid letter has put me in." Andrea thought with a smile. "Yes this may be just what I need, a night out with the fine, fine, fine Dr. Quentin Taylor."

Andrea poured herself a glass of white zinfandel, entered the master bathroom and prepared to soak her body in the luxurious marble whirlpool bathtub. Relaxing in the whirlpool tub with its 14 jets, hand held shower head, FM radio /CD player combination and pillow cushions was a luxury that was well worth the five thousand dollar investment.

A few drops of pure Lavender Essential Oil in the Elemis Burner would definitely set this bath off Andrea thought as she lit the candle under the oriental burner. Soon the oriental burner warmed up and the smell of lavender filled the room, providing an uplifting, unwinding, and calming effect. Andrea clicked PLAY on the remote and John Legend began to croon "Ain't this what you came for...Don't you wish you came, oh Girl what you're playing for." She eased her body into the tub for a stress reliving soaking hot bath and sang along, "Come on, let me kiss that. Ooh, I know you miss that...What's wrong, let me fix that...Twist that." Resting her head on the pillow cushion and slowly sipping zinfandel, she closed her eyes and thought of Quentin as John Legend song "Tonight's the Night" continued playing in the background. The tub's 14 jets massaged her entire body like tiny hands, pushing and pulling tightness from her tense muscles, Andrea soon began to feel her stress level and her blood pressure lower. She lifted herself out of the tub and ran her hands along her curvaceous body. The exotic bath oils had soothed her skin, leaving it silky to the touch. She patted her body dry and indulged herself with a silky exotic body balm.

3

Chapter 2

Quentin arrived at Eat Street Bar a half hour early, coming directly from his office. He felt a tremendous need to relax after a grueling day in the surgery suite at the Avon Northwestern Hospital. As he sipped his Hennessey, he thought about the procedures he had performed on his last patient. Helen Harrington's body lift went exceptionally well. The Belt Lipectomy, as it is called, involved a circumferential incision around the Helen's waist and back. He had given her an Abdominoplasty Lower Body Lift along with the Belt Lipectomy. The procedure was performed in a hospital and required a planned two night stay.

Quentin had some initial reservations about performing the surgery because Mrs. Harrington was the wife of his colleague, Dr. Phillip Harrington. Operating on Helen seemed too close to home until Phillip assured him that Helen was hell bent on getting the procedure and he felt that Quentin was the only one he trusted to do it. The aging Helen had fought long and hard to lose fifty-five pounds but still felt fat because of excess skin, back rolls and loose, saggy abdomen. Since her gain and loss of weight was circumferential, her surgical procedure for correction of this problem needed to be circumferential.

4

Quentin was a member of the American Society of Plastic Surgeons and was certified by the American Board of Plastic Surgeons. "Quentin, unlike some of these so called plastic surgeons, who start out as general practitioners or worst yet ophthalmologist who take a three month crash course on cosmetic surgery, you have been specifically trained in cosmetic surgery," Harrington pointed out. "You have hospital privileges to perform any type of plastic surgery that is offered in a cosmetic surgical facility or hospital. And since Helen wants this so badly, I will not feel comfortable with anyone other than you doing it. Hell, Man, I've known you for eight years now and you have never fucked up a procedure. So what the hell is the big deal about operating on Helen's fat ass?" With Dr. Harrington's blessing, Quentin gave Helen a procedure that would make her body look fifteen years younger.

Quentin was about to order another drink when Andrea approached him. He immediately stood up, took her hand and kissed her on both cheeks. "Wow Babe, you are looking fantastic." Quentin said, still holding her hand as he stood back to admire what he hoped would be his latest conquest. Quentin eyed her up and down. Her flawless caramel skin, penetrating cocoa hued eyes, and pouty merlot colored lips were sheer perfection and every inch of her 5'9 frame was just as fine. Taking in the body hugging platinum knee length dress with the twisted bodice that showed just enough cleavage to let him know that what Andrea had was the real deal. No fake boobs there. Thank God. "Uhmm, Uhmm, Uhmmm!" Quentin laughed and turned her around three hundred and sixty degrees still holding on to her hand as in the middle of a dance floor.

Andrea went along with the program. After all, she had spent time and effort trying to get her hair, nails and make up just right. Hell yeah, she wanted to look dazzling this evening. So when Dr. Quentin Taylor, otherwise known as Dr. Q.T., lavished her with compliments in front of everyone sitting at the bar, Andrea took it all in stride.

Andrea smiled and said "Q., Honey you are as fine as always. You look marvelous. Is that Hennessey you're drinking?" "Yeah Babe, would you like me to order one for you?" No, I think I'll wait until later." "Well, our table should be ready, I went online for reservations." Quentin said. "The food here is amazing." "Did you have any problem finding your way here?" "Not really. Thanks to the On Star navigation unit in my ride, it was a breeze. And the valet parking was right on."

The head waiter escorted Andrea and Quentin to their table without delay. Quentin pulled out a chair for Andrea and after she seated herself, he took his position at the table. Their waiter came almost immediately with menus. "Good evening, how are you tonight? My name is Jon and I'll be your server. Would you like a few moments to look over the menu?" "You should try the Seafood Brodetto." He suggested as he poured glasses of ice water. "Forget the water for now and bring us a carafe of wine. "What do you want, Babe?? Red or White??" Let's have white Q., she answered. "Pinot Grigio, Sauvignon Blanc, or Chardonnay?" Q. quizzed. Being somewhat a wine connoisseur, Andrea asked Jon "Do you have Pinot Grigio-Banfi-San Angelo 2004 available?" "Indeed we do, Madam." Campiello was an upscale Italian Restaurant and Bar, well known for its impressive wine, cocktail, and martini as well as food menus.

This was Andrea's first visit to this particular restaurant. Quentin frequented the bar at least two or three times a month. He would usually order a light meal after a few rounds of Hennessy.

Dinner started out with appetizers. Quentin ordered first "Do you have the Spicy Fried Calamari with Lemon Paisley Aiole tonight?" "Indeed we do" replied the waiter. "Then, I'll have that." Quentin said. Andrea chimed in, "I'd like to try Minestrone Romagna." "Indeed, Madam. Would you like to order a Salad?" "I will have the House Salad and the Spaghetti Alla Chitarra with Shrimp." Andrea answered. "Indeed, Madam. Would you like a vegetable to go along with that? We have freshly grilled asparagus." "Sounds great, Jon. I'll have the grilled asparagus." After Andrea finished ordering, Quentin resumed his order. "I'll have the Seafood Brodetto with halibut, clams, mussels and Saffron Orzo. And make my vegetable grilled asparagus also."

Andrea picked a piece of the bread from the basket the waiter left on the table for them to snack on until the meal was served. Careful not to spoil her appetite, she tore off a tiny piece and popped it into her mouth and followed it with a sip of water. "How's the bread?" inquired Quentin. "Delicious." "By the way how did that procedure go? Did you actually do a body lift on that woman?" "It was a combination Abdominoplasty and Lipectomy, otherwise known as Belt because it was like cutting a belt around the entire waistline." Quentin replied. "Yes, it went without a hitch. The patient was surprisingly in excellent health to begin with and that was a tremendous help." "But enough about my day. What about you? Did you get that account that you were working on?" "You can bet your bottom dollar, I did." Andrea beamed. She had worked on

7

the Denico account for almost a month, doing research on the business, and putting together an impressive financial report to present to the board. It had paid off big time. "Well Babe, this calls for a celebration. I propose a toast." Quentin said as he poured a glass of wine for the both of them. "Here's to us." Quentin toasted. "Hear, Hear!" chimed Andrea, lifting her glass in a toast. Andrea sensed a slight tongue prickle as she sipped the mild peach, apple and ginger flavors of the flowery, fruity smelling wine. "A very good choice, Babe" Quentin said as the waiter approached the table with the appetizers. "The Minestrone looks yummy." He took a bite of his food and Andrea asked. "How's the calamari?" "Best damn octopus I've ever tasted."

Pretty soon, Jon was back again with the main course. "The dinner presentation here at Campiello is remarkable, Q." "It truly is, Babe. This Seafood Brodetto and saffron orzo is superb." "I hear they have a Campiello's in Miami and it's operated by the same family." Quentin added "Great, I have a conference in Miami next month, I'll check it out. Meanwhile, I'm going to check out this here fancy smancy Spa-get-tae." Quentin quipped as he refreshed each glass of wine.

As they polished off their dinner, Andrea thought about the fine specimen with whom she was dining. His close trimmed goatee and mustache made his handsome dark brown skinned face look so masculine. His dark brown eyes could hypnotize and seduce any woman Black, Yellow, White, or Puerto Rican. She hated to take her eyes off of this fine man with his L.L. Cool Jay looking lips.

"Damn", she thought "When I get this fine looking specimen alone, Whew" "Help me Lord, Don't let me get ahead of myself.

Give me patience." As she continued to stare at him through those long lashed smoldering, smoky lined eyelids of hers, Quentin locked eyes with her in a very seductive, penetrating way and thought "She's coming along, Not ready just yet, but almost ripe for picking. Give it awhile longer." Finally, he broke their seductive eye fuck, and picked up the Visa Platinum card that the waiter brought back to the table and said "Let's get out of here, Babe. The show at the jazz club starts in a half hour."

Jeff "Tain" Watts and his group were the featured performers at the Dakota Jazz Club. Quentin had taken great care to reserve a table that was in an intimate corner of the room yet provided a good view of the performers. Just as they took their seats, the announcer said "Welcome to Dakota where we present the best in live jazz seven nights a week. We play host to world class jazz singer, instrumentalist, and bands every weekend.

Just back from performing at the Copenhagen Jazz House in Denmark, tonight ladies and gentlemen, it is our pleasure to present to you Mr. Jeff Tain Watts. A working man's drummer, Tain has worked with, Micahel Brecker, Hiram Bullock, Robert Thomas, Jr., Joey Calderazzo, and both Wynton and Branford Marsalis. Performing with Tain tonight is his group featuring Ravi Coltrane tenor, David Budway on the piano, James Genus on bass, Paul Bollenback (guitar) and Gregoire Maret on harmonica."

While the group blasted out its opening number, "JC is The Man," a perky waitress took their drink request. A Hennessey for him a Courvoisier for her. "Ravi is working that saxophone. Did you know that his father is none other than John Coltrane?" "Does JC refer to John Coltrane?" "I don't know some folk say it may refer to Jesus Christ or James Carter." The Hennessey had kicked in and put Quinton into a real mellow mood. "As if he wasn't already laid back and smooth enough." Andrea thought.

The group performed their next number, "Stevie in Rio," a tribute to Stevie Wonder. Quentin listened attentively to Maret's harmonica while Andrea was enthralled by Bollenback's superbly lush guitar backing, "Stevie in Rio," "That guy's is right on the mark with that Stevie tribute" Quentin stated "Budway's very assured piano playing is certainly adding some great touches." "I am just in awe of Watts' polyrhythms." No doubt this is one of the best performances I've seen in a long time." As a sweet melody called "Kiss" that pushed softly, Coltrane's soprano soared over the beat and the melody slowly caught fire Andrea closed her eyes and swayed along with the rhythm. The group continued to conjure up a variety of tunes, some with a jazz flavor, and others with a bluesy aura. Tain's group was passionate and proficient in both.

The waitress came back as perky as ever. "Would you care for another Hennessey and Courvoisier? "No Thank you that was it for me. I don't want to take in any more calories than I've taken in already tonight." Andrea answered. Quentin gestured "no thank you" and asked for the check. It was already 1:15AM and he had to check in on Mrs. Harrington by 9AM. He wouldn't get nine hours of sleep, but he got accustomed to getting only a few hours of sleep during his residency at Chesapeake General Hospital.

When they reached Andrea's Condo, Quentin escorted her inside. "This is a very fine looking place you have here. Is it always so cozy?" "Maybe you should spend the night and find out." Andrea smiled. Quentin took her into his arms and she pressed against him, her face against his neck. Quentin's masculine Bvlgari cologne mingled with his own pherones and sent an intense, sensuous aroma to Andrea's nose that was so seductive her knees almost buckled. Sensing her weakness, Quentin tilted her face towards his and kissed her passionately. Then as quickly as he held her, Quentin stepped away from Andrea and reminded her that he had a busy morning. "Get your beauty rest, Babe. I'll get in touch with you as soon as I can." Andrea opened the door for him and blew him another kiss.

Chapter 3

LaShondra hit the Mall right after she got off of work at the Bank of Minneapolis. Her first stop was Bed, Bath and Beyond where the sheets were on sale for forty percent off. The newly purchased queen size bed, armoire, and nightstand were waiting for the finishing touches. LaShondra had not wasted any time cashing her paycheck. It was a far cry from the minimum wage she earned as a Big-Mart cashier. "Is that it, Madam? Three queen size sheet sets, three queen size comforters, two Hello Kitty twin size sheet sets, two Hello Kitty comforters, two Hell-o Kitty pillows, one Hell-o Kitty shower curtain, wastebasket, and bath ensemble. Someone sure loves Hell-o Kitty or have twin girls." "Uhh, No twins here honey. The extras are for her little girlfriend or a cousin who might stay over." The cashier rang up the rest of the merchandise. Rose Garden Bath Ensemble, wastebasket, shower curtain, shower curtain hooks, three Turkish bath towels, three bath mats, twelve hand towels, twelve wash cloths, two Egyptian cotton bath rugs, and one Hello Kitty tub mat. "That'll be eight hundred seventy eight dollars and forty-three cents after your forty percent discount." "You saved five hundred seventy five dollars and twenty-nine cents." "Is this cash or charge?" "Charge" responded

12

LaShondra. Relieved that she had stayed under the one thousand dollar credit limit, LaShondra happily swiped the Visa card made out to Andrea McNair. As soon as the last package was loaded into the shopping cart, LaShondra made a bee line out to the parking lot and loaded the bags into the rented Ford Fusion that she had picked up from Avis Car Rentals. "I could grow to like this car. It runs so smooth and I know I look good driving it," she thought.

Just six months ago Shondra, as her friends and family referred to her, and her five year old daughter KeKe were living in a six hundred and seventy square feet five hundred sixty nine dollars a month 1 bedroom apartment bedroom right off of Marion Street in St Paul, MN. Shondra was not too unhappy with the arrangement until her beau, Eric, started to complain and stopped coming around to visit her as often as she liked. Shondra noticed a gradual difference in him. At the beginning of the end, Eric would say that he was at his mother's house when he couldn't be reached at his place. If she'd phoned his mother's house and his mother said that she hadn't seen him, he'd say that his band had a gig in Columbia Heights, a nearby suburb, and when he found out about it, it was too late to ask her if she wanted to come along. Shondra didn't believe that Eric was being monogamous but whenever she would question him about other women he would always reply "Babe, stop doing this to yourself. Stop worrying about something that isn't even happening. You know that you are the only one I want. Why don't you believe me.?"

After seeing a text message on his cell from someone named Mae saying "Hey Sweetness, you were hot last night, can't wait to see you again. Phone me." And when she questioned him about

13

it, Eric denied having an affair with anyone named Mae and told Shondra that she needed to see a therapist. "If you are seeing someone else, just leave me alone and stop coming around here trying to lay up with me. I don't want to get some damn STD because of your two timing ass." Eric's large eyes tightened as he shook his head and slammed his right fist into the palm of his left hand repeatedly. "I told you that I am not seeing that woman. The only time she has seen me is when I played at a club last week." LaShondra put one hand on her hip, moved her head and neck side to side and pointed her long finger toward his face. "What fucking club, Eric" "What night did you play? Where was this club?" "Why wasn't I invited? You lying motherfucker. How in the hell did Mae end up with your phone number" When he didn't answer her question fast enough, she snatched a lamp from the table. Eric grabbed her as she tried to fling a lamp at him. Little did he know that LaShondra had been having repeated dreams about busting his brains out with the very light she was aiming at him and his quick reflexes may and saved his life and kept her from doing some serious jail time.

LaShondra had truly loved Eric and thought that they would eventually hook up together. Things however changed. She gained full custody of KeKe and her baby girl moved into her bedroom. Eric moved out of the bedroom onto the couch and then he started acting like a damn fool. Disappearing every other night, taking a shower before leaving the house and after returning, always being short on cash, checking his phone for text messages didn't add up.

Eric didn't know what had come over him lately. He had always been selfish when it came to his woman. He wanted her undivided attention. He had a great thing going on with LaShondra but he just didn't want to play second fiddle to a five year old and since she was not his child he just couldn't feel fatherly toward KeKe. Hell, he had a fourteen year old daughter named Jazmine that he was not close too. And in the four years that he's been with Shondra she had to prod him into giving his own daughter an occasional birthday or Christmas card or gift. And in spite of all her prodding, he had never attended any school plays or school functions that his own daughter, Jazmine was involved in. Hell, if he had wanted to be a father, he would have married Jazmine's mother Nakia. Instead, he left Nakia before Jazmine cut her first teeth.

Eric had a reputation for lying, but LaShondra never believed people when they told her how big a liar he really was. Shondra thought about the first time that someone had accused Eric of lying. It was a co-worker who had told her that Eric, an electrician for the city of St Paul, had parked his city van in no parking zones on many occasions and had received an excessive number of parking tickets. This tidbit of information may have seemed trite at the time, but when he almost lost his license because he had three hundred dollars' worth of unpaid tickets, he insisted that someone else must have driven his van. LaShondra had to admit his was lying because he went to work every day and no one else drove that van enough to get three hundred dollar worth of tickets.

Eric sat the lamp back on the coffee table and pulled LaShondra close to him. Something about LaShondra being that upset at the thought of him with another woman turned him on. The fire in her eye, her pulsating temples, and the flaring of her nostrils made his libido increase. Hell, Mae will just have to see him another time. He could not pass up what he damn well knew would be an emotionally and physically intense sexcapade. Make up sex with Shondra tended to be more strenuous as their anger and frustration found its outlet in rough sex. Afterwards, Shondra would end up feeling relaxed and believe that he only loved her. Eric always felt high after a bout of aggressive sex. "There was absolutely no sex as good as make-up sex." He thought. That was one reason why he didn't mind provoking Shondra more and more these days.

Chapter 4

erry massaged Michelle's scalp with his fingertips distributing the rich soapy lather of his own creation on head. Michelle was happy to have this miracle worker perform his magic after her traumatic experience at Ermalina's Hair Salon. As Terry continued, the shampoo lulled her into a semi sleep state. Michelle thought back to the day she almost ended up as bald as Mr. Clean. Ermalina had been Michelle's stylist for years. But that fateful day, Ermalina's nine year old son was struck by an auto as he rode his bike and she had to leave the shop before Michelle got there. "Tell Michelle that I had to leave and she can call back for another appointment." Ermalina said out loud to no one in particular as she rushed out the door to see about her son.

Several stylists were in the shop but the stylist that she was familiar with were all at work with customers waiting. Except for one, the new girl. Michelle reluctantly let the new stylist relax her hair. The stylist informed her that Ermalina would not return until the next day and then she would have to work her in because she was booked solid. Michelle thought about her job interview for a position on the Minnesota State Child Advisory Board and decided to let the stylist, a young gal who looked like she had just graduated

17

from the beauty school relax her hair. After all the woman who she had just finished looked okay. In fact, the style made her look ten years younger. Michelle decided to take a chance. Bad move.

The next day, as she prepared to go to her job interview, Michelle noticed several thin places in the front her hair. She had never been able to see her scalp after a perm before. After the interview, she went directly to Ermalina's salon. "What the hell did you do to my hair?" Michelle screamed as she walked into the salon and spotted the offending stylist. "Did you get your damn beautician's license from dumb school?" I am going to sue the drawers off of your no perming ass." Michelle had gone in for a simple touch up and had ended up looking like a plucked chicken.

Terry finished the shampoo by applying a deep conditioning treatment. "I don't know what you put in that conditioner Terry, but it smells divine. You should sell your products in beauty supply stores all around the country." "Honey my products are selling like hotcakes since I did that hair shows on the West Coast. And you are absolutely correct; they should be selling all around the country. They will be after I do the shows on the East Coast. The D.C., Virginia, New Jersey, and Georgia shows are coming up in three months. Why don't you come with me? Honey, you would be a terrific model. I have just the do for you baby girl." Michelle thought about it. She wanted to visit the East Coast and this would be a good reason to go. After all she had nothing holding her back. Her beau, Todd, was scheduled to be in Los Angeles for the next six months. Terry had managed to nurse her hair back to normal getting rid of those conspicuous bald spots at the front of her scalp and now her hair was looking better than ever. "Terry that sounds like the best proposal I've heard in months. If you are serious, I'm game." "Child, I am as serious as a heart attack! I can do some serious styling with that hair of yours." Terry said as he undid her styling cape, shook off the clippings, and handed a mirror to her so that she could take a look at her finished hair do.

Michelle looked in the mirror and was amazed. Terry was a miracle worker. The Sistah Curls were gorgeous. She was happy that in the six months that Terry had been caring for her hair, he had managed to reverse the effects of her damaged hair and return her hair back to its natural, healthy state. Not to mention that he has styled her hair better than Ermalina had ever styled it in the five years that she had worked on her hair. Maybe the mishap at Ermalina's salon was a blessing in disguise. Michelle picked up a few products from the product counter and paid for them. "I'm glad that you are using the shampoo, conditioner, and moisturizer between visits." Terry beamed. "I wouldn't dream of not using these fabulous products Hon. See you the next time."

Michelle left Terry's In2Hair Salon and made a bee line to her favorite nearby Chinese restaurant. She placed an order and paid the cashier. When her order it came up, she got it, and headed back to her apartment. "I should never go to a grocery store or restaurant when I am hungry because I will buy everything," Michelle thought. "Look all of at this food! It's enough to feed a small army. How could I even think about participating in a hair show if I don't keep my weight down?" Michelle sat the take out containers on the kitchen table. She had bought more than the usual order of sesame chicken. Although she had eaten a short stack of pancakes, two eggs, hash browns and four strips of turkey bacon for breakfast before she left out for her 8am hair appointment, she was suddenly ravenous.

Michelle was happy to hear the doorbell ring. She opened the door without looking through the peephole or asking who was there. Just as she expected, it was her girl Andrea. "Hey, girl! Come on in." "You are just in time." "Just in time for what?" "Just in time to help me eat this moo goo gai pan, sesame chicken, wonton soup and pork egg rolls." "Michelle, why do you have all this food?" "Did you have a lunch date?" "I had a lunch date alright. Me, myself and I." "Seriously, I don't know what has happened to me lately, Andrea. I just eat and eat and eat." It's like the more I eat the hungrier I am. Michelle said as she put plates on the table. Andrea helped by placing the glasses and silverware on the table. She worried about her friend. After all, Michelle had been her friend since high school. They were both in the same homeroom class all during high school. They both joined many of the same clubs and organizations all during high school. They both were debutantes their senior year. And they both won scholarships to the University of Minnesota, Twin Cities. Winning the scholarships had been a breeze because their competitive spirit had helped them both maintain GPAs of 4.0. In fact they were almost mirror images of each other intellectually. The only difference was Andrea received a PhD. in Business Administration and Michelle earned both a J.D., Juris Doctorate which allows her to practice in the United States and Canada as well as a J.D. / LL.M. allowing her to practice International and Comparative Law.

How did your date with Mr. Q.T. go, Andrea? Is he as good as he looks?" Girl what do you mean, is he as good as he looks?" "You know what I mean. Don't play dumb?" "Is he packing or what?" "Girlfriend, don't even go there. You know I don't do anything like that on my first date?" "Are you forgetting who you are talking to, Andrea?" "This is me! Your girl from way back when!" "Way back when what? Andrea asked as she first dipped her egg roll in the spicy mustard and then in the sweet and sour sauce. One bite and she gasped "Whew!

"Whew, it should burn your lying nostrils and you're lying sinuses out, you lying heifer! You know Dr. Q.T. hit that thang last night." Michelle paused the chopsticks filled with sesame chicken midair. "Michelle, Quentin was a perfect gentleman. He gave me a goodnight kiss and said goodnight." "What's wrong with him? Didn't you wear that new dress that you bought from Sak Fifth Avenue when we were in New York last month?" "You don't think he's one of those down-low brothers, do you?" "Yes I wore the dress and Hell to the no! He is definitely no down-low brother. The way that man kissed me and made my knees buckle he has got to love women." "Girl, why am I here letting you talk me into that juvenile kiss and tell thing?" "Because that's what we do. We kiss and tell." Michelle laughed as she cleared the table and placed the dishes into the dishwasher.

Michelle told Andrea about Terry's invitation to the hair show on the East Coast. Michelle thought that it would be the perfect opportunity to search for a location for the law office she had been planning to open. Being a child advocate attorney who worked to protect the rights of minors in divorce, child custody, neglect and abuse cases here in Minneapolis was wonderful, but Michelle had long dreamed of doing her own thing. She now planned on starting a private law firm in Georgia that would provide a full range of legal services. Her law degrees as well as a four year stint as prosecutor in St. Paul were sure to work in her favor. Andrea thought that was a wonderful idea, although she could not imagine her best friend being so far away. After listening to Michelle's enthusiastic plans for law office, Andrea temporarily forgot about mentioning the bill from Beneficial Finance.

Chapter 5

erry sat in the styling chair looking through hair design magazines just to make sure that the hair styles that had been swirling around in his head were as original as he imagined. He had not seen anything remotely resembling the three hair styles that he planned to present at the East Coast Hair shows. "Ms. Terry, why are you buying so many hair style magazines?" "You have enough magazines in this salon to open a hair style magazine stand?" Caroline asked as she carefully took the rollers out of her customer's hair one by one. Caroline had been working at Terry's In2Hair salon for four years and she could relax, cut, blow dry, color and roller set hair with the best of them. Caroline had never seen any reason to be original. She had perfected approximately nine hairstyles in beauty school. Terry kept her around because she had loyal customers who were happy with the same-o, same-o hairdo. "Caroline don't you ever get tired of doing the same hairdo time after time? Don't you ever want to try out something different?" "Here, look at this. Why don't you talk one of your customers into letting you do that to her hair?" "Terry Yarborough, you must be a damn fool. What customer do I have who wants to sit in this chair for an hour and leave out looking like Fee-Fee the pink

23

poodle?" Caroline laughed as she spun the styling chair so that her customer, who had glanced at the photo in the magazine, could get a look at her own hairstyle. "Take this hand mirror so you can get a look at the back." Caroline knew she had done a fantastic job and waited for the customer to respond. "It looks 100% better that it did when I came in here honey." "You like it?" Caroline asked "I love it! There ain't nuhthing wrong with your styling, honey. You don't need to do that poodle style hair do to get no customers"

Terry could not tolerate mediocrity or mundane routines. He had always endeavored to stand out and excel. Terry took fashion design classes in high school and learned to sew his own clothes. Wearing brightly colored clothing and wearing his long dark hair in a ponytail, his uniqueness in high school earned him the reputation of being gay. Girls wore gowns designed by Terry to the prom. In fact, he had saved enough earnings from his prom gowns to pay his way through Fashion Institute of Design. Although Terry enjoyed designing and sewing gown, his portfolio did not fare that well when he applied to attend art school. Instead of taking a fashion design course in junior college and re submitting a portfolio a year later as the art school recommended, Terry decided to go beauty school. He had come a long way since receiving his beauty school diploma. He had opened In2Hair beauty shops in three neighboring cities. He also owned and managed a beauty school and did a weekly In2Hair TV infomercial that highlighted his shops, his products, and his beauty school. His next endeavor was to franchise In2Hair.

Terry laughed and yelled out, "That's it!!! My next entries in Hair Style Monthly will be inspired by Shitzus, Poodles, and other long haired dogs. Each picture will include a hair model holding a dog that looks like her." "Terry you are a freakin fool. Talking about fixin someone's hair so she can look like a dog." Caroline said. "Yeah, what woman in her right mind wants to look like a dog?" asked the customer in the next chair. Terry looked at her and smiled. Not because of the question, but because the woman looked so much like a bulldog. Terry had to get out of there quickly before the smile turned into a full blown laugh. The bulldog looking woman looked at him like she was going to growl and start barking. "I'm going to check on the shop in St. Paul. Text me, if anything should come up." Terry said as he walked toward the coat rack in the corner of the room. Although he had a cell phone, Terry did not like receiving calls because they could be very annoying during a meeting or during a meal with a client. Terry slipped on his coat, put a Jimmy Jam hat on his head leaving his long hair exposed, and wrapped a scarf around his neck to ward off the frigid Minnesota weather. As he walked out of the door the bull dog looking woman growled "That freaking faggot's got some nerve hating on women and putting them in the same category as dogs." 'Fucking asshole" she barked.

Shop Number 2

Terry arrived at shop number 2 and was greeted by Douglas, the head cosmetologist. "What's happening man?" He asked. "It's poppin' up in here man. I haven't had a break all day." Douglas answered. "How many have you done?" "Too many, man. I haven't had time to take a break." "You are all about the business, Douglas, all about the business. but right now you need to take time out to rest up a few minutes. I told you about wearing yourself thin like you do." Sit your ass down and let me finish up this client. You don't mind if I take over from here, do you darling?" Terry asked the young brunette sitting in the stylist's chair. She smiled and shook her head indicating that it was okay for Terry to take over. "You know what would look good on you; Terry asked as he grabbed a styling smock from the hanger and put it on. "Some strawberry blond highlights would give you a fun, young sexy look." He said to the forty-something lady who now had an apprehensive look on her cute oval shaped face. "Don't worry." Terry assured her "When I finish with you, Beyonce had better keep an eye on Jay Z." Terry first created a layered look by cutting around the perimeter of her head. The woman in the chair prayed that he did not cut off too much of her hair since it took a long time for her to grow her shoulder length hair. "He's in shear heaven snipping away like there was no tomorrow," she thought.

After he finished working on the perimeter of her head, Terry started snipping away at the top of her head with what he called texturing scissors. "This will give your hair texture and allow it to be bouncy." He explained. Next he created an inverted triangle above her forehead that looked something like a long bang. Working quickly he sectioned off the hair around her face, applied color, and wrapped foil on the hair. After Terry completed the coloring and the color was left to process for about twenty five minutes, a shampoo girl rinsed and deep conditioned the patron's hair.

Terry walked over to the display cases and inventoried the beauty products. "You need to get in more of your avocado and more of your pomegranate facial masques and more of the anti-aging cream." "I see it sold out quicker than I thought it would," responded Terry. "Did you do something special to promote it?" Well, two weeks ago, we did give free facials with each hair do over $85. Most of the patrons who got the facial, bought the product while other's in the shop that saw the results bought the product also. It didn't take too long for it to all sell out." Douglas said. "I'll get a new shipment out to you by Tuesday and I'll make sure that you get enough. Also, let's do that promotion again. I'll get the other shop to do it also."

Terry noticed that his client had returned to the stylist chair and went over to inspect the results of his cut and color task. He then used the blow dryer and a paddle brush to complete the job. Just as expected the client new hairdo was marvelous.

He couldn't help feeling like he had been a hair god transforming a toadette into a princess. Just as he planned the color flowed beautifully around her face. "Wow, looks fantastic and it is soooo bouncy." "Now you got to know how to work it girlfriend. Douglas laughed. Didn't you say you were going to a club tonight? Well, when you walk in show some serious attitude honey. Douglas demonstrated by throwing his shoulder back and pushing his pelvis slightly forward creating the illusion that he was leaning back slightly. Lifting his knees high and pushing them to the ground--almost spider-like. Douglas made his stride look long and commanding. "You have to look real sultry. Do you know what I mean? "When you first walk into the club pause at the entrance and give them this look. Demonstrating how she should walk into the club, Douglas lazily scanned the room while holding his head high and

27

shoulders back. He gave the impression that he was looking for someone. "This way all the ballers, playas, and haters can get a good look at you." When you see someone who looks good noticing you, toss that hair over your shoulder girl." "Toss my hair?? She asked. "Yeah girl, toss that hair over your shoulder. It's long enough. Don't tell me you never tossed that hair." "No I haven't," she answered. "Well get over here and practice he said helping her out of her chair. Start with the walk. She walked the way she had seen him walk, gave a sultry pout and then tossed her hair with a laugh.

Everyone in the shop laughed. Someone even clapped their hands in approval. She was quite pleased with her makeover and gave both Douglas and Terry a hug. Terry asked her if she was interested in participating in the LA hair show. "Are you kidding?" She asked. "No, just give me your name and phone number, I'll save it in my I-Phone and give you a call with the specifics." "Can I schedule my next appointment with you?" she asked. "I can't take on any new clients now, girlfriend because I am stretched to the max developing my products, trying to develop my franchise, and planning to represent my shops in the LA Hair Show. But, if you are serious about being a model in my LA Show, I will certainly hook you up." Terry replied as he put his coat on and cocked his Jimmy Jam cap on his head. In the meantime, just bring your hips on back here and let Douglas take care of you."

Chapter 6

*A*ndrea was livid when she received a bill from a Best Buy store in Minneapolis totaling one thousand and eight dollars. The same card was used a day later to purchase an X-Box and game related computer software for four hundred and eighty five dollars. She went to Best Buy to discuss the bill with the store manager and urge him to file a criminal complaint. Andrea guessed that the person who was using her personal information was not a seasoned identify thief because she wasn't clever enough to put in for a change of address right after applying for the account. That way Andrea would have not received the unpaid bills or known something was amiss. "Doesn't this person realize that she is ruining my credit, and is causing me a host of problems? What the hell is her problem?" Andrea yelled out.

She wanted to question the Best Buy worker who sold the electronic equipment to the imposter. "Shouldn't the retailer ask for identification whenever a customer makes a purchase with a credit card?" She wanted to know. After meeting the store manager, showing him a copy of a bill and explaining that she was not the person who charged the electronic equipment, Andrea was led to the security office. Without bothering to make any introductions,

29

the store manager addressed one of the two security persons in the room. "This lady has a bill for an Xbox One and some games that she did not charge. Go back to the date of purchase and see if you can pull up anything on the surveillance cameras that matches an Xbox bought on that day and charged to the person whose name is on this bill. See if you can get a picture of whoever used that name."

Without waiting to be asked, Andrea sat down in an empty seat in a corner of the room. While the security person searched video files for the transaction, Andrea looked at several large screens in the room that intermittently displayed real time customer activity throughout the store. The surveillance cameras seemed to capture every activity in the store except for the restrooms and break room. Although she knew that stores had cameras installed for loss prevention, she had no idea the extent of coverage was involved. She learned by looking at the dozen of screens in the security office, there were cameras situated at the entrances and exits monitoring shoppers entering and leaving. There were views of the sales floor as well as individual aisles. Cameras monitored storage rooms, supply areas and the parking lot.

Andrea noticed one camera zooming in on two teen aged customers. They were wearing big coats and saggy pants. They took turns picking up one game after another, looking at the packaging and walking down different aisle passing several games back and forth to each other. Andrea noticed that the security person who was sitting near a control panel remotely zoomed and panned cameras on the two kids until they reached a checkout counter. Each boy paid for the games they had picked up with cash from their pockets. Andrea did not know why but she was relieved that the boys did not attempt to shoplift the games. "God knows there are enough of our young black men in the system as it is. Those two boys may go on to be doctors, lawyers, or teachers one day," she thought.

The security person who was searching digital surveillance footage for a fraudulent transacting using her name and credit information finally found what she was looking for. She turned to her and said. "I think this recorded footage will be extremely useful for investigating the credit card crime that was perpetuated against you. Take a look at this video. Do you know the person who is paying the cashier?" Andrea took a long hard look at the woman after the security person froze the picture. The woman was not her height or weight. The woman on the video appeared to weigh ten or fifteen pounds more than she and appeared to be five or six inches shorter. The woman in the video wore her hair in a short blonde bob. Andrea's dark hair was at least twenty two inches long.

The store's security supervisor made some notes on his computer and then had Andrea sign a paper for a copy of the video. He assured Andrea that he would get back to her after he sent the information through the proper channels.

Chapter 7

Andrea headed to the 26th floor lobby of the Seattle Westin Hotel. She had forty-five minutes before the start of the National Financial Forecasters Conference. She decided to put something into her stomach before going to the conference. Even though she wanted to get a good seat in the Cascade Theatre Room so that she could view and hear the keynote speaker without distractions, she knew that it was not a good idea to skip breakfast. Andrea had been 'cognizant of her weight since she was a teen. She didn't want to end up overeating later in the day simply because she missed the most important meal of the day. As she selected fresh cantaloupe, strawberries, honeydew melon and a bagel, the handsome gentleman in front of her loaded his plate with scrambled eggs, hash brown, biscuits and bacon. "Didn't you forget something?" he asked. Andrea looked at his over-stuffed plate and said "No, this is it for me. You can really pack on pounds at these conferences if you're not careful." "You don't look like you have anything to worry about in the weight department." He smiled and then joined several other men at a table in the banquet room. Andrea picked up two packs of cream cheese and walked into the banquet room.

As she entered, she looked around and was amazed at how many people were having breakfast before the conference. Wondering if she would be able to find a seat, she noticed an older looking Caucasian woman with blond hair and bangs. The woman adjusted her stylish dark frame eye glasses with one hand and signaled Andrea to join her group at their table with her other hand. Although Andrea had no problem sitting with or engaging in conversations with people she didn't know, she wasn't in the mood for small talk this morning. "Thanks, but I am meeting someone and I'll just look around until I find them." She lied.

Andrea remembered the first time she visited Seattle. Not knowing anyone who lived there, she decided to stay in a first class downtown hotel and she chose the Westin. It was her twenty-second birthday, 9/11/2003, one year after the World Trade Center was bombed. While most people were skeptical of flying that day, Andrea was determined that 9/11, this year, her birthday would be happier than it was one year before. She stayed in the very same hotel, met two white guys in their late twenties, had drinks with them at the bar, and at their suggestion went on a day trip to Canada with them. Although the men did get a bit tipsy, they remained perfect gentlemen whose only motive was to have fun partying and making a beautiful young lady's birthday memorable.

She finally spotted her old friend Nicole Davis seated a few tables toward the center of the room. She walked toward Nicole who didn't stop waving her hand until Andrea stood directly in front of her. Andrea said good morning to everyone in the group and was greeted warmly as she sat down at Nicole's table. "Nicole. When did you get in?" "I checked in around twelve am this morning. I took a later flight out here. I was hoping to hook up with you?" "I'm glad that I spotted you this morning. Are you planning on attending the conference opening program and listening to the keynote speaker this morning?" "Yeah girl, the motivational speaker is supposed to be outstanding. And God knows I need all the inspiration and encouragement I can get."

Nicole laughed. One of the many food servers arrived at the table with coffee and juice. As he filled her cup with decaf, Andrea caught a glimpse of the man who had been in the breakfast buffet line with her. He and several of his cronies were looking in her direction eyeing both Nicole and her. "I know who wants to hang out and party with us later." Nicole said as she simultaneously looked in the same direction and spotted the group of professional black males. Nicole tilted her head and gave a quick flirtatious look at the very dark skinned hunk that was checking her out with his piercing dark brown eyes. "I have a feeling that this conference is going to inspire me and give me the opportunity to do lot things that I had always wanted to do." Nicole said tongue in cheek as she returned her attention to the ladies at her table.

Andrea and Nicole finished eating and went on to the grand conference room where Andrea found third row seats. She usually made a habit of sitting up front because she felt that the movers and shakers and big wigs were in that area. As she sat down she noticed that all three of the black executives that she was eyeing during breakfast were heading toward the same row. They sat a few seats away from her separated only by a heavy set matronly looking woman.

The woman had made small talk to Andrea about the keynote speaker and the other people seated on stage. She gushed as she told Nicole that the keynote speaker was none other than her husband of twenty-five years. The woman took a few pictures of her husband and some of the other speakers. "Just a few pictures for posterity, something he can look back on in his old age and smile about." She told Nicole and handed her the digital camera so that she could get a look at her handiwork.

As Nicole looked at the photos on the LCD screen, she noticed the fine looking chocolate man smiling at her. Although he was two seats away, she could feel the vibes he was sending her way. He made eye contact with Nicole and she flashed him seductive smile. The woman took a few more photos before eyeing an empty seat closer to the stage. "I guess I'll move up front now honey, so that I can get some better shots. Even though they have professional photographers and videographers in here, Delmont just loves my pictures." Nicole watched the woman as she eased her heavyset body out of the seat she was in and walked in front of her in an effort to navigate toward the aisle. Nicole moved in her legs and feet so that she would not get her Jimmy Choos stepped on. As she looked back at the stage, a new presenter had taken the podium. Her peripheral vision could detect that Mr. Dreamy had moved closer now that there was no one sitting between them.

Soon Nicole was also listening intently to the dynamic speaker. She had forgotten about the flirtatious man who was now sitting right next to her right. Nicole thought about how she could apply this information to her own place of business. "Delmont really laid out the 411 on demand-driven forecasting and how does it differ from traditional demand forecasting." McChocolate said trying to impress Nicole whom seemed to be hanging on to every word of Delmont's speech. "It is amazing how demand forecasting can drive profitability within a company." He told his audience.

Nicole turned to directly face this chocolate man and asked "Are you a financial forecaster?" No, but I do use forecasters in my wholesale distribution business." "Wholesale distribution business? What do you distribute?" Nicole quizzed. "Let me introduce myself, my name is Linwood Cary. I am the owner and CEO of Cary Distribution, one of the largest distribution warehouses in the U.S. and dare I say that it is a Fortune 500 company. In fact, Delmont who just finished speaking is one of my employees." "Is that a fact?" Nicole stated trying to sound unimpressed because she assumed that Chocolate man used that line to amaze every woman that he wanted to seduce and she was not one to be used and tossed aside by some arrogant asshole no matter what he owned. Sensing that he had turned off this beautiful caramel colored woman, Linwood redirected his attention to the speaker onstage.

Nicole spoke to Andrea whose attention was focused on the speaker. "Isn't that your former supervisor? "She asked. "Yes" answered Andrea and that motherfucker is using one of my financial planning research reports almost word for word." His plagiarizing ass did not think you'd be here responded Nicole. "Let's meet that bastard after the conference and let him know that you do not appreciate that shit." Although Andrea and Nicole could be sophisticated, well-spoken business women, they were straight up with each other and it was often reflected in their speech.

After several speakers completed their presentations Andrea and Nicole decided leave the auditorium. "Let's walk around and check out the various venues that are part of the conference." Nicole said. "I saw that fine mahogany hunk talking to you when we were in the auditorium. "I noticed that he eased his way next to you after Delmont Wilkins wife moved to another seat. Did you two plan to meet up later tonight?" Andrea quipped. Nicole told Andrea about Linwood Cary and his wholesale distribution company. "Mr. Fortune 500 strikes me as an egotistical braggadocio." "That never stopped you before. Remember Hal Jenkins, who owned the Cadillac dealership? He never missed a chance to brag about his Cadillac business in fact, are you're still driving that Escalade that he gave you?" Andrea asked. Nicole couldn't resist laughing out loud. Hal did run his mouth off about his money and his Cadillac dealership. Why was Nicole so turned off by Linwood Cary's apparent pride in his accomplishments?

Just then she sensed someone behind her. She turned to face Linwood Cary. "You are even more beautiful when you laugh like you just did. How did you get her to laugh like that?" He asked Andrea. Not wanting to be rude, Nicole properly introduced Andrea to Linwood. "You are the gorgeous young lady that my friend, Phillip Parker, can't keep his eyes off. If he knew that we were just introduced, he would flip out." He said "You introduced me to your friend Andrea however, you have not told me your name "Linwood smiled as his dark almond shaped eyes locked on Nicole's own grey green eyes. Nicole felt compelled to answer him in a decent manner even if she did have some reservations about speaking to him. "You seem like a person who enjoys laughing. What do you think about joining me to attend a Chris Rock comedy show." "I thought those tickets were sold out. Nicole answered. "I tried to order two online last week and learned that they were out of tickets twenty-six hours after they went on sale" Andrea added. Well, I have four so if you want to go also and have no problem with my friend coming along, we all can see that crazy Chris Rock tonight. What do you say?" Nicole looked at Andrea for a response and Andrea assured her that attending Chris Rock's comedy show seemed harmless enough."

Linwood and Nicole exchanged phone numbers. She learned that they were both staying at the Westin during the conference. With that bit of business taken care of the two women excused themselves from Linwood's presence and went to the hotel's parking garage to retrieve a rented auto. They decided that they could come to Seattle without visitng Pike's Place Market. "You know we could ride to monorail to Pike Place." Nicole reminded Andrea. "I know but hauling back anything that we may decide to buy would not be fun. Anyway, parking at the market is easy and we can ask any merchant to validate our parking and get a discount rate." Traffic was not bad and since she knew her way around Seattle, Andrea had no problem reaching her destination. Once they reached Victor Steinbrueck Park, she drove just down the hill toward the Market's parking garage on Western Avenue. Andrea parked the car and they started walking down the cobblestone street towards the intersection of First and Pike. They stopped at Pike Place Fish Market and watched as the fish throwers tossed eight consecutive salmon without dropping a single one. Andrea placed an order for two large smoked salmon to be shipped by UPS to her home. The salesman took her order and assured her that they would arrive fresh on the date she had specified. They continued walking, passing street performers and tourist until they reached a descending staircase. The staircase led to the Main Arcade where they found a variety of restaurants, candy shops, and ethnic vendors. They walked around the arcade and bought a few trinkets and souvenirs and then decided to go back to the hotel.

Back in her room Nicole decided to skip lunch take a power nap and rest up before attending the Chris Rock show. After several hours she woke up, took a shower, and picked through the three outfits that she had brought with her. She wished that instead of going to the fish market and the arcade that she had spent that time buying something sexy to wear to the show tonight.

Chapter 8

Chris Rock ran onto the stage and the filled to capacity audience began to applaud wildly. Rock called out "Hey, Seattle, What's up? Yeah!" The casually dressed comedian paced back and forth the length of the stage and began telling a joke about people complaining about how bad off they are. "Everybody's bitching about how bad their people got it. Nobody's got it worse than the American Indian. Everybody needs to calm the fuck down. Indians got it the worse. You know how bad the American Indians got it. When was the last time you met two American Indians?" Linwood laughed and slapped his leg when Chris Rock delivered the punch line. "Shit I've seen a polar bear ride a tricycle, but I've never seen an American Indian family just chilling out at Red Lobsters."

Chris Rock ranted about everything including sex, race, and women's hair styles, his delivery was absolutely impeccable. Even though his show was laden with obscenity and profanity, the crowd apparently thought it was pretty good. Andrea thought his commentary on relationships was right on and she had to laugh when he stopped pacing and looked directly into the audience and said "Black women will say to a black man 'as soon as you get a little money you want a white girl.' Hell, we want a white woman before

40

we get a little money. If a black woman sees a black man with a white girl she will get mad. Yeah, I said it! I said it! The real reason black woman will get mad about interracial dating is because black women are not attracted to white men. Black women won't date ugly white men. Black men don't care. They love big fat ass white women! They will drop kick Keara Knightly to get to Rosy O Donnell." Andrea and Nicole laughed along with the rest of the audience. Chris Rock continued his routine. "Black women know Rosy O Donnell can walk into any club and get her a black man and she don't even like men!" He is so right about that Andrea thought. "If you see a black woman with an ugly or old white man that means her credit is fucked up. She'll tell you 'They was ready to repossess my car.'"

Soon he was on the subject of re-electing a Black man as President of the United States. "Is America ready for a second term black president? Is America ready for a black president? They should be. They let a retarded one serve two terms. White folk are turning out in droves for Mitt Romney because he's white. Here's a special message for white voters. In times like this, you need a white president you can trust. The best white man for the job is Barack Obama. Let's take a look at the facts, Rock quipped. For the first two thirds of his life, Barack Obama was known as Barry, which is the third whitest name on earth right after Cody and Jeff. Barack Obama supports gay marriage. Most Black men don't support straight marriage." Rock paced the stage and went on, Barack Obama has a dog. Is it a pit-bull or a Rottweiler? No, it a Portuguese water dog named Bo after one of the Dukes of Hazard." Linwood laughed as though he was about to split his side. The show went on with more quips about Obama, Romney, Clint Eastwood's empty chair routine, and other issues. Finally, the show was over. As the light came on, Nicole noticed that Linwood was wiping tears away with his monogrammed handkerchief. "Damn, baby, if you get this teary eyed during a comedy routine, I wonder how you would react at a funeral.

Linwood Cary laughed, "I can't help it. He's hysterical! I cracked up the entire two hours that fool was on stage! He is one dude who doesn't mind saying what a lot of people may be thinking. That bit about the differences between men and women was hilarious." Nicole protested "I don't know. Sometimes he takes it a bit too far. I think he went too far during President Obama's first run for presidency. He joked about why a black First Lady wouldn't know how to act. I didn't like it back then when he said he didn't think a black woman should be First Lady of the United States because a black woman could not stay in the background of a relationship. Too many people really feel like that. I still don't understand why did he had to blurt out that crap?" "What did he say?" Andrea asked. "He said A Black First Lady would be too much work for the secret service and black president to would have to get a white First Lady because she would play her position and do exactly what he tell her to do." Listening very carefully to Phillip and reading between the lines Andrea wondered if Phillip Parker would be the type of man who would get a white woman for that or any other reason." "We all know that crap he said back then about a black First Lady was not and continues not to be true. Michelle Obama, in many people opinion, is the best first lady ever. She stays out of his business and does her own thing. As first lady, Michelle O. is involved in various

42

causes that she is interested in such as supporting military families and ending childhood obesity." Nicole remarked. "Michelle Obama once told an interviewer who was fishing to find out if she influenced the President's decision-making that she tries not to tell President Barack Obama what to do because as she saw it, he had enough people in his ear." Andrea added.

"Chris Rock is known for saying the unthinkable. His comedy is brave and challenging and five years ago that was a funny thing for him to say. You can bet your bottom dollar a lot of other people thought the same thing. He just had the unmitigated gall to say it out loud before an audience. I think it's classy and downright hilarious the way he deals with subjects like popular culture, celebrities' scandals, politics, war, love relationships, and race related issues. I have to say that tonight's show was one of the slickest, most high-octane stand-up shows that I have seen." Phillip added.

What was your favorite part of tonight's show Nicole?" asked Linwood." "Oh God, the part about how you have to be careful of what you say and to whom you say to." She recalled the comedian walking back and forth holding the microphone and saying "Fat girls can say whatever they want about skinny girls. But skinny girls can't talk about fat a girl that's just mean. Short guys can say whatever they want about tall guys. But tall guys can't talk about short guys that's just mean. Poor people can say whatever they want about rich people but rich people can't talk about poor people. Even some black people have to watch what you say." It reminded her of a heavy girl receptionist in her office who got caught in a three way conversation talking about the office manager's weave. She would have been highly insulted if the office manage had called her a fat slob.

They exited the Paramount Theatre arena and walked toward the chauffeur driven limo that Phillip had provided. The chauffer opened the door for Andrea to enter first followed by Phillip. Then he walked to the other side and allowed Nicole to enter followed by her chocolate man. The Lincoln limo's wrap around seating allowed all four of them to sit together. Andrea liked the way she and Nicole ended up sitting next to each other with the men seated on opposite ends. It was good seating because one woman would not be sandwiched between the two men. Although being a tasty morsel between two luscious pieces of meat may have been a wonderful treat, she knew she could not tolerate all of that testosterone. She would save that for her dreams.

"Seems to be a gentleman," she thought. "I wonder what kind of man he really is." A few minutes after they were seated, Linwood asked Nicole if she and Andrea wanted to take a limo tour of Seattle and its surrounding area. "It's kind of late but what do you want to do Andrea?" "I am up for whatever; I don't have to be anywhere until noon." "Is that right?" Phillip said easing himself a bit closer to Andrea who seemingly showed no objections. After all, he was a good looking man and even though she was dating Quentin, she was not engaged, married, or otherwise committed. Phillip poured a drink for Andrea and Linwood poured one for Nicole. They all toasted each other. "Here's to the beginning of a beautiful friendship" "Hear, Hear" they all said as they touched wine glasses together and sipped. Andrea stared out the window dreamily as the limo cruised by Columbia Center. Phillip put his arm around her shoulder and pulled her closer toward him and the window. As she leaned, he said "That building there is Columbia Center. Can you guess how many floors are in that building?" I don't have to guess, Andrea said. I know it has seventy-six floors. It has more floors than any other building west of the Mississippi River." "Oh so you are a know-it-all huh?" "I know that much!" Andrea laughed, feeling a bit tipsy. "What else do you know, Ms. Know-It-All? Do you know that you smell wonderful? Do you always smell this good?" Phillip asked as he moved his nose close to her breast and took in a deep breath. He let his nose linger there for a few minutes when Andrea instinctively touched his head with her hand. He took this as an indication that she wanted him to go further. He began to slowly move closer his face toward her cleavage. The low cut blouse that she wore allowed him easy access to her firm breast. He first kissed them with his lips and feeling her hand rub his head, he began to lick the exposed part of one of the twin mounds with his tongue while cupping the other in his hand. When Andrea rubbed on his head harder, he could not stop himself from pulling her both of titties out and sucking on them one at a time. He went from one titty to another sucking on them like he had never seen a titty before.

Nicole and Linwood were oblivious to what was going on. They had long moved to the other end of the wrap around seat. Linwood and Nicole were locked in a deep French kiss. Andrea snapped to her senses, pulled her blouse back up and said loud enough for Nicole to hear. "I guess we'd better call it a night." Phillip brushed her hair behind her ear with his hand and whispered in her ear "Can I spend the night with you?" Before she could answer, He licked around her the front and back of her right ear, sucked her earlobes and nearly caused her to pass out when he stuck his tongue inside her ear and moved it around and around while holding her close.

Andrea had been seeing Quentin for several months and he had not gotten this far with her. She did not want to be unfaithful to him but she did not know how much more of his stalling around she could take. She hadn't known this man twenty four hours yet he had done to her some of the things that she wanted Quentin to do. "I need to get some rest. I've been up too long." Andrea said breathlessly. "Don't tell me it's pass your bedtime?" Linwood told the driver to take them to the Westin Hotel. "Would you like another drink?" Phillip asked as he poured himself another. "Why not?" Andrea responded. As she looked out the window, the limo drove past Washington Mutual Tower, Two Union Square, Nordstrom's flagship store and several art museums back toward their hotel.

When they arrived at the Seattle Westin Hotel, the chauffeur assisted them in exiting the limo. The intoxicated and somewhat gregarious foursome entered the hotel lobby and headed toward the elevator. Andrea asked Nicole if she was going to be okay. "Do you want to come to my room for the rest of the night, Nicole?" "Hell no, I'm going to my own room. I'm fine. I'll see you tomorrow." Nicole answered as she held Linwood's hand like she did not want him to get away. "You sure you're okay, you look a little tipsy." Nicole said to Andrea. "I'm okay; I just want to get some sleep." Phillip held Andrea by her waistline steadying her. When the elevator arrived at her floor, he walked her to her room. Andrea opened the hotel room door and turned to look at Phillip. Instead of coming in he just stood there.

"Look Baby, although you are sweet and sexy as hell, I don't want to impose or take advantage of you. I don't know if I should come in after all." Andrea looked him in the eye and said "I have something you may be interested in checking out." "Oh yeah, just what might that be?" "Come in and find out." Phillip looked around the room after entering. Andrea took off her blouse, slacks, and underwear. "Is this what you want me to see?" Phillip asked as he walked up to her and held her close. "No." Andrea answered woozily and walked over to the bar, poured two drinks. Handing one to Phillip, she sipped on the other as she pulled out a revealing night gown she had bought while she and Nicole was out shopping. "I want to show you this and ask you a question. "What would you do if you were my man and I wore these especially for you?" "Baby if you wore that for me I would do anything you wanted me to do. Name it and I would do it." He said as he finished the drink. Andrea poured him another drink overfilling the glass until it flowed over. Phillip wiped the glass off with a napkin. Then he took a few sips and sat the glass down on the dresser. He pulled Andrea close to him and if he were some sort of vampire he began sucking on her neck after a few brief kisses. He left her neck to focus on her mouth. He gave her a long deep kiss and grinded against her until she felt weak. Andrea moaned and he lifted her up and carried her to the bed. After he laid her down and sucked on her nipples until they were hard, he said "I don't want to take advantage of you he said. "Don't worry you won't" she said as she saw his sizable erection. Feeling aroused, she took it into her hand and moved it back and forth rhythmically until he thought he would explode. She got him to stand up and then pulled him toward her breast. She placed his hard erection between her breasts while he stood in front of her. He moved it around on her between her titties. He touched her nipples with it. He could hardly contain himself as she put her hands on the side of her breast and enclosed his brick hard erection in between her titties. Phillip moved back and forth rhythmically, reached a crescendo, let out a yell and fell to the floor. "I have never experienced anything like that in my whole life he panted. Never!" "Great, I'm glad you liked it, Andrea said, now I really need to get some rest. Why don't you get dressed and I'll call you tomorrow." She said. "What? You are going to throw me out?" "I'll call you." She promised as she walked him to the door and gave him a quick peck on the cheek. "See you tomorrow." Phillip let himself out and Andrea was so spent that she fell asleep without double locking the hotel door.

Chapter 9

erry drove around the streets of St. Paul thinking about beauty products, hairstyles, and upcoming hair shows. He knew that hair shows were the perfect venues for introducing his products and getting the recognition that he needed to start his In2Hair franchise. The only thing holding him back was capital. He had scrimped and saved enough to open the two salons that he presently owned. His beloved Grandma Alice had left him a sizeable estate after her death. He did not want to dishonor her by wildly spending the money that she had passed on to him in her last will and testimony.

He moved into the duplex that she had bequeathed him and hired a real estate agent to rent out the upstairs apartment to a young working couple. He told the agent that he did not want the tenants to know that he owned the property because of the possibility that they would try to skip their rent or hound him when things needed fixing. Paying the agent a small percentage of the rent that they submitted was a great way to manage payments, repairs, and if needed evictions. All he had to do was check his bank account each month to make sure that the agent had deposited the payments into his account. He was thankful that the tenants didn't present a lot of problems.

The only real issue that he had with them was when the water heater broke. They complained to the agent. The agent informed him of the situation and he gave his consent for the installation of a new water heater. The money for the heater was taken out of the next month's rent and the balance was placed into his account. Terry managed to keep the home that his grandmother had left him without refinancing it or getting a loan on it. He was proud that he didn't have to worry about a roof over his head and have steady income in these tough times when many people were losing their homes and jobs. Happy to be unattached to anyone at this time, Terry focused on one thing and that one thing was keeping his head above water, an In2Hair franchise. He had read so many self-help books and perused so many get rich quick videos that he added writing his own book and producing his own how-to videos to his bucket list. He told himself with a smile, "Of course, on the cover of my *How to Become a Millionaire Like Me* book and video, there will be a picture of me on my luxury yacht vacationing in Portofino."

As Terry eased his body into his automobile, he thought about his Grandma Alice or "Mother Dear" as he often called her. He remembers how protective she was of him when he was a youngster." He remembered how he stayed with her after his own mother had married and moved to another state when he was just nine years old. "Mother, why are you packing all your clothes into that suitcase? Where are my clothes? Aren't you going to put my clothes in there too? Are we going to visit Cousin Vicky in North Carolina?" "No, Baby you are not going with me this time. Mama and Mr. Bryant are getting married and we are going to move to a new house in Detroit. When we settle in, we are coming back for you. Meanwhile, you are going to stay with Mama Alice and keep her company." "I don't want to keep Grandma Alice company! I want to go with you!"

Terry remembers crying and falling out on the floor. He cried so much that night that he woke up with a tremendous headache. "You don't look so good baby? How do you feel?" "My head hurts. Take me to my mama. Take me to Detroit. I want to go with my mama." "Baby, we have to wait until they send their new address. Detroit is a big city. We will never find them without an address. How about a bowl of Trix or Captain Crunch?" "No, I don't want any cereal, I want my mama. Why did she leave me for Mr. Bryant? I hope he drops dead." "Don't talk like that Terry. Your mama loves you more than anything. She just wants the best for you and Mr. Bryant is going to make sure that you have everything you need." Terry just lay on the floor and cried himself back to sleep.

Mama Alice knew that Terry was going to go through a period of shock and denial. After losing her own husband, she herself went through the very same feeling before she finally accepted and learned to deal with the reality of her loss. She knew that Terry was going to experience the very same feelings. In the meantime she would do everything in her power to keep her one and only grandchild happy. She pulled out a mixing bowl, flour, eggs, nuts, Hershey chocolate chips and made the tastiest, fudgiest chocolate brownies that she ever baked. Terry awoke to the aroma that filled every room of the house. Mama Alice handed him a big slice on his favorite little plate. "I know just what will go good with that baby." She assured as she hurried to the refrigerator and poured him out a glass of whole white milk. "Drink all of this milk so that you will have strong bones and pretty white teeth." Terry looked into the mirror and ran his tongue across his pearly white teeth. "Thanks Grandma! Thanks to you I have pearly white teeth. That sorry excuse for a mama didn't care if my teeth rotted out. That's why that no good Mr. Bryant showed his true colors when he got her away from family. I could tell by the way he smirked at me the day he took her away that he was nothing but trouble." That's okay, I had Mother Dear. I had Mother Dear and she took care of me better than you ever did," Terry thought.

Terry felt himself getting melancholy so he turn on his CD and joined Tye Tribett in singing I Need You. "*Lord You are so amazing, Lord You are so amazing, Lord You are strong and Mighty. Lord You are full of mercy. Lord, Your name above all others.*" The stylists in his shop often kidded him about singing religious songs, quoting the bible, and spewing out a bunch of expletive, deletives whenever the opportunity presented itself. Terry knew he had a lot of demons but he also knew that basically he was a God loving, God fearing individual. His Grandmother had made sure of that. Grandmother had also made sure that he'd never have to want for anything as long as she lived and after she died. At the age of fifty five, his Mother Dear was a healthy, one hundred and sixty pound non-smoker who did not eat badly. So when an insurance agent tried to sell her life insurance many years ago, she opted for a million dollar policy. During his sales pitch, the enthusiastic young black agent told her that Jewish people and white people always left something behind for their children to live on and remember them by. Whether it was true or not, it got her thinking. She wanted to leave her one and only grandchild a legacy. Terry's a good child she thought and it's his birthright just as much as anybody else's to live a good life. I'll buy that policy and I can look down on him from heaven and know that he is okay financially. Her late husband had worked hard to leave her debt free and she knew the benefits of receiving a large insurance payment.

She took out a million dollar insurance policy and made him her beneficiary. She left the house and the two buildings that housed the beauty shops to him. He would never sell them or get a loan on them. Cherishing her gifts to him would be the way her would honor her forever. The one luxury that he permitted himself was the Lexus LLF-A that he bought with part of his inheritance.

Terry eased the black LLF into the driveway of his home and let out a sigh. He was happy to finally get a chance to have some time for Terry. "Terry Time today will include a wonderful sea-food dinner and a glass of wine," he said out loud. "First I'll pop these babies into the steamer." He said as he took the jumbo shrimp and Alaskan Crab leg out of the refrigerator. "What a magnificent dinner!" he thought as the smell of shrimp and crab wafted from the food steamer and filled the kitchen. "This is the life." Terry's thoughts were soon interrupted by the house phone. "This is Terry speaking," he said.

A deep Don Cornelius sounding voice on the other end answered "Hell-o Terry, This is Jonathan Belington, a personal care contract specialist for Mansfield-King. We met when you con-tracted us to manufacture your hair care products. I decided to give you a call because I was wondering if you wanted to meet and discuss your products. Do you have any ideas or questions about formulating new products?" "As a matter of fact I do have some questions as well as suggestions." Terry responded. He held the phone between the left side of his face and his left shoulder as he put a prepared baking potato into the microwave oven. He walked over to the fridge, pulled out a salad, and placed it on the dining table. "What kind of questions did you have in mind? Manufacturing, packaging, or do you have questions about formulation of a product?" asked Belington. "I have questions about expanding my products and I have some suggestions that I suppose could come under the heading of formulation," Terry answered. "Great!" Belington responded. "When can we sit down and go over your concerns and concepts.

As you know Mansfield-King offers a complete range of services for development of hair care products. My company would be happy to help your brand achieve the goals you have set." Terry liked what he was hearing. Someone wanting to help him achieve his goals gave him a boost to get the ball rolling as fast as he could. "Give me a date, and time and I will be glad to come in and discuss the products with you." "Great! How does one p.m. on Monday sound?" "Sounds Fine! I'll see you then. Your office is still in the same location, I assume. It was just ten months ago that I last met with you to arrange the initial creation of my line of hair care products." "I'm still in the same office." Belington responded. "I have you on the calendar for Monday. We will discuss how we can meet all of your manufacturing, packaging, and formulation needs for In2Hair hair care products. Before you know it, you'll be as well-known as the Bonner Brothers."

Terry sat down in front of his big screen HDTV with his plate of steamed shrimp and crab legs, a baked potato loaded with butter, sour cream, chives, and bacon bits, a tossed salad complete with bite sized pieces of romaine lettuce, red leaf lettuce, black olives, cherry tomatoes, thinly sliced red onions and Italian salad dressing. As much as he ate and drank, his rail thin six foot one frame never got beyond one hundred and fifty five pounds. After eating the entire seafood diner, Terry drank two glasses of Riesling and fell asleep while watching America's Got Talent.

Chapter 10

The smell of coffee mingled with cinnamon raisin toast woke Eric out of a deep sleep. He heard LaShondra singing happily in the shower and looked at the clock on the nightstand. Damn, I'm late. "Shondra, why didn't you wake me? You know I have to be in by 6:45am, or they will dock my pay." "I tried to wake you. You just kept saying you were getting up." Eric was always hard to wake up. But this morning LaShondra had no time to keep trying to get him up. She had to stop by Valerie's place and pick up KeKe who had spent the night with her playmate Ginger. LaShondra wished that she could afford a nice place where KeKe could have her own room and invite her friend to spend the night.

Eric grumbled "I've got to go home and change." "Eric, you wouldn't have to go through all that if you hadn't moved out." Shondra said. "Why did you move out anyway?" "Let, not go through that again." "I can't be sleeping on no couch, Shondra." "If you chipped in more money we could get a larger apartment." "Maybe two or three bedrooms." "You make more than I do LaShondra, I don't think it's fair for me to pay half of everything when you make more." "I didn't ask you to pay half Eric. You know that. But two hundred dollars a month when you make over twenty-two hundred a month is nothing." "What do you mean nothing? I have bills to pay, girl." "And I don't? Shondra shot back. "Let's not start this again." Eric snapped as he hurriedly dressed. "Aren't you going to have some coffee before you leave?" "I told you that I was late and I've got to get to work." "Will I see you later? Are you coming over after you get off of work? I'm going to cook dinner tonight." "Yeah, I'll be over, right after I check on my mother." Shondra immediately became alarmed. She knew that was a cover up for going to his other woman. Eric had never shown any interest in checking on his mom in the pass. He always left it up to his younger brother, Ronnie. Eric felt that since Ronnie was his mother's pet and stood to inherit the home as well as most of her insurance benefits, Ronnie could handle the day to day care of the eighty-seven year old woman who was growing more senile and dependent by the moment.

The taxi came soon after Shondra phoned for one. It was four p.m. Eric got off at five p.m. As soon as Shondra entered the taxi the driver began to flirt. "What's that fragrance you're wearing?" the driver asked. Shondra assumed that from his accent and features, he was from Somalia. "Red" she replied. "Where to, lovely lady?" Shondra gave the driver directions to the parking lot where Eric parked his car. "I want you to wait until I check something out and then you can drive me back home." "You want me to wait?" "Yes, I will pay you and I'll give you a nice tip." They arrived at the parking lot and Shondra asked him to circle the lot. When she saw that his car was there, she directed him to park three rows behind Eric's car and then she slid down in the back seat so she could not be seen. "I want you to keep an eye on that green nineteen ninety-eight Ford that I showed you." "What? Why are you down there? What is going on?" "I'm just checking out my man. I think he's cheating on me." "What? Him cheating on someone fine as you?" "When he gets in his car, follow him but not too close. He may get suspicious." "Follow him? Follow him where?" "Wherever he goes." "He is getting in the car now." "What does he look like?" asked LaShondra. "He has on a uniform." "That's him! Don't get too close to his car just follow him." Eric drove off and the cabbie followed several cars behind.

LaShondra chose to knock lightly on the front door of the apartment instead of ringing the doorbell. She didn't want to give Eric a chance to take cover just in case he did see the cab following his car. LaShondra wanted to catch him off guard and find out exactly what was going on. She was surprised when an old man opened the door opened and stared her in the face. Sure that Eric had to be in this apartment LaShondra asked, "Is Eric here?" "EER-IK?" responded the old man who backed away from the door with a limp. "Yes, Eric" she answered. "The guy whose car is parked right out there." "EER EER-EER-IK KAR" he stuttered as he nodded his head. EER-IK BAC DAR WIF MUH MUH-MAE" "Mae? Who is Mae?" LaShondra didn't wait for an answer before she walked down the hallway and turned towards the door where the sound a TV was blasting. "As loud as this damn TV is blasting, I can see why they didn't hear the knock on the door and the conversation between me and that old man." LaShondra thought. She stood there for a moment and listened as a female's voice asked. "Do you want me to get you something to eat, baby?" "What you got?" Eric asked "I don't know what the hell she's got." LaShondra yelled as she pushed

58

the door open. "But I damn sure know what I got for your sorry ass" as she pummeled Eric on the head with her oversized, overstuffed purse. She managed to get in three or four good hits before Eric who had been sitting on the side of the bed stripped down to his tee shirt and boxers snapped out of his surprised stupor and managed to hold her wrist and keep the purse away from his head. Mae, who had been sitting beside him in her bra and panties jumped up and ran out of the room when Shondra burst in on them.

Wanting to get a butcher knife from out of the kitchen to defend herself in case this heifer decided to come after her, Mae thought that it would be better if she just let Eric handle it. Also, she didn't think it would be a good idea to mess with LaShondra because Eric had told her many times that LaShondra was crazy and would surely hurt her if she found out about them. In a way, she was relieved that Shondra had finally caught them. Now Eric would have to make up his mind and choose between the two of them. After all, Eric had been creeping in to see her for almost a year now and it was time for him to either shit or get off of the damn pot. "How did she get into this house?" Mae asked her brother. NOC ON DA-DA-DO" he answered. Knowing that her brother did not have the mental faculties he had before his stroke, Mae decided not to blame him. "Instead she decided to follow Eric, who had quickly put on his clothes, and was heading to his car." LaShondra stood in front of Eric's car. Right in front of the driver side door, she cursed him out as loudly as she could causing nearby neighbors within ear-shot to stop and listen. LaShondra yelled, "I knew your no good ass was up to something and asked you over and over again to be straight with me. You just kept lying and lying. You know what.

You can have this old ass hag with her titties damn near touching the ground. Just don't ever come around me again."

Mae didn't like to fight, but she didn't like to be degraded either and what Shondra had said was fighting words. She stepped up to LaShondra and looked her straight in her eyes and said. "If you don't get from in front of my house right now with all that cussing and fussing you are going to wish you had. And if you don't like my titties, do something about it right now." LaShondra saw the cab slowly back out of the parking lot and she decided that it would be best to leave. "Wait up!" she yelled to the cabbie who now had the taxi in drive and was pulling off. "Why did you start to leave me?" she asked. "I did not bring you here so that you could get into a fight. If they call the police, I will have to spend a day in court." "I don't get paid to sit up in court; I get paid to drive a cab." "Anyway is it worth it? As fine as you look, you don't need to be running after a man, busting into somebody's house, raising hell." "If the police come, I'll be tied up in this mess. Lose money, lose time because you fuss at your man for doing what he does. They may send me back to Somalia for all your fighting," he complained. "But the police didn't come and instead you are going to get a big tip. Probably the biggest one you've gotten in a long time. Shondra assured him.

Back at her apartment, Shondra had a long cry. Then she sucked it up and vowed to never let Eric or any other man dictate how she behaved. She would use every man she came across. She would never depend on a man for love, money, companionship, friendship, or home repairs. "If you can't trust or depend on them, what good are they?" Shondra wondered out loud. "I can do bad all by myself," she continued talking to herself out loud. "Eric was not all that anyway," she mumbled. "Didn't cook, clean house, wash dishes, or carry on an intellectual conversation," she fumed. "He was not that great of a companion or friend. Where was he when KeKe got chicken pox and you had to stay up all night with her until she felt better? A friend would have been there by your side. Eric was nowhere to be located. Didn't show his sorry behind until the next week," she yelled out. Roscoe, her ex-husband, had his ways but he was in no way as low on the food chain as Eric. The phone rang snapping Shondra out of her conversation with herself.

"Miss McNair?" "Yes." Shondra quickly answered. "This is Gwen from Larsen Realty. How are you this evening?" "I'm fine" Shondra replied. I'm just phoning to let you know that the condo that you applied for has been approved." "Really? When can I move in?" Shondra asked excitedly? "How soon can you rent a U-Haul?" laughed Gwen. "You can pick the key up today. We are open until 7pm tonight." "I'm on my way right now." Shondra said.

The condo could not have come at a better time. Shondra thought. "Too bad you had to lie and steal someone else's identity to get it," her alter ego thought. "Well, why should some people have everything that life has to offer while some people end up with the crumbs?" her ego responded. "Because some people work hard for what they have in most cases." Alter ego told her. "And I don't?" ego retorted. "I don't stand on my feet eight hours all day a Big-Mart making minimum wage? I don't wait tables at a restaurant on my time off from Big-Mart to pay for a lousy one bedroom apartment in this hellhole of a neighborhood?" Shondra thought. "Aren't you're tired of this crap. You need to live a better life by any means necessary." Shondra's ego suggested.

61

Shondra sat across the desk from the real estate agent and looked at the paper work in front of her. There was a copy of the application that she had fraudulently filed out using the name of Andrea McNair. "Miss McNair my I see your I.D. please?" the real estate agent asked. I know you already showed it to Gwen when she took your application, but we are required to take another look at it when you sign the actual rental contract," she said with a cheerful smile. Shondra looked through the small red wallet that she had carefully place all the cards that referred to Andrea. Careful to keep them together so that she would never inadvertently pull out her own I.D. when she was operating as Andrea, she kept it all in a red wallet. Shondra wrote the name Andrea McNair on the line next to the word tenet. As she wrote the date next to the signature she thought this is the first day of my new life. As soon the keys to 1089 Rio Lane were in her hands she thought about how she was going to furnish the condo with upscale furniture. "I'm not taking any of that secondhand thrift shop furniture from that tacky apartment with me."

Shondra left the Realty office and headed straight to the furniture store. Once inside the showroom, she fell in love with the South Sea Rattan and Wicker furniture. It made her feel as if she was on top of a tropical island. She selected the Pacifica dining room for the breakfast nook. The matching Pacifica sofa, chair, loveseat, end table, and coffee table would look fabulous in the great room, she thought. Then she signed the contract for furniture. All Eight thousand, nine hundred and forty nine dollars of it. She would have to go somewhere else for the bedroom furniture because she was afraid to go over ten thousand dollars. She would go straight to another furniture store before the first store would have time to post the information.

Once inside the furniture store, LaShondra asked the salesman to show her the bedroom sets that had a tropical flavor. "I want to feel like I am on an island every night." He showed her a beautiful King sized sleigh bed that had warm, brown colors found in nature. And the reeded posts, turned feet, and woven rattan surfaces are all inspired by Hawaiian Islands." Not wanting to sound ignorant, LaShondra commended on the palm leaf hardware handles on the dresser and nightstand. "I think one or two six or seven foot palm plants would be a great accessory." "Brilliant!" exclaimed the happy sales associate. "Please text me a picture of it when it's all set up."

LaShondra penned Andrea's name on the contract and the salesman confirmed that the delivery date would be in four days. As far as she was concerned, that was perfect timing. She would have enough time to clean out her old apartment, box up and dispose of the things she would not be taking with her. She would donate anything that reminded her of Eric to charity.

After LaShondra arrived back home she took off the light colored makeup, put the contact lens into a liquid solution, placed the wig on a Styrofoam head and locked it all in overnight bag. She tucked the overnight bag into a small closet in her bedroom. She did not want anyone seeing her "Andrea look" and questioning her about it. Andre would have to remain her secret.

Chapter 11

ndrea opened another letter from a creditor. This time it was a pay day loan company threatening to garnishee her checking account at the Bank of America. This was the first lead that she had on the identity thief who had been wreaking havoc with her credit. Andrea had been unable to assess her bank account because unauthorized money was taken out and she had requested that the bank freeze both her checking and saving accounts. This latest letter forced her to visit the bank's personnel office to gather information about this perpetrator.

The bank manager led her to a small office and introduced her to Sterling Steingold. After briefing Steingold on why Andrea was in his office, the branch manager assured her that her problem would be taken care of and left. Steingold looked over the bills and a copy of the loan application that Andrea had acquired from the pay day loan company as well as the Best Buy DVR. "May I see some ID" Steingold asked. Andrea gave him her driver's license, "I wonder if the strumpet who is using my identity is using the same damn picture," she thought. Steingold looked at the ID and thought that this was the perfect time to get his flirt on. "This is a great picture of you. Usually driver's licenses do not do justice to how people really look. But then, you look like you couldn't take a bad picture if you tried to." Andrea blushed. She had felt certain chemistry when she entered the handsome information security analyst and acting personnel manager's office and laid eyes on his fine specimen of a man. Feeling a pulsating, throbbing in her crouch, Andrea crossed her legs in effort to contain her feelings. "Damn, you act like you never seen a man before. What would Quentin think if he knew you had the hots for a man you met only fifteen minutes ago?" He then placed the Best Buy DVR into his computer to exam at her request. "The woman in this video looks nothing like you." He said, telling her what she obviously already knew. Steingold sensed her tenseness and frustration and decided to get on with the job.

First, he checked the data base for all employees with the last name McNair. There were twenty-five working for the bank in the city of Minneapolis but not a single Andrea. He next assessed branches of his banks in St. Paul and the surrounding area. Not a single Andrea McNair. He did find an Ann McNair. "I may have something here. There is an Ann McNair who works at the one of our branches in St. Paul." "How would we know this is the person I am looking for? ....the one who has turned my life upside down?"

For some reason Andrea began to sob. Steingold offered her a tissue and tried to console her. As she took the tissue she felt his hand brush ever so slightly on her own and immediately felt a rush. "Don't worry Andrea, I hate the idea that someone like you who worked hard for everything you have can be ripped off by a conniving thief like the one who has done this to you. I will do everything in my power to help you not just because she has dragged the name of our bank into it, but because someone could do the same thing to me or some other unsuspecting hard working person." He said to her relief. "There is one last thing that we need to do before I can delve deeper into this matter. I have to get copies of your signature to compare with the perpetrator." He pulled up a copy of Andrea's signature that the bank had acquired when she opened her accounts. He then pulled up legitimate copies of paid checks that Andrea had signed and were on file. He then asked Andrea to sign her name on a form ten times. "This is just a procedure that we use to help us determine whether your handwriting is the same as the forged document." Andrea obliged and wrote her name ten times on the sheet of paper. "This certainly does not appear to be your signature. The lines on this apparently forged signature are shaky. The dark and thick starts and finishes for first and last name indicate frequent pen lifts that come from carefully, slowly forming letters instead of writing quickly and naturally. Yes, there is definitely seems to be some check fraud going on here. Of course if it goes to court, a handwriting analyst may be called on to testify."

And I will definitely be there to testify on the bank's behalf when we do find the person who is responsible." "If I can ever find out who she is." Andrea retorted, "You look like you need to unwind. How about having dinner on me? It's 5PM and I will sign out in about fifteen minutes? What do you say?" He looked at Andrea with a smile that could melt chocolate. Andrea thought for a moment "It is Friday. I'm not in the mood to cook dinner. Quentin is out of the city at a conference. I suppose I could have dinner with Michelle, but girlfriend ain't nowhere near as fine looking as Sterling." He broke her trance by asking, "What's it going to be? We could drive to St. Paul and swing by Ann McNair's place while we're at it." "Dinner in St Paul sounds great. I will be waiting outside in my car. I'm driving a red Lexus," she said.

"Fine, I'll tidy up my desk and then I'll see you in a few minutes. Promise me, no more tears while you're waiting. We are going to get to the bottom of this thing, I promise." He assured her as he led her to the bank's exit. Several of the tellers eyed him as he walked with the lovely young lady, wondering whether he would walk out the door with her.

Andrea pulled the sun visor down and looked in the mirror. Thank God for waterproof mascara she thought. "Why on earth did I start blubbering in Steingold office? I am a professional woman perfectly capable of taking care of myself. Maybe it's because he was the first person who could actually help me unlock the mystery to what is happening to my identity. After touching up her lipstick and blush, Andrea put on her Gucci sunglasses. She looked amazing, her face framed by a freshly styled hairdo. "Terry certainly knows what to do with my hair. The time I spent in his chair today was well worth every minute. The next time I visit the shop I will triple his tip." Andrea had just flipped the visor back into place when Steingold appeared next to her window. She was relieved that he did not catch her primping. She did not want him thinking that she was getting dolled up to impress him. "We'll take my car," he motioned to a black Mercedes S Class sitting in a far corner of the parking lot.

The drive to St. Paul was exuberating. Sterling had put the top down. After letting Andrea select from a music CD from his collection, he popped in the Michael Jackson analogy that she selected.

The music was upbeat and they both sang along. Sterling looked at Andrea and smiled. She couldn't help noticing his naturally curly shoulder length black hair had a nicely groomed gelled look. His clean shaven skin the color of honey and warm chocolate colored eyes, perfectly complimented his luscious lips that appeared to move in slow motion hypnotizing her as she stared longingly and lustfully at them. Andrea had a thing for men's lips. Even though she thought Quentin had the perfect L.L. Cool Jay lips, she couldn't stop stealing glances at Sterling's perfectly formed mouth. She finally broke her fixation on his lips by focusing on his nose. The slightly broad bridge had a small hump in it. "Someone must have whacked him pretty good she thought of perhaps it was from an accident."

Her thoughts were broken when he announced, "There's a quaint little restaurant in St Paul called M.P. Island Soul Café. They serve the best Caribbean food." Andrea thought "Here's I am with a guy that's obviously married or in a relationship. Does that Jamaican-Jew playa think that I am so dumb and needy as not to know what is going on? Hmmph, taking me to St. Paul and then to some hidden restaurant." "Well, what the fuck! I just want a little distraction from my problems. There is nothing this MF can do that my man, Q, can't do except help me find the bitch who stole my identity." "What harm can a dinner in a 'quaint' restaurant cause as long as the food is good?"

Sterling proved to be quite a gentleman rushing out of the car to open the door for her. Inside the restaurant, pulling the chair out and waiting for her to be seated before he took his seat. "The jerk chicken with yellow rice and peas is absolutely fantastic." Sterling offered. "Then jerk chicken it is and I'll take a side order if plantain." Andrea beamed. Sterling ordered a pitcher of ginger beer after checking whether Andrea preferred that or something else.

Sterling had not exaggerated when he described the jerk chicken. It was the best she'd ever tasted. As they enjoyed the fine Caribbean cuisine, they shared tidbits about themselves. Andrea learned that Sterling who was originally from St. Lucia had grown up New York. He had been transferred to Minneapolis by his bank temporarily to get the newest branch's personnel department up and running. He expected to stay in Minneapolis six or seven months. His job was to staff and train the new employees hired by the new branch. Having worked in many different capacities in many different banks, Sterling was no stranger to identity theft. He had even trained bank personnel how to recognize and deal with identity thieves. He seemed confident the he could help bring the Andrea McNair wannabe bring to justice.

"How can something like this happen, Sterling?" Andrea asked. "Very simply put, it can start with a lost or stolen wallet. It can start with pilfered mail or documents thrown out by a business." "Thrown out documents? You mean my personal information could have been breached?" Exclaimed Andrea. "It happens more often than you can imagine. Some info is thrown out without being shredded and someone comes along dumpster diving and before you know it they have hundreds of phony I.D.s. The perp then commits credit card fraud, financial identify or criminal identity theft." "I can't wrap my head around this, Sterling. Why me? Why did my identity get lifted?" Sterling sensed that this was a good time to get intimate with the exquisite looking, sweet smelling woman.

Not in a sexual sense but in way that he could give her a warm hug or a friendly brush up against her cheek. He urged Andrea to come home with him for a Mojito like only he could make. She agreed to go but only after he took her back to the bank to get her car. Sterling quickly paid the tab and escorted her back to his car before she changed her mind.

Once inside his sophisticated, somewhat staged condo, Sterling led Andrea to the living room and urged her to have a seat on the sleek blond leather sofa. Instead of sitting down, Andrea was drawn to the dramatically lit aquarium in the dining area. "This is amazing! You can actually see the back of the aquarium from the kitchen." She said. "I kind of like it myself," he said as he took off his tie and undid the first four buttons of his dress shirt. He went to the bar area of the big room and mixed two drinks. He passed one to Andrea, sat down on the sofa close to her, and said. "Now aren't you glad you came with me. Andrea fixated on his sensual mouth and beautiful white teeth that were movie star perfect. "It does feel good to talk to someone who may be able to help find who is using my name to acquire credit." She said. Then suddenly realizing that they had not gone anywhere near Ann McNair's apartment while they were in St. Sterling, Andrea bought it to his attention. "Sterling, why didn't we check out her place while we were in St. Paul?" "I know, we didn't get to see where she lives. I have someone in mind that will do that for us. We'll leave that up to a professional because we don't want her to know that we are on to her."

"This aquarium, the drink, and my great company will help you feel better." "I don't know Sterling, every time I think of what that person is doing with my good name, I get bent out of shape all

70

over again. Whoever it is has got to be stopped." She cried getting all riled up again. "Don't worry doll, he said as he took the glass out of her hand and held her close. She did not resist his warm and sympathetic embrace. She needed to be comforted and reassured right then and there. Not wanting to rush things, Sterling said to her. "What you need is a good massage. Don't you agree? Here let me help you take these shoes off." He said as he got down on his knees and slowly undid the ankle straps of her Pradas. He gently placed her right foot in his hands and began making long, slow, firm stroking motions with his thumbs. He started at the tips of her toes, slid back up toward her ankle, and watched her face as he retraced back to the toes with a lighter stroke. Sterling braced Andrea's foot and leg by cupping one hand under her heel behind her ankle. Then he grasped the ball of her foot with his other hand and slowly turned it in different directions three or four times. Andrea's lips curled in a smile as she felt the joints in her feet loosen and relax. "Feels nice doesn't it?" Sterling asked. "Hmmmm, I didn't have any idea this foot could feel so good. It feels 180% different from the other one." "Don't fret. I'll make that one feel good too." He smiled and directed his attention to Andrea's neatly manicured toes. Sterling ran his finger slowly across Andrea's toes. Detecting that she was extremely sensitive to his touch, he held her foot beneath the arch and began grasping the base of her big toe and began slowly sliding his fingers to the top and back to the base. Just as Andrea thought it could not get any better, he began to slowly and firmly pull each toe, sliding his fingers from the base to the top and back to the base. Sterling finished the massage on that foot by doing a few toe slides between each toe with his index finger. Eyeing the gold ankle bracelet on Andrea's left ankle, Sterling took a few sips of his drink before continuing his task. "Does this mean that you are some lucky man's love slave?" He asked as he touched it with his finger. "Does it really matter?" Sterling then ran his hands up from her ankles to her knees and back down to her ankle again. As Andrea felt more relaxed, she let her legs fall slightly open as her body lost all signs of tension. Sterling rested his head on her thigh and although he was immediately intoxicated by the closeness of her body, he thought "The next move is hers." Andrea ran her fingers through his hair and remarked, "That was quite nice. How did you learn to give such a great foot massage?" Oh, I've had a few foot massages myself. I picked up a lot just from having my own body massaged every now and then." "How often is every now and then? And does that come with a happy ending?' She laughed. "How often is whenever I feel like I need to get the kinks out?" He responded as he began to give her other foot the same sensual treatment. "And just what do you know about a happy ending?" "Oh, I've heard of the famous happy ending, who hasn't?" "Well, what about you? Do you want a happy ending?" He asked as he finished up the foot and directed his massage efforts towards her ankle and upwards. Sterling ran his hands slowly up her legs and Andrea began to quiver as he worked his way up to her thigh with his magical hands. Andrea's cell phone rang. "Don't answer it." Sterling urged. Andrea impulsively looked at the Caller I.D. and picked up when she saw that it was Quinton. "Hell-o." Andrea said trying to focus on the caller as Quinton spread her legs open a bit more. "Tell them to call back." He said as he peered at the seat of her panties. Andrea squirmed as she felt her crotch begin to tremble, throb, and quiver all at the same time. "You need a ride from the airport?" I thought you would be out of town for the rest of the week." "Tell them to call back." Sterling said again as he pulled her panty crotch open revealing her wet cunt which he immediately began to inch his finger into. To Sterling's delight, Andrea told Q. that she would call him back. She gently pushed him off of her, thanked him for the dinner, drink and foot massage. "So that is a slave bracelet on you ankle." He said as she got up to leave. "I just have to take care of some business." "I thought that finding out who stole your I.D. was taking care of your business." Sterling responded. "Are you saying that you are not going to help me? And do you try to seduce all of your female clients?" "No, I don't know what got into me. I don't usually mix business with pleasure. I promise that it will not happen again. I want very much to help find out who stole your I.D. and put a stop to it. Please accept my apology." "There is no need to apologize. I enjoyed every minute we spent together tonight. Everything was great." She gave him a warm hug and a kiss on the cheek. "Great, I got her all worked up for what to go out a screw some guy named Quinton."

Chapter 12

Terry entered the elevator and pressed the button that led to the 17th floor of the prestigious fifty-seven story I.D.S. Tower. The entire seventeenth floor housed offices for Mansfield-King Products Inc. He told the receptionist that he had an appointment to see Jonathan Belington, a personal care contract specialist for Mansfield-King. She picked up the phone, dialed a number and informed the man of his presence. After a short wait, the receptionist escorted him to Belington's office.

Belington stood up and shook hands with Terry. "It's good to see you man." He invited Terry to sit down. Welcome to Mansfield-King. "After speaking to each other on the phone a few days ago, we set up this appointment to have a face to face meeting. I'm happy to meet you." Terry responded. "How did you find out about us?" Belington asked Terry. "I Googled you." Terry smiled. "I don't know how much you know about us, so I would like to give you a little information about what we do here. "I've done my research interrupted Terry, I know that Mansfield-King laboratories custom formulates and manufactures hair care products.

Okay, since you have obviously checked us out, I would like you to take a few minutes to fill out this questionnaire. Then I'll go over each response with you. Terry filled out the first page of the form which included name, company name, address, city, state, zip, phone, fax, cell-phone and website. "I don't have a website yet, I'm working on it however. "It doesn't have to be finished yet. We just need the name of your website and the web address." Belington said. "It's Terryzin2hair.com" "Wonderful" Belington said as he pulled a package from a file draw in his desk and handed it to Terry. We'll be referring to this as we talk about your product but let us finish this form.   As you can see the next part of this form asks you to discuss your product idea. Tell us about your product idea." Terry look at the questions under the heading "Tell Us about Your Product."

Let's start with the first question. "What is your product idea?" Belington read from his copy of the questionnaire. "Basically it's a line of hair care products; I want to start off with a shampoo, conditioner, and a moisturizer." You don't want to add a perm? It may be best to go on and put that out there along with the products that you mentioned. "How would I develop a perm?" Terry asked. "All perms have the same basic ingredients." Belington responded. "We can provide you with a list of vitamins, oils, and other interesting and functional ingredients that you can select in order to make this your own special product." I don't want to put something out there that will take someone's hair out or burn their scalp" laughed Terry. "I can't be going to court over a lawsuit."

"If we manufactured it and put that out for you, we would have to go to court right along with you. Our company uses only products that have been proven safe. So don't worry about the product being unsafe." Hell in that case, I may as well add a dandruff cream and a hair grower!" "Go for it man! You will be catching up with those Bonner Brothers in no time."

"Let's discuss your products' performance characteristic?" Belington suggested. "Performance characteristics?" Terry repeated quizzically. "What will your product to do that other product may not do?" Belington answered. "My shampoos would be formulated to cleanse thoroughly but not strip African American and super-curly hair types of all its natural oils. My shampoo will replenish the hair's own natural oils. The styling products would contain conditioners and polymers that form protective barriers around the clients' hair so it can withstand heat from styling tools." Terry answered. "Those are great characteristics for hair care products that I am sure that enable you to successfully market your products. It will also help with the test marketing." Belington said. "I don't want to sound naive but what type of test marketing are we talking about? Are we talking about testing the products on laboratory rats?" Terry asked. "No, Sir. We are simply talking about the limited introduction of the products along with a marketing program that will gauge the reaction of potential customers in a market situation. Our marketing department will handle that so that is not something that you have to worry about. I'm sure that the test marketing will go well." He assured Terry. This is more involved than I thought it would be, Terry thought to himself as watched Belington type something on the computer's keyboard.

"Next question, what do you want to say about the product on the label?" "I want it to say "intensive moisture treatment rescues even the most dehydrated hair strands, for all hair types, uniquely formulated to repair damage to the outer protein layer of the hair," because that is basically what it will do." "Uhmm hmm" Belington said while continuing to type. "What is your target market? Women, men, natural hair, and chemically treated hair?" he questioned. Terry answered also adding "My target would be specifically for black women. The products could be used on both natural and chemically treated hair. I'm not just saying that to get more bangs for my bucks. I'm saying it because I have used it in my shop and I know it works." Terry said.

Terry read the next question from his copy. "What form do you want the product to take? Do you want lotion, gel, paste, cream, etc.?" "I want the shampoo and conditioner to be in lotion form, the moisturizer to be in cream form and scalp treatment to be an oil." Terry answered readily.

"What about the next question? Do you have special ingredients you want us to use?" Terry said that he had mixed a concoction that included Shea butter, Vitamins C oil. "On the next page, you'll find a list to standard and exotic butters and oils. Do you see any that you want to use?" Terry read the list. "I guess we can add mango butter and olive oil. I've used those ingredients and they are very beneficial. Oh yes, the jojoba oil is good too. Let's add all of those. However, I do not want any, I repeat any mineral oil or petroleum oils in the products because they clog the hair follicles and prevent the hair from growing. I want my customers' hair to grow." Belington jotted down the list of oils and said. "Now take a look at the vitamins." A, D, E, C, Beta –Carotene the list started off. "Let's add the Panthenol. That's vitamin B5 and it is excellent for repairing the hair shaft." Terry said. Seem like you know your vitamins, Belington chimed in knowing that the more ingredients

Terry added to his products, the more his products would cost to manufacture. Terry went on, "I do hope that you include various polymers & resins to give shine, conditioning, detangling, softening, and styling hold."

"Are there other ingredients you specifically don't want in the product?" "I don't want any alcohol or other drying ingredients." Belington asked the next question. "As far as this product is concerned, what takes precedence?" "I am not trying to go for an economical price because I do want to make some money off of the products or at least break even. I can't say that the ingredients are new because all of the ingredients have been used to some extent. Maybe not in the same combination. I'll say that high end ingredients would take priority. That's my answer. My products have high end ingredients so they would expect to pay twenty dollars for my shampoo."

"We are getting close to the last question." Belington said. "I hope we are, I did not know that I had to go through all of this." Terry said and glanced quickly at his watch. He had been in this office almost an hour. "What type of container and cap do I want to use?" "I want the shampoo and conditioner to be in plastic bottles. The moisturizer and hair grease to be in a jar. And the scalp treatment in a small tube with a snap off cap." "What sizes do you intend to provide? Two, four, eight oz., etc. We can also ship bulk in one, five, or fifty-five gallon drums." "I won't be needing any drums yet Terry laughed "I have to see how those four ounce jars are going to sell first." "Do you want us to use our stock scents or provide your own?" "I have decided to use the stock scent since I have not come up with any scent of my own." Terry looked over the list of scents that the company offered. I would like to sample some of those fragrances before I decide on any one in particular." He said. "Sure, I understand. We have some swatches that are pretty much like the perfume samples that come in magazines. If you choose some from the list that you want to consider, I will see to it that you get samples to take home with you. You can fill out the part of the contract that indicates the scent of your choice, sign it and fax it back to me. You won't have to come back in for that." He said sensing that Terry was growing tired of his many questions. With a broad smile on his face, he stood up and walked from behind his desk toward Terry and gave him a large envelope that contained the contract that they had just drawn up.

"Well, Mr. Yarborough that takes care of everything. I will get this over to our business office and they will set up payment arrangements and from there it will go on to production. Do you have any questions?" "Yes, what kind of time frame are we looking at? How long will it take from our meeting today to receiving my products?" Terry inquired. "I'll say that after you take care of the financial arrangements, it will probably be two or three months, maybe sooner. You can keep abreast of what's going on with your products by going online to our products department. After you get those papers back to us, we'll give you a password and you can go to our site to track the progress of your products.

Chapter 13

LaShondra was sitting at the kitchen table putting finishing touches on her home manicure. Revlon's rum raisin nail polish made her long dark skinned fingers look stunning. She looked up from her handiwork and saw KeKe standing in the doorway leading to the kitchen. Her glossy raisin colored lips smiled as KeKe entered the room. "Good morning baby, how did you sleep?" KeKe whined "My throat hurts mommy" as she eased herself onto Shondra's lap. Shondra noticed that she felt warmer than usual. "You feel pretty warm baby, let's get you something cool to drink. Shondra went to the fridge and poured a small glass of orange juice for KeKe. The girl sipped a little of the juice and quickly dropped glass on the floor and grasped her neck. "Mommy it burns.

"I 'm sorry mommy. I broke the glass." "You don't have anything to be sorry about baby. Don't worry about dropping the glass, I'll clean it up. I may have to take you to the doctor," she said.

How would she manage to get medical attention for her daughter when she was scheduled to be at work in three hours? The idea of being late again worried LaShondra. After all, it was just two weeks ago that Shondra clocked in late. "This is the second time this week that you have been late" barked her supervisor. "If you

80

are late one more time, we will have to replace you with someone who will be on time." Shondra needed this job in spite of the poor pay and lack of sufficient medical benefits. She had seen many of her more dedicated fellow workers spend weekend after weekend on the job and still make less than eighteen thousand dollars a year while employees at other retail stores earned over twenty four thousand a year. "These cheap bastards have some nerves." Shondra thought. She hated the fact that she and other employees had to wear a uniform consisting of a blue shirt and khaki pants. Only the blue shirt had been issued. As much as Shondra hated khaki pants, she had to buy at least three pairs of khakis and two more blue shirts because she liked feeling fresh. After working such long hours, she didn't always have the energy to wash pants every other night. She didn't mind that the khakis and blue shirts were purchased from a thrift store. They were in good condition and they would keep her from going to the laundromat so often.

Today, no matter what that ignorant supervisor threatens, I am going to take my daughter to the doctor. Shondra did not have anyone else to rely on. Her parents and other close relatives were in another state and she did not have friends that she could entrust the care of her only child to. She didn't even leave KeKe with the one person closest to her, Eric. Although she did not consider Eric a child abuser or molester, she did not trust any man alone with her young daughter. Shondra had read too many newspaper accounts and seen too many TV shows like Nancy Grace and Issues with Joan Velez Mitchell that depicted horrific child abuse. The babysitter that she occasionally used was trustworthy but she was only seventeen and could not sign permit forms required by doctors and hospital. Taking care of KeKe during her illness was something that only she could do and she didn't give a damn whether it would cost her that piss ass Big-Mart job or not.

Even though KeKe had just awaken from what Shondra now remembered now as a night's sleep interrupted by occasional tossing and turning, KeKe was still acting drowsy. She refused to try some warm chicken noodle soup crying "Mommy my throat still hurts." "Baby, we are going to the doctor to find out what is wrong. Shondra phoned in to let her supervisor know that she would be late because she had to take her baby to the emergency room. Shondra and KeKe arrived at the emergency room and were soon in a small office where the intake clerk asked a few questions and inputted Shondra's information into a computer. Name? LaShondra Jackson. Address? 5500 Leeway Drive. Phone? 957 328 4911. Insurance? "I don't have insurance."

Shondra thought about the fact that she had worked three years at the same Big-mart and did not have ample medical benefits because the policy would reduce her scant paycheck even more. She was barely making enough to pay the monthly $550 rent and keep food in the house. She had put off applying for Medicaid as her supervisor and some of her fellow employees suggested. She thought about her co-workers Booby and Precious. Several of Booby's teeth had cavities. He had to go without dental care because he didn't have medical benefits. He ended up having to pull two of those rotten teeth himself. She pictured Precious and the three children to she had to support. Precious, couldn't afford a new pair of shoes even though she worked in the shoe department. LaShondra knew she would have to get a better job. The sound of the receptionist snapped her mind back to her own problem, "You must sign this form acknowledging that you will be responsible for paying for this visit within thirty days of receiving the bill." LaShondra thought about phoning Eric or KeKe's dad to ask for the money. But that thought fled her mind quickly when she realized that it would only provide them with an excuse to try to get back into her good graces. Knowing that it would only complicate matters, she quickly put that thought out of her mind.

Shondra and KeKe sat in the reception area for almost forty minutes. A nurse finally called them into a small room and asked questions about KeKe's medical history and what was bothering her now. She measured her height and weight, took her temperature, pulse, and blood pressure. Then she escorted them into a room with a bed and asked KeKe to put on a robe. "Can you get up on that bed for me honey?" she asked. "Do you want me to fix this bed so you can sit up and watch TV?" KeKe nodded and the nurse cranked up the bed so that the child could comfortably watch the cartoon channel that her mother had chosen for her. "A doctor will be in to see her shortly." She told Shondra. Shondra wondered just what she meant by the word shortly. She hoped it meant soon.

After what seemed like an eternity but actually was only twenty minutes, a doctor entered the room. "Let's see what's wrong with you little lady. Can I peek into your ears with this little spy scope? It may feel a little cold but it won't hurt a bit," he assured her. Now, let's listen to your chest? He placed the stereoscope onto her chest, listened and said "Your chest sounds good. Now I want you to open your mouth real wide and say AHHHH" KeKe stretched her mouth as wide as she could. The doctor peered in and said, "Oh, I see why your throat is giving you a bad time. I want you to tilt your head back and open your mouth wide and say AHHHH again." This time he scraped a sterile cotton swab along the back of her throat causing the little girl to gag and cough. He offered her a sip of water and said "I'll return to talk to you after the results of the throat culture comes back from the lab."

Twenty five minutes elapsed before he returned to the room. "We're going to get you all fixed up." I'd like to ask you a few questions while the nurse gives KeKe something that will make her feel better. Shondra and the doctor stepped outside of the room as the nurse stayed in. "What are you giving her?" Shondra asked. "It's an antibiotic." He responded. "What's wrong with my baby?" "She has a streptococcus infection." "A strepto-what?" "She has a streptococcus infection called strep throat." "Is it serious?" "It could be. Has she ever had this before?" "No, she's never has this. Will she get better?" "She will but she has to take the entire dose of antibiotic. Missing a dose or stopping before it is all taken she could cause her illness to get worst. If she does get worst or develop joint pain or swelling, fever, stomach pains, weight loss, or fatigue, bring her back in right away because these are all signs of rheumatic fever which can develop from one to five weeks after your child has been infected with the streptococcus bacteria." "Are you saying my child is going to die?" "No I am not saying that. While rheumatic fever is a complicated and involved disease that affects the joints, skin, heart, blood vessels, and brain. It does not always occur after strep throat. But it is something that we want to watch out for. I am almost sure KeKe will be just fine." "How do you know she'll be fine?" He gave LaShondra the standard textbook answer to her question. "Children five to fifteen are more at risk of developing the condition if they have experienced frequent strep throat infections. You can tell strep throat from a plain sore throat that accompany a cold because it will be more intense and you'll end up here or at some other doctor's office. Also, rheumatic fever is also more common in children who have a family history of the disease." I'm sure that KeKe will be better before the week is over, just make sure that she takes all of the medication. That is very important because we don't want her to relapse into that achy throat." The doctor shook LaShondra hand before leaving the room.

LaShondra closed her eyes and said softly "Thank you, Father, I don't know what I would do if anything happens to my baby girl. She is the best thing that has ever happened to me. She has been such a blessing. Please Father, make her feel better." The nurse bought KeKe into the room and handed Shondra some paperwork that included follow up instructions and several prescriptions. Shondra read the follow up instructions to herself as the nurse read them aloud.

"Be sure that she drinks plenty liquids and take all of the antibiotics. If she does not show signs of improvement in a few days, you may return to the ER. She should show signs of improvement a day or two after she begins her meds. Are there any questions?" "No questions but thanks for helping us." Shondra replied,

Shondra took Ke home and tucked her into bed. She phoned in to tell her supervisor that she had to take the rest of the week off. "Just be sure that you bring a note from the doctor saying that your child was sick and you needed to be with her all week. If you don't have a note I'm afraid that we will have to let you go." Shondra was already ticked off because her job did not provide medical insurance. She bit her tongue to keep from cursing and acting ignorant. Instead, she vowed to look in the classifieds for another job all week long.

Chapter 14

Shondra thought that she was dreaming when she heard the doorbell ring. It was not unusual for her to have dreams so vivid that she would actually experience sound effects. She fluffed her pillow, turned over on her right side and pulled the blanket up to her chin. Just as she found a good spot to snuggle comfortably in the lumpy bed, she was sure that she wasn't dreaming. The doorbell had stopped ringing and now someone knocking on the door loudly and rapidly. Now fully awake, Shondra got out of the bed and walked into the living room. She tiptoed to the door and peered through the peep hole. It was Eric and he was as drunk as a skunk.

The knocking got louder. Afraid that he would awake KeKe, Shondra opened the door and told him that he could not come into her house at three o'clock in the morning. "You need to go back where you came from. My baby girl is so sick, I had to take her to the hospital and I don't have time to be messing with your drunken ass, Eric." "What's wrong with your baby girl." "Don't worry about what's wrong with her, just go back to where you got that liquor because you sure didn't get it from here." "Look Shondra, I am getting pretty fed up with your whining about where I go, where

87

I been, who I see, and all the rest of those ignorant questions you always asking." "You are getting fed up. You are getting fed up. I have been fed up Eric." So if you are so fed up and I am so fed up why the hell are you ringing my door bell and knocking on my door. Get the hell out of my house Shondra shouted. Get the hell out before I call the police on your ass." "I'm going to give you something to call the police for. You want to call the police. Call them." Eric shouted as he backhanded Shondra across the face causing blood to ooze from her bottom lip. "What you waiting for call the mother-fucking police." Eric shouted. "Eric, please don't wake my baby up, She is real sick." "You are the one who's sick bitch." Eric shouted as he grabbed Shondra by the neck and started to choke her until she passed out.

Shondra woke up and saw two policemen standing over her along with a paramedic. She didn't know where she was or what happened until one of the officers told her that a neighbor had heard a very loud argument in her apartment and had phoned the police. Fortunately, these two officers were in the neighborhood. The paramedic insisted on taking her to the emergency room because Andrea had bruises on her neck and her lip was severely swollen. LaShondra tried to protest, but her voice was barely audible. All that she could get out was a faint whisper. "My baby girl just came from the ER and I need to be here with her." "Don't worry about her, Ms. Jackson, we will take her to the children's shelter and you can check her back out as soon as you're done at the hospital. But you need to go there right away because they will take pictures of your bruises and we can use them as evidence against the man who did this to you."

As the paramedics drove LaShondra to the Emergency room, they told her how Eric was caught choking her and the police had to beat him with a blackjack to get him off of her. All she could think was that the liquor had driven him crazy. She wondered why he didn't beat the woman who he had been seeing. Why did he come to her house and jump on her. She started to cry as she thought about Eric's abuse toward her. All she had ever done to him was to try to please him and make him happy. No manner how nice she was to him, he never gave her with the same respect, love and appreciation that she bestowed upon him. She vowed that if he ever got near him again he would be sorry that he even met her. No one had ever laid hands on her like he did tonight. Hell, her own daddy never abused her. Eric is going to pay for this she vowed.

"Are you LaShondra Jackson?" asked the same intake worker that assisted Shondra when she bought KeKe in a few hours earlier. "Weren't you here earlier today with your little girl?" Shondra tried to answer her question but when her voice would not respond, she nodded her head. "Don't worry about answering the questions about hospitalization and employment. I'll just use the same info that you gave me this morning. My shift is over in twenty minutes but I'll print out your info and bring it right back. You can look it over and sign it if it's correct." Shondra signed the papers without really reading them thoroughly. She had a good idea that all they were interested in was being paid for their services. She wondered where she would get the money to pay two hospital bills she knew that if she did not pay them, her credit would go from bad to worst.

The ER nurse took Shondra's vital signs. She recorded the information on a Chart. BP 141/54, pulse -113, respiration -21, pulse oximetry -99% on room air. "You may need tetanus shot since your tetanus status is not up to date." She told Shondra. Soon a tall, lean, blond man seemingly not a day older than twenty five came in and extended his hand to Shondra. "My name is Dr. Hatton and I am an intern here at North Memorial Hospital. Your chart indicates that you were strangled. Let's take a look. He asked Shondra to look up toward the ceiling as he examined her eyes. Next, he took a look at her neck and asked her if she remembered what happened to her. Shondra croaked out a no as she shook her head from left to right. He asked her to take a few deep breaths as he checked for difficulty breathing. "Swallow for me." Shondra held her neck as she tried to swallow. "Swallow again, please." He said. Shondra held her neck as she desperately tried to swallow. How does your head feel? Do you have a headache? Damn straight, I have a headache she thought as she nodded yes. "My throat is sore too." She croaked. The doctor asked Shondra to stand up and then he asked "Are you lightheaded?" Shondra didn't have to answer. She slightly swayed back and forth. She thought it was because it was the first time that she stood up on her own since the police and paramedics transported her to the hospital. "I'm going to order x-rays of your neck and then the social worker who handles abuse cases will come in and take photographs of your injuries." Seeing the quizzical look on Shondra's face, the doctor explained that photographs would be taken for legal as well as medical purposes. He explained that photographs will document all of her injuries including the placement of the perp's hands during her strangulation. "If the x-rays indicate that you suffered laryngeal or hyoid bone fracture, we may have to admit you. Since you are very obliviously hoarse, I am going to order a laryngoscopy to evaluate your vocal cords and trachea. I'll see you after I get the test results back." If that sorry, poor excuse of a man messed up my neck, he's going to wish he never met me vowed Shondra. Her thoughts returned to KeKe. My baby is somewhere spending the night with complete strangers she thought. Thanks to Mr. Asshole coming to my house in the middle of the night drunk or stoned. He had to be stoned she thought. She had seen Eric high off of alcohol before and he had never demonstrated the type of madman behavior as he did tonight. Shondra concluded that Eric must have tried crack or some other drug. No matter what he took, drank or smoked he should have kept his dumb ass away from her. She was not going to make excuses for him. Shondra was not the type of woman who would put a man before her child or excuse a man's stupidity. That's why I wanted him to go on about his business and leave me alone anyway. Shondra snapped in and out of her thoughts as she moved to the various positions dictated by the lady who was operating the x-ray equipment in the small room adjacent to her. Every now and then the lady would come out and reposition her neck and the x-ray camera.

The X-ray technicians laid the large x-ray envelop on top of Shondra's tummy and rolled the hospital bed back from the X-ray area to the room on the fifth floor of the hospital. Shondra glimpsed out of the window and noticed that it was now daylight. She wondered what time it was and looked on the walls for a clock. When the technician rolled her into a small room, she saw a clock on the wall and noticed that it was now seven-fifteen a.m. "Why are you leaving me here? Take me back to get my clothes. I have to go and get my baby girl. I need to give her the antibiotics that that doctor gave me. Shondra began to cry. I have to give my baby her medicine at 8AM. Shondra explained as best as she could that KeKe had a strep throat and they had taken her away to someplace called a shelter. The technician listened patiently. She then picked up the phone and asked to speak with a social worker. She explained the situation to the person on the other end, hung up the phone and told Shondra that the social worker will phone the shelter and see to it that KeKe gets her meds.

It wasn't long before a doctor came in and introduced himself. This time it was a heavy set black man with a pleasant smile that showed all of his perfectly even, beautiful white front teeth. He could have modeled them for toothpaste commercial "Why does every doctor feel they have to introduce him or herself? I don't care if you do have pretty teeth, I can read the damn name tag" Shondra wanted to scream out. "Did you eat or drink anything in the last two hours." He asked. She whispered "No." "This will take five or ten minutes. I want you to sit straight up in your chair and stick out your tongue and far as you can. I am going to place this small mirror in your throat. It may feel a little uncomfortable when I pull on your tongue. If this becomes too painful, I want you to signal me by pointing to your tongue. In that case, I may have to give you a local anesthetic." He gave her a smile and a little pat on the back and reassured her that this would be over shortly.

Then pressing down her tongue with some gauze, he held a small mirror at the back of her throat and shone alight into her mouth. "Say eeeee." He peered down her throat and told her to say ahhhhhhhh He then wrote a few notes on a chart and smiled that toothy Colgate toothpaste smile at her and told her that her larynx did have a bit of swelling and inflammation but there did not seem to be any kind of narrowing, scar tissues of paralysis involved. I am going to recommend that you follow up with your family doctor if the hoarseness doesn't go away in one or two days." "Thank you Jesus." Shondra croaked. "No, I'm not Jesus. Contrary to some folk's belief that doctors are gods." He chuckled. Very funny, Shondra thought. Is he full of it or what? "Just a little humor to try to make you feel better" he smiled. "Oh now he thinks he's funny. You should really try out for Comic View. Let me get out of this looney bin," she thought. As if reading her mind, he assured her that someone come to escort her back to her room.

Back in the original room Shondra stared at the clock. I was now nine forty five a.m. I don't care what they say I am leaving this place she thought as she took off the hospital gown and put her clothes back on. She was looking around for her shoes when she remembered that she did not wear any. I guess I just have to wear these hospital slippers out of here, she thought.

Still feeling woozy, Shondra found her way out of the examining room and managed to get to the waiting room. Spotting a phone on the wall near the intake desk and seeing a "Please limit your call to 5 minutes." sign posted above the phone, Shondra decided to phone Booby and ask him for a ride home. "Miz Boo-beeee some fish is calling uuuuuuuuuu," the sweet sounding she-male voice that answered the phone called out. Right away Shondra felt a little apprehensive about having to ask Booby for a ride home. But being the loner that she was, Shondra didn't have any female friends to call on and she had no relatives in the area. She realized that she had only Eric. Why did things have to be so fucked up between them she wondered? She

93

was a good mother, a good lover, a good worker, a good person. But what had it gotten her? "The short end to the stick," she said aloud. "A short dick?" Booby asked as he came up behind her. "Who has a short dick?" Ain't say nothing about a short dick, you freak Shondra laughed. That's what I heard you say Ms. Thang. Didn't you hear her say something about a short dick, Frieda?" Frieda, formerly known as Freddie before his gender re assignment which consisted of wearing falsies, tucking his penis backwards between his thighs and wearing tight panties, smacked his lips, looked around, and exclaimed "Where? Where? Yall is some crazy ass heifers!" Shondra laughed painfully. "Please don't make me laugh, it hurts. And stop referring to me as a fish, you frisky bitch." Booby and Frieda got serious when they finally saw the extent of Shondra's injuries.

Booby put his arm around Shondra and scanned the room for a nurse or doctor for answers. "Were you in an accident? Where is KeKe? Was she hurt too? Is this why you didn't show up for work today? Shouldn't you be admitted? Why didn't they keep you? Girl, answer me!" He said loudly. Shondra broke down and started to shake and cry. "Can anybody tell us anything?" Frieda yelled. Two intake workers seated at their desk and the patients that they were checking in eyed the three as the waiting room security guard walked up to them. "I just want to go home," Shondra cried. "I just want to go and find my baby girl." "Your baby girl is lost? You can't find KeKe? Lord what is going on here? Why can't anyone tell us something in this hospital? Who is in charge?" Demanded Booby. "Who is in charge?"

"I see that you have a hospital ID on. Did the doctor see you yet?" asked the tall, muscular, light skinned security guard who came out to see what all the fuss was about. Frieda got up close to him and batted her eyes. "We just want to find out what happened to our friend here and we can't get any answers. Can you help us?" Booby chimed in very lady like. Shondra interrupted "I just need to get my baby girl. She is sick and the police took her to a shelter." After reading Shondra's name on her wristband, the security guard asked an intake worker who had just come back from a break to find out if she had been seen and discharged.

The doctor who had attended Shondra came out into the waiting area and spoke to her. "Ms. Jackson, we were wondering what happened to you back there. We need to release you." How long is that going to take? Shondra asked, I need to get out of here? "Why are you in such a hurry? You need to get your follow up instructions in order to insure that you heal properly." The doctor responded. "The police took my baby to social services and I need to get her back. "It will only take a few minutes," he assured her. "We'll wait out here for you, Shondra," Booby said.

"Is he the one she's talking about with the short dick?" Frieda sniggered after they sat down in the waiting area. Booby smacked Frieda playfully on the knee and laughed. "He's too fine for that, honey. He looks like he packing." "You can have Dr. No Dick, I'll take the hunk in uniform. He looks like he's packing more that gun on his side. Girl, we should come here more often" Booby said with a laugh.

Fifteen minutes later, Shondra came back into the waiting area with her discharge papers. Together they left the emergency room and headed for the parking lot. Once inside of Booby's multicolored hoopty, Shondra filled them in on what happened. She told them about KeKe's doctor visit. She told them how Eric had come to her house in the middle of night and then committed assault and battery on her in a drunken rage. Shondra had been friends with Booby and Frieda since meeting them poolside at the apartment complex where she lived.

They struck it off right away that hot summer day. Shondra had taken KeKe to the pool to cool off since her air condition units had stopped working and the heat inside of their apartment was unbearable. That summer, Booby and Frieda taught KeKe to swim and bought all sorts of water toys and swimsuits for her. They called themselves her fairy godmothers. Booby and Freda had even helped Shondra get her job at the local Big-mart.

Pretty soon they were walking Shondra to her door. "Do you want us to stay with you tonight? You don't have to stay but I do want you to let me hold on to your mace if you don't mind Frieda." "Honey I am going to let you hold something better than mace. Frieda pulled out a pink C2 Taser. This will drop him to the floor fifteen feet away." Shondra's eyes popped as Frieda started to hand it to her. She backed away. "I don't want to kill him, Frieda," she said. "Oh you won't kill him but he may wish he was dead after you blast his ass with this cute little C2 and make him lose control of his bladder and anus at the same time. You know what I mean?" "No Frieda, I'm scared of that thing. Put it back in your purse." Frieda laughed and Booby chirped in, "Girl put that thing back in your purse. Shondra don't need to be tasing nobody. I have a feeling that ignorant ass man ain't dumb enough to come back in here messing with her tonight." "Well, if you are sure that you don't want us to stay with you tonight, you can use my mace." Frieda said and reached back in her purse, pulled out mace and handed it to Shondra. As bad as Shondra's throat hurt, she couldn't help from laughing because Frieda, at that moment reminded her so much of the Tyler Perry character, Madea. I'll keep this for a while if you don't mind. "Well, let's just hope that spaying him with that mace won't just piss him off and cause him to whup up on you some more. You sure you don't want my little taser? It has a LED light so that if he pops up in the dark you can see him. This baby also has a laser so that you can't miss him when you aim at him." "Frieda, didn't she say she did not want that thang??? Huh, Ma-D-ah? Huh? Let's get on up out of here. We'll keep in touch with you and if you need anything, a ride or anything tomorrow, just phone us." LaShondra got into bed and cried herself to sleep. She tossed and turned all night thinking about how she could get away from Eric and make a better life for KeKe and herself.

Chapter 15

Andrea was on her way to the airport when her OnStar phone rang. It was Quinton. She was relieved when he informed her that he did not need a ride home from the airport because he was able to get the airport limo. She thought with a sigh of relief, "Great, now I can go right straight home and not face Quinton after that close call with Sterling. What the hell was I thinking? What the hell was I doing?" Andrea asked herself, knowing quite well what she was thinking and doing. She knew exactly what she was thinking. Sterling was a one hot hunk. She knew what she was doing. She was letting him get her all worked up. "If my cell phone had not snapped me back to my senses, I would have willingly let him seduce me." She tried to put him out of her mind as she drove 15 miles over the speed limit all the way home. She felt an urgent need to take a cold shower and get as far away from Sterling as fast as possible.

Andrea reluctantly checked her mailbox after arriving home. This was a chore that she had grown more and more hesitant to perform because she feared that she would get another bill for something that she did not buy or borrow. She reached into the mailbox and pulled out Oprah, Elle, and Lucky magazines, a magazine from her university alma mater, and an envelope from In2Hair Salon. She was happy that there were no letters sent in window type envelopes that were dead giveaways for collection agencies. "I guess no news is good news." She told herself.

After a brisk cold shower, she dried off and rubbed vanilla scented body butter all over her body. She opened the door of the lingerie closet that contained all her night clothes and decided to put on the fuchsia colored silk Le Perla robe that she had purchased for two hundred and five dollars in Seattle while on a shopping trip with Nicole. Andrea checked out herself in the full length mirror rubbing her hands lightly over the short robe's sheer blouson sleeves. She loved the lace inserts with the flower pattern at the shoulders. Two hundred and five dollars was a lot to spend on a bath-robe but it was worth the sensual feeling that she experienced just from the short time that she had been wearing it.

She sat at the vanity blow drying and brushing the long thick locks of her jet black hair, she thought about how skillfully Terry had cut her hair, making every strand fall into place. With just a flick of a comb of brush, she could make every strand fall into place. She had perfected the hair toss as well as any white girl. Andrea laid the brush on the counter and gave her hair a couple of quick tosses before leaving the mirror behind. She poured herself a glass of merlot and sat on the sofa perusing the newest copy of Oprah magazine checking out all the sage advice, fashions, cosmetic and book reviews.

She picked up the Lucky Magazine that also came in the mail and checked out the latest spring fashions for the spring season before being interrupted by her land line phone.

"Hell-o Michelle. This is Andrea." "Girl I know it's you but how did you know it was me calling?" Michelle asked. "Caller ID dum dum." Andrea laughed. Michelle ignored the dum dum reference because she knew Andrea was saying it in a playful way. "I know you have caller ID, big head, but do you always check it out before you answer the phone," asked Michelle. "Most of the time, I do. I guess it's what old folk refer to as force of habit." "Force of what?" Michelle asked as if puzzled. "Force of habit" that means something you do without thought, or something that you do automatically." "Thanks for the vocabulary slash trite expressions lesson but the reason that I really phoned you was to find out if you received an invite to Terry's launch party." Michelle asked not waiting for an answer, she went on to read her invitation out loud to Andrea. "Wait a minute let me look at this envelope that came in the mail today. It's from Terry's In2Style Salon but I don't know if it's an invitation. It is an invitation," Andrea said. "There's a glossy open face card that looks like an invitation inside." "Have you ever seen that girl on the card inside the shop?" Michelle asked. Andrea looked at the beautiful caramel colored young lady on the card. The model was posed very strategically wearing absolutely nothing except a head full of waist length naturally curly hair. Even though she was nude the eye was drawn to the lovely thick mane of hair. "No I can't say that I've seen her before. She must be someone Terry handpicked to be the face of his product. He picked the right person because any woman would want a head of hair like that." Michelle continued reading "In2 Hair Launch Event, 883 S. Smith Ave, West St. Paul, November 14, 7 until 9PM. That's a good day and time for me. What about you? Are you going to attend?" Michelle asked Andrea. "I don't have anything planned for that time. I'll probably be there Andrea responded. "What's all this stuff on the back of the invitation?" "It's just a little info about Terry. It seems like an advertisement that touts his credentials." Andrea answered and read the back of the invitation.

"Terry is a celebrated hair stylist and beauty expert. Over the last decade he has attracted a loyal following of trend setting, style conscious individuals. At Terry's In2 Style Hair Salons, Terry and his carefully selected team offer fresh looks, techniques and advice receiving praise from clients of all backgrounds and lifestyles. Terry's hairstyles and innovations have been featured in numerous hair shows and national magazines. Mary J. Blige, Gabrielle Union and Taraji P. Henson are a few of the celebrities who visit Terry's salon when they are in the twin cities area. Limited VIP Guest List, RSVP: TerryTaylor@in2hair.com, First fifty guests to RSVP will receive a Twenty five dollar gift certificate. There will also be drawings for twenty five complimentary product gift bags." "I guess I should go on line and RSVP so I can win one of those fifty dollar gift certificates." Michelle laughed. "Girl you know you don't need a fifty dollar gift certificate with all the money you have stashed away." Andrea said. "I can always give the certificate to someone else as a birthday, Christmas, or some kind of present." Michelle said." My phone is beeping. I'll get back with you later." Michelle said and hung up.

Andrea had just finished reading an article entitled 'Are You a Fashion Frugalista' and feeling so bad about spending two hundred and five dollar on a silk robe when the doorbell rang. Who could that be? She wondered as she looked toward the direction of the door. The bell rang again. This time the ring was longer, more urgent. She was aware that she was not fully dressed so just in case it was a stranger, she tip-toed to the door and peered through the peephole. She was surprised to see Quentin outside her door holding a bouquet of assorted flowers in one hand and a bottle of wine in the other. Andrea opened the door, Quinton walked in and as soon as he saw her in the silk, fuchsia colored robe he dropped the flowers and the wine bottle and put his arms around Andrea, pulled her close to him and kissed her passionately. Andrea's knees began to buckle and she became light-headed. Quentin sensed her weakening state and opened his eyes to look for a spot to sit her down. He did not break the kiss and she did not resist when Q lifted her up and walked toward the same sofa on which she had been reading the magazines. He sat her down and they both looked at each other and Andrea laughed. "Welcome back," she said. "I missed you. I didn't know your favorite flower, I bought an assortment." he managed to get out before kissing her again. She leaned back in a reclining position as she felt his muscular body press against her.

The self-tie robe must have also been a self-untie robe because as the couple's bodies moved in sync to the kisses, the tie slipped open on its own an inadvertently presented a full frontal view of Andrea. Quentin, for the first time saw her in all her magnificent womanhood. As a plastic surgeon who had performed hundreds of breast implants, tummy tuck, and butt lifts, Quentin could not remember many women who had a body as beautiful as the one he was looking at now. Andrea did not try to close the robe. Instead, she ran her hand slowly over her full breasts one at a time. Quentin watched in awe as she ran her long manicured fuchsia colored fingertips over the mounds of each of her perfectly symmetrical breasts. Quentin was quick to notice that not only were they symmetrical in size, they were also perfectly paired in shape and projection as Andrea continued her breast "sexamination."

Andrea's watched Quentin become even more excited as she moved her fingertips to center of each mound toward the chocolate colored areola and then to the sensitive nipples. When she reached the nipples, she stopped and Quentin knew instantly that was his cue. He began his own breast exam gently running his tongue over each breast mound, areola, and nipple. By the time he reached the second nipple, he was also doing a vaginal exam. Andrea moved rhythmically as Quentin licked and sucked her breast. Her vagina throbbed in response to the motion of his fingers. She pulled his head closer to her breast and ground her pelvis fiercely as Quentin proceeded to give her the best finger fuck of her life. She shivered and let out a series of moans each louder than the other. Her groans turned to a shriek as she felt her wet cunt spasm uncontrollably. Andrea opened her eyes and noticed that Quentin had somehow managed to undo his shirt and tie. Pulling him closer, she unfastened his belt and helped him un-zip his pants. Before Andrea could touch his private part, Quentin, took it out and put in in the spot where his finger had been. Once she felt him inside of her, Andrea quickly got over being deprived of fondling him the way he had pleasured her. She was so glad that she did not go all the way with Sterling. She was so glad that she had waited for Quentin. She promised herself that she would not put herself in that position with Sterling again.

Chapter 16

Denico Corporation's 'Powers That Be' wanted a financial forecast in order to think about and prepare for the future. The corporation was an international manufacturer of paint and coatings based in Minneapolis, Minnesota. One of largest paint and coating corporation in the world, Denico produced everything from house paint, varnishes for decks, to automobile paint. The Fortune 500 Corporation sold its products under a number of separate brand names, many of which were acquired through a series of buyouts over the past twenty years. A quarterly forecast would provide a means for the firm to express its goals and priorities and to ensure that they were internally consistent. A financial forecast would also assist the firm in identifying asset requirements and any needs for external financing.

Andrea sat at her desk reviewing the information that she had put together for her client before presenting her final report to the board. Each person who sat at the long shiny mahogany table in the board room of Denico Corporation would receive a copy. She had the fifteen copies needed to hand out at the presentation. In a column headed "Denico's assets for 2013", she listed current assets, cash, accounts received, and inventory. She added them all up to

104

get total current assets. She listed fixed assets and added that to the total current assets and derived total assets. "All these figures look good," she decided. "Now let's take a look see at Denico's liabilities for 2013 and see if those numbers check out."

The next column headed Liabilities and Owner's Equity listed current liabilities, accounts payable, and notes payable. Andrea added the three up and came up with total current liabilities of three hundred and eighty million. She next studied Long Term Liabilities. Long term debt she notices was one hundred and sixty million dollars. She went on to study owner equity; common stock, retained earnings and added them all together to come up with total owner equity of seven hundred and sixty million dollars. She looked at the bottom line and determined Denico's total liability and owner equity. Although she could use a computerized program to figure out assets and liabilities, Andrea who was great at math enjoyed figuring it all out in her head. She would use the computerized program in the board room and project the same information on the smart board. Working this out without the help of a computer program always helped her better retain the information in her head and allowed her to present dynamically without benefits of using notes.

Andrea noticed the light to her phone flickering indicating that she had a call on the other end of the line. She picked it up and said "Hell-o, Andrea McNair speaking, how may I help you?" The voice on the other end responded. "Hell-o, this is Sterling Steingold calling from Bank of America. I have some news that you may be interesting in hearing. This may be something that you prefer hearing in person and not on your company's phone." "You are right; I prefer to keep my private life away from the office as much as possible." "Good, when can I see you again? I mean when can we get together to discuss my findings." "I'm going to be tied up all this week with several meetings that may go on after office hours. I can't even get away for lunch." Andrea responded. "No problem, just phone me at the bank whenever you have an opening in your schedule. I think you'll be pleased with the progress that we've made." He concluded, "I'll be sure to do that. Thanks for phoning, I'll get back to you as soon as possible." Andrea waited for his response. "Fine, we'll talk later. Good Bye, Ms. McNair."

After placing the phone on the receiver, she went back to her calculations. "Where was I? She asked herself and looked back down at the balance sheet. The column headed Income Statement in Millions listed sales eighteen million, Cost sixteen million, Taxable income two million, and tax, seventy nine million. Andrea made a few calculations and said to herself, "just as I thought that seventy nine million is incorrect. It should be seventy six million." Then she started talking to herself out loud as if she was working a problem on the chalkboard in from of a group of students. "Subtract the cost from the sales and we get a total taxable income of two hundred million. Now subtract the seventy six million in taxes from taxable income and we come up with a net income of one hundred and twenty four million dollars." After checking dividends and addition to retained earnings, Andrea came up with a growth forecast rate of thirty three percent in sales for 2014. "So that's the bottom line for Denico's 2014 forecast. They stand to gain by thirty-three percent if they continue going the way they are financially. "She ran off copies of her report and checked her PowerPoint presentation to make sure that everything was in order."

Before leaving she asked her assistant to place the reports in individual folders embossed with the name of her company on the front cover and place her business card in the cardholder on the inside front cover. "Sure thing Ms. McNair the young assistant replied. Would you like me to put them in your mailbox or on your desk?" "Please put them on my desk, Susan. That way we won't have to worry about anyone inadvertently taking them." "Sure thing, Ms. McNair, I'll get it done right away." Andrea liked having Susan as an assistant. She was very efficient in getting any task that she was given done in a competent and timely manner. She knew that Susan was bucking for a promotion and when the time came she would give her a glowing evaluation if she kept up her good work. "I'm going to call it a day. I'll see you tomorrow morning." "Have a good evening Ms. McNair."

Chapter 17

$\mathcal{S}$terling sat at his desk and listened attentively as the handwriting analyst examined the credit application filed by the identity thief who was masquerading as Andrea McNair. Someone applied for a charge account with Wells Fargo Bank. Ralph Daniels was one of the best handwriting analyst in the field and had been called upon to testify in fraud court cases initiated by banks around the country. Sterling had been able to successfully recoup stolen money for his bank using the Ralph's expertise many times in the past. He listened as Ralph Daniels compared and contrasted the writing on the bogus application to the authentic application.

"You know handwriting analysis involves comparing two documents, one by a known author, in this case Andrea McNair and one by an unknown author whom we will refer to as Andrea Wanabee. I am going to start off not with checking for similarities, which even you, Steinny could do with a fair degree of accuracy. I'm going to start by checking for differences." Steingold looked at Ralph a bit irritated. First, he was irritated because he did not like being referred to as Steinny and secondly because he had heard Ralph's how to compare handwriting spiel every time he has used him to determine fraud. He knew the procedure. Hell, he could probably analyze the damn handwriting himself if he put his mind to it. His only drawback would be what the judge or jurors thought of his handwriting testimony in court. He would not be the expert witness Ralph Daniels was. But he damn sure wasn't going to let Ralph give him another lecture on how to distinguish one a, b, c, or d from another. In fact, he was going to help Ralph lecture. "It's the differences that initially determine if the same person possibly wrote both pieces of text. If there are key differences in enough individual characteristic and those differences do not appear to be an attempt to disguise one's handwriting or copy someone else's handwriting, the two documents were not written by the same person." Steingold said. "You're absolutely correct." Daniels beamed and went on to say "We refer to that as simulation and simulation has its own telltale characteristics."

Ralph looked at each letter with a magnifying glass. "I have had ample time to examine both the credit application completed by Andrea Wanabee as well as the exemplars and bank application written by Andrea McNair. And I have concluded that there definitely a case of fraud on the part of Andrea Wanabee." "Would you be willing to give your expert opinion and testify in court if need be?" "If I am available, of course, but my report should be enough to convince the judge and juror. All your lawyer has to do is put my report in PowerPoint format and they will see that the letter form which includes curves, slants, and even the proportional size of letters written by the perpetrator is different from that of your client." "What about how smooth and dark the lines are and the spaces between the letters and words and all that crap." Steingold asked now wondering how he could have ever thought that he knew enough to convince the court that he himself was a handwriting expert. He could repeat some of the tidbits that he remembered from Ralph's many lectures but he was no Ralph L. Daniels, professional, forensic handwriting analyst. "That will also show the handwriting is a forgery."

"Every person on earth has a unique way of writing. Do you remember being in primary school and everyone in your class learned to write based on a particular copybook or a style of writing" "In fact I do remember our teacher using the Zaner- Bloser Handwriting workbooks. We all wrote in a similar style." "Right, but as we grew older our handwriting changed because the writing characteristic that we learned in school or our style characteristics became only the underlying method of our handwriting. We developed individual characteristics that are unique only to us and distinguish our handwriting from someone else's." He's going into another lecture Steingold thought and decided it was time to wrap up his session by once again showing that he knew a little something about handwriting analysis. "I know that most of us don't write the way we did in first or second grade. And while two or more people may share a couple of individual characteristics, the chance of those people sharing twenty or thirty individual characteristics is so unlikely that many handwriting analysts would say it's impossible. So even though the person who forged Andrea McNair's handwriting tried to slant or curve some of her handwriting characters, there is no way that she can pass off her handwriting as Andrea's." "Ye Gads Steinny, you don't need me in the courtroom. You can win this case on your own testimony." "Well, if you want to let them pay me the big amount that they pay you to be an expert witness, maybe I will do it myself." Steinberg said as he stood up and shook Ralph Daniel's hand and thanked him for coming.

Glad to bring this meeting to a close, Sterling decided not worry about whether the handwriting expert would testify. He was confident that Ralph's fat ass would show up in court and give his expert opinion. Ralph got a kick out of trying to act like he was unavailable. In all the years that the bank had used him as an expert witness in counterfeiting cases, he only missed court once and that was when he had to be admitted to the hospital for an appendectomy. Ralph had a way of managing to juggle his time so that he could get every penny that was offered to him for his expertise. Now that Sterling had that out the way, he needed to focus on getting other leads before he turned the case over to the authority. Steingold wanted to be certain that he could point the police in the right direction. If the case was going to be airtight he had to cross all his "T"s and dot all his "I"s.

Chapter 18

*L*aShondra had been eating in the restaurant that Saturday splurging on a steak sub combo when Andrea and Michelle had come in for lunch. Shondra looked at the shopping bags they bought in with them from upscale dress shops and shoe stores. She wondered what it would be like to be in their shoes for one day. She watched as a waitress soon came and took the two women's lunch orders. She noticed that both women seemed to be watching their weight because they only ordered soup and salad. She guessed that they were both a dress size five. She herself was a size 10. Shondra continued eating her lunch but she couldn't help glancing in their direction from time to time. She wondered what it would be like to just have some leisure time to spend with a girlfriend over lunch. She had not had close girlfriend since her college days back in Atlanta. In fact she couldn't remember ever having lunch, dinner, or breakfast with anyone other than a man or her queer friends Booby and Frieda since she moved to Minnesota. As Shondra continued eating, she noticed that one of the two women were finely dressed and were wearing enough gold on their wrists, neck, and fingers to pay her rent for three or four month. She knew the price of jewelry although she didn't own any diamonds or gold. She had always liked the way it looked and priced it whenever she would go window shopping. She could tell that the gold on Andrea's wrists as worth some serious money.

Andrea savored rich tasting the celery soup as Michelle talked about her recent engagement to Todd Shepherd, an up and coming architect in Minnesota. "Todd really surprised me when he popped the question last week. I had no idea that he was going to asked me to marry him when he took me out to my favorite restaurant." "I can imagine that your jaw dropped five inches when you found the fifteen caret diamond engagement ring inside of the chocolate dessert that he insisted you try," Andrea said. She then asked, "When is the big day?" Michelle answered. "I haven't decided yet with all the cases I have pending." Michelle, a court appointed child advocate and public defender, responded. "Also, Todd has to spend a lot of time out of state planning and developing a new municipal center for some city near Los Angeles. But don't worry girlfriend you will be the third person to know the date after Todd and I decide. That's because you, my friend will be maid of honor." Andrea let out a squeal and Shondra sitting at a table next to them stopped chewing and held the bite of steak sub in her mouth as she strained to hear what all the commotion was about. She listened as Michelle assured Andrea that she was her first and only choice for the title of Maid of Honor at what promised to be one of the best weddings in the city. Shondra began to feel a bit depressed thinking about her present situation and involvement with a no good, two-timing, sometimes volatile man who she would never walk down the aisle with because she knew she could not change a leopard's spots no matter how hard she would try.

The two sophisticated sounding women finished their lunch and prepared to leave. Shondra watched as Andrea picked up the tab, paid for the meals and insisted on leaving the tip. She watched as Michelle headed to the restroom to "Fix my makeup." She watched as the waitress bought back Andrea's credit card and Andrea placed it into her purse as she eagerly answered a call on her cell phone. She saw Andrea looking at the phone before answering it, obviously checking to see who was calling. "Must be someone she is looking forward to talking to." thought Shondra as she resumed chewing the piece of sub she had bitten before deciding to eavesdrop on the two women sitting at the table next to her. "Maybe your man is going to propose also. Maybe you two bitches will have a double wedding." She said under her breath. Shondra continued to watch and listen in on the conversation as Andrea chatted gleefully with whoever was on the other end of the phone. Shondra watched as the woman who had gone to the restroom returned and the two women started toward the exit. She also watched as Andrea clashed into the bearded guy who was standing outside of the restaurant asking for change. The contents of Andrea's purse spilled onto the sidewalk and Shondra watched as the group scrambled to pick up the makeup bag, purse, and other items. She smiled and shook her head as she thought "That's what that uppity bitch gets for trying to act so saditty." As she went to the door she glanced back at the table where the pair had sat and noticed a twenty dollar tip under a plate. She reached to pick up the tip and saw a cell phone on the table. She quickly picked up the cell phone and the twenty dollar tip and walked out of the restaurant.

Sooo this is what an I-phone looks like, she thought as she used the track ball to scroll all over the screen. She knew better than to phone anyone who knew her because the call could be traced back to her. However, she could keep it to go to her favorite internet sites none of which required an internet I.D. She went to YouTube to check out videos, Google to check out employment opportunities, and TMZ to check out gossip on the celebrities she liked. "Yeah this I-phone is the bomb. Now I see why so many people are buying them. The internet was not all Shondra looked at on the I-phone, she also checked out the other icons on the small cell phone's LCD screen. She checked out the messages that Andrea had not looked at. She checked out the contacts and saw the names of friends, businesses, and associates that Andreas had stored in the phone. She saw a folder listed ICE which stood for *in case of emergency*. She clicked to open the folder and saw several contacts listed including: Mother, Sister, Best Friend, and Me. Curious about the "Me" entry she decided to check it out. She felt a sense of glee when she discovered "Me" was aka Andrea. Andrea listed her own information into the contact book in order to remember certain important phones number. However, she also listed everything that the contact feature allowed her to enter including title which was Miss, first name, last name, picture, company, business address, e-mail address, work number, extension, pager, fax, home phone number, and home address. She had entered all this information on herself, her friends, and business associates into the I-phone's contacts feature. Andrea was a corporate finance manager with Denico Paint Company. The I-phone had been provided by her company. The company also paid the monthly phone bill so that she could be reached at anytime, anywhere even while vacationing in the Bahamas.

It was almost week before Andrea missed the I-phone. She tried phoning it but no one picked up. She found out that it had not been used and thought that it was in her car or condo hiding out in some nook or cranny. Meanwhile, armed with key pieces of Andrea McNair's personal information which included date of birth, Social Security number, utility account numbers, and mother's maiden name, Andrea applied for and received a new driver's license online. At first, she had not planned on using the information that she found on the I-phone. But she just could not get the picture of Andrea coming into the restaurant dressed like one of the Real Housewives of Atlanta. "Shit. What gives her the right to be stylish while you have to look like Cinderella before the ball? You should look like Ne-Ne, Kandi, Phaedra and Kenya all rolled into one. Open up an account in the uppity heifer's name and get yourself some clothes that suit the real you. Also looking good is the best revenge." Shondra thought about Eric running out on her every chance he got. She would show him.

Chapter 19

Almost two weeks went past before LaShondra decided to use the bogus driver's license to apply for credit. Before she left home, she sat in front of the mirror for almost an hour giving herself a makeover so that she could look something like the person on the driver's license. She left the apartment feeling like she could pull this lie off.

Shondra's heart was beating a mile a minute as she gave the items to the Nordstrom's cashier. The young girl who somehow struck Shondra as an energetic new hire, eagerly rang up the black Boyfriend Blazer at two hundred and thirty-five dollars, two pairs of leggings, two pencil skirts, a low V-Neck silk wrap tunic and a white ruffle blouse, Sergio Rossi Aramis boots, a pair of Valentino cutout lace-up boots and a pair of kitten heel slides. "Did you find everything okay?" the young girl asked while taking her time to ring up the items. Shondra's heart was now in her throat as she stuttered a mere "Y-Y-Yes" Her hand shook visibly as she handed over the credit card and signed a receipt that bore the name Andrea McNair. Her legs were wobbly as she walked quickly toward the exit trying not to look back fearful that security was going to grab her before she got out of the mall. She let out a sigh of relief as she found her rented econo car in the parking lot. Shondra threw the bags in the trunk and hauled her butt away from Nordstrom's, away from the Mall of America and away from that part of the city. She drove and drove until she reached Northeast Minneapolis. She finally decided to stop and eat at Jax Café. Shondra's nerves settled down and her appetite kicked in. She ordered a salad, a seafood platter and a Jaxburger and a glass of white zinfandel. Shondra was grateful that the waitress served the zinfandel out immediately. She was not big on drinking but she did need to get her nerves back to normal. After a few sips of the wine, she began to think about KeKe. KeKe was in daycare. Now that she had lost her job and was collecting unemployment. She was able to take advantage of the reduced daycare tuition.

Although Shondra was reluctant to have her daughter out of her sight since Ke's medical ordeal, she thought it would do the child a world of good to mingle with other children and get some pre-school instructions a few hours a day. "Damn, how could I buy all of these clothes for myself and not get anything for my baby girl." "Yeah, do you see Cynthia Bailey's or Kandi Burgess' daughters walking around looking like a rag-a-muffins?" her alter ego asked. "Shut the hell up." She answered out loud. "What did you say?" an old lady sitting near her asked. "I didn't say anything to you. I was just thinking to myself." She said. "You can't have KeKe looking like a rag-a-muffin the voice inside her head repeated" She held her hand up to her temple and whispered "I said shut up." The old lady's eyes cut toward the mumbling woman, shook her head, and made the sign of the cross while silently praying "Satan get thee away from me." Shondra's meal came but she could only eat the Jax Crabroll and the Neptune Salad that she ordered. After having a second zinfandel, she asked the waitress to box up the Jax Burger so that she could take the half-pound Angus burger home with her. She would share it with KeKe later on tonight. The second zinfandel gave Shondra the confidence and nerves to go shopping for KeKe's.

She decided to go into Kohl's and pick up a few things for KeKe. She scooped up two pleated and one ruffle tiered scooter skirt, a Juicy Couture velour hoody dress, one denim jumper, four pairs of leggings, three sweaters, socks, and two pairs of shoes for KeKe. This time Shondra didn't feel nervous and her hand did not shake when she swiped her forged credit card. In fact she felt extremely exhilarated. I guess Jamie Foxx had the right idea when he sang "Blame it on the Alcohol." Shondra thought as she put the car in gear and sped off from the mall. She had only forty-five minutes before the day care center would begin charging her an additional fee for picking up the child after the contracted time.

Shondra arrived just in time to avoid additional childcare cost. She gave KeKe a big hug and told the caregiver "Thanks for taking good care of my baby." KeKe was now enrolled in New Horizon Montessori Preschool. "This center is so much better than the YMCA daycare center that Ke attended before we made our move." she thought. "Have I steered you wrong yet." The voice inside her head whispered. "Haven't things been a lot better since you have been listening to me?" "Just leave me alone." Shondra said aloud. "Mama, you want me to leave you alone?" KeKe asked very innocently. "What?" "You said "Just leave me alone. I heard you." "I wasn't talking to you baby, I was talking to this headache I'm having." "Oh, said KeKe I thought you were talking to me."

"No Pumpkin, you can talk all you want. In fact how was your day today? What did you do in that school of yours? Did you learn anything interesting or did you do anything fun today?" "It was fun today mommy. I made a picture for you." "You did?" "The teacher let us put buttons, combs, forks, keys, and things from her goodie box on a sheet of black paper." "And that made a picture?" UH Huh, we had to let it sit in the sun until after lunch and them when we took the buttons and keys off the paper, there was a picture." "I see the sun faded the paper and the places that were covered stayed black." "Uh hum" "That was a good idea."

Once inside of her apartment, Shondra opened all of the packages and tried on all the clothes. She was pleased that she was able to get everything in the correct size. She did not try anything on in the store because she was fearful the longer she stayed in the store, the harder it would be for her to go through with the identity theft.

Just as she finished trying on the last garment and looking at her reflection in a full length mirror, her new cell phone rang. She picked it up after the third ring. It was Booby. "You didn't forget that we are giving Ms. Thang a pard-day tonight to celebrate her birthday?" "Hell no, girl. You know you told me that you wanted me to hang out with you bitches tonight." She answered. "I made arrangements for your sister to baby-sit KeKe." She added. After a brief phone conversation about what time she was leaving, LaShondra went into the bathroom and flat ironed her hair into a short, sleek bob. Next, she meticulously applied the Cover Girl Make up that she had picked up from the drugstore. She thought, if it was good enough for Queen Latifah and Rihanna it's good enough for me. She told her reflection in the mirror before pressing her newly painted lips together. She opened the door for Booby's sister and thanked her for coming to sit with KeKe. "Eric is going to flip when he sees you, girlfriend." LaShondra was flattered. Ain't going out with Eric. I hope I never see him again." "Be sure that KeKe gets in bed by eight and don't give her any sweets. You can have a snack if you like."

She slid into the rented Ford Fusion and with laugh started to sing "Don't Be Tardy to the Pardy. Ooo, ooo, don't be tardy to the pardy. Ooo, ooo."

Chapter 20

LaShondra thought about how she had ended up in Minneapolis in the first place. She had never gotten accustomed to Minneapolis' cold weather. It was a far cry from 'Hotlanta'. Minnesota was the home state of her ex-husband, Raynaud and he had moved back to take care of his ailing grandmother after graduating from Morris Brown. In time, she learned not to think about the cold too much. She learned to dress in thin multiple layers instead of wearing a thick coat. And she always wore gloves and hats to keep her extra warm. If she had to get the rail, or be outside for any length of time, Shondra would wear a scarf and boots. After a few frigid months, she learned to embrace Minnesota's cold winter. Pretty soon, Raynaud had Shondra were out sledding.

After Raynaud left her and the baby, Shondra had to fend for herself. The meager hundred dollar a week that Raynaud had to pay for child support did not cover the cost of groceries, furniture payment, rent, phone, and electric bills which were not included in the rent. KeKe needed clothes and shoes. Although she kept good care of her clothes, she was growing like a weed and a few clothes needed replacement almost every year. Shondra had managed to eke out a living by working at Big-Mart. Pinching pennies and robbing Peter to pay Paul, she often went without so that KeKe could get a new coat. Her panties and bras were so worn that she was embarrassed to wear them. She bought generic everything when she shopped for groceries. She hated it, but just like learning to cope with the weather, Shondra learned to cope with no name brands and their feeble attempt to taste like the real thing.

Although Shondra didn't like to think in terms of could have, should have, or would have, she sometimes found herself thinking about the past. She remembered Robert Frost's poem "The Road Not Taken." Shondra recited part of the poem softly "Two roads diverged in a wood, and I---- I took the one less traveled by, and that has made all the difference." She began to think about her life before Minnesota, before she married Raynaud, before KeKe was conceived. She had never imagined that the road she had taken with Raynaud would lead here to her present state of affairs.

Why didn't Shondra relocate to Richmond, Virginia where she could get a job working at her aunt's child care center? After living in Minnesota and getting a taste of being on her own, Shondra now considered it her hometown. In spite of the cold winters, LaShondra had come to appreciate the beauty of Minneapolis. She enjoyed the outdoor activity. She loved the fact that no home in Minneapolis was more than six or seven blocks away from a city park. There was a total of one hundred and forty three parks and there was always something going on. Shondra often joined the many joggers or in line skaters in the park near her home. The twenty-two lakes within the city were always lovely and teeming with people, even in winter. She loved watching the canoeing, sailing, water skiing,

123

and windsurfing enthusiasts who were out for a good time. She remembered the few times Raynaud had rented a canoe and taken her out for a ride on the lake.

Even though she felt more at home with people of her own ethnic background, Shondra had gotten accustomed to the fact that the city was three-fourth white. And unlike Atlanta, Blacks here were a minority. Shondra appreciated the diversity that the city offered. There were significant number of Somalis, a few Hmong refugees, a few Mexicans, and the highest percentage of American Indians of any major city in the country. Shondra was glad that she was a part of the largest minority. Minneapolis would never afford her the number of Black friends and acquaintances that Atlanta offered but she could live with that.

Minneapolis was the only home that her daughter had ever known. Shondra did not want to uproot KeKe and move back to Atlanta where she attended college or back to Richmond, her hometown. She had established herself in Minneapolis. She had a job, an apartment, and a few good friends. She could not say the same thing about Atlanta where she had to drop out of Clarke because she could not work and keep up her grades at the same time.

The thought of asking her parents to pay for her out of state tuition was unimaginable. They had tried to get her to consider going to Hampton Institute since she wanted to attend a historically black university. When she was a high school junior, Shondra checked out Clarke Atlanta University yearbooks in Mrs. Pernisha Patrick's math class. She also looked at Morehouse University yearbooks in Mr. Rodney Patrick's chemistry class. The two Patrick teachers instilled a sense of ambition and determination in her.

Although the Patricks were staunch believer in promoting HBUs, they encouraged all of their students to think about and plan on attending college. Without really trying to convince students which place of higher learning they should attend. Their fondness of Morehouse, Clarke, and other HBUs was evident and rubbed off on many of their black students. Shondra's parents had always encouraged her to get good grades so that her grade point average would not prevent her from attending college. Mrs. Patrick encouraged Shondra to sign up for the after school SAT Prep class that was being offered twice a week. Since she knew a high SAT score could be her ticket to Clarke, Shondra took Mrs. Patrick's offer. Her grade point average and SAT scores earned her a partial mathematics scholarship. She had just enough to pay for tuition and books. She still had to find a place to stay because living in the dorm would put her way over her budget. "Several of my best friends live there and Sister Henrietta Vaughn who rents several duplexes in the area said she would hold a room for you. Phone her and let her know when you will arrive and you can meet up with her to sign a lease." She hugged both Pernisha and Rodney Patrick and accepted a graduation card that contained a gift of one hundred dollars. "You shouldn't have." She said through teary eyes. "Nonsense, I wish it could have been more. Rodney and I saw such potential in you and your desire to attend an institution that means so much to us. Give it all that you've got and do not let anything come before your goal. We are here for you if you need us." Shondra's parents gave the Patricks a hug and thanked them for all of their support. She was able to find a part time job in less than a week after moving into the duplex that Mrs. Patrick had arranged for her to live in.

Try as she might, it was difficult to study and think about how she was going to pay her part of the thirteen hundred dollar rent on the small West End duplex she shared with three other students. The duplex was within walking distance to the campus that they all attended. Working at the Black health food store/restaurant until 10PM and then going home and do research for some paper that was always due was hard.

Shondra thought about how she dated Raynaud for two years. She met him when he was in his sophomore year at Morris Brown University and she was in her freshman year at Clarke. She remembered how she had just sat down in window seat of the Marta when a fine looking brother sat next to her, the scent of Aramis radiating from his well sculpted body was intoxicating. Shondra looked up from her biology book and met his smiling face. Her heart almost melted when he flashed those pearly whites at her. "A fine looking brother with not one damn gold tooth", Shondra thought. The dimple that creased his left cheek was the sexiest thing she had seen all day. "That brother knows he's fine. Probably has so many women after his ass it ain't even funny." Shondra told herself.

It was Saturday and although she did not have class, she went to the campus library to add the final touches to a research paper. Shondra got off and headed directly toward the science building. She noticed that "her fine looking friend" got off at the same stop. As she headed toward the college complex, he walked in the same direction. I hope pretty boy here ain't no damn serial killer, Shondra thought. Pretty soon she realized that pretty boy had turned toward Morris Brown Hall. "Well don't you feel cheap, Pretty boy is a student and he was not following your tired ass," a small voice inside of her head told her. "He was just trying to make your day and you immediately think he's after you. You should be so lucky."

Well he's probably a punk ass art major with his fine, hot cocoa looking, long dreadlock wearing self. She said out loud. "He is an art major and he is downright gorgeous, Marlene." She turned around and saw her best friend, Marlene Parker, walking a few steps behind her. "Girl, what are you doing talking to yourself?" "Child you don't know the half of it. Since I that man sat down next to me on the Marta, I have been carrying on a two-way conversation with myself. Who is that fine brother? Is he bi? Married? Spoken for? Give it up girl. What is the 411 on him?" "His name is Raynaud Jackson." Marlene answered. "And he is an art major, but he ain't no punk. He ain't gay, and he ain't married." Losing the Ebonics, Marlene asked Shondra, "Are you ready for the Biology test. Did you study the chapter on DNA and Molecular Genetics? I am so ready to get this test out of the way and get on to the chapter on Human Genetics." LaShondra replied "Okay Miss Egghead, let go over the structure of DNA for the umpteenth time. However, I still can't figure what biology has to do with being a math teacher."

A few days later Shondra saw Raynaud on the Marta again. Again he sat next to her and this time, looking directly into her eyes, he smiled and introduced himself to her. She was transfixed by those deep dark brown irises that were surrounded the clearest, brightest eyes she's had ever noticed. She watched as his full lips seemed to move in slow motion as he asked her if she attended Clarke or Spellman. Shondra just sat there staring at him, amazed that he could hypnotize her with one look. And that damn scented oil that he had on was fit for an African king. Lord, even the dreads 'look-ded' good on him today. "Isn't this your stop, too?" He asked as he took her books out of her hand, stood up and made a gentlemanly gesture toward the door of the Marta with his free hand, while he waited for her to head toward the exit. "He can be the damn Boston strangler," she thought as she stood up. "I'm getting off this Marta, I don't care who he is!" "Not only am I getting off this train, I am going to be his baby's mama." She smiled to herself. "But first, I have to play hard to get." Still unable to verbally respond to him, she reached for her books and he handed them to her. "So, how long have you been attending Clarke?" "Two years." "Where are you from?" "Virginia" "Are you ready to tell me your name yet, or are you going to keep me in suspense?" "My name is LaShondra Richards. I'm sorry that I didn't answer you when you first asked. My mind was somewhere else."

Raynaud was persistent in making her acquaintance in spite of the Shondra's repeated excuses that she was too busy. In reality she was always busy studying for a test, late for work, or was working late. She did not lie to him because she was working her ass off trying to pay the high cost of tuition. "If I can just make it this year, I can get more financial assistance next semester," she kept telling herself. Shondra could barely make ends meet yet, she continued to go to classes and put forth her best effort.

Chapter 21

❋

Andrea had a standing once a week beauty appointment at In2Hair every Thursday at six pm. The salon was just thirty minutes from her office and she was usually on time since she was always Terry's last customer of the day. She walked into Terry's salon and was cheerfully greeted by a pretty young girl who was seated behind a semicircular receptionist desk. "Hello Ms. McNair, it's good to see you again. I'll let Terry know that you are here." "That will be fine, thank you." Andrea sat down in the reception area and took a quick look around the trendy salon. She was always impressed by the salon's warm and inviting look. She sat down on a comfortable chair and waited to be sent to the styling area. Even though she had been in the salon numerous times, she still enjoyed checking out the place.

Directly above the reception desk was recessed lighting. The decorative pendant lights that shone toward the back wall of the reception area highlighting the salon's logo undoubtedly increased In2Hair salon's name recognition. The salon's pristine white walls and beige marble floor were accented by the addition of lush green tropical plants. A large wall fountain with copper trim and brown rain forest marble added a level of style and sophistication to the reception area. The sound of water not only gave the salon a calming feeling, it added a touch of class. Andrea could not think of one hair salon she had visited that had a waterfall feature. Themes of copper, cracked glass, and brown rain forest marble were repeated throughout the salon providing such a relaxing and soothing atmosphere a patron would not mind if the stylist was a little late getting to her. However, Andrea had never waited more than five or ten minutes before she was seated in Terry's stylist chair.

She walked over to the display area and took a look at the new products that Terry had put out since her last visit. "Very shrewd, Terry, placing your products in the reception area is a smart move indeed. This reception area is a prime location with easy access to entice your clients to make a purchase." She thought. By her calculation, about one fourth of the salon's profits came from selling hair care products. Andrea watched as a woman who had just finished getting her hair done walked up to the display and picked out a bottle of shampoo and a jar of conditioner then happily paid the receptionist.

"Ms. McNair, Terry is ready for you now. You can go on to his station." Andrea thanked the young lady and walked to the styling area where Terry had the honor of the prestigious first chair in studio of ten chairs. "Hell-o friend girl, you are looking good in that Versace." "Hi Terry, I need a shampoo, conditioner, a trim, and style." Do you want to keep the same style or do you want to try something different?" "I kind of like this style for now. I just need you to trim it a bit because it's too long." Terry signaled a young hair styling intern who came over and escorted Andrea to a shampoo bowl. The girl shampooed and massaged Andrea's hair and scalp and then gave her a deep conditioner. After a final rinsing, Andrea was directed back to the stylist chair where Terry stood waiting with a stylist cape. After she sat down Terry placed the cape around her chest and shoulders fastening it in the center of her chest.

Terry applied a light product on Andrea's hair and then began blow drying with a round brush. "Terry, I got that invitation that was sent out." "Did you RSVP yet?" "Yes I mailed my RSVP the next day. Didn't you receive it?" "It probably arrived; I am not handling any of that. I provided a list of who I would like to attend to my event planner and he is handling the invitations, RSVPs, and all of that stuff." Terry said as he started to craft Andrea's hair in loose waves with a large curling iron. "Terry I am so impressed by what you are doing with your hair products. You have actually started your own brand. You know that? We hear those athletes, movie stars and other celebrities talking about their brand. You have actually started your own brand." Andrea said. "It was all God's doing, honey. All God's doing. It was like He lead me each step of the way because seriously, I did not know what the hell I was getting into when I started doing hair. But I took it one step at a time and then I opened one shop and then another and then another. I guess I have been blessed." Andrea shook her head in agreement and said. "You were blessed but you also had the good judgment to stay focused. Now look at you. You have your very own hair products out there." "Yes they are out there. I just hope they sell." Terry laughed. "They will because they are good products. They made my hair grow." Andrea said. "Girl shut up, all this Indian hair on your head was going to grow anyways. But I would like to use your picture in my magazine ads." "You got magazine ads?" "Yes, honey. My products will be in advertised in Essence, Ebony, and Black Hair for the next three months." "You are a regular entrepreneur, Mr. Terry." Terry laughed as he finger combed Andrea's loose waves. He finished up by spraying a few squirts of holding spray a five inches above her hair and let the particles lightly fall down on her tresses. Terry spun the chair around until it stopped in front of a large mirror. "Like it?" He asked. "Love it." She answered. "I'll see you at the launch party on Saturday night." she said. "Okay Love," he said.

Terry was glad that Andrea was his last appointment of the day. He had quite a few loose ends to tie up before the launch party. After tidying up his work area and speaking with his assistant salon manager about some minor shop concerns, Terry put on his coat and hat. "Before you leave, be sure that all of the damp, dirty towels are placed in the washer, dried, and neatly folded. And be sure to add the fabric softener. I don't want any funky, mildew smelling towels in the shop when I open up on Tuesday." He told the shampoo girl. "I'll see you all next week."

Chapter 22

ndrea contacted Bynum Finance and was fortunate that the loan company shared application information with her. The application listed two credit card references. One credit card company not only provided her with a copy of the application, but also gave her with a list of all the purchases that had been made in her name. Andrea wanted to burst into her impostor's house and scratch her eyes out but, at Sterling's suggestion, she decided to coordinate her efforts with the investigator assigned to the case. After she photo-copied each document, she would hand over all the documents she was able to obtain. Andrea wanted to be certain that detectives would be armed with enough evidence to get a search warrant of the perpetrator's home. She hoped the search would turn up enough evidence to get an arrest warrant for suspect.

She was so excited about her latest discovery that she could not resist phoning Sterling to make an office appointment. She knew it would be better to meet with him in an office environment because she wanted only to discuss business with him. It was hard not to be distracted from the real reason she met him outside the office. The chemistry between them was so undeniably strong. If she was not

133

in love with Quinton, Sterling would, without a doubt, be someone she could be seriously involved with.

Sterling picked up the phone and answered politely. "Good Morning, Sterling Steingold speaking, May I help you?" After a brief hello, Andrea identified herself and began explaining the reason she wanted to set up an appointment with him. "I have been gathering what I hope can be used as evidence against the woman who is using my name to get credit. I am going to take my findings to the authorities, but I want your opinion before I make that move. I want to make sure that what I give them is relevant and can be used in a court of law to bring this woman to justice and clear my name." Sterling decided not to probe her about what evidence she had. Instead, he decided to let her bring it in. "Hell if that is the only way I can see her, set up an appointment. Just make sure it's late enough to ask her out for a drink after the meeting is over." He thought. "Sure, Andrea I have an opening at 4PM tomorrow." He told her. "That sounds good to me; I'll see you tomorrow at four o'clock." She said. "See you then." Sterling answered. She thanked him and said goodbye.

Sterling thought about the case after she hung up. He really wanted to get to the bottom of this case not only because if would clear Andrea's name but also because each time he brought a fraud investigation to a successful closure, it put a feather in his cap. Solving this case would help further his career should he decide to go up for a promotion instead of pursuing his dream of becoming an investment banker.

His banking position was all well and good but it was not the career he had planned on when he got his M.B.A. His current salary of $108,895 was better than most of the workers in his bank, but with the cost of living going up, his exquisite taste, and penchant for the finer things in life, a raise or promotion would be welcomed. The bank was in the process of looking into hiring a credit card fraud investigator. However, until the person was actually on payroll, Sterling was given the responsibility of investigating credit card fraud and abuse of cardholder information. He was also responsible for interviewing individuals involved and providing assistance to law enforcement. In the short time that he had been working at this particular bank, he had participated in two court trails.

Sterling glanced at his watch and noticed that it was a half hour before his workday would end. He opted not to stay any longer than necessary tonight because he had a full day tomorrow. He had scheduled several meeting including a training session for his workers that would last at least an hour and a half. He had arranged for all the bank's employees to come in an hour before their normal work day to attend the monthly employee meeting. He had determined that the theme for this meeting would be customer focus. He had made arrangements with Bo Jangles fast food restaurant for them to prepare enough steak and cheese, chicken, sausage, and ham biscuits for everyone who was to attend the early morning meeting. He would pick them up on the way to work. The head teller would bring in orange juice and coffee. And the branch manager would bring in a fruit tray and donuts. Sterling had long ago learned that when people are fed, they are more receptive to a business meeting or workshop. He knew that most would show up early, in good spirits, and happily participate in workshop and training activities.

In fact, he had sent out an e-mail reminding everyone in the office of the meeting and included the words "Come hungry."

The following day, the scheduled meeting went without a hitch. After everyone had their fill of breakfast foods, juice and coffee, the branch manager officially opened the meeting. First on the agenda was a review of the number of new customers who signed up the previous month. He awarded certificates and checks for five, three, and two hundred dollars to the top three employees who recruited the most new customers that quarter and encouraged others as he passed out each check. "This could be you!" He exclaimed as he presented the five hundred dollar check to the employee who opened the most new accounts. After posing for a photo with the first recipient, he presented the second check and said "This too could be you!" He then presented the two hundred dollar check to the last employee and said to the on lookers in the audience. "Remember, this could be you! All you have to do is ask everyone who comes up to you. Do have a checking account? Do you have a saving account? If they don't have an account, persuade them to open up one. Go over the advantage of having that account. Tell them you would be happy to help them open an account." Sterling presented Spirit Celebration Cards. "I like to present this card to the team for behaviors exemplifying The Bank of America spirit and core values." Lastly Spirit Awards for associates who go above and beyond is awarded to the some more outstanding workers." Employees anticipating more prizes clapped enthusiastically. He continued, "These awards are worth two hundred and fifty dollars each and can be redeemed for merchandise on the company's web site."

Sterling passed out flyers that highlighted the bank's annual nationwide conference. After everyone had a flyer in hand and were admiring the highlights of Atlanta, Georgia's famous hotels and restaurants, Sterling said "Bank of America periodically sends employees to meetings, conferences, and other industry events. The bank considers participation at these events beneficial to its representation in the industry and the development of and retention of their best employees. If you are selected to represent this branch in Atlanta, your registration fee, travel, lodging and meals will be paid for in accordance with the A/P Policy and Procedures. What does that mean to you? It means all of your expenses will be paid and you only need to take money for souvenirs. How will we choose representative to attend this meeting? We will consider attendance, performance, productivity and other traits that an outstanding employee would exhibit. As I said earlier, "This too could be you!"

"We need three volunteers from this bank to join others from this area in educating homeowners about the loan modification program. This is a three day workshop that would allow homeowners to meet face to face with bank employees and go over their mortgage troubles. Hopefully, we can help homeowners achieve affordable modifications. Our goal is to offer permanent modifications through the taxpayer funded programs we have access to. Seven of you have been trained specifically in home modification. We can't send all seven. Five of our banks in this district are sending three representatives each. If you are interested in participating, please put your name on the sign-up sheet that's on the table in the back of the room." "Are there any questions?" A hand went up in the back of the room and after being recognized a woman in seated on the second row asked, "If we volunteer, would it count as time and a half or regular work hours" "It would count as time and a half since you will be working after regular banking hours." After a going over a few concerns regarding security issues, the branch manager bought the meeting to a close.

The morale boosting meeting went over just as Sterling had planned. Workers went to their assigned post in a cheerful and pleasant mood. Sterling, happy that the meeting was out of his way, went to his office after being assured that several workers would tidy up the conference room and place the leftovers in the fridge for anyone who wanted breakfast foods for lunch.

Chapter 23

The knock on her front door seemed urgent. Shondra wondered why someone would knock when there was a perfectly good doorbell that was obvious to anyone who approached the door. Maybe the doorbell is not working she thought as she wrapped a towel around her head and walked towards the door. She peered through the peep hole and saw a police officer standing there. He had obviously heard her approaching the door because instead of knocking again, he stood there looking intently back at the peephole. "Who is it?" She asked nervously. "Minneapolis sheriff's department miss," he answered. She opened the door and he said "I'm looking for a Miss LaShondra Jackson. Are you LaShondra Jackson?" "Yes, I am. What is this all about?" "I have a subpoena for you to appear in court involving a case against Eric Randall." He answered. "Oh" she said. "The subpoena tells you the date and time as well as what courtroom you have to appear in," he said. "Just sign this saying that you received the papers." Still standing in the doorway, Shondra signed the paper and returned them to the uniformed officer. After she gave him the papers, he thanked her and left. She briefly read the criminal subpoena that

139

summoned her to Eric's trial and made a mental note of the trial date. "I hope they lock him up and throw away the key."

The phone rang and when Shondra answered the call she was happy to hear from her friend Frieda. "Frieda, where on earth have you been hiding out? I have been trying to reach you for days," she said. "I and Booby went to Atlanta to the Tyler Perry Studio. Yes girlfriend, you heard me right. We were in Atlanta at the Tyler Perry Studio. Don't you listen to your phone messages?" "I didn't get any phone message "You need to check again because we called you several times." "Why did you go to Tyler Perry's Studio in Atlanta?" Frieda told her that Tyler Perry had a contest on the internet to get someone to play Mr. Brown's illegitimate son who he did not know he had. "I videotaped Booby as she pretended to model a gown she made for that reality show Project Runway. Tyler Perry's casting agent thought that it was hilarious and asked us to come to Atlanta to film a segment called 'Mr. Brown is a deadbeat dad'." "Why didn't you phone me as soon as you got the news? I could have gone with you." "Girl, when we found out that they had paid for our ticket online and all we had to do was go to the airport and pick them up, we left this town quick, fast and in a hurry. Booby is going to be a STAR-RAH! And I am going to be her agent!" Frieda exclaimed. "How did it go? Did she get her lines right?" "Did she? Girl, Booby hadn't been on the set three minutes and she was already a Diva! I bet there's going to be a recurring part for her because Mr. Brown had to take a DNA test and it came back positive. The storyline took them to the Maury show and Maury said, 'Brown, you ARE the father!' Mr. Brown ran off the stage to that little spot where they always fall out and cry. You should have seen him fall out and brawl like a baby." "It sounds funny as hell." Shondra said. "When is it going to air?" "The agent is going to let us know. We took pictures with Mr. Brown, Cory, and the rest of the cast." "Great, I can't wait to see them," she said.

Shondra agreed to meet Booby and Freda for breakfast at the pancake house on Saturday morning. She was relieved when she saw their hoopty in the parking lot because it meant that she did not have to sit there waiting for them. Booby was all smiles as she stood up and gave Shondra a hug. Shondra didn't know whether Booby really stood up just to give her a hug or because she wanted everyone in the restaurant to get a good look at what she was wearing. "Hey, you diva you! How does it feel to be starring on one of the best comedies on television?" Shondra beamed. Booby gushed. "It happened so fast. One minute Frieda and I was surfing the net. We came across this Tyler Perry site and read about the contest. It was the last day to enter. Girl, God must have had a hand in this because Frieda came up with the idea and I acted out the skit she wrote for me. We uploaded the video and BAM, we got a call asking us if we can come out for filming." Frieda said. "Booby, Frieda told me that you were fierce!" "Damn straight, you know how I roll!" Booby answered. "What have you been up to Miss Thang? We couldn't get you on the phone. I sure hope that you did not go back to that Eric character."

Speaking of Eric, I got a subpoena to go to court to testify against him for choking me that night." "Good, I hope they subpoena me and Frieda. We will make sure that he get some time." Booby said. "You weren't even there, how can you testify?" Shondra asked. "I can testify that I saw him leave the house and when I went inside your house, I saw that you had been hurt." Booby said. "Thanks but no thanks. I don't want you going to jail for lying under oath. Shondra laughed. "I don't even want to show up, I don't see why you two want to go."

"We may not need to show up, but make sure that you show up Shondra because if you receive a criminal subpoena and you fail to show up, you can be held in contempt of court." Booby warned her. "What will happen if am sick on that day and can't get there?" She asked. "If you don't get admitted into the hospital or die, the judge may issue a bench warrant for your behind." Booby replied. "What's a bench warrant?" "You will find out what it is if you don't show up in court." Frieda laughed. Booby told her. "It is a piece of paper issued by the judge that authorizes the po-po to find you and bring you to court. You may even end up doing time or paying a fine. So don't plan on missing that court day. You better be on time too." "They act like I'm the one who committed the crime. Do I need to get a lawyer to go with me? She was now somewhat worried." "Don't even sweat it girlfriend, all they want you to do is give your side of the story, answer questions and provide testimony." Booby assured her. "Yeah when they look at those pictures of your bruises, you may not have to say a thing. A picture is worth a thousand words." Frieda added. Even though they made going to court seem less intimidating, she still had some reservations. If she did not show up and they could not find her, they may toss out the case and forget about looking for her. Maybe Eric had learned his lesson and would stay away from her if he did get out.

Chapter 24

Shondra had promised Booby that she would attend the special party that a group of his friends were giving during the local airing of the episode of the Browns. Even though it was a house party, Booby and Ms. Frieda were expecting a huge turnout of both straight and gay friends. Ms. Frieda's boss and his wife had insisted that the party that would air Booby's appearance on Tyler Perry's hit TV series, The Browns, be held at their twenty three room luxury home. She tried on almost everything in her clothes closet. Some of the outfits were new and never before worn. She was not happy with any of the garments even though she looked fine in all of them. Her mind went back to the outfit she tried on a few days ago in the ladies apparel section of an upscale department store.

Shondra thought about how good she looked in the six hundred dollar Rachael Roy pantsuit. She was afraid to get it on her Andrea credit card and she would have shoplifted it had it not been for the salesgirl poking her head into the dressing room just as she was trying to get the security ink tag off the jacket. Even though she had sensed a strange man following her, it was if she was being compelled by some unknown force to acquire and possess things that she could not afford. She knew that stealing someone else's identity was wrong. Something inside her head told her that she had gone too far and at the same time, another voice told her to get all she could get, any way she could, and as long as she could. Deep down inside, she knew that her double life would come to an end but she wasn't sure how. She thought about leaving the country until it all blew over. Another option was to leave KeKe with her parents and join the navy or the merchant seamen. She did not consider leaving KeKe with her ex-husband because she was afraid that his significant other would try to take over her maternal position or worst yet treat her baby girl like a doormat. Shondra vacillated between wanting to stop her criminal activity and pushing her luck as much as she could. Today, her mind was on getting back to that Rachael Ray pantsuit. She hoped that it was still on the rack. She planned to waste no time looking at anything else in the store. Since she had already tried on the suit, it would only be a matter of taking it off of the rack and paying the saleslady with the fake credit card that she had been careful to put in a separate compartment of her wallet.

Shondra turned into the LaSalle Court Parking Garage, took a parking receipt and parked her car. Before she got out, she checked her reflection in the rearview mirror. She applied a fresh coat of rum raisin lipstick, finger combed the medium length honey blond wig she wore, checked out her hazel contacts, and winked at herself. After tearing herself from the mirror, Shondra gathered her purse and exited the car. LaSalle Court Parking Garage was central to most of the downtown stores that she enjoyed visiting. Macy's, Marshall's, Target's, and the Gap which were all within walking distance. She had planned on getting into Neiman Marcus, grabbing the Rachel Roy pants suit and leaving right away, just in case that man who kept watching her happened to be in the store again.

Shondra walked quickly pass the shoe department, pass the cosmetic department, and pass the jewelry department. Although she would have loved to buy a pair of new shoes, a new tube of rum raisin lipstick, and a pair of earrings to wear to Booby's party, she kept stepping. "Don't worry about that stuff now. Just get the pants and jacket and get the hell out of here," a voice warned her. "You should really turn your ass around and get out of here fast!" another voice said. "Too late, Shondra said. I'm already here and I can see the suit is still on the rack." She said as she sped up her pace. A young lady wearing a Neiman Marcus name tag responded, "I am sorry, what did you say?" Shondra, oblivious to the woman, went directly to the rack and grabbed the suit that she had been coveting since she tried it on a week ago. Just as she began to take it to the saleswoman, she could not help noticing the white linen jacket, open back top and matching slim leg pants from Narciso Rodriquez's spring collection.

She knew that she would look sophisticated in this elegant ensemble. "No time to try this on, you know it's your size. Buy it and if it doesn't fit bring it back and get a refund or sell it to one Frieda's freaky ass." The voice told her. "Where would Frieda get eight hundred and ninety five dollars to pay for this suit?" Shondra answered out loud. "Pardon?" the bespectacled grey haired saleslady asked. "I was just asking myself if I really needed two suits. I have to speak at two important meetings and I want to look impressive, so I guess I need them both." Would you like to try them on? The saleswoman asked. "No, no, no. Shondra responded. I know my size and these will do just fine." The saleslady said. "You must have a really good job as she rang up the one thousand, eight hundred and ninety five dollar purchase and pointed to the credit card machine for a signature. "I don't have a job, but I do have a career as a motivational speaker. You know like Iyanla Vanzant. I give speeches that motivate and inspire employees and other audiences. "Shondra lied. "Is that right? That sound like a good job." The saleswoman said, emphasizing the word job. "It's not a job Shondra protested. A job is something you hate to go to. A career is something that you enjoy doing." "Well, I must have a career as a saleslady, the sales associate teased, because I sure do love selling women clothes, especially expensive one." She thanked Shondra and gave her two garment bags which contained the ill-gotten gain. The saleswoman turned to another customer and Shondra left the woman's department.

Chapter 25

ndrea arrived at Denico Corporation's board room thirty minutes before the meeting was to start. She noticed that she was not the only one to arrive early. There were a few other speakers and presenter setting up tables that contained brochures, flyers, and other paraphernalia pertaining to their particular presentations. Andrea did not need to set up a table or put out any flyers. She simply came early to make sure that her presentation, which had been saved on several flash drives in case one was misplaced, showed up perfect on the large screen projector.

"The topic of this meeting was Current State of Denico Paint and Coating Corporation. The discussions would revolve around where Denico Corporation stood in relationship to other paint and coating companies. The focus today would be on answering the following questions." The meeting's facilitator said as he clicked on a PowerPoint list. What is the total market size? Has the market grown or declined? What is the market growth rate? Are long term forecasts positive or negative? What are the color trends for this year?" The meeting went on for three hours with a fifteen minute break each hour. Andrea's presentation took place without a hitch during the bottom half of the first hour. She was relieved to present

147

her findings and readily answer three related questions. Now she would spend the remaining hour and a half learning more about rumors of the potential acquisition of Denico Paint and Coating Corporation by a Polish paint company. Denico Group's CEO and owner quashed the rumor that a Polish owned paint company would acquire Denico Paint and Coating Corporation and said, "Anything that you have heard about a merger and me becoming a member of the Teknos-Denico's supervisory board is absolutely false. Don't worry about it. Denico Paint will continue to operate as usual."

During the final hour of the meeting, Henry Franklin presented information about ten new colors being producing by the company. "Denico was a one of the leading producer of chemicals including base coats, clear and top coats, enamel paints, lacquer paints, and primers. We are also known as trend setters in the world of color. Each year, color experts at paint companies around the world develop trend forecast for consumers and industry. Many variables affect the direction of design and color. Such trends as demographics, changing consumer desires, social and economic changes and technology all come together to influence color themes. This year, our main focus will be on industrial hues for architectural and interior design."

No other brand delivers the complete spectrum of colors for laminated glass like Valencia colors by Denico," Henry Franklin, nationwide architectural applications manager for Denico, boasted. "Used in curtain walls, atriums, skylights, partitions and conference rooms, Valencia color interlayers allow the most expressive designs with distinctive hues from the subtle to the dramatic,

Denico has developed 10 unique colors for the Valencia Color by Denico's line of poly vinyl butyral for laminated glass, he continued, No longer reserved for paint and wall coverings, architects and designers continue to push the envelope, developing innovative color design methods for every glazing application. When exploring light, form, and space in the design process, glass can be the answer for all three considerations with the addition of Valencia colors by Denico. Now hospitals, living rooms, and urban facades can showcase color in the glazing design. Valencia color by Denico gives architects and designers more creative freedom with glass than ever before."

As part of his presentation, Franklin displayed and discussed PowerPoint illustrations of glass samples that were strategically placed on the table so that each person in attendance could experience the colors. Some of the attendees looked at the informative brochure on industrial glass coloring which included advice and tips for successful color design. He began to call out the new colors and go over the aspects of each color. The names of each color were perfect: Olive Oil, Sun Flower, Baked Clay, Raspberry Tart, Caribbean Spa, Pacific Treasure, Spout Green, Caramel, and Smokescreen. "Pacific Treasure 8379 is a refreshing color bridging green and blue. This color revitalizes hospitality, healthcare and office environments and works well with more neutral palettes found in flooring, furniture and wall coverings." He said as he clicked on a picture showing the color in a children's hospital glass painting of a colorful seascape.

Kimberly Love, a Denico color stylist, added that Valspar had a version of this color called Sea Kiss. She went on to say that water is a source of life and the start of spring and the clean blue color of Denico's Pacific Treasure symbolized looking forward to a new year, a new beginning, and a fresh start.

Franklin showed his appreciation of Kimberly Love's input and readily agreed with her. After several others commented on the new paint colors, Franklin ended his presentation and the meeting came to a close.

The meeting was about to wrap up when Andrea's phone vibrated. Instinctively, she looked at the screen to see who was calling. She'd hoped that Quinton would phone her and ask her out to lunch. Instead it was Michelle. Anxious to answer her phone, Andrea gathered her briefcase and headed out of the building. "Hey Girlfriend, what's happening? I am so glad that this meeting and my presentation is behind me. I can't wait to get somewhere and unwind." She told Michelle. "Where are you, Michelle? How long are you going to be there? Great, I'll be there in thirty minutes."

Andrea arrived at P.F. Chang Chinese Bistro and spotted Michelle sitting at a table for four. "Hell-o Michelle, how's your day been so far?" "You know me, girl. I'm not complaining about a thing. It's all good." Michelle replied. "I heard that!" Andrea quipped back at her and placed her purse on the chair next to her. Andrea and Michelle always made it a habit of sitting at a table for four when they joined each other at a restaurant because it left two chairs empty in case two great looking guys wanted to join them and also it gave them more room for their purses, more elbow room, and more space for their plates and silverware.

"Have you been fitted for your dress for my wedding yet?" Michelle asked. "I plan on having that done on Tuesday after I get off of work." Andrea answered and then turned her attention to the menu. It was six thirty p.m. and Andrea was famished. She ordered the Chang's Chicken Lettuce Wrap as an appetizer while Michelle went for steamed shrimp dumplings. "Why did you order an appetizer Michelle? We can share the lettuce wraps." "I know, Michelle answered. I just wanted some of those shrimp dumplings. They are banging." They both ordered egg drop soup.

Chapter 26

"Quinton, I like you to meet my friend and stylist, Terry Yarborough. He is the owner of In2Hair Beauty Salons in both of the twin cities. Terry is throwing this party to launch his new line of hair care products." "Hey Man, I'm pleased to meet you. This is some gathering you have going on here." Quinton remarked. "Dr. Quinton Thomas, famous plastic surgeon, star of the reality TV show, Before and After?" Andrea and Quinton laughed. "The honor is mine, Doc." "Please man, call me Q or Quinton." He said. "Of course, Q, enjoy the party but don't forget to check out the products. Maybe you can recommend them to some of your patients who have hair problems." Terry said. "Sure, we are about to make our way to the buffet line right now. And again, congratulations on launching your own line of hair products." "Thanks." Terry responded.

Quinton and Andrea picked up dinner plates and headed toward the buffet table. Although the food was laid out buffet style, servers stationed at each table plated the food that each guest requested. Andrea selected crabmeat stuffed mushrooms and marinated scallops wrapped in bacon" "Would you like to try the Maryland Crab Cake prepared with lump crab meat and Remoulade Sauce?" the server asked. "It looks absolutely delicious." Andrea said. "I know I'm not passing it up." Quinton said. The food server placed a crab cake on Andrea's dish and then added one to Quinton's dish to accompany the Oyster Rockefellers and jerk seasoned chicken drummettes that he had already selected. "You better save some space on your plate if we are going to visit the carving station." Andrea laughed as she looked at Quinton's plate. "I honestly don't know how you can eat so much and keep that six pack." "I work out every day baby, and judging from that fine looking ass on you, the gym is your friend also." The chef at the carving station put on quite a performance. The meat presentation was outstanding. The options included roasted turkey breast, prime rib, baked ham, sliced steak, roasted pork tenderloin, steamship round and Peking duck. "How can Terry afford all of this?" Andrea wondered as she indicated to the server that she wanted prime rib and baked ham to go along with the brown rice and fresh vegetable bundle of broccoli, string beans, asparagus, and carrots tied with a leek ribbon. Quinton chose the Peking duck. The server carefully placed Quinton's choice of Peking duck next to his serving of julienne yellow and green squash.

Carefully balancing the dinner plates, they headed toward one of the beautifully decorated tables and found the one with their names on cute little placeholders adorned with the In2Hair logo. A waiter who stood by asked what they wanted to drink. They both asked for a glass of wine and the waiter obliged them. Quinton took a drink of wine and nodded approvingly. Then he took one of the Oyster Rockefellers from his plate and placed in on Andre's plate. Laughing, he quoted Lewis Carroll. "O

Oysters, come and walk with us! The Walrus did beseech. A pleasant walk, a pleasant talk, along the briny beach: We cannot do with more than four, to give a hand to each." To show her remembrance of ninth grade literature, Andrea quickly added the next stanza. "The eldest Oyster looked at him, but never a word he said: The eldest Oyster winked his eye, and shook his heavy head—meaning to say he did not choose to leave the oyster bed." Quinton looked at the oyster and laughed. "I'll bet you are one of the oysters who chose to leave the oyster bed and follow the conniving carpenter and the deceitful walrus." He then slipped an oyster with creamy spinach and pancetta into his mouth and said "Uhmmm, Uhmm, Uhmm. I am glad you left the oyster bed." Quinton eyes narrowed as he laughed and continued his humorous banter. "If anyone had told me in ninth grade when I was in Ms. Brown's literature class reading Lewis Carroll's The Walrus and the Carpenter that I would be dining with a nut like you, I would not have believed it." "You wouldn't have? I don't know why. Mr. Carter, my teacher always told me that there were students in ninth grade classes all around the world reading the same selection and we may run into them later in life." Andrea said. "I guess he was right because here I am with you, twenty years later, eating oysters and discussing that eighteen stanza poem." He responded. "At the time I thought it was a funny poem about two predatory characters that were walking on the beach one night when they came upon an offshore bed of oysters and invited them to join them." Q said. "I know she said the oldest oyster warned them not to go along with the walrus and carpenter but they didn't listen and after they got a few yards away, the walrus

154

and the carpenter made a meal out of them." Andrea remembered aloud as she watched Quinton eat another oyster, and playfully smack his mouth and lick his lips.

"I know the food was good but you look like you are ready to smack your mama, Dr. Q." a nice looking middle aged man said as he stood next to Quinton. ""I hope that I am not imposing. You seem to be enjoying yourself so much. Do you mind if we join you?" Not at all Quinton said gesturing to the man and the woman who was with him to be seated in the empty chairs across from Andrea and him. "Andrea, please meet Dr. Richard J. Vaughn and his lovely wife Dr. Megan Richardson. They are both specialize in E.R. plastic surgery. Megan and Richard please meet the very lovely Andrea McNair. Andrea is a financial analyst with a prominent chemical cooperation here in Minnesota." They politely acknowledged each other. "Does Dr. Quinton always smack his lips when you eat out?" Dr. Vaughn asked kiddingly. "We were just talking about a popular Lewis Carroll poem as we tasted the Oyster Rockefellers." Andrea said. "Let me guess, Richard said and looked at his wife. Together, they chimed, 'The Walrus and the Carpenter.' They all laughed. Quinton raised his wine glass and offered a toast to Lewis Carroll. Andrea and Quinton finished their meals and after server came over and took their dinnerware, they excused themselves. "I suppose we need to go mingle." The gathering was attended by the who's who on the Minneapolis and the St Paul's social circuit. The guests were enjoying themselves chatting with friends at the bar, and serving stations. Andrea spotted Michelle and her fiancée, Todd, having a great time. "I know about one fifth of the people here," said Andrea, looking over the room. There were editors from Black Hair magazines. There were several people who looked like advertisers and publicists. Andrea stood along the side of room while Quinton stopped to talk with a former patient. She took this time to scan the room and people watch. She noticed two women she previously had seen in the salon walking in her direction. They were nicely dressed and very obviously happy to attend the gala event. She smiled at them as they went by. They smiled back and continued chatting.

"There are a lot of beautiful people here," a heavyset woman dressed in a tight fitting red dress said making her way across the room toward the bar. "I haven't seen so much glitz and glamour in quite awhile." Another woman answered. "Are those drinks on the house also?" "No honey, but since there was no admission charge and the food is free, I'm not mad. Besides, I won this hair care kit just by watching a demo over there in the styling area!" "Can I take my drink over there and watch?" the heavyset woman asked. "I sure had mine with me and no one said anything. It didn't stop me from winning this seventy nine dollar kit." The plump lady said.

Terry took a break from circulating around the room doing photo-ops with anyone who would join him for a picture, taken by a photographer he had hired just for that purpose and strutted toward the stage. The D.J. turned down the music and made an announcement. "Ladies and Gentlemen, Let have a round of applause for our man of the hour, stylist extraordinaire, the owner of In2Hair, the developer of a new line of Black Hair Products, Mis-sterrr Terrrrrrr-rayyyyy Thommmppp-sssson! The crowd gave a loud applause as Terry approached the D.J. and took the microphone. "Thank you. Thank you." He said and signaled for them to stop clapping. Thank you all for showing out tonight. It's great to see you. Take a look around you and say to the person on your left *You look fabulous!*" Everyone echoed Terry's compliment and Terry laughed at his suggestion and said. "You know, I picked that up in church. You know how the pastor always tells you to look at the person next to you and say *God is good, Isn't God good.* Seriously, this room is full of beautiful people!" Terry gave a few shout outs to special guest and then said, "I would like for everyone to enjoy the food but don't leave without stopping by the In2Hair beauty products booth while stylists demo the products and give away raffle prizes.

Andrea told Quinton that she was going to say hell-o to Michelle. She left him talking to several of his medical associate. As she headed in Michelle's direction, she walked pass a giant flat screen plasma TV that repeatedly aired an advertisement for In2Hair products. In another area, party goers took turns striking poses in front of a backdrop that prominently featured repeated images of the In2Hair logo. A prominent local photographer made everyone who lined up for a keepsake photo look like Hollywood stars for a small price of fifteen dollar for an eight by ten or ten dollars for a five by seven color photo. Andrea and Michelle took several photos. "Looking good ladies. Smile with your eyes." Click. Click. Now let's see you look fierce. That's it! Give me your fiercest look. Now vogue, vogue, vogue." He urged in an effort to get at least two or three good poses out each person.

Michelle's fiancé said "This Terry fellow must be some hair stylist. I must have cost a pretty penny to pull this off." "Terry has styled hair for countless magazine covers and for top models including Tyra Banks and Eve. Just about everybody who is anybody has been to Terry." Michelle told him. "Andrea and I are lucky because he is not taking on any new clients." "He's that good huh? Maybe I will talk to him about investing in those In2Hair products."

"Ladies and Gentlemen we have a special guest who is going to perform for you tonight. It's Atlanta's newest superstar Victor Grimmy Owusu, also known as V.I.C. Let's give it up for V.I.C." The crowd went wild when they broke out on stage and one of the singers yelled out. "Hey, Minneapolis! How y'all doing out there? Everyone who's enjoying this launch party say In2Hair! The crowd responded and yelled back In2Hair! "Let's hear it again. Say In2Hair!" The crowd yelled even louder In2Hair! "Now we don't want anyone leaving this damn party without a bag of In2Hair products in your hand. If you didn't win some, buy some damn it! It's on sale out there in the demonstration area." He laughed and the crowd laughed with him.

"Now I have another question for you." The young handsome rapper with the long braids said. "Are there any big girls in the house?" "I want you to bring your big asses out here on the dance floor and show everybody what you got. Come on out here." Three big ladies went out on the dance floor. "Are there anymore big girls out there?" Two heavy set shy ladies stepped out on the dance floor. "That's what I'm talking bout." Now that I got my big girls, all you shawtys in the house come on out here. Come on out here shawtys, come on!" He said. V.I.C.'s band started playing the infectious party jam "Wobble." As the shawtys came out, Victor began singing the hip hop lyrics and soon almost everyone joined in the popular line dance. V.I.C. sang *"Oh, oh, oh, oh all the shawtys in the club, let me see you just back it up, drop it down, let me see you just get low n scrub the ground, let me see you just push it up, push it up, let me see you just wobble baby, wobble baby, wobble baby, wobble, wobble baby, wobble baby, wobble baby, wobble, yeah get in there, yeah, yeah."* The crowd formed a dance line and were doing the wobble slide, a series of steps, the included cha, cha, chas, turns to the right, and turns to the left. Quinton motioned Andrea to the dance floor and proceeded to do a jazzy version of the wobble. He not only knew how and when to jump up, bounce, jump back and bounce, look right and rock eight times. He did it with swagger. Andrea was impressed and honored to be on the dance floor with one of the best dancers there. She managed to keep up with him with some pretty good moves of her own. Terry was on the floor next to them proving he could wobble with the best of them. The rapper sang out *"ey big girl make em' back it up, make em' back it up, ey big girl make em' back it up, make em' back it up."* Those honeys did the Beyonce booty shake and the crowd went wild. *"Yeah, Ha-ha, Woo, Ahhhh, Get it, Get em mama"* could be heard around the dance floor.

The group performed two more songs, each giving their audience the opportunity to show their electric slide skills while others learned new moves. The Dee Jay got back on the mic and thanked V.I.C. for the short but impressive performance. "V.I.C. is on tour and can be seen tomorrow night at the Twin Cities Celebration of Hip Hop better known as The Hip Hop Fest hosted by YO." "This is not a commercial for the festival but a shout out for V.I.C.'s performance. Thanks again V.I.C." Then he slowed things down with the swing dance song, 'As I Gave My Love to You' by Sonja

Marie. Quinton escorted Andrea back to the table and headed to the bar to get drinks for the both of them. He ordered a Hennyville Slugger for himself and a champagne martini for Andrea. He felt someone staring at him and turned to look at a familiar face. "Dr. Thomas, so that was you on the dance floor." Quinton reached into his memory and realized that she was one of his patients. Checking her five foot eight inch frame he recalled implanting size thirty six D silicone breast implants and performing lipo on her waistline. She was wearing a form fitting gold colored cocktail dress that features an asymmetrical one shoulder design. The fully ruched short dress hugged her curves giving her tremendous sex appeal. "It's been awhile since I last saw you. You look fantastic," he told her. He soon noticed that her black clad male companion was giving him the once over.

Seeing that Quinton and Sterling were checking each other out, Amy quickly introduced them to each other. Sterling this is Dr. Quinton Thomas who lasered a couple of sunspots from my shoulder she lied. Doctor, this is Sterling Steingold. Sterling is an information security analyst with Bank of America. Dr. Thomas, aren't you associated with the local reality TV show 'Before and After'?" "In fact, I am." Quinton answered. Sterling said "I have a friend who tried out for that show. He wanted to get receding jaw line repaired." "I think we did chose a young man by the name of Charles Christian for a jaw line improvement," Quinton said. "The show will air in February." "Well I guess the adage that everyone is just seven people away from knowing someone is true." Sterling remarked thinking about how close he and Andrea had been. He had been checking out Andrea and Quinton ever since he spotted them at the buffet table. He took notice of them enjoying their meal as he and Amy sat a few tables away. He observed them on the dance floor as he danced a few feet away, with several different partners. He noticed them as they headed back to the table and Quinton left her there and headed to the bar for drinks. He wondered if she was pretending not to notice him. How could she have not seen him? After all, the place was not that damn large. Sterling was trying to find an excuse to approach her when Amy said "Dr. Q. I hope you will dance with me before the party is over." "Well, we'll see about that." Quinton answered and headed back to Andrea with drinks in hand. "That's it Sterling thought! If the doctor didn't ask Amy, he would insist that she walk up to him and ask him to dance." In fact, he would make sure that it was a slow dance. Then he would ask Andrea to dance with him.

Andrea and Quinton finished their drinks and she excused herself to go to the ladies room. Quinton looked at his watch. It was getting pretty late and he had to make his hospital rounds by six a.m. However, he wanted to spend some time with Andrea alone before turning in for the night. There was just forty five minutes before the launch party would be over. The lights were lowered and the D-Jay slowed the music down with John Legend's song, 'Best You've Ever Had'. Amy arrived at the table just a few minutes after Andrea left. "Would you like to dance with me," she asked as she reached out for his hand. "I'd be honored," he said and led her to the floor. On the dance floor Quinton and Amy slowed dragged, strutted, fish tailed, did a little shake and bake, and grinded all in one dance getting quite a few smiles from less agile dancers on the floor.

Sterling watched as Andrea headed back to the table only to find her man on the dance floor having a grand time with someone other than her. Sterling intercepted her before she could reach the table and said "Fancy meeting you here." Trying to look surprised she said, "Sterling, what a surprise!" "I don't know why it would be that much of a surprise. Terry invited almost everyone in the twin cities to this launch party. Are you having a good time?" "Yes, how about you? Are you enjoying yourself?" "I will if you will dance with me." He whispered in her ear letting his lips linger close to her ear until she answered affirmatively. He took her hand and escorted her to a spot on the dance floor that was out of Quinton's and Amy's view. Sterling pulled her close and placed his right hand in the small of her back and held her right hand at shoulder height with his left one. He guided her movements by pushing and gently pulling her hand and body. Their foot movements were minimal but in sync as they hugged and swayed back and forth and sideways effortlessly. Never losing the rhythm of the music, he slipped his hands around her waist and went into an intense slow grind. She draped her hands on his shoulders. They danced cheek to cheek and just before the song ended, Sterling spoke softly in her ear. "Please phone me, baby. You know that I've been trying to reach you." "I've been busy," she answered." "Don't you want to know what I found out about the person who have been using your name? Or are you afraid of how I make you feel?" He said as he inhaled the scent of her skin. Feeling the warmth of his breath as he spoke to her, Andrea was aroused by the closeness of his mouth to her ear. The song ended too soon and he had to lead her back to Quinton who was now sitting at the table joined by Amy. He pulled the chair out so that she could be seated. "I see you have met Amy, Sterling's date." Quinton said. "Actually we know each other professionally though our dealings at the bank." Andrea responded. "Well it is a small world." Quinton said. "Have you met his lady friend who also happens to be a client of mine?" "No I have not met her. Why don't you introduce us Sterling?" Andrea said as she looked Sterling directly in the eye.

Sterling continued to stand next to the seated threesome. "Andrea, this is Amy. She is a Senior Banking Operations Risk Specialist at one of our branches. Amy, meet the lovely woman whom I just had the honor of dancing with, Andrea McNair. I hate to introduce you two and run, but the party's close to ending and I want to get our wraps before the crowd lines up to check out their coats." He said as he helped Amy from her chair. "It was good seeing you. Take care." He said. "You too." Andrea responded. "Bye." The blonde said as she reached for Sterling's hand and led him to the coat room.

Chapter 27

Sterling walked quickly through the parking lot until he found his car. He did not know if it was the report in his hand or the memory of the night he almost spent with Andrea that initiated the urgent need to see her again. It had been two days since he last saw her and he'd decided to wait until he had a reason other than wanting to knock some boots to see her again. He now had new information on the case and a legitimate reason to phone her, but he decided to hold off. Hell, there were many women who would jump at a chance to knock some boots with him. Instead of hooking up with Andrea and trying to take her away from her man, he was going to wait until she was willing to come to him on her own. The thought of the slave bracelet around her ankle flashed across his mind momentarily and he remembered his mother and another woman discussing anklets when he was young. "In some cultures heavy, chiming anklets were worn as a sign of dancing girls," his mother's friend commented. Sterling smiled to himself and imagined a more elaborate bracelet around her ankle. He pictured her as a belly-dancer wearing a bracelet of coins or tiny bells around her ankle.

164

Sterling decided to expedite the search for the person who was forging Andrea's name. The credit card application listed several references which he had already started to follow up. He phoned the one listed as a landlord reference again for the third time. He was curious as to why the landlord did not answer or return his call. He decided to check the number for the apartment complex in the phone book and to his amazement it was not the number listed by the forger. In fact none of the numbers matched. Sterling dialed the number listed in the phone directory. Maybe they have a new number. "Lakeside Apartments, Sam Donovan, Manager speaking." "Yes we have and Andrea McNair living here. She moved in about a year ago. Nice lady. Never gave us any trouble." Sterling was excited that he was getting closer to solving the fraud. He had a good mind to call the real Andrea, take her to the 972 Lakeside Drive address and to check her out. The phony Andrea imposter deserved an ass whipping for all the trouble she had caused Andrea. Instead, he decided that he had worked enough for one day.

Sterling noticed Tanya Riddick coming out of the vault. She looked in the direction of his office as she always did when she was in close proximity. Today he decided to mess with her. "Hey, Tonya. How's it going?" "Fine" she said with a cute southern accent. "You sure?" "Sure, I'm sure." She said. "How's it going with you?" Sterling decided to mess with her some more. "Fine" he said in a pretend southern accent. "You messing with my accent again. Mr. Steingold. I can't help how I talk. I'm tryin to change it." Don't you dare, Sterling laughed. "I think it's cute." "You just playin." Sterling looked around to see if anyone was looking and pulled her inside his office. "How about dinner tonight and I promise not to tease you about your cute little accent again." "Well" she hesitated. "Please" he begged. I'll take you anywhere you want to eat." "What time?" She asked. "Right after work." "I'll phone my carpool and tell them that I have a ride. You are going to give me a ride home after dinner, right." "Right. You know I'll take you right up to your door. I'll even tuck you in if you let me." Sterling said as he pulled her closer to him and gave her a kiss on the cheek. He released her and she moved away from him knowing that there were many busybodies working in the bank and neither of them wanted to be the focus of negative attention. Here take this report and make two copies so that they won't wonder why you are in my office as he said as he handed Tanya the envelop he received from Ralph. He needed several copies, one for his use, one for the lawyer and one backup copy. Tanya took the envelop and turned to walk away, he couldn't resist slapping her on the ass as she walked away. He hoped she would not file a sexual harassment suit against him. He had never done anything like that in his entire career. "Damn it, Andrea you got me so worked up, I'm in here jeopardizing my career. How am I going to get out of smacking Tanya on the ass like that? What if someone saw me? He wondered as he quickly looked around. "I've got to get the hell out of here," he said as he put on his jacket and went out to his car.

He sat there smoking a cherry flavored blunt while waiting for Tanya to come out with the original report and copies. She had seen him in his car many times so he knew she would have no problem finding him in the parking lot. Thirty minutes later Tanya came out with the copies. She opened the door and seated herself in. "Look

Tanya, I'm sorry that I smacked you on the behind in there. Are you angry with me about that? If you are, what can I do to make it up to you?" "What are you talkin about? I ain't angry about nothing. I'm just glad we didn't get caught. I don't want any trouble." Sterling took her hand into his, kissed it and held on to it as he put the car into gear and drove off. "You are so sweet." He said to her. "Are all the girls as sweet as you where you come from? If they are I must be living in the wrong town. Tanya blushed and said "Sterling you are such a charmer. Are all the guy as charming as you where you come from?"

Inside the restaurant, Sterling urged Tanya to order whatever she wanted. He really liked her innocence. Tanya order a rack of baby-back barbeques ribs, a tossed salad, and a baked sweet potato. Sterling ordered a T-bone steak, a baked potato with sour cream and a tossed salad. They both drank a beer while waiting for the meal to arrive. "This beer is sooo good." Tanya said. "Just what you need after going in and out of that vault all day. What do you do in there anyways? Count the money 10 times a day?" Sterling laughed. "You know what I do. Crazy man. You know what 'erbody' in that bank do." She laugh as she lifted the beer mug to take another sip. "Erbody, who is erbody." Sterling asked. "Sterling you promised not to tease me. I said everybody." "No you didn't, you said erbody." She pouted and he made kissy faces toward her and she burst out laughing. Sterling liked Tanya a lot. She was easy to get along with. He reached out and gave her hand another kiss. The meal arrived and they talked about their different backgrounds and experiences. He liked the way Tanya made him laugh. He really didn't want the evening to end and it really didn't matter if he had sex with her as

167

he initially intended of not. He just wanted to spend more time with her.

He was surprised that she invited him in for a beer when they reached her door. He readily accepted her invitation and was surprised that she had a good supply of beer in her fridge. Her apartment was a modest one room flat that served as a kitchen, dining area, living room, and bedroom. He sat in one of the two chairs in the kitchen area while she served him a cold beer. "What do you think of my crib?" she asked. "Crib? Are you a baby?" "Do I look like a baby? Do I act like a baby?" "No and no. So why do you call your apartment a crib?" "I don't know. Why you got to pick at 'erthing' I mean ev-er-ry-thing I say?" she whined. He pulled her to him and sat her on his lap. Then he kissed her on the mouth and she kissed him back. "You don't look or act like a baby. But you can be my baby." He said as he kissed her harder and held her closer to him. He got a boner as he felt that same butt his hand had smacked on its own volition earlier that day grind against his lap. Tanya gave him one of the wettest kisses he'd ever experienced. He wondered if she her other orifice, the one in his lap, was as juicy. He slid his hand into her low cut blouse as he began to kiss her on her neck. Tanya turned around to straddle him and give him better access. Sterling wasted no time in massaging her breast. "Are you sure that you want this?" Sterling asked "What do you want me to do?" "I want what you want." She replied. "You have to say it so that I know you will say later I raped or sexually harassed you." "After all we do work together." He said as he pressed his manhood against her. Her answer was another wet kiss and more gyrations. "You know I want you to make love to me, silly." "You know I walk pass your office everyday just to check you out with your fine self." "Hey where did my innocent county bumpkin go?" "Ain't so country I don't know a fine man when I see one." She said as she pulled her low cut blouse off and dropped it on the floor. "Kiss me again." She begged. Sterling obliged by returning a kiss as wet as her kiss. He teased her by retracting his tongue from her hungry mouth and gently sucking her bottom lip causing her to impatiently squirm and pull his head toward her breast. She took one breast out of the bra and popped it into his mouth. Sterling acted like he was in titty heaven sucking and licking one until he had to try the other one to see if it was just as good. Tanya, by now, was ready for action. She pulled his pants down, hatched up her skirt to reveal that she was not wearing underwear. "Do erbody where you come from go without underwear?" He panted. "Don't worry about erbody where I come from, just worry about me coming." She panted. "Just worry about us coming." She said as she rode him as hard as she rode Ole Pete, the race horse that she had left back home in South Carolina. Sterling loved the way she rode him as they sat in her dining room chair. He loved the way she let him rest a bit before riding him on her sofa in the living room area. He loved it when she straddled him on the bed and rode him more fiercely than ever. She likes being in control. Sterling thought as he dozed off into a sex induced sleep. He had intended to leave before daybreak but he was whipped into such a relaxed state his muscles refused to let him get out of bed.

Tanya woke up early and made pancakes, eggs, and sausage. Sterling got dressed and came over to the kitchen area. "Good morning Sleepyhead, I didn't know what you'd like for breakfast before leaving." She said "I did make coffee though." "That's good, Baby. I like coffee." "Can I call you baby now that I stayed at your crib last night?" He asked and without waiting, he pulled her to him and kissed her. "You know there is one place that we did not have fun last night." He said looking around the kitchen area. "You got me 'erwhere' in the crib except the kitchen, Baby. Why? Why didn't you get me in the kitchen?" He asked as he turned her around to face the kitchen counter. He bended her over and pulled up her skirt. Tanya knew what he wanted and butted up against him. She helped him find the way into her feminine wiles. "You were in control last night. Now it's my turn to show you that I like control too. Who's in control?" He said as he humped harder and harder slapping her on the ass. Tanya groaned. "You are in control." "Who?" "You are" "Who?" "Lord Jesus!" She screamed "Lord Jesus?" "Baby, I going to ask you again. Who is in control?" He demanded and humped her so fast it felt like rapid fire and so deep she thought he was going to bust through something inside of her. "You Sterling!" She screamed and fell out on the counter. He ejaculated inside of her and they both slid to the floor. "I guess we are two control freaks." Tanya laughed and Sterling responded. "I guess we are." Tanya laughed and started singing Control by Janet Jackson. "Control now I'm all grownup. I'm in control, I'm in control. Don't make me lose it." "Don't make you lose it. Girl you are tripping." Sterling said as he left the crib.

Back home in his condo, Sterling thought as he showered, "Man if that didn't beat all." Using a new bar of his big manly smelling soap on a rope, he shampooed from head to toe. He even washed his mouth out with soap. I pray to God that she did transmit any HIV into my mouth with those sloppy wet kisses. He thought knowing that he was just as bad as she was. I guess I'll find out when I have my next HIV exam. Man what was I thinking? Messing around with no condom. All the new soap in the world won't help me if I screwed up. Sterling made a mental note to ask her about her sexual partners on Monday when went back to work. Meanwhile, he would not spend his whole weekend crying over spilt milk. What I did was irresponsible and if I get out of this without getting HIV this will be the one and only time I screw up like that again. It's Andrea's fault. He thought. If she had not been such a tease that night. He wouldn't have pounce on Tanya the way he did. Tanya started working in his branch office six months ago and although she was eye candy, he never even flirted with her. "I'd better call my boys and hang out before I lose what's left of my mind. He made a mental note to hook up with several of his guy friends the next time they held a card party."

Chapter 28

LaShondra made her grand entrance to Booby's house party an hour late. She wanted to be certain that all eyes would be on her when she stepped into the scene. Miss Frieda opened the ornate French doors and Shondra entered the foyer of the fabulous, upscale house. The floor to vaulted ceiling windows, panoramic view, and a unique curved staircase briefly captured her interest. "Now this is the life" She thought as Frieda led her pass the staircase to the great room where the party was taking place. "You can mingle in here or you can get a drink from the wet bar through that door." If you want to get something to eat, the gourmet kitchen over here." Frieda said as she led the way to a huge kitchen and showed LaShondra an elaborate spread of party foods.

The celebration of Booby's appearance on "Meet the Browns" could be described in one word "Boojey." "How in the hell did Miss Frieda and Booby get to throw a party in such a luxurious home. I hope that they aren't in here illegally." She thought. Everyone was happily drunk and enjoying themselves. Booby's guests were smoking it up, drinking it down, dancing it all out and having a good time. "Frieda didn't even have to rearrange the living room furniture in order to create a "dance-floor" in the center of the room." Shondra noted. The room had more than enough space for everyone in the room to dance if they wanted to. The lighting was low and the music was loud. The DJ seemingly played to the energy of the crowd. His playlist started off with something light and upbeat and then worked up to more energetic songs the got the party jumping.

A small group at the wet bar were doing tequila shots. A cigar smoking, ebony skinned man wearing dark sun glasses toasted by saying "One tequila, two tequila, three tequila, FLOOR!" A response from his Latino companion was "One Shot! Mas Tequila! Two Shots! I can't remember! Three Shots! Eureba!" After the toasts, they all tossed down their tequila shot. The novices licked salt off the back of their hands and sucked on a slice of lime. While the real tequila enthusiast ditched the salt and lime theatrics and drank their shot straight. "One more," someone urged. "Not for me. Too much Tequila will give you an epic hangover mañana." "Not this brand. This is one hundred percent blue agave." Frieda and Shondra left the Tequila drinkers and walked toward another group of party people.

"Help yourself to whatever you like to eat or drink. We were able to throw the party in this swanky house but we did not get anyone to wait on your ass." Freda said. "This is fabulous Frieda, how on earth did you get your boss and his wife to let you use this place?" "I lied to them. I told them that Tyler Perry and the whole cast of Meet the Browns would be here." They both burst out laughing uncontrollably. "When they don't show up, what are you going to do?" "The hell if I know. I guess I'll cross that bridge when I get there." Frieda said. "Meanwhile, they get the closest thing to the show in this area, they get to say they partied with Booby." They broke into laughter again. Booby came into the room and wanted to know what was so funny. "I need a drink Shondra said. Do I just go to the wet bar and get what I want?" "Yeah," Booby said. Drink it all up. The bar is stocked to the hilt with the good stuff and we didn't have to buy any of it." "I swear Frieda, when these fine brothers and sisters get through drinking all that fine liquor and that white couple figure out you two pulled a fast one on them, you are going to have to find a new job." Shondra laughed. "Fuck it, we'll be living large and working in Hotlanta." Frieda said.

Shondra got her mixed drink and strutted into the great room intent on delivering a fair amount of delicious drama. She stood in an unoccupied spot and chose one of the seemingly straight men to mess with. She looked him up and down purposely trying to make them break her flirtatious stare. Booby noticed Shondra standing off to the side drink in hand and decided to break up the flirtation. He introduced her to a few of the guess who happened give her an approving glance. "You look like you just stepped out of a Cosmopolitan magazine with that suit on. I didn't know the bank where you work pay that type of money. I know that suit is a Rachel Roy and it had to cost at least five hundred dollars. And girl you are rocking them black stilettos with the gold tone metallic almond toe and the gold heel accent." "How you know so much about fashion and the cost of clothes?" she asked. "I know your ass is not making enough at that bank as a teller to buy a suit and a pair of shoes like that? Did you use your rent money to purchase it and are you going to take it back and get a refund after the party. Don't be ashamed. Girl, white women have been doing it for years." Booby said.

Frieda asked the DJ to stop the music and made an announcement as she pointed to a large banner of Booby and the cast of Meet the Browns. "Since the theme of this party is Booby's Guest Appearance on Tyler Perry's show 'Meet the Browns', we will take a break from all the dancing and watch Boogies scene. I must tell you however, we only have that one clip. You will have to tune in on this coming Friday night at eight p.m. when it's aired to see the whole thing. Also, your tuning in is good for the ratings. Maybe Booby will get a reoccurring part if the rating go up." Frieda explained. "Humph. Like someone really want to see that face on TV every week." Sylvia murmured just loud enough for her date to hear her. "Ease up." He laughed and hunched her with his elbow. "Did you say something Sylvia? Frieda asked. "I said I'd better get his autograph now." She lied. "Everyone is going to get a signed picture just like the one on the banner as a keepsake." Frieda responded.

After they watched the clips, Frieda bought out three decks of trivia cards that he had purchased from the souvenir shop at Tyler Perry Production Studio when he was filming in Atlanta and asked a few of his guest to get together for a game called Meet the Brown Trivia. Seven of the twenty-five or so house guests sat down around the two card tables Frieda had sat up in the game room to play the game. "We need one more person. Who else wants to play?" a woman sporting a long blond Mohawk haircut. "Tina is going to play. She getting something to eat right now.' Soon the heavyset red-bone wearing a leopard print low-cut cleavage revealing top and a short tight skirt joined them. Tina placed a plate of sweet and sour meatballs, buffalo hot wings, potato salad and macaroni and cheese on the card table and flopped down in the empty chair at the card table. "That mac-n- cheese looks good. Save me a forkful." The girl with the Mohawk said. "You better get your own. I'm crushing this myself." Are you all ready to play this Trivia Game?" Yeah go on someone said, "The other table seems like they are having a good time. I hope our questions are different because I heard almost all of their questions and answers revealed a short, gray headed man wearing gold rimmed eyeglasses. "Name two items of clothing that Leroy Brown likes to wear?" The Mohawk woman asked. "Tight ass suspenders, bold ass patterns, and jacked up bright colors" was the response that came quickly from the gray hair guy. "That was too easy." Someone remarked. "Okay get this right for twenty points. What did Brown call his senior group home?" "Group home? I didn't know he had a group home," was Tina's response. "It was called the Meadows, no it was called Brown Meadows." A wearing long dark artificial eyelashes and a flowing black wig answered and pulled a card from the deck. "What did Brown inherit?" She asked and then bit down on a spicy mustard chicken drummette from her own plate of party food. "Everybody knows that one. His daddy left him an old broken down dilapidated house. Brown turned that house into a boarding house for old people." Responded the guy in the gold rimmed glasses who was now puffing on a Newport. "You should receive the "Boss of the Year" award for letting this group of people have a bash like this in your home, a snooty looking white woman standing at the bar next to Frieda's boss remarked.

He responded, "You know I locked my bedroom doors and I hid the extra beer and good liquor until I need it." "Did you stash your valuables? Someone once clipped me for a brand new bottle

176

of expensive volumizing coconut-scented Ojon shampoo from my bathroom medicine cabinet during my last party. Who ever heard of someone stealing hair products? Whoever it was caused me to have a bad hair day every day for one solid week," the woman recalled.

Frieda interrupted the conversation when she walked up to the group and said "May I borrow Boss Man for a few minutes? This is my song and I need a dance partner." Feeling flattered he immediately accepted the invitation and walked Frieda, a man who looked remarkable like a woman, to the center of the dance floor. Flo Rida's Good Feeling was blasting from the speakers and Frieda was definitely feeling the music.

"Oh, oh, oh, oh, oh, sometimes I get a good feeling, yeah. I get a feeling that I never, never had before, no. I get a good feeling, yeah. Oh, sometimes I get a good feeling, yeah. I get a feeling that I never, never, never had before, no. get a good feeling, yeah"

Flo Rida's lyrics blasted. I don't know if I can keep up with you Frieda, her dance partner said. This is club music and I don't get out to the clubs that play this kind of music." He whined. "Just stop thinking, let go and allow the music to be your master. You will have so much fun and feel so good." Frieda urged. She started out doing the Halle Berry Dance. Then, in the middle of the song, she put her hands on her knees, dropped it like it was hot, and scrubbed the floor with it a few times. She then straightened up, leaned the top of her torso forward, stuck out her booty and shook it like it was made of Jell-o. Boss Man got close up behind her and slapped her on the butt a few times. Everyone thought the dance was hilarious. "That's it Frieda said. "That's good Boss Man. Go with the flow. Soon, his wife joined them and a few of his associates. "See what I mean, Boss! You have impressed others and inspired them to get their asses out here and dance also."

As Frieda danced, Booby checked out the guest and tried to make sure everyone was having a fine time. LaShondra joined Booby as he walked from one group to another chit chatting and making introductions. "This is Sylvia, my next door neighbor, I invited her because whenever I had a party at my place, she was always cool with it. She would never call in the noise violations on me like someone else I knew would. Her roommate would turn me in every time and Sylvia would always warn me. Wouldn't you Boo? I would always invite both of them to the party. Sylvia would come and have a good time and that old heifer who shares her apartment would not come for all the money in the world." "And where is she tonight? Sitting home watching television while I'm here enjoying myself Sylvia laughed." Booby added. "I also invited you because I knew you would bring that fine looking specimen of a boyfriend with you just to taunt my fine ass. What's his name?" Booby asked. Sylvia laughed and without answering moved closer to her male companion. "For real Bitch, I asked what his name is." Booby reiterated a little tipsy from the three drinks he had thrown down. My name is Shawn and her name is Sylvia not Bitch." The good looking dude answered. "Well excuse me, I just thought I know you from somewhere. Didn't we meet at the Pure Diamond Lounge or the Ambassador Club before?" Booby quizzed him with a knowing look. "I have never been to either of those establishments. I do believe you owe Sylvia an apology. She did not do anything to deserve being called out of her name," he snorted. "Anyway, where in the hell is Tyler Perry and all the rest of the cast that were supposed to be here. That's the reason Sylvia and I came to this tired ass party." "Oh no he didn't Booby yelled. I'm about to kick your ass, Mister. Why you so interested in seeing Tyler Perry, You think you might have a chance in getting on one of his television shows of his next movie?" "If he put you on his show, I know damn well I have a chance." Sylvia's friend went on. "Let's go home. It's getting late." She urged him. "That's right, bitch you need to get him up out of here right now or I'll beat the crap out of his punk ass." Booby warned. "Call her Bitch one more time. Call her Bitch one more fucking time and see what happens. He opened his jacket to reveal a silver colored glock. Undaunted by the gun, Booby looked him in the eye and said. "I don't care about no mother-fucking gun. Get the hell up out of here." Booby threw his head back defiantly and pivoted in the opposite direction, seemingly unafraid of getting a cap busted in his behind by Sylvia's irate escort as he strutted off toward the dance area.

"I have an announcement to make." He said. Unfortunately, the plane from Atlanta that Mr. Perry and the cast were on was delayed. However, they do send their deepest regrets." Several people sighed or expressed their disappointment. Most of them were too drunk or having too much of a good time to even care whether they saw Tyler Perry or Katie Perry. Two people who had passed out on the sofa wouldn't know whether Tyler Perry showed up or not. Boss Man was sitting next to Shondra trying to push up on her while his wife sat on her opposite side sipping a drink and trying to talk Shondra into "doing lunch sometime or better still going out shopping together." After Shondra learned that the wife was one of the city's leading criminal lawyers, she promised to get back with them. "She may come in handy if I ever need an attorney." Shondra thought. "Booby, why didn't you tell us you had such a fascinating beautiful friend?" Boss Man's wife said. "She is gorgeous. Where have you been hiding her?" "Ms. Shondra have been doing her own thing. I haven't had time to hide her. She's been kind of busy these days." "I hope she has enough time to show me where she got that fine looking suit she's wearing." "I'd love to try on that jacket. Do you mind dear?"

Boss Man's wife looked directly into Shondra's brown eyes until Shondra said yes. "Well come with me because I need to try on the shell also. And I don't want everyone watching in case it doesn't look as good on me as it does on you. Shondra followed her into the most beautiful bedroom she'd ever seen in a showroom, movie, or magazine. Once inside, the woman tried to put Shondra at ease by asking her what size she wore. "It seems to be about the same size you wear." Shondra answered. "Can I help you take it off? I can't wait to try it on," she said." Shondra said. "I'm sure you can't," as she took the woman's hand into hers and put it on the lapels of the Rachel Roy jacket. The woman slowly took off Shondra's jacket and the shell that she wore under the jacket. She was surprised to see that Shondra was braless. Shondra helped the woman take off her own blouse. She was surprised to see that the woman was more fully endowed and perkier than she in the Ta-ta area. Seeing that Shondra was amazed at her tits. Boss Man's wife laughed and said. "They cost a fortune to get lifted and enlarged." "Shondra laughed along with her." Who did them" Shondra wanted to know. "Dr. Q. He's the best breast man in town. Feel them."

She said and without hesitating she took Shondra's hands and placed them on her tits. "What do you think? Do they feel like your's or can you tell they are fake?" "No they feel like mine." The woman took both of LaShondra's breast into her hands and after pausing a few seconds she slowly massaged them, squeezed them and pinched each nipple. Shondra began to moan. She had never entertained the idea of letting another woman touch her. Now this woman was awakening feelings in her that she did not know she had. Her breast were being manipulated like they were a delicate treasure of some sort. Shondra didn't even know this woman's name. Whoever she was, she was much gentler that Eric had ever been. The woman saw that Shondra's eyes were closed and her lips were pursed. She felt Shondra tremble slightly. She licked Shondra's soft bottom lip a few times before sucking on it causing Shondra to squirm a bit. Then she licked both of tits before sucking them. She sucked Shondra's tits until Shondra began to moan. Then pushed Shondra against the wall and unbuttoned her Rachel Roy slacks and again was surprised when she saw that Shondra was not wearing underpants said "You are full of surprised aren't you," as she knelt down if front of Shondra. She left a trail of kisses from Shondra's belly button to her clitoris. She licked and sucked on her until Shondra began to cry. Then she ran her tongue in and out Shondra's sacred orifice in a succession of rapid fire motion. Shondra pulled the woman's long blond hair and gyrated and undulated her hips while the woman continue licked, suck, and prod faster, deeper, and harder. Shondra climaxed and fell to the floor. Soon there was a knock on the door. Shondra heard someone on the other side snigger. Is everything alright in here? Did the jacket fit?" "Yes we were just talking about

181

going shopping tomorrow to look for a gray pin striped one for me." The woman said. "We're coming right out." She added. I hope so because you've been in there almost an hour, all the guest are gone and Frieda and Boss Man are lost somewhere in this big ass house. I'm ready to go home and call it a night." "Okay, okay. I'm coming." Shondra said. "That's what I afraid off." Frieda mumbled under her breath. "You didn't try on the jacket." Shondra told the woman who was studying her prey, wanting to devour her one more time. "We can do that tomorrow when we go shopping. That is if you want to. She said as she ran her finger into Shondra's wetness and finger fucked her until she cried "Yes, I'll see you tomorrow" "What time, the woman asked." "What time do you want me to meet you?" Shondra asked and she ground her hips frantically. The woman suddenly stopped and asked. "What time do you want to meet me?" Shondra said "I have to work tomorrow, but I'll call in sick and I'll meet you when you tell me." The woman resumed finger fucking Shondra's throbbing, wet honey pot until Shondra collapsed into a fetal position and cried like she had been hurt. She kissed Shondra and told her that everything was okay. After getting dressed, they gave each other a quick hug. Shondra said. "I don't know how to say this, but I don't even know your name." She smiled and said. My name is Lana Irwin and my husband who you all have been calling Boss Man name is Lester Irwin. Les own a restaurant and Frieda does work for him."

"As you can probably tell, Les is crazy about Frieda." "And you're okay with that?" "Of course," she said. "We have an understanding. I know what he likes and he knows what I like. And right about now, I'm liking you. I hope you like me too." LaShondra didn't respond. She was not a lesbian and she was not about to become one. If Lana got her kicks out of playing around with her tonight, good for her. She thought. Sure she may meet her again tomorrow for fun and games, but she was definitely not going to get trapped into that lesbo stuff. Some party this turned out to be. She came hoping to find a good man and hooked up with a horny ass woman. Shondra found her friend nodding off. She shook her and said "Wake up Booby. Let's go home. Frieda has her own car. She can leave when she get through doing whatever she's doing."

Chapter 29

Sterling decided to phone Andrea as he left his office. He wanted to assure her that he was still working on her case although it had been a little over a week since he talked to her. He was certain that he could get to the bottom of this fraud episode. After all, he was no stranger to credit card theft. Since he had been employed with the bank he had become quite an expert at all types of rip offs. To him, credit card fraud was a small meatball when he measured it against employee embezzlement.

His job required that he frequently work with the Identity Theft Assistance Center. The center was set up to aid victims of identity theft fraud and share data with the Federal Trade Commission in order to help law enforcement apprehend credit card thieves. This morning he would check the FTC's Consumer Sentinel database which is used as a source of information for ID fraud investigations. "Something has to show up if this person is in the system. More that thirteen hundred federal, state, and local law enforcement agencies can access the system." "I have never heard about this Identity Theft Center." Andrea said. "Most people haven't. It's a bank sponsored service set up to help victims access credit reports, place fraud alerts with credit bureaus, and notify companies that may have had fraudulent accounts opened under other people's names." "Do you think this can help me?" Andrea asked. "I'm certain that your good name will be restored one way or the other." He said. "The bank is only responsible for fraud associated with the bank. Anything else should be handled by your credit card companies. They will fix their own accounts. I will be happy to give you a few pointers on how to deal with them if you like." He offered. "Of course, if you can save me from any unnecessary hassles, I would be happy for your input." She assured him. "Don't worry Andrea. The last thing that I want is for you to go thru any more than you have already gone through." He responded as he looked her up and down. They locked eyes and she remembered his touch the night she went to his apartment. "Would you like to accompany me to the Identity Assistance Center so you can find out if they have any data concerning credit cards, or medical identity theft? Or should I go by myself and report back to you what I found out concerning only your bank account." He asked. "Yes. I want to go with you. I want to find out about everything concerning my credit." She answered. He smiled like a cat that had just swallowed a canary.

He had successfully found a way to spend time with her alone. "Okay, do you want me to pick you up or would you prefer to meet me there? I'll give you the address and if you don't know the area, you can check out MapQuest." He said. "Since you obviously know your way there, I'll ride along with you if you don't mind. It's already noon and I hope we can accomplish a lot in order to get this mystery solved." She said. "Your man will not get upset if I swing by to pick get you?" He teased. "I would be furious if you were my woman." Andrea laughed and commented. "Sterling, don't be silly,

I would explain everything to Quinton if I had to." "You mean he doesn't know about this identity thing?" "No he doesn't. But now, I need to put down this phone and get ready to go with you on this mission. How far are you from my house?" She asked. "I'm right outside your door." He answered and rang the doorbell two times. Andrea looked through the peephole and swung the door open to greet him.

Sterling entered her condo and she gave him a warm hug and a quick peck on the cheek. He in turn gave her a smile and a compliment her on how lovely her home was. "You have exquisite taste, my lovely. Did you have an interior designer come in?" He asked. Andrea "No, I'm totally responsible." "Really, how did you manage that? Did you get some ideas from Nate Berkus or one of those Home and Garden Magazines?" He probed as she looked around the room. "Make yourself comfortable while I find something warm to wear. I know it's freezing out there. You know that there was a forecast for snow tonight." "I know. I think we can beat it if we head on out now. I think we can get there and back before it starts." Andrea put on a sweater, wool slacks, and fur lined boots. She layered that with a red wool coat, a hat and a pair of gloves. As they pulled out of the parking garage, Andrea noticed the overcast sky. "Do you think we should wait to do this on another day?" She asked nervously. "Can't you access it online?" "We'll be in and out in no time, he assured her.

After a short forty minute drive, they arrived at the center. He signed in and she signed in as his guest. He put his password into two computers and showed her how to use the data program to find out if her name or social security number had been compromised.

186

"Andrea we need to put a stop to this before you begin to feel the full impact. Identity theft has destroyed many people lives and I don't want it to happen to you." He said and then proceeded to pull up data on his computer screen. After Andrea got a feel for the program and figured out how it worked, she pulled up two recent credit card inquiries that she did not authorize. She printed out the information and used a yellow highlighter to mark the names, addresses, and phone numbers of the credit card companies. Sterling advised her to immediately contact the companies and let them know what was going on. After an hour and a half, an office worker told them that the place would be closing and they had about twenty minutes to finish their research. He also told them that it was snowing. "Let's call it a day, Andrea." I have what I need. Did you find anything?" "I think so. I'll show it to you later and you can tell me if it has any merit." Sterling helped her with her coat before putting his own back on. "Once outside, he scraped the snow off of his windshield and let the car warm up for a few minutes before heading back to Andrea's condo. "It took twice as long to get back home as it took to get to the center." She said. "Well, I was transporting precious cargo and I had to take my time." He said. "If it took you that long to get me home, there is no telling how long it will take you to get home." She said. "You live so far from here." "Are you worrying about me? Does that mean you care?" he teased. Andrea looked at the handsome hunk and blurted out. 'Damn right I care. If you go slipping and sliding out there and God forbid something happen, who is going to help me solve this case?" He stopped smiling and gave her a serious look. "Is that all I am good for? Is that all you want from me, to help find out who

187

is using your identity?" "I want you to as a friend." She said as he moved closer to her. "A friend?" He repeated as he lightly touched her chin and tilted her face upwards so that she could look directly in his eyes. "Yes a friend." She reiterated. "Can I give you a friendly good night kiss before I leave?" He asked. She responded by wetting and pursing her lips. He immediately kissed her lightly. "I'm sorry; I didn't wait for an answer." He said as he drew her closer in his arms. "Would it be okay if I give you a kiss good night? This time I'll wait for an answer, he said. As he held her close, he could feel her heart beating a mile a minute. Andrea had only one answer in her head and that was "Yes Sterling, a good night kiss would be okay." After that response, he gently brushed her hair behind her right ear, pressed his mouth next to the exposed ear and whispered "I believe that I can be a just a friend because I don't know if friends can hold each other like this." Andrea made no effort to move away from his embrace. His warm breath felt divine. She moved to face him and found out that she could not resist kissing him full on the lips. They started sucking on each other's lips and ended up French kissing.

They didn't break their embrace or unlock mouths as Sterling artfully led her to her bedroom. He slipped off the layers of sweater, blouse, camisole, and bra that she wore. Then he slipped a breast into his mouth. He licked and sucked until she begged him to do the other one. He readily obliged until Andrea stopped him long enough to tear off her boots, pants, legging, and panties. Suddenly the phone rang. She picked it up and it was Quentin. "Andrea I have been trying to call all night. Are you okay?" "Yes, she answered as Sterling began to kiss her stomach, paying special attention to her belly button. "You know it's snowing hard out there? Are you going to be okay? I'm stuck here at the hospital." "I- I- I'm fine." She said as Sterling kissed her thighs. "Okay, then. I'll check on you later." "Don't try to come out here Quentin." "I can't, Honey. I have to stay here and check on my patient." "Okay. You do that. I'll talk to you tomorrow." She said and hung up. Sterling kissed her on the mouth again. She had never been French kissed like that before. Not even Quentin titillated her tongue like that. She pushed Sterling on his back and relieved him of his dress shirt and tee shirt. She was amazed at how sexy his six pack was. She rubbed his chest lightly before he pulled her head down so she could kiss him. He couldn't take her mouth on him like that for more than a few minutes. He lifted her off of him, rolled her on her stomach, and positioned her on her knees. She shivered as he pressed his body close to her. He cupped her breasts in his hands and massaged them until she moaned. When he penetrated her, she propped herself up on her elbows and forearms to keep her balance. He rode her so furiously that sweat dropped from his chest onto her back like raindrops falling from a cloud during a sudden downpour. When she could take no more she screamed "Oh God! Oh God! Oh God!" Sterling continued stroking her, pulling his penis almost all the way out and pushing it back into her as far as he could. Sweat continued to drop on her back. She screamed "Oh please Lord! Please! Please! I can't take it." Sterling growled like a tiger, shook uncontrollable and fell over on his side. "Are you okay?" he asked. While she rested on her stomach, he wrapped his arm around her. Soon the both fell into a deep sleep.

Chapter 30

Terry's In2Hair products had been selling all around the country since being advertised in hair style magazines and on TV. He had done make overs on the Wendy Williams, The View, and even Kathy Lee and Hoda TV talk shows. Each time he appeared on a show, he plugged the fact that he was going to be featured in an upcoming Hair Show. This Friday afternoon, he was a guest on Steve Harvey's TV talk show. "Why do professional hair stylists do these hair shows? Is it going to be anything like the Bronner Brothers Hair Show in Atlanta that the movie was based on? Do you plan to come out there with a marching band like that guy on Chris Rock's movie "Good Hair" did?" Steve Harvey quipped. "Stylist and people who plan on becoming stylist attend hair shows to brush up on their skills. They come to take part in exciting competitions and to get ideas about what is hot and trendy in the world of hair care." Terry responded. "Is it going to be off the chain like the Bronner Brother Hair Show?" Steve asked. "The Bronners do put on quite a show. You know, Steve, all and I do mean all hair shows are very theatrical and I dare say some shows have a circus-like quality. Now, don't take the circus part the wrong way. There are no clowns or tigers and horses in hair shows, at least none that

I've attended." Terry responded. "Audience what he means is that the circus has a lot going on and a hair show has a lot going on as well. Even though a hair show may be like a circus, hair is the "mane" attraction." Steve chimed in. "Exactly!" Terry said "And may I add, hair care professionals also attend these shows to learn what's new in hair care products. My hair company and others will be offering samples of products." You heard it folks, the hair show will be in Hampton, Virginia on August 16th. Let's give Terry of Terry's In2Hair Styling Salons and hair care products a big round of applause. Thank you for doing the show, I hope you come again. "Today, everyone is going home with a bag of In2Hair products!" Steve told the audience.

Terry left the impressive set of the Steve Harvey television talk show pleased with his performance. He was glad that he had the opportunity to walk into Studio A on the second floor of the NBC Tower in Chicago where the Steve Harvey show was aired. He was always impressed by the many elements that came together to produce a talk show. He would notice the cameras, lighting, green rooms, dressing rooms, and audience holding area each time he was a guest on talk show. He marveled at the way the production manager, engineers, stagehands and everyone associated with the show handled their business.

Terry couldn't help smiling as he thought about his appearance on today's show. The makeovers were well received by the audience. The In2Hair product audience gift bags were sure to convert customers to his product line. And the plug for the hair show that he was to be featured in was sure to gain hair care pros attention and the following that his brand was seeking.

He decided to celebrate his television appearance by taking in a few Chicago sights before returning to his room at the Downtown Hyatt Regency Hotel. Terry's first stop was Catch 35 Seafood and Premium Steak Restaurant which was just a short walk from the theater district. Terry ordered Seared Scallops with Szechwan glaze, bone in rib eye, shrimp and crab bisque and a Martha's Vineyard salad. The server was very attentive and accommodating. He kept refilling Terry's glass of iced tea and he didn't seem to mind changing the three course rib eye meal to include the seared scallops that Terry wanted to add. Terry was surprised that the food was very fast and came out hot. He thoroughly enjoyed the Martha's Vineyard salad which contained an ample mixture of baby lettuce, raspberries, pine nuts, blue cheese, red onions, tomatoes, and raspberry dressing. As he took a sip of iced tea, several diners smiled his way as they were seated at a nearby table. He nodded and smiled back at them thinking that they looked like a celebrity couple who he just couldn't place at the moment. "I'll probably see them again in People or Star Magazine." He thought.

Terry soon finished his meal, placed an appropriate tip under his salad plate, and left the restaurant. He decided to burn off some calories by taking a one mile waking tour of the Loop. His walk started off on East Wacker Dr. As he continued walking on Wacker, he approached Willis Tower. "My trip here won't be complete without checking out Skydeck Chicago, stepping out on The Ledge and experiencing what it feels like to view the city through a glass floor thirteen-hundred and fifty-three feet above street level." I'm definitely going inside this building," Terry thought. "This will be a great photo op for my Facebook page."

After standing in line briefly and going through a metal detector, Terry paid his seventeen dollars admissions fee. He had to stand in line again to get inside in the venue's movie theater where he would view a short video on the Sears Tower as well as a short history of Chicago. He stood fifteen minutes in yet another line before he finally stepped into the glass box. The elevator ride up was fast and quite nerve-wracking. Traveling one thousand, six hundred feet per second, the ride up to the observation deck was fast and maybe furious to some people. But Terry was thoroughly exhilarated by it. The elevator took him one hundred and three floors high and his ears began to pop as he traveled upward. "I could have prevented this ear popping if I had bought along a stick of gum or a pair of earplugs." Terry thought.

A couple with two young children was also on the elevator. While the woman nursed the youngest child perhaps to prevent painful ears, the father held the older child's hand. He estimated that there were at least fifteen other people in the glass elevator with him. When they finally reached the ledge an African American woman who seemed to be nervous from the time was coaxed on the elevator two other women cried "Holy #@$(*#, this is scary. Whooooaaaa this is really scary!!!" She took a very cautious step, and another. And cried again "Whoahohoho this is scary." Her friends, who seemed somewhat nervous themselves, put their arms around her. Eyeing Terry, one of them nudged the other two and said "Look, this is the stylist who did those makeovers when we were at the Steve Harvey show this morning. Can we get your autograph? Better yet can we take a picture with you?" Terry signed their Skydeck passes and took pictures with each of them. The one who was so terrified said. "I am scared shitless, but I want to take a picture with you and tweet it to my friends." She bravely moved next to him and focused her cell phone camera on herself and him to get a shot of them together. "I wish Steve Harvey had picked me for a makeover this morning," one of the ladies confessed to Terry. "Sweetheart, you look beautiful just the way you are. You don't need a makeover. Your hair and makeup is just fine. But if you are ever in the Twin Cities, come on to my salon and I will be happy to serve you and your two lovely friends." Terry told her. He learned from his Grandmother and her friends long ago that a woman loved to be flattered. "Enjoy the rest of you observation." Terry told them as he moved away from them to get some photos of the view.

"I love being able to look down on this beautiful city to see tourists rushing about and yellow taxis moving rapidly across the streets of the windy city." An older lady told her escort. "Look over there. The beach and navy pier are also really neat to look at." He responded. "We are having a blast! My husband and I are celebrating our twenty-five year anniversary of meeting for the first time. We met in Chicago and we couldn't have picked a better spot to visit!" The woman exclaimed. Terry smiled and congratulated them. "It was nice talking to you."

Terry finally found a space inside the glass box where he could turn his attention to the magnificent view outside of the elevator. "I am on the ledge of the Western Hemisphere's tallest building literally standing in a glass box, and the 360 degree view is breathtaking." Terry said as he used his camera phone to record this part of his trip to the Windy City. "The view is simply spectacular! I can see skyscrapers, sport stadiums, sculptures, green roofs, Lake

Michigan and miles of lakeshore from this vantage point. Visibility is over thirty miles. You can see all the way to Wisconsin and Indiana he said as he pointed his camera in the direction of the cheese state." He continued. Several teenage Japanese boys moved closer to him to get videos of their own and he put his cellphone video camera on pause to oblige them. The boys talked in Japanese as they used their expensive looking Nikon and Sony cameras to capture the panoramic views of the downtown Chicago skyline.

"Would you mind using this camera to video tape us together?" one of the boys asked in perfect English as he gestured toward Terry. "It would be my pleasure Terry answered and after a pointing the expensive looking Japanese camera at the boys for a few minutes and taking a few pictures, Terry handed the camera back. "You want me to get some shots of you on your cell phone camera?" the teen asked. Terry handed the friendly fellow his cell phone and did a few jumping jacks as his new friend videotaped him. He then got down on the clear see thru floor of glass ledge and did pushups. He knew that the shot of him doing pushups on the glass floor of the Skydeck above the city's best sights which included: the Water Tower, Wrigley Field and Millennium Park would be an interesting conversation piece.

Terry was pleased that the Hyatt Regency where he was spending the night was within walking distance from the Skydeck at Willis Tower. He decided to make a quick trip to nearby North Columbus Drive before heading back to his hotel room. He stopped to take pictures of the Wrigley Building before heading toward the Museum of Contemporary Art. He snapped pictures of outdoor sculpture by such well known greats as Picasso, Miro,

Henry Moore, and Marc Chagall. "After I post these pictures on my Facebook page, I'll think about giving a few copies to Michelle."

Terry continued walking and snapping pictures with his cell phone. He took photos of street juggler, mimes, and musicians until his cell phone battery became low. "I'd better get back to the hotel, charge this phone and get some rest so that I can get to the airport on time." He thought. The concierge greeted him as he walked back into the lobby and Terry thanked him for suggesting that he visit Willis Tower Skydeck. "

After taking a shower in the contemporary bathroom, Terry dried himself off and put on the complementary white lush bathrobe that he found in the closet. He got a beer out of the small refrigerator that sat on a counter next to a mini bar. "Am I tired!" he thought as sat down in a comfortable chair behind the desk in the room's oversized work area. "As soon as I check my e-mail and follow up on my tweets, I am going to call it a night." He was appreciative of the Wi-Fi and high speed Internet access as he clicked on Facebook to find out what his Facebook friends were up to. Terry yawned and walked over to the room's king-sized bed, turned down the luxuriously soft down blanket and plumped up two large pillows. He took off the robe leaving him in his black Tommy Hilfiger boxers and plopped down on the bed. He fell asleep within the first fifteen minutes of watching Jimmy Kimmel Live on the thirty-seven inch flat screen TV.

Chapter 31

The Profile Event Center proved to be a dynamic and exciting setting for both Michelle's wedding and reception. She appreciated the idea that the venue was conveniently located in the heart of the Twin Cities with easy access to hotels and major freeways. Of the two halls that the Profile Event Center offered, Michelle had chosen the smaller of the two, the stunning Diamond Hall, which would accommodate the one hundred seventy-five guests she'd invited to her wedding. The hardwood dance floors, gorgeous high tech dance lighting, disco balls, a state of the art sound system and performance stage would ensure that both the wedding and reception would be memorable. The event center included a bridal changing room located conveniently close to the wedding and reception area. The beautiful dressing room included lighted makeup mirrors, changing screens, a big-screen television, full-length changing mirrors, a couch to lounge on and a pretty bathroom. Michelle was also delighted that Maxine Stone, the wedding planner, showed her this particular venue because the photographer and videographer wouldn't charge extra to shoot her getting ready since there's no additional location to visit.

Maxine had handled all the logistics of the event perfectly. All that was left for Michelle and her groom to do was simply relax and enjoy their big day. But as she and Andrea walked toward the dressing room door with her wedding clothes in tow, she turned towards Andrea and confided that something was bothering her. "When I woke up I was completely relaxed. Now, all of a sudden, I get a case of bad nerves. I keep thinking that something is going to go wrong before this day is over. What if I can't brush it off my shoulders and not let any of it affect my mood." Andrea tried to reassure Michelle. "Sweetie, have fun! Relax and enjoy! This is your big day! It's wonderful that you are sharing it with all the people who mean the most to you! So what if something does go wrong? So what if someone who's not related to you sits on the bride's side or someone who you really want to attend does not show up, or something else pushes your button? Who cares, just let it all go and have a great time." After a few minutes, Michelle took in a deep breath, exhaled, and relaxed. "Andrea, girl you are so right. Why the freak should I worry? My big day is finally here and I am marrying the man of my dreams."

They entered the bridal changing room where the excitement of the bridesmaids clad in magenta colored halter shouldered, knee length, taffeta sheath dresses were either checking themselves out in the mirror, snapping pictures of themselves, or applying makeup lifted Michelle's spirit and erased all traces of apprehension. She picked up one of the bridesmaids bouquet of pink and white calla lilies which had been tightly placed in an ornamental bouquet holder called a tussy-mussy and inhaled the flowers' sweet aroma. "I guess I'd better get dressed so we can get this show on the road."

She said to no one in particular. After getting into her bridal under-garments, she began putting on the gown.

Andrea assisted one of the bridesmaids in helping Michelle cover her head with a silk tee-shirt so that she could slide the gown on easily without damaging her hair or getting make up on it. After this maneuver was completed, they pulled the snug fitting gown with its mermaid silhouette down over Michelle's shapely bust, hips and thighs, all the way to her knees where it then flared dramatically into a soft flowing skirt all the way to the floor.

"I sure hope you don't have to go to the bathroom after this thing is fastened," one of the bridesmaids said. "Don't worry, I took care of all my business beforehand and I haven't had a sip of anything to drink since last night." "Instead of those sexy panties I know she's probably wearing, she should have put on some Depends," A perky bridesmaid added. "Hey, ease up Baby Girl, you know I ain't wearing no damn diaper under this thirty-two hundred dollar wedding dress. I don't care what Lisa Gibbons and those other damn movie stars do on those silly ass Depends commercial." Michelle warned in her best sister girl voice. They all laughed at the thought of that funny commercial.

"I swear this wedding gown is unlike any other piece of clothing I've ever owned, although all of my debutante gown, prom gowns, and beauty pageant gowns were a hassle to get into and out of," declared Michelle. "I definitely agree," Andrea responded. "Putting this gown on and maneuvering around in it has got to be unlike the way you've worn and moved around in anything else." "I'm so glad that you are here to help me, Friend Girl, because getting dressed in this gown is definitely a two or three person job and I can't think of anyone else I'd rather have overseeing this operation." "Well, just in case your dress or one of the bridesmaids dresses need emergency an alteration, I have bought Mattie with me. She is an expert seamstress who can make sure that the dress is fitting properly. She will help us examine the gown to make sure every fastening has been secured, every inch is lying smoothly and there are no last minute smudges or spots." Mattie can attach a loop to that long train on the back of your gown. You can slip the loop over your wrist so that you can easily lift it for walking and dancing if you don't want your train bustled," "I am going to wait until after the first dance to bustle." Michelle smiled and winked at her cousin, Deidre. I have a bustler who will take charge of my train in the meantime. Right Deidre? Deidre is going to drape it over the chair when I sit, and help transport it when I walk." "I'll even help her get it in the car when she takes off for her honeymoon." Michelle's cousin, who was handling the task added. "Hold up, what's a bustle?" asked one of the bridesmaids. The cousin quickly responded. "You've seen it before. It's that extra fabric in the back of wedding gowns that drags along the floor for the ceremony. It's called a train. The bride can trip and fall while she's dancing at her wedding reception, so the train essentially needs to be folded up so it's out of the way. There are different ways you can fold it. Deidre is going to fold it into a French bustle."

"Let me do that," Andrea offered. The bridesmaid who had tried to get the first of fifteen buttons on the back of Michelle's gown handed over the crotchet hook that she had been trying to use to button Michelle's gown. "It's hard to get those buttons through those tiny buttonholes." Michelle used the hook to grab each elastic button hole carefully pull each hole over its corresponding button. "Oh, so that's how you use that crochet hook. Fastening all those button by hand would take about an hour and leave your fingers sore" The bridesmaid said as she intently watched Michelle fasten the last of a series of buttons lined down the back of Michelle's dress. "Whew! I'm glad that's over. Why did you need so many buttons in the first place? You know those buttons don't do didly." "Stop criticizing my dress. I thought you liked it." I love it, I just had no idea fastening them buttons would be such a job." Andrea, do you know that this damn gown has seven large fish bones in the bodice?" "What? You've got to be kidding me," laughed Andrea. "I kid you not. They're supposed to make sure this dress holds its shape." "It's great that the dress has built in foundation but are those bones poking you girl, like those damn underwire bras poke you?" "They haven's so far. The bones are capped so they don't push through the lining and they follow my curves to add support and make my body look great, even without a bra." "Well that foundation's got you looking like a 'brick house' as the song goes."

Andrea looked at Michelle and smiled. She knew the wedding guests would surely fall in love with Michelle's gown at first glance. "Michelle, honey, this has got to be the most beautiful gown I've ever seen. You look fabulous." Michelle's ivory colored satin and organza mermaid wedding gown was elegant yet sexy. The gown was absolutely flattering on Michelle. Fitting her snugly at the hips and thighs before flaring out at the knees, it showed off the full shape and curve of her hips. The gown also emphasized her well defined waist and fairly proportionate bust.

One hour before Michelle was ready to walk down the aisle, the photographers and videographer arrived. The wedding planner had timed their arrival for the latter portion of the bride's hair and makeup styling when Michelle was closer to being finished so that photos would be more flattering. "They will have plenty of time to capture the details of your gown, shoes, jewelry, and so on in addition to the hustle and bustle of the room." Michelle remembered the planner telling her.

The videographer and photographer moved around the dressing room getting candid shots of the bride in various stages of preparedness. They also captured interactions between Michelle and her bridesmaids and relatives. "Michelle, sweetheart, I've never seen you look so beautiful! Your hair, nails, makeup, and gown are impeccable! You look like a bride out of a movie!" Her grandmother exclaimed with tears in her eyes." "Now, now Nana, don't cry. Your eyes will be all red when we take the family photo." Michelle said as she extended he arms and gave Nana a careful, brief hug. Nana wasn't the only person in the dressing room who noticed how radiant, relaxed, and ready to start a new existence. Michelle's mother was almost floored when she caught a look at her only daughter. "Your father may not let you go when the pastor asks who gives this woman to this man?" she said with a smile.

"Now that you have your gown on, are you ready to get the final touches of your makeup applied?" Vicenza, her makeup artist and god-brother asked. Vicenza was a New York makeup artist who had done Tyra Bank's, Vivica Fox's, and Kerry Washington's makeup at some point. He had also appeared on both the Oprah Show and America's Next Top Model as a makeup artist. Vicenza had flown out to Minnesota just for the occasion. "I'm ready Vicenza, just don't let anything get on this gown." "Stop worrying, Hon. I got you. Michelle pulled her gown up before perching herself on a backless stool. Vicenza draped a clean white satin sheet over the entire front of dress before applying last-minute face powder and makeup. "There's not much more that I need to do Michelle." "Cenza, will the makeup that you applied earlier today last all day?" "It should carry you through all the crying, hugging, kissing, eating and dancing you are going to be doing before, during, and after the ceremony." He said. "Damn, Vicenza, did you buy your makeup from Pittsburgh Paint Store?" Andrea asked. "No but the mascara is waterproof, and the lipstick is kiss proof, and her skin makeup is bombproof." Vicenza answered as he gingerly applied Model in a Bottle makeup setting spray onto Andrea's face. Vicenza finished up by applying foundation on her neck in order to making sure that her face did not look different from the rest of her body. Michelle signaled the photographer and said, "Some foundations and powders look different in pictures, since they reflect light differently. Do you mind if we get my makeup checked and photographed with a flash before you take any more photographs of me." "The photographer obliged by taking a few shots at various angles. He showed Michelle the test shots and assured her that the makeup would not affect the reflection of the light and her photographs would come out just fine.

After Vicenza finished working his magic and the photographer finished showing her the test shots, Michelle walked towards a full-length mirror in the dressing room and took a long moment to marvel at how stunning she looked. The photographer and videographer took several quick shots of Michelle looking at her reflection in the mirror. The photographer's assistant announced, "We're ready to take the pre-ceremony photos of the bride with her family and attendants. We'll take approximately forty shots allowing two or three minutes per shot before we move to the groom's dressing room to take pictures of him and his family and attendants. The wedding planner, Maxine Stone, stepped forward and untangled Michelle's veil from her tiara. "You ready to walk?" she asked. "Yes," Michelle said. "Let's get you to your man." Stone said and led Michelle out of the dressing room toward a waiting area.

At approximately five-thirty pm, thirty minutes before the ceremony, the wedding music began. Four male ushers took Polaroid pictures as guest entered the Profile Event Center's Diamond Hall. Four female ushers who had been instructed to begin seating guests thirty minutes before the wedding were reminded to stop the seating five minutes before the processional was to begin. The room grew quiet with anticipation as the prelude music began. A recording of 'You Are' being sung by Charlie Wilson resonating from the sound system prompted the wedding party to assemble and at five after six pm the attendants proceeded down the aisle.

The audience grew attentive as the minister and groom entered the room from stage right. The Groomsmen escorted the Bridesmaids down the center aisle, followed by Andrea, the Matron of Honor and Matthew Morgan, the groom's Best Man. They were followed by five year old twin cuties Muffin and Mikey, Michelle's brother's children. Muffin, the flower girl threw petals as she slowly strolled down the aisle. Mikey the ring bearer carefully carried a satin pillow with a ring resting on it. After all of the members of the wedding party had taken their places, the entrance to the hall was closed by a sheer curtain. The processional music began. The audience continued standing and looking on in anticipation.

Michelle, who was escorted by her proud father paused at entrance of the Diamond Hall. Suddenly, the curtain opened and the lighting changed so as to enhance Michelle's special moment as she completed her walk down the aisle. A backlight was cast on her, making her appear to glow and look as if she was floating down the aisle. Michelle and her father proceeded to walk down the aisle. The thirty second walk was the most serene, almost out-of-body experience that she had ever felt as the words from one of her favorite love song resounded from the speakers. During those few brief moments, she felt as if she was watching herself from another vantage point as she choreographed her walk to accompany thirty seconds of Atlantic Starr's *'Always'* was being sung by Michael and Mariah Newby. She did not select the traditional wedding march because it was so generic. She'd told the planner "Even though the traditional march would be safe to play, it's played so often at weddings my guest could close their eyes and when they hear it, they could be at anyone's wedding. I want them to know they're at my wedding."

The audience swooned as Mike's smooth voice sang and the lovely bride made her way to her beaming groom.

> *"Girl you are to me*
> *All that a woman should be*
> *And I dedicate my life to you always*
> *A love like yours is rare*

205

It must have been sent from up above
And I know you'll stay this way for always
And we both know
That our love will grow
And forever it will be you and me"

The minister, Reverend Charles T. Watson began the Call to Worship. "Dear friends and family, welcome to the marriage of Michelle Denise Robinson and Todd Shepherd. With great affection for Todd and Michelle, we have gathered together to witness and bless their union in marriage. To this sacred moment they bring the fullness of their hearts as a treasure and a gift from God to share with one another. They bring the dreams which bind them together in an eternal commitment. They bring their gifts and talents, their unique personalities and spirits, which God will unite together into one being as they build their life together. We rejoice with them in thankfulness to the Lord for creating this union of hearts, built on friendship, respect and love."

Michelle's dad finally heard his cue. "Who gives this woman to be wed?" He answered proudly. "I do!" The minister said "Todd you may now recite your vows to your bride." Todd looked drop dead handsome in his white bespoke tuxedo, tailored exclusively for him, as he looked at Michelle adoringly and said. "Michelle, sweetheart, I give you my promise to be by your side forevermore. I promise to love you deeply, to honor you fully, and to listen to you truly as we share our thoughts, our hopes, our fears, and our dreams. It is your heart that moves me, your head that challenges me, your humor that delights me, and your hands I wish to hold until the end of my days. From this point on, you are my life. I give you all my love, all my life, now and forever."

"Michelle, you may now recite your vows to your intended." Michelle recited her vows. "Todd, today, I take you to be my husband. I promise to love you without reservation, comfort you in times of distress, encourage you to achieve all of your goals, laugh with you and cry with you, grow with you in mind, and spirit, always be open and honest with you, and cherish you for as long as we both shall live. I vow all of these things from this day forward."

Reverend Watson turned to the bride and said "Michelle Denise Robinson will you take Todd Shepherd as your husband, in happiness and with patience and understanding, through conflict and tranquility?" She responded "I will." Michelle placed the ring on Todd's finger and vowed. "Todd, my love I give you this ring as a symbol of my love. As it encircles your finger, may it remind you always that you are surrounded by my enduring love"

The Reverend then asked the Groom, "Todd Shepherd, will you take Michelle Denise Robinson as your wife, in happiness and with patience and understanding, through conflict and tranquility?" I will, Todd responded. "You may now place the ring on your bride's finger." "This ring I give to you as a token of my love and devotion. I pledge to you all that I am and all that I will ever be as your husband. With this ring, I gladly marry you and join my life to yours."

The Minister went on to say "In the years which shall bring Michelle and Todd into greater age and wisdom, we hope that their love shall be ever young; that they shall be able to always recover from moments of despair. In this hope, may they keep the vows made on this day, in freedom, teaching each other who they are, what they yet shall be, enabling them to know that, in the fullness of being, they are more than themselves and more than each other, that they are all of us, and that together we share joyously the fruits of life on this earth, our home."

"By the power vested in me by the State of Minnesota and inasmuch as you, Michelle Denise Robinson and you, Todd Shepherd have declared your love for each other before family and friends, I now pronounce you husband and wife. You may now seal your vows with a kiss." "Alright now," one of the guest said loudly. "Go on kiss her," a male voice blurted out. "Yeah!" Someone else added. As laughter and applause filled the room Todd and Michelle engaged in their first kiss as man and wife. "I present to you Mr. and Mrs. Todd Shepherd."

After briefly adjusting his gold rim eyeglasses on his nose Rev. Watson said, "Please stand and join with me as we ask God's blessing on this new couple. "Eternal Father, redeemer, we now turn to you, and as the first act of this couple in their newly formed union, we ask you to protect their home. May they always turn to you for guidance, for strength, for provision and direction. May they glorify you in the choices they make, in the ministries they involve themselves in, and in all that they do. Use them to draw others to yourself, and let them stand as a testimony to the world of your faithfulness. We ask this in Jesus name, Amen."

The guests stood and watched as the couple and the recessional lead out. Some of the audience members took pictures with their cell phones while others used cameras they bought along. "There's always someone who gets in the way of a good shot with their camera flashes that show up in the video or photograph," the videographer grumbled. "The wedding coordinator told them if they must take pictures to be aware of their surroundings and not get in our way and she asked them not to use flash cameras. But, as you very well know there is always some amateur jackass that don't give a crap if their flash interferes with hired cameraman's photo." The assistant complained. "Well let's just get in there and photograph the family and wedding party while everyone else is taking part in the cocktail hour." The cameraman said as he led the way to get shots of the wedding party.

The photographer and his assistant had worked with Michelle and Todd in detail prior to the ceremony to compile a list of all the necessary shots and who was to be in each one. The list, they informed her, would ensure that the bride and groom and their families had all their needs met, while saving a lot of time and confusion while they shot. "It also allows us to politely manage family members and others who ask for additional shots during the session. We simply tell them we are covering the list first and, if there is time at the end, we'd be happy to add any additional shots they'd like." They had followed the couple's list regarding the before and during the wedding photography shots. "Well, our video and still cameras have captured everything from the bride looking into a mirror, the bride and bridesmaids putting on makeup, the bride pinning a corsage on her mother and a boutonniere on her father all the way up to the groom getting ready in his dressing room, the groom looking into a mirror, the groom pinning a corsage on his mother and a boutonniere on his father." The assistant said as she read over the must have wedding shots list that the couple had contracted. My shots of the bride and her father walking down the aisle, the parents being seated, the wedding party walking down the aisle and the groom waiting for the bride all look great." One of the still photographers bragged as he and his cohort rushed to take posed pictures of the bride and groom before the reception. "I got great shots myself man. Let's get started on the after ceremony session."

Cameras flashed as the assistant called shots. "We are going to spend two minutes on each shot. So get ready. When I call you, please come up and take you position." The wedding party waited for their turn be photographed. Some even took pictures of each other. They were careful not to get in the way of the photographers. "Let's start with the beautiful bride. Michelle tear yourself away from that marvelous looking man of yours so we can get a shot of you alone. Maid of Honor and Bridesmaids, get ready because you are going to come up and join her after two or three minutes, the photographer's assistant instructed. The photography session went on for exactly one hour. Photos of the Bride and her parents, were mirrored by the groom and his parents. Finally, shots of the groom with the bridesmaid and shots of the bride with the groomsmen concluded the after the ceremony photos and video.

While the wedding party was being photographed in another location, the cocktail hour for guests was in progress. "Why the hell didn't I eat something to tide me over? Taking pictures may take a while, probably over an hour." Michelle's Aunt Emma complained as if her two hundred and eighty five pound body couldn't afford to miss one or two calories. "Emma you are not going to starve. Bring your fat ass on into the cocktail lounge with me and let's see what's popping," her equally ample escort prompted. Trust me, the food at this cocktail hour will probably outshine the reception dinner!" He went on to say.

As soon as Emma and her escort entered the room they marveled at the layout. Servers were stationed near the door with trays of Champagne, ice water, wine, and the couples' signature cocktails. Guest were offered the drink of their choice. "I'll have one of those blue drinks, thank you." Emma said and he'll have a glass of water." "How you gonna order my drink?" Her escort asked. "You don't order anything for me. I order my own damn drink." He snapped. Here we go again, thought the server. There's always one crazy acting couple at every wedding or funeral reception that I've ever worked. "Willie, you are driving and you are not going to get sloshed and drive me back home." "Don't worry about it girl, I'm going to put something in my stomach. Plus, this little old weak ass champagne ain't gonna effect my driving." "What's that blue drink?" He asked the server. "It's the bride's signature drink. It's called Something Blue. It's the bride's way of sharing her good luck with her wedding guest." "Yeah, but what the heck is it?" He wanted to know. The server responded, "Its rum, blue curacao, and pineapple juice." "It taste pretty good too. Having all these drinks right close to the door sure is an interesting way to greet guest." Emma, who was Michelle's second cousin observed.

Willie wasn't the only guest who was ready to unwind and get their drink on after the ceremony. Many of them decided to forgo the champagne, water, and wine offered by the servers and went to the main bar that offered hard liquor. Some of them went to one of the two satellite bars which were located at opposite corners of the room and got a glass of beer or a can of soda. Others went directly for the food while the line wasn't too long. "Where's the guest-book?" "It's over there on a podium next to the table with the wedding presents," "I guess we'll spend sixty plus minutes sipping drinks and nibbling on gourmet hors d'oeuvres while they get their pictures taken," Willie said. "You know this may just one of the best times of the night." He added and headed to the bar to get a shot of vodka before Emma could try to stop him. Emma was impressed by the cocktail hour food selections. There was a variety of cheeses, beautiful garden fresh vegetable crudité with dips and fresh fruit beautifully displayed on a mirror. There was chicken brochette or skewers of marinated chicken with roasted bell peppers and onions, cocktail franks with sauerkraut and mustard wrapped pastry puffs, mushroom caps filled with spinach and pine nuts, beef Sirloin on a skewer, miniature spinach quiche filled with egg and cheese, and pot stickers. Emma filled her small plate with as many beef and onion filled pastry puffs, miniature crab cakes, vegetable spring rolls, and chicken quesadillas as it would hold and headed toward a table to sit down. After she checked to make sure that the two empty seats at the table were available for the taking, she put here plate on the table and introduced herself. "That's smells good. What is it?" An older woman who was sitting next to her asked. Emma ignored the question because she thought the woman was fishing for a sample from her plate. "If she likes the way it smells so much, she can get her old butt over to the buffet line and get some for herself, she thought as she bit into a miniature crab cake then licked her lips with a smile of approval.

Terry and his date Sandy, as well as Douglas, and several In2Hair stylist sat in the lounge area on couches or ottomans and sipped cocktails. "Is that Quinton over there?" Douglas asked Terry. "That's Q. alright. Who are those women he's talking to?" Caroline asked Douglas as they eyed the tall table to their right. Quinton stood at a bistro table socializing with several attractive females. Some folks walked around the room and mingled with old friends and made new friends. Most of the attendees took a few moments to check out a video montage of Todd's and Michelle's childhood. A photographer dedicated to the cocktail hour event took digital photos that would be placed into a keepsake folder inscribed with their names and wedding date. The nine member Rise Band and Show created a laid back atmosphere with their performance of memorable R&B, Funk, Jazz, and Motown numbers. The female vocalist Ivory Staton and male vocalist Tennyson Price sang hits from the "50s" through the "90s". The male lead had the dance moves of James Brown, Michael Jackson, M.C. Hammer, and Morris Day. The band delighted the guest with their rendition of *The Girl from Ipanema*.

After Michelle took a few moments to freshen up and grab a drink, she got into positions at the receiving line to greet her guests for the next thirty minutes. During this time, guests mingled and had drinks and hors d'oeurves. Seven-fifteen pm arrived and guests were directed towards seats for the reception. The bride and groom were scheduled to arrive ten minutes later. Michelle and the planner had allowed five hours for the reception allowing an hour for cocktails, two hours for dinner, and three hours for dancing,"

After briefly introducing himself, the Master of Ceremonies thanked the guests for attending. The MC introduced the wedding party into the room in the traditional order. "Ladies and Gentlemen, the wedding party is now set to enter the room. Let's have a round of applause as I introduce them to you. The Bride's parents, Mr. and Mrs. Bobby Robinson. The groom's parents, Mr. Samuel L. Shepherd and Mrs. Cynthia Parker. The bridesmaids and groomsmen in couples, Gina Goodman and Kyle Brock, Angela Bromwell and Carlos Torres, Kimberly Vance and the groom's brother Samuel Shepherd Jr., and Vanessa Johnson and Joseph Liberman. Next, there's the maid of honor, Andrea McNair and the best man the groom's other brother Ricky Shepherd. Last but not least, the lovely flower girl and handsome ring bearer, Muffin and Mikey Shepherd. The audience remained seated until the M.C. said, "Ladies and Gentlemen, may I have your attention please, at this time I would like to announce the newlyweds have just arrived, please stand and join me in welcoming Mr. Todd and Mrs. Michelle Shepherd! Please give a big round of applause for the new Mr. and Mrs. Shepherd!" Michelle and Todd made a dazzling ta da entrance into the reception hall. They both were relaxed and ready to have fun. Their warmth and happiness radiated throughout the room.

With the audience and bridal party still standing, the Michelle was the first to be seated, as her new husband, Todd, held her chair. Todd then took his seat beside her. The female members of the bridal party were then assisted by their male partners holding their chairs. The guest sat down after the men in the bridal party were seated. The color palette of fuchsia, light orange, green, and white was the perfect complement to their enchanting affair. Each place setting featured green hued napkins and chargers, garnished with a pink

Asiatic lilies. The M.C. briefly announced the formalities set for the evening and then said "Ladies and Gentle, please bow your heads as the groom's brother, Samuel Shepherd Jr. will now say Grace before the meal." After the prayer another announcement was made "Ladies and Gentleman at this time we are going to open the buffet line. First let's have our bride and groom, wedding party, and parents help themselves." Once they were almost finished through the line, he announced that the buffet was now open to all of the guests.

By the third hour, dinner had been completed and it was time for the couple to have their first dance. "Folks this is the moment we've all been waiting for! Please focus your attention to the dance floor and get your cameras ready." He paused until the room quieted down. "For the first time as a married couple it is my pleasure to announce our bride and groom, Mr. and Mrs. Todd Shepherd." The D.J. played *All My Life* by K-Ci and JoJo as Michelle and Todd danced the first time as man and wife. Todd softly sang along as he and Michelle danced.

> *I will never find another luva sweeta than you,*
> *Sweeta than you*
> *And I will never find anutha luva more*
> *precious than you*
> *More precious than you*
> *Girl you are*
> *Close to me you're like my mother*
> *Close to me you're like my father*
> *Close to me you're like my sister*
> *Close to me you're like my brutha*
> *You are the only one my everything and for*
> *you this song I sing*

And all my life
I've prayed for someone like you
And I thank God that I that I finally found you
All my life
I've prayed for someone like you
And I hope that you feel the same way too
Yes, I pray that you do love me too

Although they danced very well together, they had practiced the dance many times just to make sure they looked good on the ballroom floor during their wedding reception.

The father-daughter dance immediately followed the first dance to the somewhat slow tune of '*Hero*' by Mariah Cary. After dancing to Mariah's song for less than a minute, the DJ enthusiastically announced "Michelle and her dad like to boogie. We're going to switch it up alright." Michelle and her father immediately stopped dancing a somewhat slow two-step and broke into fast paced steps like which included the dougie, the body wave and slides when the DJ switched to *Let's Groove* by Earth, Wind, and Fire. "Folks it is now time for the groom to dance with his mother!" After a slight pause he went on to say, "Put your hands together for the mother/son dance!" Todd's mother opted for the more traditional dance style when Three Times a Lady blasted from the sound system. Finally. The M.C. invited the guest to dance when he said "Ladies and Gentlemen the dance floor is now open. Let's get this party started!" With that announcement, Kool and the Gangs' *Celebration* got almost everyone on the dance floor. A mix of popular, classic and current dance tunes followed. Guest line did a variety of line dances including all-time favorites such as the wobble, cha slide, and cupid shuffle. Folks who wouldn't dance to *Boom Pow* or *Gangnam Style* didn't hesitate get on the dance floor when *At Last* or *When a Man Loves a Woman* was played.

"Ladies and gentlemen, the bride will now cut the cake and in about an hour from now cake will set on a table alongside other fun sweets for those of you who may want a sugar boost after dancing for a while." Michelle cut the cake and paused just long enough for the photographer and videographer to capture the moment. "The money has been counted and guess who's wearing the cake? All of you think the bride will wear the cake, say k-ache." There were a few responses since most of the guest had already noticed the giant champagne glass with the word groom was filled to the brim. "All of you who think the groom got the most money and will wear the cake, say wear the k-ache." At the M.C.'s urging, the guest responded overwhelmingly "Wear the k-ache." "I can't hear you guys what did you say?" The guests yelled out again, "Wear the K-ache." "Did you hear that Mrs. Stephenson? The audience wants your new husband to wear the cake." Michelle responded by smushing the first slice of her wedding cake in Todd's face after she first fed him a forkful.

Right after the cake cutting, or about two hours before the end of the reception the master of ceremonies said "All right we are ready for the bouquet and garter tosses. All the single ladies! I said ALL THE SINGLE LADIES!! Who are interested in catching the bouquet come up and give it a try." As Beyoncé sang the lyrics to her hit song, single women eager for a chance to catch the bouquet women walked out, ran out and danced out into the dance floor. Michelle waited until the song got to the part where Beyoncé sang.

Wo oh ooh oh ooh oh ooh oh
Wo oh ooh oh oh ooh oh oh ooh oh oh oh
'Cuz if you liked it then you shoulda put
a ring on it
If you liked it then you shoulda put a ring
on it
Don't be mad once you see that he want it
If you liked it then you shoulda put a ring
on it....

Michelle turned her back to the ladies on the floor, closed her eyes and tossed the bouquet over her right shoulder. The rest of the guests laughed as the women ran and reached for the bouquet. Michelle then sat in a chair in the middle of the dance floor. "Folks let's get all single guys to the dance floor... it's time to toss the garter." First our groom has to remove that garter from the bride. Everyone make lots of noise to help him out!" Todd came up to his bride carrying a football in one hand. He knelt before her, placed the football on the floor beside him, and took off her garter. To make things fun for the men, he placed the garter on the football and the men in the room roared with laughter. "Now that's the way to toss a garter." Terry called out. The D.J. cut to *Who Let the Dogs Out* by the Baha Men. The single men went out on the floor and Todd asked his dad to act as a center and snap the ball to him. "Come on old man you can still snap a football with the best of them. My dad used to play for Virginia Tech in his day, people." Todd laughed. Mr. Shepherd bent over as the audience roared with laughter. After Todd said a few random numbers and yelled 'Hike'

Mr. Shepherd snapped the ball. Todd caught it and turned toward the single men and threw it out just enough that it would not go out into the area where the guests were seated. Carlos Torres, one of the groomsmen caught the toss and did a crazy victory dance as if he had just made a touchdown.

After the garter toss the D.J. walked out onto the dance floor and said "Ladies and Gentlemen as you all were out here on the dance floor shaking your groove thing or whatever, a secret, stealthy, undercover judge infiltrated the room. This surreptitious judge, whose name we will later disclose, picked the best male and female line dancer, the best male and female steppers, the best male and female swing dancers, and the best male and female slow dancers." Almost everyone attendance stopped talked and waited to see who the best dancers were although most of them knew their names would not be called. "At this time we invite Dancing with the Stars Season Three Mirror Ball Trophy Winner, former Dallas Cowboys running back, Pro Football Hall of Famer," He paused and asked is there anyone in here who do not know who I am talking about?" as the audience began to applause.

"Ladies and Gentlemen our secret judge is none other than Mr. Emmitt Smith." With the help of a pair of sunglasses and a toupee, Emmitt Smith, a longtime friend of Todd's had kept a low profile during the event. The room erupted with applause. "I guess I can take off these sunglasses and this toupee now. I wouldn't have done this stunt for anyone else but my friend Todd." "Will the people who received magenta colored cards with numbers come up and receive your own mirror ball?" After all the winners were on the floor, the DJ asked each their name and after they spoke their name on the Microphone, Emmitt Smith gave them their mirror ball as well as a handshake. Of course this was a photo op for each winner and it would make Michelle and Todd's wedding video more sensational. "Todd you owe this man big time." Todd's father exclaimed. "We have a few more gifts to give away before the last dance. Everyone look under the seat of your chair and if you see a magenta colored card with the word gift on it, you get to keep the beautiful centerpiece that sits in the middle of your particular table." Winning guests happily let the D.J. know who they were. At Michelle's urging, he called all the winners up for a group picture. Each and every one of them came to the center of the dance floor to be a part of the group picture. "Folks this night seemed to go by so fast but our bride and groom wanted to dance to one last song before they exit. Please feel free to join them." Michelle and Todd were joined by bridesmaids and groomsmen who did not have Grand Exit obligations as they danced to T-Pain and Chris Brown's song *Best Love Song.*

> *Homie kiss your girl*
> *Shawty kiss your man*
> *We can see you on the kissing cam*
> *Now show me some love (yeah yeah)*
> *Show me some love (yeah yeah)*
> *Now look her in the eye, say baby I love you*
> *I never put no one above you*
> *And if you feel that way*
> *Go ahead and kiss your baby*
> *And now we've got the whole stadium in*
> *love like eh*

And if you feel that way
Go ahead and kiss your baby
And now we've got the whole stadium in
love like
Eh, eh, eh, eh, eh, eh. Oh, oh, oh

Although many of the older guest hadn't heard the song before, they liked the part of the lyrics that told them to kiss their lover. They also enjoyed seeing couples kissing on the ballroom's digital projection screen. Before the reception ended, almost every couple in the room shared a kiss.

The D.J. made an announcement for guests to line up for the bride and groom's exit. "Alright folks at this time our bride and groom are exiting the building. I'd like to invite all guests to line up to see them off!" Right before the last dance Andrea and several bridesmaids had made sure the guest had everything together for the bride and groom's grand exit. "Why didn't Michelle pass out sparklers instead of these things?" One of the guest wanted to know. "Sparklers would have created a high spirited closure of the night but Michelle decided against them because they emit toxic smoke and they are usually tossed on the ground when they burn out, Ms. Nosy. Do you want one of these glow sticks or not." The bridesmaid who was also Michelle's cousin answered the inquisitive woman adding a question of her own. Instead of having someone be responsible for picking up sparklers from the ground and disposing them, Michelle thought it would be better for guests to wave various colored glow sticks with their logo printed on them. Those who wanted to could take the glow sticks home and keep them a few hours later until their light extinguished." Andrea and a two bridesmaids gave each person in attendance a glow stick. "These colorful glow sticks will make for great photos since its quite dark outside," one of the attendants said as she peeled the wrapper off of a glow stick and cracked it to activate the light. "What are you doing? Don't light them up now because everyone will start using theirs. You all are supposed to wait until everyone lines up outside and receive the signal to light them." Andrea gently scolded her. "Oh, my bad. I was just testing it out." The girl replied with a giggle. Andrea queued the guest outside and had everyone who wanted to participate line up on each side of the walkway and form a human tunnel. Guest enthusiastically waved the glow sticks and loudly wished the couple bon voyage as they walked briskly toward a waiting limo. Several groomsmen made sure everyone cleared the premises and moved on after the bride and groom make their grand exit.

Chapter 32

❀

Andrea was not expecting the letter from Dell Computer Outlet that arrived in her mailbox that Saturday afternoon. She opened the envelop and found a new credit card in her name. The following week, Toys R Us, Macy's, Sony, and Bloomingdale credit cards landed in her mailbox. She was dumbfounded by the flood of unsolicited plastic cards. Her first call to Bloomingdale's confirmed what she had suspected. Someone had applied for those cards using her name. By Thursday, she was at her wit's end when she picked up the phone and called Sterling. "Sterling, it's happened again. Someone has managed to spend more than $7500 using my name, my credit, and my identity. Sterling, this is becoming scary. I'm beginning to wonder if this is someone who has some sort of vendetta against me." "Hold on, Babe. I thought we were making some progress toward catching this person but now you're telling me that you think they are still at it? Do you want to meet with me to talk about it?" "Yes Sterling, I do want to talk to you about why these damn cards keep ending up in my mailbox. How soon can you get here? I need you to be with me when I take this to the police." "I can get there in about an hour. Can I bring you anything to eat or drink?" "No thank you. I'm not hungry. I'm just

223

tired of being caught up this tangled web of deceit." Although she was grateful that she would not have to pay those fraudulent bills, Andrea could not help feeling violated and vulnerable.

Sterling arrived with a bag of burgers and fries for the both of them despite being told that Andrea was not hungry. He had been working out at the gym and he was ravenous. He could not pass up grabbing a couple of burgers from the near-by Shake Shack Burger Restaurant. "I can't understand how anyone would have the unmitigated gall to keep breaking the law over and over again," she said as she planted the newly acquired cards on the table next to his double cheeseburger topped with lettuce, tomato and Shack Sauce. She politely refused the vegetarian 'Shroom Burger, which was actually a crisp-fried Portobello mushroom filled with melted Muenster and cheddar cheeses, topped with lettuce, tomato and Shack Sauce. She also passed up the side order of sweet potato fries he'd bought for her. "I can't eat now. My stomach is in knots because of these crazy charges." It seems like the police is not trying to find out who's doing this."

Sterling took a bite of the burger and chewed while nodding in agreement. After swallowing and taking a sip of his milkshake, he dabbed at his mouth with a napkin and said. "Whoever the culprit must somehow have your name, your driver's license number, and your picture on a fake driver's license." Sterling said. "It's a very easy crime. It's an easy crime for anyone to commit if they have a desire to do it. Fighting against identity fraud is hard because credit card companies are rarely willing to prosecute suspects of I.D. Credit card companies should be considered accomplice to the thieves because they refuse to file charges. She got over seven grand from Victoria Secret, Dell, and Bank of America. Sterling said. "You'd think they'd want to prosecute, but they don't care. That's why the police don't spin their heels looking for them," Andrea added.

"I've notified my bank immediately as you very well know." I don't know what the police have been doing as far as your case is concerned but, as a bank representative, I have worked with you in an effort to make appropriate corrections concerning the unauthorized transactions in your account. I've tried to correct any incorrect reports submitted by the bank to credit bureaus. And, I've attempted to help protect you from any future identity theft or account fraud." He reminded her.

"Yet, that has not prevented this person from masquerading as me in order to steal money from my account, opening new credit cards, applying for loans, renting an apartment and committing only God knows what other crimes she's committed using this charade. This bitch will not be happy until she has demolished my credit, left me with unwanted bills and caused me countless hours of frustration trying to clear my good name."

"We alerted the fraud departments of all three credit bureaus and they put a fraud alert on your file. Didn't these creditors call you before they opened these accounts in your name?" He asked. "I didn't get any calls. I think they called the impersonator instead." Andrea answered.

Andrea picked up the phone and dialed the police department. She asked if she could file another report to go along with her initial report. "Even if the police can't catch this bitch identity thief, having a copy of the police report should help me clear up my credit records later on." She told Sterling who had agreed to drive her to the police station. She was placed on hold. As she waited for someone to come to the phone and speak with her, she watched Sterling devour the rest of his Shackburger and wished that she could tolerate the Portabella Mushroom burger that he bought for her.

She was finally connected to Detective Beverly Rose in the forgery and fraud crimes unit. The fraud unit was responsible for investigating felony related cases that were involved financial crimes such as forgery, unauthorized use of credit, check, debit and EBT cards. The fraud unit also handled swindles, scams, con games, embezzlement, and I.D. theft. Andrea later learned that particular unit consisted of only one police sergeant and four detectives. "Hell-o Detective Rose, I am Andrea McNeil. I came to your office a couple of months ago to report that someone was using my I.D. to open credit accounts in my name. I haven't heard anything back from you, so I'm assuming that you have not learned anything." "The case is still open," Rose assured her.

"I figure that the case is still open Detective since I'm still getting copies of credit cards that I haven't applied for. Mr. Sterling Steingold, a representative of Bank of America have been working with me in an effort to learn what's going on with my I.D. He's even had private investigator follow a lead on someone who he thought was responsible. Mr. Steingold and I would like to come in and give you some additional paper work." "Of course, I'll be here until eight pm." The detective said. Steingold finished his meal, disposed of his food wrappers and placed Andrea's meal in the refrigerator. "Let's go, Babe." He said as he put his jacket back on.

Forty-five minutes after they left Andrea's condo, they arrived at the Forgery and Fraud Unit of Minneapolis 4th police precinct and made their way to Detective Rose's office. After exchanging greetings, Andrea got down to discussing the reason for her visit. She gave documents and the new credit card billing information to Detective Rose. "As I mentioned during my phone call a few hours ago, I am still being targeted for I.D. theft. Here is a copy of a complaint I filed with the Federal Trade Commission along with a copy of an identity theft affidavit that I've completed in hopes it would assist me in reporting to various companies that a new unauthorized account had been opened." Andrea asked Rose why it was so difficult for authorities to put a stop to her problem.

"This thief or these thieves could be anybody including people you know. It could be neighbors, friends, relatives, or coworkers, unemployed friends living the lifestyle of the rich and famous, someone without impulse control, drug addicts or gamblers in desperate need of money." "Did you forget to add organized crime rings, restaurant and service employees who swipe credit cards?" Andrea asked. "Don't forget possible security data breaches that could happen on the internet," Sterling pitched in.

Rose added the new paperwork to Andrea's existing file and gave Andrea a copy of the police report. "Send a copy of this police report to each and every one of these creditors. Ask the credit bureaus to send you a fraud alert application. Tell them that you want the alert to remain on your credit report for longer than the standard ninety days. This will validate your claim. Send out all correspondence via certified mail with a return receipt at the post office." Andrea and Sterling thanked Detective Rose as they shook hand. Rose assured Andrea, "We will find out how your information got out there when we catch the perpetrator." She strongly emphasized the word when. "I didn't say if. I said when because it's only a matter of time." "I hope you catch her before I do Detective because if I ever run across anyone using my name and social security number, I may not be responsible for what I will do to that person," Andrea shot back. "Detective Rose Shook her head and said "I hope I didn't hear what I thought I heard." "She's doesn't mean that. She's just upset." Sterling tried to explain. He put his arm around Andrea's waist and led her out of Rose's office, out of the fourth precinct and back to his parked car.

"It seems like credit card companies sign up anyone. Why should they care if it's the wrong person? All they care about is money, the bottom line. It's a damn shame that I must go through all these changes in order to convince, Victoria Secret, Toys R Us, Macy's, Sony, and Bloomingdale that I was a victim of some sort of credit card charade. How can I convince them that they should disassociate these charges from my name and social security number?" Andrea asked as she got into Sterling's Mercedes. "Calm down, Love. You are not responsible for any losses that those companies incur. The bank and card companies must repay you any money that you lost." "Can the credit card companies and bank rebuild my reputation? Can the bank and credit card companies guarantee me that I will not lose my job over this fiasco? I am a financial analyst at a prestigious fortune five hundred company. What happens when one of those payments goes unpaid and my company gets a whiff of my bad credit? I can hear human resources asking me; How can you plan our company's multi-million dollar finances when you can't even manage your own two hundred and fifty grand a year salary?" She began to sob and before starting the car, Sterling turned toward her and gently wiped tears from her eyes with his finger before giving her a Kleenex from his glove-box. He said, "I hate that this has happened to you. I vow to you that I'll do all I can to help you. I'm going to personally look over each and every application, follow every clue, and try to run down any and all suspects myself. And when we take the responsible party to court, I'll be there to testify against the unscrupulous scoundrel." Sterling put the key in the ignition and drove her back home.

Chapter 33

*L*aShondra could feel the man watching her every move as she returned the dresses to the saleswoman. "Did they fit you okay?" "They were too tight." LaShondra lied. "I see this is a size 10. We have both of them in a 12 would you like to try them on? I can get them off the rack for you." "No Shondra laughed nervously as she cast a sly glimpse in the direction of the man who was pretending to look at a navy blue dress on the rack. He seemed to have followed her to every section of the store that she had visited. Shondra decided not to let him spook her. "I think I'll just take a look at some of your pants suits instead."

The salesgirl asked the man if he needed help. Shondra listened for his reply. "I'm looking for a dress that would look good on my Aunt Edna. Her birthday is tomorrow and she asked me to get her a dress to wear on women's day at the church she attends." He answered. "What size does she wear?" asked the sales girl. . "Fourteen, sixteen, I don't know." He answered. The salesgirl showed the man several dresses and he pretended to like them but insisted that he did not know her size. One dress seemed too big while the other seemed too small. The salesgirl decided to give the man some space and returned to help LaShondra.

Shondra checked out a Rachel Roy polyester pantsuit. She liked the looks of the laser cut jacket and high waist trousers. Shondra examined the straight leg, high waist trousers. "Don't you like the legs on those pants? I think the center pleat on these relaxed fit pants makes all the difference. Try them on and see how they fit." Shondra looked at the pant suit and thought there no harm in trying it on even if the pants are two hundred and ninety five dollars and the jacket is just as much. Striking poses for which America's Next Top Model celebs, Tyra and Miss Jay, would give her props, LaShondra could not stop admiring herself in the dressing room mirror. She did not want to leave the store without that Rachel Roy pants suit. Shondra thought about removing the security ink tag that was attached to both the jacket and the pants.

Shondra removed a cigarette lighter from her purse along with a metal fingernail file. She had watched Booby and his friend take a lighter and melt the top part of the cone on an ink tag and then scrape the melted part of the cone off with a knife. She remembered how they took the knife and popped the first ball bearing out allowing the rest of the ball bearings to pop out easily. She tried to remember what Booby did next. "Once the ball bearings were gone, Booby slid apart the two pieces of the security tags and the tag came apart easily." Shondra clicked the cigarette lighter and stared at the flame when suddenly the sales girl came near the dressing area and asked.

"How's it looking? Let me see you in it." "Oh, I've already taken it off." Shondra said. "Are you taking it with you today?" I was before you showed up, Shondra thought as she returned the lighter and file to her purse. "It's just as well, the fire alarm would have

231

gone off the minute I tried to burn the plastic cone." "What did you say about the fire alarm?" asked the clerk. "Nothing, I just got a text message from my neighbor that my fire alarm is going off." She said as she shoved the pants suit into the salesgirl hand. Shondra would have charged the pantsuit but for some reason, she did not go through with it. As many times as she had used the fraudulent charge cards, she never purchased a single outfit that cost as much as the Rachel Roy pant set that she had just tried on.

LaShondra noticed that the man who seemed to have been following her around the department store was no longer in sight. "I can't believe that I came that close to shoplifting that pantsuit. What's wrong with me? How did I end up like this?" Shondra asked herself as she turned on the ignition. "If I had gone through with it and popped that security ink tag on that suit and walked out of that store without the alarm going off, they still could have caught me. My picture from the store camera would have been on the news." "So what! Who would have known who you are with that wig on and you know the images on those video cameras always come out grainy, bleary, fuzzy, or unclear." Shondra's alter ego told her. "Shut up. Leave her alone. You did the right thing Shondra." Someone inside her head screamed. "I just need to get away from this mall." Shondra said to herself. "I need to get away from this mall." "Yes, let's am-scray and go to the bis ar and get a ink-dray." "Oh so now you speak pig Latin?" "Just go home Shondra, go home." She told herself. She drove the car out of the garage and pulled off so fast that she almost hit a car that was in front of her. Shondra's heart fluttered in her chest like a wild fist-sized butterfly. She took a sip of Pepsi that was left in the car's cup-holder.

The drink had become warm and flat but she drank the rest of it because her mouth had suddenly become extremely dry. "I don't want to go to jail. Why would I risking my freedom? What would happen to KeKe?" "It's a bit late to be asking those questions." Shondra's palms suddenly felt clammy and her stomach hurt. Feeling beads of perspiration on her forehead, she began to hyperventilate. Shondra drove the car off of the highway onto a shoulder in the road and began to cry as soon as she turned off the ignition. She sat there crying off and on for a half hour before a highway patrol officer pulled up beside her. "Are you having car problems Ma'am?" "No sir. I just started having some sort of dizzy spell." "Do you want me to call an ambulance to take you to the hospital" "No, officer. I feel better now." "Please step out of the car and show me your driver's license and car registration, he said as he held his hand on the gun that was in a holster around his waist and stared at her intently though mirrored sunglasses.

Shondra slowly and carefully pulled out the cards out of a small pocket on the outside of her purse. She then stepped out of the car and gave the officer the identification cards He asked her to sit inside of his car while he checked her driver's license. Shondra did as he asked. He sat down in the driver's seat of the patrol car and looked at her Minnesota state driver's license. Then he punched the information into a computer in his car. Almost immediately a picture of Shondra came up. The only problem was she looked nothing like the picture on the computer. "You look different." He said. "I know. I look different because I'm wearing a wig." The officer looked at her without showing any signs of shock or amazement. "I am also wearing contacts." Can I take them out and show you my real eyes." He nodded and she took the contacts out. "I am also wearing a wig. You want to see my real hair?" Shondra took the wig off before he answered. The officer looked back at the computer screen. "I see that you do not have any violations Miss Davis." You are free to go now, but do you feel well enough to drive. Do you want me to call someone to come and get you?" "No, I feel better now." I'll follow you until you get off of the interstate?" The tall, ruddy face, red head officer said. "Thanks, I appreciate the help that you are giving me." LaShondra said. Once she was inside of the car, she was relieved that she was back on the road and feeling better. She was even more relieved that she did not give the officer her Andrea I.D. She was relieved that she had purchased the used car in her own name from a dealer who did not care about bad credit as long as he got his inflated payments on time. Thank God I did not have a stolen Rachel Roy black pantsuit in her possession, she thought.

Shondra picked KeKe up from school and stopped by the nearest McDonald's. "Mama is going to buy something from here for dinner." Yeah! KeKe exclaimed. "I want Mc Nuggets, fries and a chocolate shake. Thank you Mommy!" They placed their order and LaShondra drove to the apartment. "Baby, Mommy needs to rest up. Will you put my food in the refrigerator for me? I'm going to take a little nap. After you eat and read one of your library books, you can look at TV." "Okay Mommy." KeKe said. Shondra gave her daughter a hug and reminded her not to open the door for anyone. She then went to her bedroom and lay across the bed.

KeKe knocked lightly on Shondra's bedroom door. "Mommy I read two library books and then I looked at TV." "You did baby, what did you watch on TV?" "I looked at Toy Story 2." "Toy Story 2, that's a movie? What time is it?" Shondra asked and immediately glanced across the room at the time on LED screen of the TV's cable box. "Twelve thirty a.m. You've got to get to bed KeKe so that you can get up for school on time. Did you bring home any assignments for me to sign?" Shondra walked the child to her room and helped her put on her PJs. "I'm sorry you missed your bath. You can wash off in the morning." She gave KeKe a kiss on the cheek after tucking her in.

Shondra could not go back to sleep after returning to her bed. She tossed and turned as she thought about the situation that she was in. "College Dropout, Divorcee, Single Mother, Victim of Eric's Psychological and Physical Abuse, Identity Thief, and now you think about adding Shoplifter to your list of attributes? What a Loser! Add that to the list. L-O-S-E-R in all caps." She thought. How can I get myself out of this mess, she wondered. What would happen to KeKe if something goes wrong?

Chapter 34

Terry read the ad that he placed in the Star Tribune, The Minnesota Daily, and the St. Paul Pioneer Express newspapers. The ad was posted exactly as Terry wrote it.

"*In2Hair Products is in search of African American and Multi-ethnic Female models, ages twenty to thirty two, for their national print and television campaign in the Minneapolis Area. Requirements: Multi-ethnic female curly/wavy shoulder length hair in its natural state (NOWEAVES/ EXTENSIONS/CLIPS) and African American female with brown complexion straight, chin/mid length hair (NO WEAVES/EXTENSIONS/ CLIPS) Feel free to respond with photos of various looks of yourself for casting. All models must be willing to cut, color, and/or relax upon request When: Monday March 26th Time 4pm-9pm Tuesday March 27th Time 4pm-9pm Please submit today! If selected, the address will be provided by staff. Do not call if you are already appearing in an infomercial, or if you have shot one in the past. Thank you in advance for participation. We look forward to making this a great commercial. TerrysIn2Hair@gmail.com*"

Terry received so many e-mails and phone calls that his receptionist kiddingly told him "The number of women calling up to inquire about your ad is unreal. You need to hire a person just to handle the influx of responses." "I have already hired someone to

236

manage this unexpected high volume of calls from women who want to be in my hair commercial. His name is Andre Joyner. He is an unemployed mass communication graduate." Terry went on. "Almost every mass communication major I've ever met is unemployed. Nine out of ten of them have never even had a job anywhere close to mass com. I honestly don't know why they are still offering that tired old major in anybody's college." The young receptionist quipped. "That's just like young boys saying they will play professional basketball or football" Terry said. "There are not that many openings for professional sports. And there are not enough openings in television or radio." The receptionist answered. "Especially if you are ugly as sin." He laughed. "You are so mean." She said "You should be ashamed of yourself for that." "It's true. Don't No One want a news reporter or anchor person who looks like he should be on that TV show that have seemingly ordinary people transform into an ugly assed monsters." He laughed. "What's the name of that show? I think it's called 'Grimm.' I watched it one time and those beasts scared the hell out of me." He kidded. "Terry you need to get your head examined she told him before picking up the phone and taking another call about the ads. After she finished the short phone conversation, Terry informed her "Andre will also handle all potential talent information, schedule appointments, and sort through any photos or videos that may come in." "When will he start?" Terry's receptionist asked. "I hope it's soon because I have enough to do taking appointments for this shop, and doing inventories and keeping products stocked on these shelves." "He'll be here this afternoon, Doll Baby." He assured her. "He'll work right next to you at your desk unless you rather have him in that little office in the back." "He needs to have his own office because I don't need him getting in my way up here." She snapped back. "Baby Doll, I did not plan to put him up here next to you anyways. I got his office space ready yesterday. All you have to do is direct anyone who comes in for an interview to his office."

Andre Joyner was Terry's best friend in high school. Andre was enrolled in the school's Mass Communications Academy and dreamed of having his own working television and video production studio. The courses that Andre took in high school such as camera operations, the interview process, directing and producing, script writing, and broadcast video all helped him breeze through his major in mass communication at Hampton Institute where he maintained a 3.5 G.P.A. Terry on the other hand studied pattern making, machine and hand sewing techniques, and draping as he aspired to enter the world of fashion. They each went their separate ways after graduation. Andre graduated from Hampton University and Terry finished Beauty School. Terry learned from a mutual Facebook friend that Andre was lived in nearby St Paul.

When Terry phoned A.J. he learned that he had been in between employment with several communications companies and was currently laid off of his last job because of budget cuts. "I need someone to help me with two or three television commercials. I've seen some of your music videos that you posted online as well as some of the video productions that you made for the last company you worked for. How would you feel about shooting the commercials as well as screening the hair models?" "Right now, I would be grateful for the opportunity. But if something comes up that pays more, I would have to change my schedule and work for you only on my time off." He answered. "That's fine with me. I can't blame you for wanting to move up." Terry told him. "I want a commercial that can generate local, national and even global exposure by advertising on TV. It must be done correctly the first time because if it isn't, it could cost me my investment. I'm looking for "the most bang for my buck" when it comes to this commercial.

Terry really wanted his TV ad campaign to be effective and planned his strategy carefully. He knew that if he made the commercial himself the cost would be lower than outsourcing the making of the commercial to a production company. He would hire several reputable freelancers to handle all the audio and video editing needed to prepare and master his commercial for airing. He figured out how much he wanted to spend and then created a working budget for developing his advertising strategy for TV. His budget included the cost to have the commercial made and what it would cost to air it. These two costs comprised the majority of his budget. He carefully crunched the numbers and came up with a fair salary for his handpicked crew of three workers who would produce the commercial and three or four models who would appear in the commercials. Terry and Andre agreed on Andre's salary. Terry would pay Andre nine hundred a week and when the commercial was completed Andre would be paid five thousand dollars for each of three finished commercial. A.J.'s total take for the commercial would be fifteen thousand dollars plus his weekly salary for three months. Andre would make one well designed commercial a month for the next three months. One of Terry's goals was to increase awareness of his brand. "In these three commercials, I would incorporate my business's logo, branded colors, symbols, trademarked insignia and other associated imagery that make up my hair care products company's brand," Terry said. "Just let me know what you have in mind and I will come up with storyboards for each commercial." A.J. responded.

After laying out his vision of what he wanted to get across to his target audience, and being assured that Andre could translate that vision into reality, they settled on a project deadline date so Terry would know when to expect his final product. Terry wanted ample time to review the commercial before it aired. Terry would allow A.J. to offer creative input, but he would make sure A.J. didn't lose sight of his original concept and vision. Nobody knew his business better than he, so it was up to him to guide the process to the final version of the commercial and make sure that it sends out the message he intended to deliver. Terry and Andre signed a binding contract for the production of the In2Hair commercial and shook hands. He felt confident that his commercial would be done right and his business would be the talk of the town and, hopefully one day, the world.

Chapter 35

Terry submitted his ideas for an Essence Magazine article. He wrote a query letter that explained his story concept, proposed story length, and why his article would appeal to the Essence reader. The magazine's beauty editor contacted him by phone two weeks later with a response to his query letter. "Your concept for an article relates to black hair care products. I understand that you are not only a Black hair stylist, you are also on the path to becoming a hair product entrepreneur." She said. "I'm trying my best," he told her. I am nowhere near being as visible as Jose Ebar and Jonathan Austin even though my hair care line is selling well in shops and stores across the nation. I am working on selling them on QVC and Home Shopping Network." He responded with a smile. "Are you prepared to send in a short video that would be suitable for the electronic edition of our magazine? She asked. "It should be one that has not appeared in any other electronic media." "Yes, I will send in an excellent video of trend-setting hair styles that we do in my shop. This video has something for all women whether they have a short and sassy cut or long curly locks. This video also prescribes shampoos, conditioners, and treatments for each of the highlighted styles." Terry replied and went on to say. "Please take note that all of the model's hairstyles displayed throughout the entire video were done personally by the In2Hair Artistic Team using only my products. The styles you will see in any of the photos or in the video is of the models' own natural hair. Our models do not wear wigs, weave pieces, extensions or additions of any kind." He pointed out.

"We'll read your article in its entirety and view your video. We reserve the right to edit or tweak it where necessary in order to better suit our magazine's needs. We will also take a look at the video to determine if it's suitable for electronic publication in our magazine. Should we decide to feature your work in our magazine, we will send you some papers to sign prior to publication." She closed their phone conversation by saying, "When the manuscript has been accepted, it will go through the magazine's editorial workflow pattern, that is from editorial to the art department and then back to editorial. If there is no discrepancies or confusing information that requires discussion with you, the finished article will finally appear in the magazine. We'll be giving you a call to let you know where we are in the process." Terry thanked the magazine's editor for considering his manuscript and hung up. He then decided to go out for a bite to eat.

Terry thought about calling the shop and asking Douglas or Andre to join him at Fuji Ya uptown on Lakeland and Lyndale for Happy Hour. He wanted to share the news about his upcoming Essence Magazine article. After having second thoughts, he decided to celebrate by himself. He would celebrate with others once the publication hits newsstands and he knew for sure that it was indeed published. He arrived at Fuji Ya an upscale Sushi Bar in

Minneapolis, an hour before Happy Hour would end. That meant he could have plenty of time to eat discounted sushi, vegetable maki, salmon nigiri, and avocado rolls.

Terry sat at the bar and ordered a small hot ki ippon sake. He noticed a woman a few seats away from him pondering over the menu. He asked, new to Fuji Ya or "new to sushi?" She looked at him quizzically, her perfect arched left brow lifted and her hazel eyes smiled as she confessed. "New to both... How could you tell?" "The way you looked at the pictures on the menu. "May I join you or are you expecting someone to dine with you?" He asked. "I would be happy if you would do me the honor. Maybe you could suggest something tolerable for a novice like myself" He moved to the barstool next to her and said "The honor is all mine, I assure you. My name is Terry." She responded by saying, "I'm Sandy. Hi Terry, pleased to meet you." "Did you decide to be adventuresome tonight or are you just curious about sushi?" He asked. I guess you could say I am adventuresome and curious she smiled. "What would you recommend that I start out with?" She tilted her head toward him and smiled. "I hope you have time to sit and enjoy for a while." He told her.

"A sushi meal is to be savored, not rushed." "Hmmmm like so many other things in this world." She cooed. "What are you having?" She asked. "I'm having the vegetable maki, salmon nigiri, and avocado roll. However, I suggest you try either the spicy tuna roll or the rainbow roll." What's that? She asked. "Spicy Tuna Roll is made up of chopped yellow fin tuna mixed with sesame oil, habanero masago and chili paste rolled with cucumber, kaiware and yama-gobo. The rainbow roll is a California roll with crab, and cucumber on the inside, topped with an assortment of fish and avocado." "That sounds worth trying out," she told him. "Great, dinner is on me. I'll order for both of us. Meanwhile, would you like something from the bar like Long Island Iced Tea, Sake, or a sparkling White Zinfandel?" Terry asked. Terry knew that true sushi connoisseurs would first have agari, a drink of hot green tea and oshiboi along with a small cold damp towel to refresh their mouths so they are ready to begin savoring the many kinds of fish. He ordered a glass of white Zinfandel and another Sake for himself and returned his attention to her. He ordered wine and sake because he felt they did not need to tune up their mouths to eat sushi.

Terry checked out her golden brown skin, her sandy colored hair and Michelle Obama biceps. The thing about her that struck him the most was her exotic eyes. A ring of golden amber around the pupils of her eyes were surrounded by specks of brown and green and contained dark green circle around the outer edge of each eye. Her eyes seemed to be the same color as the dress she was wearing. "Sandy is a good name for you," he said as he looked at her and sized her up. He asked her. "Is that your given name or did you name yourself Sandy?" "Why would I name myself? My father named me after he took one look at me. I have a brother whose name is Dusty." "Wow, is Dusty as dusty as you are Sandy? He asked. "He is." She answered. "Oh. The food has arrived?" She changed the subject.

Eating sushi take a little courage at first, but the adventure is usually well worth it." He told her. "In Japan, it's customary to use one's hands to eat rather than chopsticks," he added. "A perfect excuse to feed each other! He picked up the spicy tuna roll and fed it to her. "I trust you've washed your hands, she said as he moved the tuna roll closer to her mouth." "I washed them and used hand sanitizer. I also used a paper towel to open the restroom door." He laughed. She took the spicy roll into her mouth and savored the taste before chewing and swallowing it. "What's do you think?" He waited for her response. "To be just a raw slab of tuna, it's insanely delicious." She admitted. "Do you come here often?" "I'd say several times a month. I like the service and sushi. In fact this is where my love for sushi began, almost ten years ago." He said as he poured soy sauce into two small side dishes. What's that for, Sandy asked. Terry answered her as he opened her chopsticks and handed them to her. "Now here's how you can use your chopsticks to eat sushi. First, turn it sideways, then invert it by twisting your wrist and dip the fish side down into the soy sauce." She did it backwards and dipped her sushi rice side down. He laughed and said. "It takes practice. You'll be able to handle sushi and use soy sauce in the right manner after a few more tries. "How do you carry the sushi into your mouth? Do you return it to the position as it was or as it was reversed?" "Most people say that sushi should be eaten fish side down so that the fish must touch first with your tongue." He took her hand into his and maneuvered the chopsticks so that she could feel the fish on her tongue. "This way the ingredients can be more fully appreciated." He told her. She savored the sushi and gave a simultaneous eyebrow lift and nod.

Sandy took a few more bites of sushi but did not finish eating the entire meal. "I can't eat another bite." She announced. "Is that because you are being polite or is it because you didn't like the food?" he asked. "Oh, the spicy tuna roll and the rainbow

245

roll was awesome. I will definitely give this place another visit."
She laughed. "When? When do you plan to come back? It was
a pleasure sharing your first sushi experience and I'd like to
be there when you try it again." He said. "Give me your e-mail
address and I'll let you know when I plan to come back." she told
him. "Oh, I'll give you my e-mail address, my twitter address,
my Face-book address, and my phone number," he answered. He
was surprised that he felt such good vibes between them in the
short time that they were together. This beautiful woman could
be The Black Widow or Typhoid Mary and far as he knew. He
didn't care, he just wanted to get to know her better. "We don't
have to meet at a sushi bar you know. There are all kinds of restaurants in Minneapolis and St. Paul as you well know. You name
the place. We can dine wherever you like." He tried not to sound
too eager. Sandy responded. "I had the best time tonight. I experienced what it's like to taste sushi for the first time and I met a
gentleman named Terry who made the experience worthwhile."
She gave Terry her phone number and e-mail address. And said
"Call or text me. I'd like to hang out with you again sometime."
"Don't be surprised if I blow your phone up with calls and texts!"
He exclaimed enthusiastically.

Chapter 36

The Chrysler Coliseum was packed with more than twenty-five hundred spectators. The audience was a mixture of hair care professionals, folks from the entertainment industry, and people out for a night of fun. "Welcome everybody! Welcome! Thanks for coming out to join us tonight for our hair style extravaganza! I'm Kevin Lawrence. Standing next to me is my brother Kroy Lawrence. We are the promoters of the 7th annual Trendsetters Hair Battle and Fashion Show. Tonight, a five thousand dollar cash prize will be presented to the winner of the Trendsetters Hair Battle. Please join me in giving our proud sponsor, Cuticle Remy, a round of applause for donating twenty thousand dollars in hair that is being used during the show." Let us also thank Kiss Red Pro, Kiss Colors, I Envy Lashes, Kiss Impress Nails, as well as TMG & JASS Product Line for their sensational sponsorship and generosity. As a montage of each company's product line played silently on a giant screen TV monitor, the audience responded with a series of hand claps, whistles, and shout-outs.

After the applause settled down, Kroy went on to say, "We are sure that you will leave here thinking that this was the best hair battle that you've had the privilege to attend! All of our outstanding

247

participating stylist are determined to win that five thousand dollars in prize money! Each of the competing stylist get ten minutes to showcase twenty models. This year our theme is 'Beauty not Moody' and the theme song is *Nobody's Gonna Stop Us* by Taylor Lee and Russell."

"We all have seen fantasy hair worn by Hollywood icons such as Lady Gaga, Nikki Minaj, Katy Perry and Rihanna. Well, tonight, our contestants are all challenged to create outrageous coifs that resemble everything from Hollywood icons to hounds and handbags. Each stylists will enter the ring to bring the drama and present their hair creations in a high octane and stylized performance. Our judges are award-winning internationally known fantasy stylist, Muffen Moses, president and CEO of Muffen International Hair Salon, and Dave 'The Hair Surgeon' Ray, a stylist slash educator slash platform artist slash author who has won almost every nationally recognized beauty competition in the country! After each challenge, the judges will critique the stylist on creativity, execution, and overall presentation." Kevin Lawrence proclaimed sounding much like M.C. Nick Cannon.

Kevin told them how the contest worked. "Each stylist has two rules to follow. Number 1, they must enter one model to be judged. Number 2, they have to reveal one final hair-do at the end of the showcase and that hair-do has to rock the runway! Stylist will be judged on a thirty point rating. There are five categories that will each carry a weight of six points. Here are the categories they will be judged on. First, contestants must adhere to the Beauty Not Moody theme. Secondly, models' outfits must be creative and complement their hair styles. Third, the models walk must be runway worthy. The fourth category is where you come in ladies and gentlemen. That category is crowd involvement. The judges will be checking out you reactions. And the fifth and last category is most exotic or most creativity."

Kroy added. "The winners of this contest will get a chance to compete for the grand prize at the Bronner Brother's International Hair Show in Atlanta. The winners of the 2013 and 2014 shows each went on to win the twenty thousand dollars grand prize. So, there is a lot at stake here at this year's competition! In addition to the five thousand dollars competition, there are other competitions. You are invited to watch and judge 10 local cosmetology students compete in a hair styling contest for three hundred dollars! You can watch seven of the baddest hairstylist in the area compete for a five hundred dollars prize. You will get the opportunity to help pick the winner of this contest. Once again, thanks for coming out to the 2015 Trendsetters Hair and Fashion Show. You can give us your input by going to our Facebook, Twitter, or our webpage, Trendsetter.com. Now on with the show!"

Backstage was bustling and electric. The pungent smell of hairspray which floated in the air as designers pressed, heated, curled, crimped, glued and teased their creations into perfection almost took Andrea's breath. "It's enough to set off an asthma attack in someone prone to that condition." She thought. Andrea watched in awe as Terry worked his magic on Michelle. She was glad that she had agreed to accompany Michelle to the hair show. Michelle was her best friend and was always supportive of Andrea's endeavors. Although Terry seemingly knew Michelle's hair and what worked for her face like he knew the back of his hand, Michelle wanted

Andrea there for reassurance. "Michelle, you look absolutely stunning." Andrea assured her.

Terry had toiled for months preparing for this hair show. He admitted that he had spent a nice chunk of change on the hair show. If he won the $5000 he probably would just break even. Terry was not in the fashion show for money. He was in it for fame, another notch in his belt, and to promote his hair products. Although he wasn't required to pay an entry fee, he purchased twenty tickets at wholesale price to sell at retail price to his customers. He had clothing made for his models and he's spent upward of two thousand dollars on props. He also bought large quantities of human hair in almost every color of the rainbow. Although he could have purchased synthetic hair for as low as two dollars a bundle. The synthetic hair was not even considered by Terry for use because of its texture and feel, as well as its inability to withstand heating implements. "All I need is for some hair to melt during my presentation." He thought. "The high cost of the Asian hair is worth the promotion, publicity, and bragging rights that comes from a show stopping style at the Hair show." He convinced himself.

A reporter from the Virginian Pilot, a local newspaper arrived to do an interview that he scheduled in advance. After introducing himself, he got Terry's consent to have the cameraman who was with him take some candid photos to go along with the article. "Terry, you are a very popular. You've had articles on beauty and hair care in Ebony, Essence, Jet magazines. Your innovative style and product ads have appeared in many hair magazines. You've given your expertise on radio talk shows and you've done make-overs on television talk shows including the Steve Harvey show, Wendy William's and the Queen Latifah Show. Should I refer to you as a hair stylist, hair entertainer, or a hair products entrepreneur?" Terry laughed and gave a witty answer. "You can refer to me as all of the above. In fact, I'm all that and a bag of chips." They both laughed. "There are a number of stylist who are doing similar styles at other hair shows and some have even been doing the exact same styles that you have come up with. How do you feel about copycats?" the reporter asked. "I don't have a problem with people copying or learning from me. As the saying goes imitation is the highest form of flattery! They can copy me, learn from me, and whatever as long as they give me the recognition" Terry responded. "I've done hair for more than a decade and in all honesty when I started out, I copied styles that I came across in hair magazines. So to answer your question, I have no problems with stylists trying out my creations. I feel proud that they're watching me and wanting to emulate me. It makes me feel like a leader in the hair field but if they don't give me credit where credit is due, then it's a different story."

As he talked to the reporter, his hands deftly whipped through one of his model's hair. Terry spoke about the concept of his hair styles for this show. "My styles are based on people who looked like their pets." He gestured toward the model he was working on, whose cotton candy pink hair would be envied by Nicki Minaj, would be accompanied by an adorable pink poodle with an identical hair do on the runway. "How does styling your models hair to look like pets fall into the hair show's theme "Beauty not Moody?" the reported asked. Terry responded, "That's a good question. I'm going to work it into the theme somehow. I could debate that most moody people generally do not own pets because their personally wouldn't be consistent enough to deal with what it takes day to day to own a pet "On the other hand I could say that some animals are moody or I could say that beautiful people gravitate to beautiful pets! I can't tell you know how I'm going to tie it in with the theme, but when these models hit the runway you will definitely learn the rationale for these doggy hairstyles."

The entire hair show was a three and a half hour extravaganza of blooming, towering, blinking, spinning, and smoking, cartoon-like hair creations. The audience applauded and roared with excitement each time various hair entertainers showcased their models. They loved the way each stylists battled in a friendly game of one-upmanship and strove to outdo each other in ingenuity and flamboyance. The crowd ate up the way each stylist emphasized showmanship, choreography, costuming and music. Trendsetter's Beauty not Moody Hair Battle was part step show, part fashion show, part dance recital, and part three-ring circus. The production was about an equal mix of stylish yet suitable-enough-for-regular wear hair, and the truly jaw-dropping creations of fantasy styles, the haute couture of hair. The audience, almost exclusively black, shelled out $30 a pop to get in.

"Canine Clone or Doggy Doubles, you be the judge." The announcer for Terry's presentation said just before the song "Who Let the Dogs Out?" blasted loudly through the auditorium's speaker system. Each of Terry's models strutted out on the runway, struck their fiercest pose, and made a U-turn back to the stage as the announcer gave a brief notation about the model and dog. The first model, a beautiful tall thin model with long red wavy curls walked her dog, a red wavy haired Irish setter, down the runway as the commentator said "If you think they kind of look alike, you're correct. It's not a fluke! Many of us, including scientists, have perceived that dogs frequently look like their owners. We have to admit that it's a phenomenon that's funny as hell."

A pink and blond poodle pranced down the runway accompanied by a Nicki Manaj look alike. Wearing heavy black cat eyeliner, glittery teal eye shadow, huge eyelashes, and pink watermelon lip color, the model sported straight blond blunt cut bangs topped by a curly blond and pink Freestar Creta Girl half wig.

The parade of doggie styles went on and included a skinny, chocolate colored Snoop Dog look alike who wore braids on each side of her parted silky black hair. As the cocoa colored model strutted down the runway, her doggy counterpart strutted right next to her, a chocolate brown long eared, pointy faced dachshund named Snoop. When she stopped in the middle of the runway to give the audience a better look, Snoop stopped also as if on cue. The crowd gave them a rousing applause.

Terry's parade of models finished their ten minute performance and it was finally Michelle's turn to rock the runway as his grand finally. She walked confidently overlapping her steps and keeping a cool gaze on a spot visible to only her. Her unleashed canine doppelganger followed suit. The dog's handsome face was set off by clearly pronounced eyebrows, a pair of large, round dark eyes, a short muzzle, square shaped lip, and a brown nose. The makeup artists did not attempt to give Michelle's face a doggy look opting to glam her up instead by emphasizing her beautiful brown almond shaped eyes with dark eyeliner, eye-shadow, and two pairs of false eyelashes and dark brown lipstick.

Terry had made a determined effort to color Michelle's long thick hair the exact same color as the cocker spaniel's reddish brown silk fur. He left the crown of her head smooth and parted down the middle making it the perfect style to compliment Michelle's face. He deliberately styled the top of her head to give her it the same rounded dome shape of her four legged friend. Her long, thick locks were dressed in loose waves through the mid-lengths to ends. Her fancy spaniel hairstyle draped well over her shoulders. The style showed off the waves Terry added though the sides and back giving this stunning canine look movement and softness. Michelle's canine companion kept pace with her as she walked the runway. "Many people would pay a lot of money to have hair like this fabulous cocker spaniel." The commentator said. The reddish brown dog's long, floppy wavy haired ears swaged just below her shoulder just as Michelle's.

Kevin and Kroy Lawrence were back onstage. Seated at an ornate desk to their right were their two distinguished hair show judges. "Our celebrity hair show judges Moses Muffen and Dave "the hair surgeon" Ray have made their decisions." Let's hear directly them who are the winners in each of our categories." The audience was quiet with anticipation. The two judges stood at the podium and as presenting academy awards, one named the category and the other opened an envelope and called out the winner. Muffen announced to the audience "For Ladies Trend Cut, Color and Style - Pro: first place goes to Chi Chi Rodrigues. Second place goes to Angela Martin" Dave Ray announced. "Ladies Trend Cut, Color and Style - Student: Antonio Darden wins first place, Tamara Parker wins second place and Patricia Mills wins third place." Muffen added. "First Place Long Hair Bridal – Pro is awarded to Oneida Thomas, Natalie Parker earned second place, and Marcellus Collins gets third place" After announcing the Long Hair Bridal student winners. Dave announced the Fantasy student winners.

Finally, Muffen announced the grand prize winner by saying "I've seen plenty women's hair styles and plenty of cocker spaniel hair in my time, but that is the cocker-spaniel-i-est cocker spaniel hair style I've ever seen." the announcer added and the audience roared with laughter. Our $5000 grand prize winner is Terry Yarborough!!!!! Terry ran up on the stage, gave a short speech and posed along with Moses Muffen, Dave Ray, Kevin, and Kroy Lawrence, and the other two prize winners. Soon the other contestants joined the photo op and grand finale. The crowd applauded and cheered as Kroy and Kevin thanked them again for attending and invited them back to next year's show.

Chapter 37

Sterling picked up the phone and the voice on the other end informed him that the fraud suspect had been tailed for two weeks. "I'm not sure this is your perp. I've followed her now for two straight weeks and as far as I am concerned, she as straight as they come." Are you sure, Sterling asked. Have you been banging her or trying to put the moves on her? He asked. "You know me better than that," the gruff sounding voice responded. "I don't let any cunt get in the way of a paycheck." Sterling knew that he was not just grasping at straws. He knew without a doubt that Shondra was the culprit. "All of the evidence points to her. I just want to catch her red handed." Sterling said. The voice on the other end interrupted him "You know she has a cute the little girl. She's somewhere around six or seven years old, I suppose. Your so called perp took that little girl clothes shopping on Saturday and paid cash for everything. I mean she bought damn near four hundred dollars' worth of clothes. Seems like that would have been the perfect time to use a bogus credit card. She bought two hundred and seventy five dollars' worth of groceries from Super-Fresh Grocery Store on Tuesday. If she had phony credit, why did she not use it then?" He went on to say "She even paid cash for gas a few days later." "Of course she paid cash, she's on to you. She knows that she's being watched." Sterling snapped back at him and then ended the phone conversation by telling the investigator that his services were no longer needed and promising the investigator that a check for his services was in the mail. "What the hell kind of gum shoe would let his subject know she was being followed?" Sterling wondered out loud. "This Shondra woman is apparently a very cunning bitch but her ass is going to jail and it will be sooner than she thinks."

He went to the refrigerator and grabbed a cold Corona Extra. After popping the cap off, he forced a slice of lime down the neck of the bottle and drank straight from the bottle. The pale golden yellow, piss colored Mexican beer with its thick white head initially felt fizzy in his mouth. The smell of this beer reminded him of stale bread and tasted like watered down malt. Sterling kept at least one six pack in the fridge to offer anyone who happened to come for a visit. It went well with the Mexican food he sometimes ordered out or picked up on the way home from work. Tonight, he was not ordering out nor had he picked up dinner on the way home. Tonight Sterling had only one thing on his mind. That was getting to the bottom of what was happening to Andrea McNair's credit and learning what part the villian had in perpetrating this fraud. I guess I am going to have to investigate this shit myself. I'll get to the bottom of this one way or the other. I'll be damn if I spend one more week trying to tie this thing up." Dealing with fraud was the least favorite thing that Sterling liked about his position at the bank.

Sterling felt that fraud cases would not lead him up the cooperate ladder in the direction he wanted to go. He had higher

257

ambitions. His sights was set on becoming the head of a Wall Street I-bank where he could earn a seven figure income. His immediate goal was to become an ideal candidate for such a position. Along with having a credible personnel track record, Sterling's management skills were great and he had gained a deep knowledge and understanding of the business when he worked on Wall Street as an analyst. Of course, along with the position as an I-bank head, a multitude of duties and responsibilities would come. His tasks would also include the hiring and firing decisions as well as determining the firm's marketing strategies. He was aware that he would deal with a larger number of clients many of whom may be politically inspired. Sterling knew that he also had to be a good political operator because banks are fairly political institutions. He recognized that as a political operator he would have to manage all sorts of egos without letting his own sometimes inflated ego get in the way. An I-bank was not like a commercial bank. People did not deposit money into I-banks. There was much, much more to I-banking. Sterling was well qualified educationally. He graduated summa cum laude from a top tier school with a MBA. However, he knew that his dream of becoming an investment banker had go to on hold until he went back to school for a law degree to add to that MBA he already had. He would then be qualified to assist individuals and corporations in raising capital by underwriting or acting a client's agent in the issuance of securities. Damn, a black man always had to be twice as qualified as a white man for anything he mused. Sterling wondered if Mitt Romney had to work on Wall Street before he assisted so many companies and involved them in mergers and acquisitions. He knew Romney had law degree, but he could not recall whether he had a MBA. Hell, with all the money Mitt's family had, he didn't need a MBA. Mitt no doubt knew how to deal with other people's money, and he probably learned about M&A just by paying attention to his rich father and family friends. Sterling learned about mergers and acquisition by watching Larry the Liquidator in Danny DeVito's movie "Other People's Money."

Sterling knew that the rationale of mergers and acquisition is alluring to companies when times are tough. Strong companies act to buy weaker companies to create a more competitive, cost-efficient company. The two companies come together hoping to gain a greater share of the market or to achieve greater efficiency. The target company will often agree to be purchased when they know they cannot survive alone because of these potential benefits. He also knew that in many cases the target company usually ceased to exist from a legal point of view when the stronger company swallows the business and the buyer's stock continues to be traded. Sterling did not cherish the acquisition end of M&A because many people were likely to lose their livelihood. Sterling did not want to be like Mitt Romney, Gordon Gecko, or Larry the Liquidator. He just wanted a seven figure income.

The phone rang and snapped Sterling's mind back to his present situation. As he walked across the room to pick up the cordless, he thought that whatever he did to get the goods on the identity thief, he had to do it in such a way that his good reputation would stay intact. He had to devise a plan that would not ricochet back to bite him on his ass. A quick glimpse at the phone's caller I.D. prompted him to saying "Andrea, what a surprise. I hope this is a social call." Hell-o Sterling, she replied. "I wish I could say

259

it was but I haven't heard anything from the police, the credit bureau, or from you. I just want to hear something from someone other than creditors sending me letters for goods and services that I did not buy or subscribe to. What is going on Sterling? When is this going to end?" she cried. "Do you have any plans for tonight?" Sterling asked. If you don't, can be there in an hour to tell you what I learned from the private investigator tonight and I can tell you what I plan to do about it. Have you had dinner? I can pick up something on the way." I don't have much of an appetite she answered. I think I've lost five pounds over all this madness. "So, I need to bring something that will stick to your ribs and put some meat back on those bones," he kidded.

"I'll be there in a little while because frankly, I am also very close to my wits end with this mess. We both need to get this thing resolved." He said before placing the cordless phone back on its cradle. Sterling decided to forgo changing his clothes because if he changed into something different, he would not be able to stop by a restaurant, pick up dinner, and arrive at Andrea's place in one hour as he promised. Instead, he opened another Corona and slugged it down before pulling a grey chunky cable sweater over his black cotton slim fit shirt. The grey sweater and black shirt looked great with the black and grey pin-striped virgin wool slim fit trousers he had worn all day. The narrow straight legged pants with its sharp crease fit Sterling to a T. Since it was cold and blustery outside, he wore his black leather coat. After zipping the front of his coat all the way up to its high fastening neck and checking his pocket to be certain he had his wallet, Sterling picked up his keys and headed out the door.

Sterling arrived at Andrea's door exactly one hour after he had talked to her on the phone. Andrea was happy that Sterling had not wasted time arriving. She had spent the morning trying to figure a way to untangle the web of lies and deceit that someone had spun falsely using her identity. As soon as she opened the door and saw Sterling, she took him by the hand and led him into the living room where she helped him place the food onto a coffee table. "Hell-o Beautiful, do you always give such a warm welcome to someone who delivers a take-out meal? Let me know right now and I'll deliver more often." You got here pretty fast, she told him as she hung his coat in the closet. "You know I'm always at your beck and call. You can call me Johnny. Johnny on the Spot" Sterling said attempting to make her smile. Andrea gave him a big hug and said "I am so glad that you came. I was so worked up today; I had a terrible headache for several hours." He pulled her closer into his arms and held her gently. She pressed her face into the crook of his neck and inhaled so deeply her nostrils could distinguish his manly pheromones from the expensive cologne he seemed to always wear. Andrea knew that each time she got a whiff of his scent; it drew her to him like a magnet. Tonight was no exception. Even though she was aware that he put the moves on her pretty fast, she knew that he was sincere about finding out who was abusing her credit. He had sworn that he would help her clear her name and she trusted him. She felt a bond between Sterling and herself.

Sterling moved away from her and sat down on the sofa and began to open the food containers. She was disappointed that the embrace did not last longer. "I bought pasta from Zelo's Restaurant. This fettuccine with rock shrimp, sweet corn, cherry tomatoes and arugula should put a few ounces on you tonight." "It smells absolutely divine!" exclaimed Andrea. "Wait I'm not finished. In this bag I have a big ole Caesar salad and two, count them, two crab cakes for you." "I know you didn't bring me two crab cakes." She laughed. "Yes, I did. I don't know how many calories are in crab cakes. I saw a lady in the restaurant eating one of Zelo's "crabby patties. She seemed to like it so much, I ordered two for you because I wanted to make you twice as happy." "You did Sterling you made me twice as happy when you walked into that door," she said as she moved close enough to him to kiss his lips. Sterling kissed her and she melted in his arms wishing the kiss would never end. "Andrea, what would Quinton think if he came through that door and saw us in a compromising position?" "Quinton is five thousand miles away performing a face lift on some famous performer." "And you don't feel guilty seeing someone behind his back? I know if you were my woman. I wouldn't want any other man this close to you." "Sterling, do I honestly appear to be the type of woman who would be in an open end relationship?" She laughed as she walked into the kitchen and pulled out several dinner plates and a pair of wine glasses. "I don't believe people in those relationships have any particular look," he answered as he took the food containers and placed them on the kitchen counter. Andrea put the plates and wine glasses on the counter near the food. As she turned to get silverware, Sterling moved close behind her, flicked away a few strands of hair, and wrapped his arms around her waist. She could feel his warm breath as he spoke in a low but strong enough voice to be heard into her left ear, "You didn't answer my question." "What question?" She asked softly as she tried to keep her composure. "Do you feel guilty seeing someone else behind your man's back?" He asked.

Each word he spoke sent warm, sensual vibrations against her ear. "I don't consider myself seeing anyone behind Quinton's back." Andrea answered. "You don't," he asked and then nibbled gently on her earlobe "Oh, that's right, you're only seeing me because I'm helping you put an end to the theft of your identity." He said. Before she could respond, he slid his tongue inside of her ear and French kissed her until her tense body began to unwind. Feeling relaxed, she pushed her tush against his body feeling an unmistakable growth in what could only be his penis. Sterling massaged her breast and waited patiently for Andrea's emotions to take over. But, Andrea regained her senses, turned to face Sterling and said "We really should eat this food before it cools off. This food smells irresistible." "Eat? Cool off? Irresistible?" Stop teasing me and put the food on the plates, woman." He said as he popped open the bottle of Moscato D'Asti he had bought from Zelo's and poured some into the two wine glasses that she had sat out for them. They each took the plates and glasses to the round glass top dining table and sat down in the woven wicker chairs. "Sterling, you certainly went all out when you picked out this meal. I didn't know you would bring so much." "When you told me on the phone that you had lost a few pounds worrying about the jam this swindler has put you in, I said to myself. Man, you can't let her lose another ounce. Get something fattening into her right away." He teased. "And if you don't gain your weight back from this meal, I'm prepared to feed you again." He continued.

"This pasta looks ten times better that Red Lobster's or Olive Garden's she said as she picked up a few strands of fettuccini on her fork and skillfully twirled them around on her fork into a nice compact sized bite which she placed in her mouth. "The sauce is so rich and creamy. And the corn, arugula, and tiny tomatoes make it so appealing." "Everything tastes so fresh. She said before picking up one of the jumbo shrimp and taking a bite. "If I eat all of this, I don't know if I'll have room for the crab ca....she started, but before she could finish her sentence, Sterling offered a forkful of his crab cake to her cupping his free hand under it in case it fell off the fork. "How good is that?" He asked amused at how much she was enjoying the meal. He was pleased with himself that he had made her feel better. The smile on her lovely face was worth his effort. He decided to forgo seducing her. Instead, he would focus on straightening out the mess she was in because of someone else's thoughtlessness. Sterling decided to go over the facts that they had and reveal his plan to meet her in person face to face.

Chapter 38

The invitation to join Frieda and Booby at the game between the Minnesota Vikings and the Chicago Bears on Sunday came as a surprise to LaShondra but she eagerly accepted it. Her social life was almost non-existing and she was anxious to turn it up a notch. Frieda told Shondra that his employer, Mr. Irwin, had given him two free tickets to the game and he had promised to give one ticket to Frieda. The seats were side by side for section 229, rows 15. Frieda explained that Mr. Irwin had a ticket for a third seat, which he usually reserved for any friend or relative he wanted to invite. He told her that the seat was right next to the two seats he and Frieda would occupy.

"I would give you the ticket but Mr. I. told me that he usually gets reimbursed by any guest who used the ticket." Frieda told her that the ticket would cost two-hundred and fifty dollars." "Why is a ticket to the game and V.I.P Tent so expensive?" "Because the V.I.P. Tent is where you get to eat all you want from a buffet table and mingle with people in the money. You may even meet a new man who will help you get over Eric, that trifling ex of yours." Shondra thought Frieda had a point. She hadn't had a steady man friend in months. "I didn't meet anyone at your Meet the Browns house party after I spent so much money on that new outfit." She said. "Hell that's because you went upstairs to let Lana try on that Rachel Roy pant suit you were wearing. No one saw you again until the party was over. What took you so long anyway? Did she get you to do a line of cocaine or something?" He asked. "Stop acting ignorant Frieda. You know what was going on. Why didn't you warn me about that bitch?" Shondra shot back. "Warn you about what?" Frieda feigned ignorance. "You keep acting ignant." Shondra said in her best Ebonics as she pulled three new one hundred dollar bills out of her wallet. "I hope you have fifty dollars," she said. "I'll get change at the cell phone kiosk" as he handed her a ticket to section 229, row 15 seat number 15. "Call me when you leave Macy's and we'll figure out where to hook up again," Frieda told her after convincing the young man at the cell phone kiosk to give him change for a hundred dollar bill. "That sound like a plan to me. Where are you going to be?" She asked. Frieda told her that she was going to Sports Authority to check out the new Jordans. "Old as you are, you know you don't need to be buying Jordan's. Your ass need to get a pair of Converse All Stars and call it a day." She cracked. "I'm never going to be too old to be stylish. Hell, I bet Jay-Z wears Jordans." "Michael Jordan doesn't wear Jordans." She laughed as they parted way.

Frieda headed toward the rack where the football jerseys were displayed. She picked out two Viking Jerseys, one for herself and one for Booby, then tried on a pair of ninety dollar PUMA women's sneaker-wedges. Frieda walked up the mirror and checked out how each shoe with its mesh uppers, synthetic overlays and suede wedge heels looked on her feet. The salesman who was helping her turned

266

his head in the direction of the cashier and gave Frieda the side eye. Frieda decided to buy the shoes since they were the exact same shade of purple as the Viking jersey she had selected. She took the shoes off, put them back in the box and headed toward the cashier carrying the shoes and jerseys with her. "That will be two hundred and sixty." The cashier told him. Frieda reached into one of her pocket for the two hundred and fifty that LaShondra had given her for the ticket. She then pulled a small wad of greenbacks out of another pocket and peeled off a ten dollar bill.

Shondra texted Frieda to get her location and find out if she was ready to catch up with her. "I left Macy's and now I'm in Nordstrom's." She told her. "Good I'm in the same corner of the mall, right below you on level three. I'm on my way to Champs Sports Store. When I finish, I'll take the escalator up and look for you." See you soon," she answered. Frieda entered Champs and was approached by a salesperson. "Welcome to Champs Sports Store, can I be of assistance?" "Yes, I'm looking for Viking warm-up pants. Do you have any that are on sale? I know they are all for sale but do you have any that have been reduced." "Right over here. We have a few that have price cuts." The salesperson said while leading Frieda to a rack of men's warm-up pants. Frieda looked at the pants and said "I don't know if these will fit me." She then walked over to the rack of women's pants. Frieda right away spotted a pair of Minnesota Vikings women's Sport Princess III sweatpants that appeared to be her size. The pants which were hanging at the front of the rack had been reduced from forty nine to thirty nine dollars. Frieda snatched them off the rack just as a blond women was reaching for them.

The blonde's face turned red as she asked the salesperson, who had watched the whole scene in amusement, "Do you have another pair of pants like those?" I don't believe we do he answered. "I moved those pants to the front of the rack along with several other pairs of pants that I was going to try on and that person took them." She continued. "Excuse me. This person took them because they were hanging on the rack. If you were so interested in them maybe you should have taken them off the rack in the first place. Don't get mad Baby Doll. You don't have enough backside to fit into these anyways." Then, as though she had a split personality Frieda decided to play nice with the upset blonde. She said in a very pleasant voice, "This is more your style as she held up a pair of 47 brand Minnesota power stretch pants. Look, it has the team's name and logo printed on the left top thigh, as well as the team color drawstring waistband. These look comfortable enough for a yoga session or a relaxing afternoon on the couch. Try them on Baby Doll. I bet you'll like them. I'm going to wait right here and if you don't like them I'll give these pants back to you." The blonde's face returned to its natural color when Booby no longer appeared to be a threat to her. She tried them on and came out of the dressing room to get Booby's approval. "Don't you look terrific in those stretch pants?" Booby exclaimed "Damn girl you look like you were made to model those pants. You can have these pants I snatched off the rack. Now I want those!" She said with a laugh. "Doesn't she look like she could be a model?" Frieda asked the salesperson. "Girl you better not leave this store without buying those pants. And don't hang them back on the damn rack." As the blonde went back into the dressing room to change out of the pants, Frieda headed to the cashier to pay for her selection.

Frieda took the escalator to the fourth level and walked toward Nordstrom's. She entered the store and proceeded to the women's section in search of Shondra. She spotted Shondra in the casual wear department. She didn't join her right away because there were a few pant-sets that caught her eye. Frieda stopped and examined several before trying to locate her gal pal.

Shondra ended up in Nordstrom's after getting strange vibes while trying on a pair of slacks in Macy's. Inside Nordstrom, a pair of Malhia Kent pieced Jacquard skinny jeans in Egyptian gold tweed that caught her eye. Shondra was now happy that she didn't waste a lot of time in Macy's. Shondra found a pair of the shimmering jeans with the golden jacquard front and solid black back and took them into a dressing room to try on. She was pleased with what she saw in the full length mirror because the jean gave the Illusion of contouring her body. "Those pants look like they were poured onto your legs, girlfriend." Booby said as walked into the dressing room area with a pair of pants that he wanted to try on. Shondra changed back into her own clothes and returned to the women's department.

LaShondra picked out a four hundred and ninety five dollar black shrunken crepe blazer with an asymmetrical body and Italian lamb leather sleeves. She added, to the items she had already selected, a top that had been pieced together from sleek silk and soft stretch jersey. The top with its deep scoop neckline, three-quarter length dolman sleeves, and high-low hem was a great match for the gold and black jeans she'd just tried on. She decided to forego buying a new pair of shoes because she had a pair of four and a half inch black leather almond toe boots with back zip closure that would go well with her new outfit.

269

Shondra looked toward the dressing room to make sure that Frieda would not see her use the fake charge card to purchase the jeans, blouse, and jacket. She made the transaction swiftly without a hitch. What she did not know was that the credit card company had flagged the card and cashier had secretly photographed the entire transaction. The cashier who had been on the job for only two days was supposed to stall her and ask for additional identification. However, the procedure for handling suspicious credit cards only occurred to her after she had bagged and handed the purchase over to Shondra. The cashier decided to keep her mouth shut about the transaction since she did not follow prescribed procedures for suspected fraud. After getting her purchase, Shondra set out to locate Frieda. She had no idea how close she was to being caught using the fake credit card.

"Frieda, are you planning on buying those leggings?" She asked as she peeped into the dressing room and smiled at Frieda who was sporting a pair of faux leather legging with sheer angular mesh inserts. "What kind of leggings are you wearing? They look like someone cut up a perfectly good pair of leather leggings and replaced the cut portions with sheer mesh triangle patches." "That's what I like about them. They are edgy." "Are you planning on wearing them to the game?" "I may. You never know." "Lord have mercy." Shondra exclaimed. Frieda laughed and decided to let her continue guessing. "I'm going to buy these. They're only thirty-four dollars." "Go ahead, I'll meet you at Ruby Tuesdays in the North Garden. Do you want me to place an order for you? I want to grab something to eat before I go home. I have two coupons. Buy one get one free. I'll buy one for me and get a take home

270

for KeKe. You can get one for yourself and take one to Booby." "That great! You must know my money is getting pretty low. Will you order a bacon cheese pretzel burger and fries for both me and Booby? Do you want the money now? Thanks." Frieda didn't' wait for an answer. He felt that he had already hit her up for two hundred dollars and fifty when he sold her a ticket to the game which he had gotten from Mr. Irwin for no charge. He gave Shondra a twenty dollar bill to cover her lunch. He thought about buying her a chocolate fudge Sunday for desert if she was up to it. "I'll join you as soon as I pay for these leggings." Frieda told her. Shondra left the dressing room and went to Ruby Tuesdays for lunch. Frieda paid for the leggings and joined Shondra at the restaurant.

Chapter 39

LaShondra took I-35W south to the Washington Avenue exit, turned right on Washington Avenue, then turned left on 11th Avenue and headed towards the parking facility near the Metrodome. She parked the rented Ford Fusion in an available parking space at a privately owned lot near Mall of America Field. Shondra, Booby, and Frieda were not diehard football fans but they jumped at the opportunity to attend a football game free of charge.

LaShondra, Booby, and Frieda had arrived earlier than usual at the stadium and entered the gate indicated on the tickets in order to avoid congestion at the stadium entrances. Frieda had confiscated tickets to section 229, row 15 seats 13, 14, and 15 from Lester Irwin, his employer and longtime friend. Lester had to accompany his wife Laura on an emergency trip to Ohio to attend her mother's funeral. When Frieda learned that Laura's mother had passed, she offered to housesit and supervise the restaurant until the couple returned. "We'll probably be away for two weeks because in addition handling the disposal of the body and holding a memorial, there are a few legal matters we need to take care of." Frieda thought the phrase "handling the disposal of the body" sounded cold. "White folk are so damn strange," she thought. "Why couldn't he just say bury her or cremate her. He could have said "We'll save her ashes in a pretty urn or throw her ashes someplace she was fond of." What the hell does he mean dispose of the body? Are they going to put it in a plastic bag and put it in a dumpster? White folk, crazy as hell, she thought.

Lester Irwin had subscribed to the Minnesota Viking's game each year. This would be the first year that he would miss the first game of the season, in his regular seat, in years. Lester paid fourteen hundred and seventy dollars for two adult season tickets this year and as much as he hated to miss the game on Sunday, he had to attend to his husbandly duties. Lester decided to give the tickets to Frieda to share with two of her friends since she would be house sitting and running the restaurant. "Hell, it was almost as if she's going to be a Black version of myself for two weeks." He laughed at the thought of being Black for two week.

Booby and Frieda each wore eighty five dollar Reebok purple home jerseys with contrasting gold colored Minnesota graphics. The replica jerseys looked similar to those worn on the field by the Minnesota Vikings Football Players. Booby wore quarterback Christian Ponder's number 7. "Hopefully, Ponder will step up his game this season because he has plenty to improve on. He had eighteen touchdowns and twelve interceptions last year." Booby said when Frieda asked him why he was wearing Ponder's jersey. "Besides it's the only one they had in my size for this price."

They were in line when the gates opened two hours before kickoff. Booby carried a large, clear standard 12" by 6" by 12" bag made of clear PVC vinyl which could be easily searched. Had Booby not insisted one bringing along a bag which had to be searched they could have used the express lane at the gate for those fans not bringing anything into Mall of America Field at the H.H.H. Metrodome. But Booby had to bring binoculars, a phone, and a camera. Because she carried a clear bag and Frieda's and Shondra's bags were very small, they did not spend too much time in line being searched.

The threesome made their way to the VIP tent which was a great place for business folk and fun seekers to gather with friends, clients and fellow Vikings fans prior to every home game. The VIP tent featured an all you can eat pregame buffet complete with an all you can drink pregame open bar, live music, free Vikings Playbooks and Gameday Magazines, along with appearances by former Vikings and coaches.

LaShondra tried to act like this was not the first time she had attended a pre-game open bar and buffet as she stood in line at the all-you-can-eat buffet with its wide variety of foods. Frieda walked around the huge tent trying to get autographs from former Vikings who were on hand to meet fans and talk football. Booby made her way to various tables set up with free Viking gifts, and game programs. After stuffing a complimentary gift of GAMEDAY Magazine into her clear plastic bag, he walked up to a table that displayed a large sign that read: "Enter to win a pair of tix to Minnesota vs. Cleveland on September twenty-second. Booby filled out a ticket, tore off the bottom part which confirmed her contest entry and stuffed it into the plastic bag along with her other belongings. She placed the remaining portion of the free ticket in a box that was on the table. "Football Paraphernalia Scratch and Win Tickets, fifteen, ten, and five dollars!" the vendor called as fans walked by a table adorned with Minnesota Viking and Chicago Bears ponchos, umbrellas, hoodies, key chains, teddy bears, as well as novelty and collectible items. Booby bought a fifteen dollar ticket and Frieda purchased two five dollar tickets. "I don't know why you bought that fifteen dollar scratch and win tickets, you can buy a Viking key chain for fifteen dollars or less." Frieda said. "The key chain is for those who bought five dollar tickets. That cute little teddy bear is worth more than fifteen dollars. So are those NFL hoodies and umbrellas." Frieda scratched one of her tickets. "Just as I thought. It's a dud." She mumbled. Then she scratched the other ticket. The ticket revealed the words. Minnesota Vikings NFL 2" long Earrings value ten dollars. Frieda gave the scratch ticket to the vendor who in turn gave her a pair of earrings. "Well at least I got my money back." Booby scratched her ticket and was an instant winner. The ticket revealed her prize, an adorable talking plush teddy bear which wore a team-colored cheerleading dress embroidered with a Vikings logo. The cute little bear even wore matching bloomers that read, "Go Vikings!" Booby squeezed the bear's stomach and it said "Block That Kick!" She laughed and squeezed it again and it said "First and Ten Do It Again!" I am going to have some fun with this bear Booby laughed as she walked in the direction of the buffet line. Frieda wondered aloud "Where's Shondra? She didn't waste any time ditching us and going her merry way." "Shondra is looking to meet a man with some money. She don't want us to get in the way." Booby answered.

Frieda was correct. Shondra had intentionally struck out on her own hoping to hook up with a good looking, well to do, eligible man. After she left Booby and Frieda, Shondra walked around the perimeter of the VIP Tent pausing here and there to check out the atmosphere. She lingered in the area of the live music performance for ten or fifteen minutes and mingled with a few people who were enjoying themselves. She didn't think much was going on there that would benefit her, so she moved on. This time it was off to the buffet line.

As she waited in line for a serving of hot wings, LaShondra listened to friendly back and forth banter between two Viking fans who were in line behind her. "The Vikings have reached a crossroad. They came off an astonishing season. They improved by seven victories, made the playoffs and watched Vikings Running Back Adrian Peterson transition from ACL rehab patient to MVP award winner." One of the men declared. "Yes but if they slide back a bit, 2013 will likely be seen as a disappointment. They need to pick up where they left off last year. We'll soon find out whether last season was just a fluke or how the Vikes will play in the future." The other one responded. The line moved up a bit and the friendly game talk continued between the two men.

"Sports writers predict that Vikes may have a slim chance at getting a wild card. I think the offensive line should be much better this year, but that defensive line really needs to pick it up. The Vikes need to be able to rush four and get pressure on a QB consistently. The only thing that will keep them out of the playoffs will be the defense," another fan chimed in. "Everyone loves predictions. "I don't think they have any idea what the 2013 Vikes can do. What basis do they have? Are they basing their views on what happened last year or the year before?" The fine looking gentleman responded and winked at Sondra. "Am I correct Honey?" Shondra shot back, "You're right Daddy." Then she added "Ponder needs to get better this season. Last year he had eighteen touchdowns and twelve interceptions. It's great to see he's sure of himself but he should mostly leave the athletic running game to Adrian Peterson." "Did you hear that, Man. This beautiful woman called me Daddy and she knows Ponder needs to get his act together." In addition to calling him Daddy, Shondra gave off several nonverbal, flirtatious cues to signify that she was interested and attracted to the man. Shondra held a lingering gaze a few seconds longer than usual and adjusted the tone of her voice to match his. He picked up on her flirtations and asked if he could join her after she sat down to eat. "Of course, I'd love to have some company in this big ole V.I.P. Tent," She assured him.

After she selected her food items, he offered to carry her plate to a table if she grabbed some beers for the both of them. Shondra got four beers and they found a table with room for Shondra, the man, and his friend. He promised to join her shortly after he got something to eat. Shondra soon learned that Daddy whose name turned out to be Danny Larson was the owner of Larson Appliances Incorporated. Danny was single, handsome, well to do. Exactly the type of person Shondra was looking for. She introduced herself as LaShondra instead of Andrea since tonight she had not gone through the motions of putting in the contacts and wearing the wig to look like her alter ego. When Danny asked for her phone number and gave her his phone number and e-mail address, she was elated. A man other than Eric had shown interest in her. "Now Darling, promise you'll call me." He said as he casually took her hand in his and looked her in the eye. Shondra raised an eyebrow and smiled suggestively. "I want to hear from you and see you again if possible.

What section of the Metrodome are you in?" He asked. Shondra showed him her ticket and he told her that is was not near his area. "So when will you call me?" He asked again. "It'll be soon." She said. "I better get back with my friends and move on to the bleachers." She said as she placed the napkin that he had written his phone number and e-mail address into her purse." "It was great meeting you Darling. I'll be looking forward to hearing from you in the very near future." "You will." She assured him.

Shondra phoned Booby on his cell phone and they met up at one of the V.I.P. Tent's exits. They made their way to their seats twenty minute before the game was to begin. Booby checked his program for the team's depth chart and number rosters so that he could identify the many players on the field. The starting lineups for both teams by their positions on offense and defense was listed. The punter, placekicker, snapper for punts and kicks, and kickoff and punt return specialists were named on the list. "I see they also list the reserves alongside the starters on the depth chart, Frieda said noted aloud. "That's good because if a player is injured, we can figure out who will replace him." Booby answered. "Speaking of injured Vikes, Robert Blanton had a hamstring injury, Carlson and Guion had knee injuries. I guess they got better because they are not on the injured list today." Frieda said after scanning the program. "Fullback Jerome Felton is out for three games because of substance abuse. He was caught driving under the influence." Shondra answered. She didn't keep up with football, but she did watch Entertainment Tonight and TMZ.

Shondra didn't really follow NFL or any other football. However, she did enjoy the excitement of football on T.V. at a friends' and associates' home while playing spades with others in the house who were not as engrossed with the game. She liked drinking beer, tequila, gin, or any other alcohol that was floating around and talking trash as she and her card partner bluffed their competitors. Watching football today would be different. She would get caught up in the excitement of cheering for the Vikes. She would watch the halftime show. Watching a game in person would allow her to see the entire play develop. She knew that as soon as the center snapped the ball and all twenty two players on the field started moving, the crowd would be revved up and rooting for their favorite team. LaShondra would be right there in the stands seeing in person what happened to the quarterback after he released the ball. She would see if he got hit, or exchange words or swings with a pass-rusher.

The first quarter went by fast with touchdowns by Viking Wide Receiver Cordarrelle Paterson, Bears' Tight End Martellus Bennett and Wide Receiver Brandon Marshall. "Blair Walsh kick is good!" shouted Frieda. Jay Cutler threw a 1 yard pass to Bennett. "It was slick how Cordarrelle Patterson returned the opening kickoff of the game 105 yards for a touchdown. That's the first kickoff return the Bears have given up since 2007 to put the Vikings on the board 7-0." A man sitting next to Booby declared to someone sitting next to him. Devin Hester took the subsequent kickoff sixty-seven yards to set the Bears up with excellent field position. A Jay Cutler to Martellus Bennett TD pass capped off the short scoring drive.

Not only did the three watch the game with great enthusiasm, they also people watched. "Do you mind if I use those binoculars for a few minutes?" Shondra asked. She scoped out trainers tending to injured Chicago Bears' wide receiver Devin Hester during the first half. She also watched Minnesota Vikings wide receiver Greg Jennings miss a catch while defended by Chicago Bears' cornerback Tim Jennings. The pace was fast during plays, but there was enough downtime between plays for the threesome to check out what was happening on the sidelines and to figure out which play may be called next. "Did you see that Bears' cornerback intercepts that pass intended for the Vikes' wide receiver Jerome Simpson?" Booby asked Frieda. "That cornerback's a beast." Frieda responded.

The second quarter was just as exciting as the first for Booby and his friends. Blair Walsh and Robbie Gould making more good kicks. Robinson made a 61 yard fumble return, Jennings made a 44 yard interception return and Rudolph caught a 20 yard pass from Ponder. "Robbie Gould, field goal. Yeah." Booby shouted and squeezed the Teddy Bear's stomach. The talking teddy cheerleader said "Shut em down, Shut em down, Come on defense, shut em down!"

Booby and Frieda got up during the third quarter after one of the players kicked the ball 28 yards and made a field goal. "We're going to stretch out legs for a few minutes. Do you want to come along Shondra?" Where are you going? She asked. "We're going to go to the concession area and the restroom. Maybe just walk around and look around." Frieda answered. "No, I think I'll just stay here and watch tie game." She answered. "I told you Miss Thang is not trying to hang around our gay asses today. She is trying to catch a man and thinks we'll get in the way." Booby said. "Booby just shut up and carrying your butt wherever it is you're going." Shondra laughed. "Look out for my bag and my teddy bear. If anyone takes them, you're going to pay for them." Booby said as she was leaving.

Shondra scanned the sidelines with her binoculars during time-outs. She watched Vike's coach talking strategy with his players and she viewed animated conversations and debates between fans in the bleachers. She also took a look at players and coaches on the Bear's team. Midway through the third quarter, Minnesota got its first field-goal drive. Shondra cheered along with the rest of the crowd.

During fourth quarter, Walsh came on again. His second 28-yard kick gave the Vikings a 27-24 lead with 8:05 left in the fourth quarter. Things were looking bleak after Minnesota's Blair Walsh kicked a 22-yard field goal to make it a six-point game with 3:15 remaining. The Bears were behind 30-24 with sixteen seconds remaining in the game, and had third and ten at the Vikings 16. Cutler then spiked the ball before connecting with Bennett in the front corner of the end zone. "Damn, Chicago is taking over at its 34, and Cutler is going to work." Booby shouted. "Cutler came through just in time when he launched that 16-yard touchdown pass to Martellus Bennett with ten seconds left." "Well, there goes the game. Vikes loose the first game of the season." Yeah, Jay Cutler led Chicago to a 31-30 victory over the Minnesota Vikings." The man next to Booby answered. "We were so close." Frieda said. "Let's get out of here. There's a party going on somewhere and someone's waiting for our arrival."

Chapter 40

Andrea and Quinton sat at the bar at Murray's Restaurant and Cocktail Lounge in downtown Minnesota. Q. texted the number to the restaurant and asked if they had a table available for later that night and they did. It was a very busy Friday night. Young couples and singles as well as older couples and groups of business people often chose Murray's Restaurant to end a work-week. For many, the sleek restaurant was a great place to impress a prospective client or romantic partner over dinner. The Maître de who escorted the couple to the bar area handed Quinton a coaster shaped electronic paging device which would alert them with a beep or vibration the moment their table was ready. Andrea asked for a menu from which she and Quinton would make their dinner selections while they enjoyed pre-dinner cocktails, or aperitifs. Like three out of four men, Q. did not need to study the menu before ordering a drink. He knew exactly what he wanted. "I'll have a Rob Roy." After looking over the cocktail menu briefly, Andrea said "I'll try a Red Carpet Vodka cocktail." Andrea watched with amusement as the bartender applied his mix magic to her drink. He combined Oval Vodka, Campari, Hiram Walker Pomegranate Schnapps, pomegranate juice, and simple syrup in a cocktail shaker

282

filled with ice. Noticing Andrea watching him work he shook the mixture vigorously and winked at her before straining the mixture into a chilled cocktail glass. He garnished the drink with a cherry and then handed it to her with a smile. Andrea picked up the glass, examined it and took a sip. The bartender waited for her approval. "Heavenly" she said, then turned her attention to several new guest who arrived in the lounge area. She imagined that they were as much in need of libations and she and Quinton. She took another sip and felt the drink stimulating her taste buds.

Quinton's perfect Rob Roy, concocted with equal parts sweet and dry vermouth, was garnished with a lemon twist which he pulled off the rim of his cocktail glass and bit into before taking a swig. "AHHHH! Q. exclaimed. Best thing in the world to wash the dust out of your throat after a long work week." Andrea held the stem of her cocktail glass and studied him for a brief moment before nodding her head in agreement.

"Honey, you seem very preoccupied. Is there something going on that I don't know about?" He asked. Andrea told Quinton about the mysterious credit and loan charges. "I can't figure out how that woman continues to get away with it. I thought the card was blocked so that other transactions would not take place. I am very aggravated that this keeps happening." "I understand. I'd be pissed off also if it was happening to me." Quinton said. He took a sip of Rob Roy and added "The criminal keeps getting away with it while the victim keeps getting held responsible for it." Andrea said. "My friend Sterling Steingold works with the Bank of America card fraud department. He has been investigating this case since I found out about it. I went to him and explained what was happening and he got right on it. He had a handwriting expert and a private investigator help out with the case. Sterling has been very supportive. He's even worked on this case during his time off." "Is he the same Sterling that you introduced me to at Terry Yarborough's product launch party?" "Yes he's the one who's been trying to bring closure to this debacle," she answered.

"I keep trying to figure out how the person or persons who's doing this got their hands on your social security number." Quinton said. "As far as I'm concerned that's the number one question I want answered." Shondra responded. "I know that you do," Q. said. "There are so many ways that someone who is hell bent on committing this sort of offense can succeed. I try to keep up with what's currently going on in the news. From what I know, there are new ways a thief get your credit card numbers. You even have to be careful when you go to a hotel because scammers are doing so many different things to rip people off right inside some of the best hotels. Some scammers use illicit computer programs and a laptop to steal usernames and passwords. Then, they log into unsuspecting victims bank accounts and credit accounts. Some of these criminals have been slipping flyers advertising pizza delivery under the doors of hotel guest and instead of getting room service, a guest may decide to call the number on the flyer. In the process of placing an order the gullible guest gives their credit card number over the phone, and the pizza never arrives."

Andrea sipped her Red Carpet cocktail and continued to listen as Q. went on. She eyed a nearby waiter as he gave a credit card back to a customer and confessed. "There was a time when I even imagined that a waiter or clerk who had physical possession of my card slipped the magnetic strip though a card reader that contained a hidden device that stored my information for their own personal use." That's a real possibility, he said. "Do you have an idea where something like this could have occurred?" "I don't have the slightest notion where or even if something like that could have happened. Usually, when I pay for something with my card, I keep an eye on what the person who is handling it is doing with it."

The coaster like device the maître de gave them began to light up and vibrate. Seconds later, a server came and led them to a subtly lit corner booth. After they were seated they gave him their dinner order. Quinton ordered a lightly charred twenty ounce rib-eye, cottage fries and a wedge salad consisting of tomatoes, iceberg lettuce, and onion with lots of chunky blue cheese and French & Roquefort dressing while Andrea had the lamb chops artichokes, and organic brown basmati rice. Andrea looked around the room until her eyes fell on a singer who was belting out popular male R and B tunes. "I love this restaurant Q.," Andrea said. "They always have pretty good live entertainment. Tonight's performer sounds almost better that the original recording artists."

The server bought an unopened bottle of Shafer Vineyards Cabernet Sauvignon to the table and showed it to Q. who confirmed the choice with a nod. He uncorked the bottle and poured a small amount of the wine into their glasses. Andrea swirled the wine in her glass before sniffing releasing the aroma. Q. took a sniff and said. "That's fine." Andrea smiled and concurred. Then the server went on to fill each of their glasses three-fourth full. "Enjoy your Cabernet Sauvignon."

The meals were soon served and Q. dove right in. "Quinton, I know there's nothing quite like rewarding yourself with a thick, juicy rib-eye steak after a hectic work week. But don't you think that twenty ounce slab of meat may add a few unwanted inches to that waistline of yours or clog up your arteries with a load of cholesterol?" Andrea tried to lighten the conversation. "Ease up, woman. Who's the doctor here? Me or you?" Quinton quipped and added." I swear, this steak melts in your mouth. Here, have a bite." He sliced off a piece, picked it up with his fork and offered it to Andrea who obediently opened her mouth for consumption. Andrea savored the dense-yet-tender bite of meat with its juicy rare center and a flavorful charred outside. Andrea took a swallow of wine to refresh her palate and made a remark about his steak. "That was magnificent but this lamb chop is cooked perfectly and I wouldn't be surprised if it will make every other lamb chop I eat in the future seem lacking." Andrea laughed. The conversation about credit card scams left her mind for a moment as she made a mental note to order a rib-eye just like the one Q. was eating on her next visit to this restaurant.

Quinton re-opened the unpleasant conversation about credit card scams. "I bought a small device to charges my phone when I travel because you can't even trust a public kiosk with your cell phone. Your credit card information can even be jacked when your phone battery runs low and you decide to charge it at one of those kiosk located in airports, hotels or convention halls." "It's called juice jacking. That's because the charging port on a smartphone is also the USB jack and it can be used to transfer information from the phone without the owner's knowledge." Andrea said. "I have used one at the airport when I flew to Seattle but I tend to think that my info wasn't jacked at an out of state airport because all the charges that I've received were local."

"Baby, let's change the conversation. I appreciate having your shoulder to cry on tonight. But I think it's time we put aside the doom and gloom and celebrate life," Andrea said. The couple continued their dinner and polished off the entire bottle of Cabernet Sauvignon before leaving the restaurant and going their separate ways.

Chapter 41

La Shondra spent nearly $2,000 at the Kohl's department store in the Mall of America after scooping up armfuls of merchandise. When Kohl's loss prevention officers noticed her unusual behavior they called both mall security and the police. LaShondra left Kohl's without a clue that security was on to her and went to Jared Jewelry Boutique. She tried to purchase a six hundred and fifty dollar, twenty two inch long, fourteen caret yellow necklace. The Wells Fargo Platinum Visa Card that she tried to purchase the jewelry with was declined. When a message from Wells Fargo Visa Card's main office came across the cash register's computerized screen and declared that the credit card was fictitious and void, the saleswoman asked LaShondra "May I please see your credit card. I need to put the account number in myself because the scanner doesn't seem to be working properly." It suddenly dawned on her. "That scanner is so working. I know what she's doing. She's trying to get me busted in here." She placed the credit card back into her purse and walked toward the store's exit without responding to the saleswoman. She made a hasty retreat to the parking lot where she quickly located her car, got in and threw the Kohl's bag onto the passenger's seat. LaShondra left the mall in a hurry, swerving through traffic and running red lights and tossing the Kohl's and Wells Fargo Platinum Visa Cards out the window of the car.

It wasn't long before she was stopped by the police. They frisked her by performing a "pat-down" of her outer clothing in order to determine if she was carrying a concealed weapon. Later, after she was arrested and transported to jail, a full-blown search of her person and immediate surroundings was performed to ensure that she did not have any weapons, stolen items, contraband, or evidence of a crime was performed. The police took possession of her automobile and searched it as well.

As soon as she was placed in custody an officer gave her the Miranda warning. "You have the right to remain silent. Anything you say can be used against you in a court of law. You have the right to consult with a lawyer and have that lawyer present during the interrogation. If you cannot afford a lawyer, one will be appointed to represent you. You can invoke your right to be silent before or during an interrogation, and if you do so, the interrogation must stop. You can invoke your right to have an attorney present, and until your attorney is present, the interrogation must stop." After her Miranda rights were given to her, she said nothing except that she wanted a lawyer. Shondra was placed in a holding cell where she waited four hours to be processed. Once processing was completed, an officer informed her, "You have the right to make three telephone calls in order to get a lawyer, to arrange for bail, and call a family member or friend to help you make those arrangements." After they performed an inventory of her belongings, the police took all of her personal property and money that she had with her and put it in a secure storage place. The police asked her to sign the inventory. "Review this list and sign on the bottom line if you agree with the contents of the inventory." During the booking procedure the police asked Shondra for basic information about herself. They fingerprinted her, took a mugshot, and had her give a handwriting sample.

"Now what?" Shondra asked the officer who booked her. "The information we gathered on you will be provided to the prosecutor's office. After the prosecutor review our report he will make a decision within seventy two hours as to what charges should be filed against you. "They did everything except put me in a lineup and ask for a piss sample." Shondra later told Booby.

Once the booking procedures were completed she made a phone call to Booby. "Hell-o Booby, Yes I know that your caller ID said the call is coming from Minneapolis Jail. That's because I am in jail." "What? You're in jail?" Booby repeated. "Yes Booby, I've been arrested. Booby, listen up do not panic. I am in jail and I am calling to ask for your help. I want you to write down this information about where I'm being held and how long I've been here." "Okay, let me catch my breath." "I have been arrested for identity theft charges." "What? You mean your name is not LaShondra Jackson? Who are you then?" "Damn it, Booby, my name is LaShondra Jackson. I can't talk to you much longer. I have to call an attorney and I need to call a bail bonding agency to get me out of here." "No profanity on the phone," came a warning from the officer who gave her permission to make calls.

"I want you to get Frieda to call her boss's wife, Lana Irwin. She's a lawyer and she owes me a favor, sort of. Next, I want you to call my friend Danny Larson. You know, the man that I met at the football game we went to. I want you to get some money for me. I should be good for about five thousand dollars. After you pick up the money, go to Tammy Paige Bond Agency and tell Ms. Paige that my bond is twenty thousand." "Twenty thousand!" Booby exclaimed. "Did she kill someone and take their identity?" Frieda asked loudly in the background. "O no you didn't put me on speaker phone so everyone in your house can know my business. Who's there Booby?" "No one is here except Frieda. I put you on speaker phone so I could write all this information down. Now, does Danny know that I'm coming to pick up the money?" Booby asked "Yes, I phoned him first and asked him to come and get me out but he said he was too busy. Probably didn't want to be seen bonding someone out of jail." "That's all right girl as long as he is going to put out all that money for you." Booby said. "I know Lana would jump at the chance to represent you. She can't even come to the restaurant without asking about you every time she sees me. Where's Shondra? When are you going to bring Shondra back to see me? Is Shondra seeing anyone?" Frieda teased. "Bail can be paid at the In-Custody Records window twenty four hours a day. Tammy Paige will come to see me and have me sign some papers. Then she'll go the records window to bail me out."

"Okay, I guess the first stop is to get the money from Danny." I'll ride along with Booby and contact Lana on my cell phone on the way to Danny's. Lana may give you a visit in your jail cell. I know she'll love that. She may even trade her designer clothing for an orange prison jumpsuit and spend the night in the slammer with you. You know that orange is the new black." "Frieda, shut the fuck up." Shondra said. "No profanity on the phone," an officer warned. Shondra hung up the phone and was taken to a jail cell where she remained until she was released on bail.

The sound of the thick cellblock doors clanging shut was more jarring to LaShondra than the ride in the patrol car and her actual arrest. Shondra ended up in a squared room called a pod with no phone or television. There was also no bathroom. Instead, there was a steel toilet and small steel sink in the cell. "I guess I'll have to piss and shit in the same room with this wacko looking broad." Shondra thought to herself as she stole a peek at her cellmate. "No privacy, she sighed." "What you in for?" The woman asked Shondra. "Busting my old man's car windows." Shondra lied. "You?" "I'm in for prostitution again." The crack head looking woman shook her head and went on to say, "You'll get used to it. The showers are nasty but at least no one tries to rape you. There are four showers with see through curtains that you could use whenever we are not on lockdown." She added, "Fights break out occasionally but if you see one just keep cool and mind your own business. If you keep to yourself and don't get involved in other people's bullshit, you'll be fine." LaShondra lay on her cot and willed herself to sleep.

Sunday morning started out with Shondra's worst breakfast ever. She was served overcooked boiled eggs and salt free grits and tasteless oatmeal. She blessed her meal by praying silently, "Lord, please let me get out of this. Being locked up is one of the most helpless, hopeless, shittiest feeling in existence. If I get out of this, I will make amends and turn my life around." After breakfast, she was allowed in the common area of the pod where there was a TV with cable, newspapers, and board games. She listened to the conversation of two women playing a board game. "I was arrested Friday night and they said that they may hold me until Tuesday." "These pigs can keep you up to thirty six hours, not including weekends and holidays, before charging you. Since you were arrested on Friday, more than likely you won't be leaving until Tuesday." A knowledgeable repeat offender told her. "As soon as I get out and get a ride home, I going to visit my mother who I have been neglecting and give her the biggest hug and kiss ever. This time I'm going to try to keep my ass out of trouble for real. I'm not going to shoplift anymore." "What did you shoplift?" Someone asked. "I put two forty ounce bottles of beer inside my jacket sleeve and the damn undercover police caught me." She answered. There was a burst of good natured laughter and the shoplifter joined in obviously amused by the predicament she had gotten herself into.

Monday morning finally rolled around and Shondra made an appearance before a judge for the arraignment. The prosecutor charged her with commercial burglary, identity theft, credit card fraud, and forgery. There was no chance that the prosecutor would drop the charges or that the judge would dismiss for lack of probable cause. There was too much evidence pointing toward her, although she did not answer any questions during the arrest and interrogation that would seemingly implicate her. She had seen too many movies and television programs not to know that she shouldn't spill her guts without her lawyer being present. After Shondra's arrest and during custody, the cops tried to get her to talk. She only said the magic words, "I am going to remain silent. I want to see a lawyer." She knew police were legally supposed to stop questioning her after she said that. She said the same thing when Detective Beverly

Rose came in and questioned her as if she had been under investigation for months. "There's no question about it. That woman knows something, but she won't get it from my mouth." Shondra thought. Detective Rose gave up. As she left, she told the officer in charge of the investigation. "She seems like a tough nut to crack, but I think we have enough on her smart ass to put her away for a while."

Her lawyer, Lana Irwin warned Shondra before they entered the courtroom. "The prosecutor may try to bargain with you by offering you a 'Plea.' You may be asked to plead guilty to some or all of the charges against you. However, if you do plead guilty, you can't take it back, so don't be in such a hurry to accept a plea. When we go into this court room today, I want you to plead not guilty." Shondra followed her lawyer's advice and bail was set for twenty thousand dollars.

Chapter 42

Frieda read aloud from the local section of the Monday Star Tribune headlines, "Minneapolis Woman Arrested on Identity Theft Charges." The article went on to inform readers that a Minneapolis woman was apprehended on Saturday for stealing the identity of another woman and racking up credit card charges under her name. "Thirty-four year old LaShondra Jackson was accused of opening various credit cards under an unidentified woman's name. She was arrested on Friday while shopping at The Mall of America. In addition to the account at Best Buy, LaShondra Jackson also opened accounts at Nordstrom and Macy," said Minneapolis police Detective Beverly Rose. "She was arrested for commercial burglary, identity theft, credit card fraud and forgery. She was at Best Buy at the time of the arrest shopping with a credit card obtained fraudulently," Rose said. Booby interrupted loudly, "She did what? I can't believe all of this was going on under our noses and we didn't know a damn thing about it."

Booby snatched the newspaper from Frieda and read out "On May 21, Jackson was approved for a total of ten thousand dollar line of credit at Haynes Furniture and spent eight thousand nine hundred and forty nine dollars of it on merchandise. Haynes sells

295

furniture such as beds, sofa, love seats, and dining room sets. At Best Buy, she had credit for nineteen hundred dollars and spent one thousand eight hundred and ninety three dollars. The amount she was approved for and spent at Dell Computer is currently unknown." "Can you believe that all along we have been hanging out the biggest identity theft con artist since Ester Reed?" Booby questioned. "Who the heck is Ester Reed?" Frieda wanted to know. "I saw her on a CBS News interview with Peter Van Sant a long time ago. She was a Montana woman who pleaded guilty to stealing a missing South Carolina woman's identity an attending an Ivy League college even though she was a high school drop out." Frieda clucked her tongue to the roof of her mouth and made a loud smacking sound then said "Come on now, your girl Shondra didn't go that far."

Booby handed the paper back to Frieda saying "I don't want to read or hear anything else the media is saying because they are going to sensationalize it." Frieda continued perusing the article her lips moving soundlessly as read each word. "The day Jackson opened the Haynes Furniture line of credit, she purchased seven thousand nine hundred and forty nine dollars' worth of merchandise which she returned to pick up on the next day. She continued to shop around for an additional one thousand worth of items while in the store. The two separate purchases added up to eight thousand nine hundred and forty nine dollars." "That heifer was bold! I wouldn't have had the nerves to get almost ten grand of furniture in someone else's name." Frieda remarked and began reading aloud again.

"The person in whose name the cards were opened under alerted authorities that credit had been opened using her identity. She contacted stores, banks and credit card companies

296

to advise them of the crime." Rose said. "It was unclear how the suspects obtained the victim's information. Police recovered electronic equipment from her home that may have been purchased at Best Buy. She is being held in lieu of $20,000 at the Minneapolis Police Jail and is due in Municipal Court on Thursday." Frieda read aloud. "I told you I didn't want to hear it from the newspaper. I want to hear it from Shondra her damn self." An irritated Booby remarked. "I'm going to head on out to get that money she asked me to pick up. You need to go on and get in contact with Lana Irwin because she is definitely going to need a lawyer."

It was seven fifteen a.m. when Booby went to pick five thousand dollars from Danny Larson as Shondra had requested. Danny Larson gave Booby cash money in return for a promissory note Shondra had written in her jail cell. Two thousand would get her out of jail on bond and the remaining three thousand would allow her to pay court cost and begin to retain a lawyer. Danny Larson met Shondra at the game between the Viking and Bears last September. He had been associated with Shondra for a short period of time, nine months to be exact, in a more or less friends with benefits relationship. As much as he cared for Shondra, he was not a one woman type of man. She was a great piece of eye candy and she was sweet and caring so he did not mind helping her out of her current situation. Danny did not think less of Shondra because she got caught using a credit card in someone else's name. Hell, he thought, I could have been arrested many times for some of the unscrupulous shit I've done to get to where I am now. "Tell my baby to let me know if she needs anything else." Danny said as he handed the money to Booby.

Booby contacted Tammy Paige Bond Agency as she was told to do. Shondra had no other recourse since her bond was too large for her to otherwise come up with. "How does this bail thing work? "Asked Frieda. "A bail bond agency writes bail for a person basically drawing up an insurance contract that says LaShondra will show up at her appointed court date. The bonding agency wants to be sure that they are not taking a risk on someone who will take off after they release."

"Good Morning, how may I help you?" a woman at the front desk inquired in a very cheerful voice. Booby answered "I would like to post a surety bond on behalf of my friend LaShondra Jackson." The woman responded "You mean you'd like to be a co-signer?" "If I'm a co-signer, what will I have to do?" If Mrs. Jackson misses a court appearance, you will be expected to help the bail bond agent find her. You will have to pay the bond agent's expenses related to finding her and you will have to pay the full amount of the bond if the she cannot be found." Booby already knew how bonding worked, she just wanted to ask the question anyway.

Booby was prepared to answer a lot of questions because she had gone through the procedure three years ago when she arranged a bail for her brother who was arrested on a grand larceny charge. Booby told the bondsman of her relationship to Shondra. She informed Ms. Paige that Shondra had been in jail for two days. "The standard rate to arrange bond for twenty thousand dollars is two thousand. Are you prepared to pay that plus thirty five dollars plus a ten dollar Sheriff's fee?" The bondswoman asked. Booby arrived at the bonding agency with cash since most agencies did not accept personal checks. Booby handed her the amount required and waited for her to draw up the necessary paperwork.

"The bond was approved. Mrs. Jackson will be released into your care. It is your responsibility to ensure that she shows up for her court date since you are the person who requested the bail bond. Otherwise, you could be responsible for the full bail amount." I'll meet you at the precinct in twenty minutes. After I pay the jailer, it may take anywhere between one to twelve hours before she is released." Booby thanked her and said "I'll meet you there. I'm sure Ms. Jackson will be happy to see you."

Chapter 43

LaShondra Jackson was charged with obtaining a driver's license in the name of her victim and using that information to gain credit in that person's name. Her defense attorney was Lana Irwin. She admitted to the crime and told Irwin she would pay the money back. "Shondra how could you get yourself into such a predicament?" Lana asked incredulously. "I know I've only met you once. However, you didn't strike me as the type of person who would steal someone else identity and commit fraud and forgery. Hell, you were in my home. I even invited you into my bedroom because I wanted to try on that gorgeous Rachel Roy outfit you were wearing." "As I remember you did more than try on that damn pant suit." Andrea said. "Let's get back to your case." Lana urged. "Why change the conversation. Did I steal anything from you that night? When I left your house, did you still have your check book and credit cards?" Shondra began the cry. "I'm not a common thief. I was going through a difficult time. And I found a cell phone that was left behind in a restaurant. At first I was just going to hold on to it until the real owner had it shut off. I didn't make any calls on it." Shondra said. "I presume that was because you knew they could be traced back to you." Lana said as Shondra continued to cry. Lana offered Shondra a Kleenex tissue. Shondra wiped a few tears from her eyes and blew her nose into the tissue before disposing of in in a nearby waste paper basket.

"My own cell phone had been disconnected for nonpayment a few weeks earlier." Go on. Lana urged, what happened next? "At first, I checked out the apps on the phone and played a few games. Then I went online and checked out You-Tube, Facebook, and Google." "Then what?" Lana asked anxious for Shondra to tell her how that phone permitted her to steal Andrea McNair's identity get credit in her name. "After looking at her pictures and video, I went on to check out the text messages, e-mails, tasks, music, and contacts." Shondra explained. "How did you get her personal information from the phone?" Lana inquired.

"What kind of time am I looking at? I can't go to jail. Who will look out for my daughter?" Shondra started blubbering again. "I asked you how you got Andrea McNair's personal information from the phone." Lana reiterated and went on to say. "The prosecutor is not going to pussyfoot with you in court so you may as well come clean with me now." "I was having lunch in a downtown sandwich shop when Andrea McNair and her friend Michelle happened to come in. They sat down at a nearby table, ordered lunch and talked girl talk for a while. After they finished eating, they paid for their lunch and left the restaurant. I finished eating my food and went to pay for it at the counter. As I was walking toward the exit, I happened to look at the area where they were sitting and saw the cell phone. I picked it up because I thought I could catch up with them and return the phone. When I didn't see them outside of the restaurant, I decided to keep it." "It never occurred to you to turn the phone in to the manager of the restaurant in case the owner came back for it?" "I didn't think about that. I guess I wanted to get a closer look at it. That phone was so much fancier than my little pay as you go flip phone." Shondra responded and then went on to tell Lana how she managed to read Andrea's email, check out her social media interactions, and snoop into some of her sensitive financial transactions. Lana knew that the stored information left Andrea's identity vulnerable and open to attack. "I managed to find her name, address, place of employment, and social security number on that phone. Like a fool, I used it. Andrea McNair was someone going places. She had a good job and a fine looking man who cared about her." "How did you know what her man looked like? You said she was in the restaurant with a female friend." "His picture came up on her cell phone each time he dialed her. I heard her talking to him on the phone in the restaurant. When I checked out her calls she had more from him than anyone else." "People don't realize that when they carry smart phones around what they actually have with them are miniature computers." Lana remarked.

"Shondra, you used information from that phone and obtained a driver's license. You then used that license to commit credit card fraud. You posed as another person in order to gain credit. They are all criminal offenses that carries serious penalties." Shondra started sobbing again. "Lana, what's going to happen to me? What's going to happen to my child? Are they going to send me away for a long time?" "That remains to be determined." Lana answered. "I don't mean to sound harsh but let's face reality. You are charged with identity theft. Your case has been filed as a felony. If you've never done anything like this, you can get anywhere from probation to twenty years. It depends on how much you stole." Lana explained. "Oh my God, Shondra cried, I can't let poor KeKe grow up without me in her life. Oh God please help me." "Your ass wasn't worried about Poor KeKe when you were out stealing everything you could get your hand on." Lana handed Shondra a copy of Minnesota credit card fraud offense code and read it aloud. "Credit card fraud offense have many variations including using representation, obtaining cash advance, fraudulent application for credit card, criminal possession of credit card forgery devices. And unlawful use of payment card scanning devices and recorders. Minnesota criminal Code § 18.2-195.2 Minnesota Criminal Code § 18.2-196 Minnesota Criminal Code § 18.2-196."

"If the items you stole were under two hundred dollars, your crime would have been considered a misdemeanor and you'd get less time. However, even a misdemeanor would stay on your record. Anything over five hundred is considered a felony and you'd be looking at more time." "Your crime, credit card fraud, can be considered both Class B and Class C felonies. A first offense Class B felony will get you anything from probation to twenty years in prison. If you committed this same type of crime before it gets classified as a Class C felony which carries an even tougher punishment. Have you ever been arrested before?" Shondra responded, "Lana, this is my first time getting into trouble. I have never even gotten a traffic ticket. You are a very experienced defense attorney, supposedly one of the best lawyers in this city. Get me out of this. I'll pay them for the things I stole." "My service don't come cheap, Shondra. How will you manage to pay me back? You claim to know that I'm one of the best lawyers in this area, you should also know that I don't even discuss a case with a client for less than two thousand dollars an hour and here I've been with you for an hour and a half." She looked at her luxurious eighteen carat yellow gold Rolex watch. Lana knew that the watch's diamond embellishments made the golden bezel and bracelet sparkle and irresistible to look at. She returned her focus to Shondra and said I am committed to providing all my clients with the best possible defense and working to help them resolve their cases as favorably as possible." "Does that include me? You alluded to the fact that I have not given you a retainer." Shondra said. "I beg to differ. You retained me as your attorney the night of Booby's Meet the Browns party," she winked. "Mind you, you only gave me a retainer. Will you be willing to pay the remainder as soon as this case if over?" "You won't have to ask me twice. I will definitely pay whatever your fee is." Shondra answered. "Now that that's settled, we have a few options as to how we are going to go forward with this case. We just have to select one that's most feasible." Lana said.

"Simply possessing a stolen credit card is not an offense. In order for the government to secure a conviction for credit card theft, they must prove beyond a reasonable doubt that you took Ms. McNair's credit card or credit card number without her consent with the intention of using it or selling it, that you used the card to buy something of value, and you had the intent to defraud. That's not a good option because we know you did all of that plus some." Shondra knew exactly what Lana was getting at. She had not stolen an actual credit card or credit card number from Andrea. She had falsified information in order to get cards and credit in Andrea's name.

She had accumulated almost nine thousand dollars' worth of furniture, more than eighteen hundred dollars' worth of electronics, and almost six thousand in clothing in Andrea McNair's name. "What the hell have I gotten myself into? I've bitten off more than I can chew." Shondra wondered aloud.

Lana suggested a way out, "The criminal justice system often allow plea bargains as an effort to alleviate courts that are over-burdened with criminal cases. They eliminate the need for a costly trial. First, I have to work out a deal with the prosecutor. Then the prosecutor will present the deal to the judge and recommend that it be accepted by the court. The Judge will then decide on whether to accept or reject the plea deal. "You can admit to attempted credit card fraud and receive a sentence right away rather than wait for a trial date and receive a harsh sentence." "Lana, do I understand you correctly? Are you saying that a plea deal will result in less jail time as well as a lesser charge on my criminal record? Can anyone who commits a crime get off by simply copping a plea?" "A prosecutor will not bargain with a defendant who does not have an attorney to represent him, or in your case her." Lana said "A plea deal may be useful in your case since the evidence against you is overwhelming. They may lock you up and throw away the key if it goes to trial." Shondra quashed that option by proclaiming, "I would rather not leaving the amount of time I serve in the hands of a jury."

"You are facing more than one charge against you. I'll talk to the prosecutor and try to get one or more of the charges dropped or reduced to a less serious crime in exchange for your plea of guilty." Shondra was guilty of posing as another person which is a criminal charge that carried serious penalties. She was charged with identity theft and her case had been a felony because of how much harm was done to the victim and the amount of monetary damage she had inflicted.

"Explain that thing about a plea deal again." "Like I said, the prosecutor may offer a plea deal as an incentive for you, the defendant, to plead guilty to a case that might otherwise go to trial. He's not doing it as a favor to you. He will do it because the courts are so overloaded it would not be productive for every case in the justice system to go to trial. In your case, I'm going to try to get the prosecutor to allow you to plead guilty to a lesser charge or to only some of the charges that have been filed. As it stands now, you are charged with credit card fraud but you may be offered the opportunity to plead guilty to attempted credit card fraud. This is a deal between the prosecutor and you the defendant. Both parties must comply with the deal. If you do not keep your end of the deal and satisfy your duties, the prosecutor will revoke the plea bargain meaning you will do time in prison."

"I'm going to sit down with the prosecutor and try to work out a deal where you'll get probation, pay restitution, and do community service in exchange for a guilty plea to a lesser charge." Lana told her. "Does that include expungement of my criminal record?" "Expungement of your record is not included in this deal. In order to get an expungement, you will need to hire a skilled attorney after this is all over." Lana told her. Lana thought to herself. "I need to wrap this meeting up, get out of here, and get me a cigarette and drink." "Maybe I can retain you to take care of that also." Shondra said and winked at Lana. "Maybe you can." Lana laughed. "I need to get out of here and get some work done if I am going to get you off the hook. When you get out on bail, phone me so that I can set up an appointment to discuss how we will move forward." Lana signaled the guard that she was done and was allowed to leave the conference area.

Chapter 44

After learning that LaShondra would not be tried in court because she agreed to a plea deal, Andrea phoned Sterling. "I can't believe the direction this case is taking. Can you believe that she was allowed to cop a plea? The witnesses from the stores who sold her the merchandise and the handwriting analyst who matched her writing to the fake credit applications will not be called on to testify." She complained. Sensing her distress, Sterling urged Andrea to attend what could have been a closed door process. "The process used to be private but now because of many victim rights statutes, you have the right to attend her plea bargain process and have input into it. Usually the details of a plea bargain aren't known publicly until announced in court." Andrea agreed that she should attend the plea bargain hearing and offer her input as to how Lahondra Jackson's crime affected her. Of course I'll be there also since my bank is involved. I will have all the files that I've collected in case I'm able to have some input. Be sure that you also bring all of the paperwork that you have involving this matter. I'll see you in the courtroom."

The state of Minnesota vs. LaShondra Jackson case was played out in a plea bargain in the Minneapolis courtroom of Superior

307

Court Judge Rebecca Obenshain. Shondra had been indicted on multiple felony counts including unlawful use of a credit card and identity theft which were dropped as a result of a plea deal. In the plea arrangement, the State agreed not to charge Ms. LaShondra Jackson.

The D.A., Mark Justice summarized the incident before Judge Obenshain. "The first count against my client involves a crime of opportunity involving a cell phone left on a seat of a restaurant in October of last year. LaShondra Jackson found the phone and used the information that she gleaned from that cell phone to obtain a driver's license in the name of the phone's owner, Andrea McNair. Bynum Finance Company alerted Ms. McNair that her name had been used to acquire credit. Bank of America also subsequently informed her that a card bearing her name had been used to make three transactions the bank was deemed suspicious."

Shondra spoke to the judge when it was her turn to speak, "Your Honor, I just want everyone here to know that I have put a lot of effort into having excellent credit. Ms. Jackson has caused my credit score to drop exponentially. If you have not gone through this you may not have any idea as to how hard it is to have all the fraudulent activity removed from your credit report. To this day, I am still working with all three credit bureaus." She said as she held up a handful of written correspondence for the judge to see. Since the judge did not offer to take a closer look at the papers, she went on talking. "Any line of credit or loan that I apply for will have a higher interest rate, if I apply for another job there's a possibility that I will be turned down because of the bad credit that has been thrust upon me by Ms. Jackson. What did I do to ever deserve this? I graduated from college and got a Masters in Business Administration degree. I worked hard to get to where I am. However, my good name is now ruined because of someone else's bad decision to sponge off of my good credit." "Ms. McNair, I definitely understand where you are coming from. What Miss Jackson did was absolutely reprehensible. The courts doesn't condone what she did by any stretch of the imagination. It may seem as if she is getting off scot-free but trust me being on probation can sometimes be worse than going to prison, doing the time, and being done with it." The prosecutor said. Lana Irwin, the defense attorney interjected, "The court is allowing Ms. Jackson to take part in a diversion program that removes less serious criminal matters from the full, formal procedures of the justice system. She is being allowed to consent to probation without having to go through a trial." "Yes, and when she completes the probation and makes restitution, which is far less than what she actually got away with, the entire matter will be expunged or removed from the records. Meanwhile, I will still be trying to clear my financial record and working to restore my good name. I will have to explain what screwed up my credit every time I apply for job and every time I apply for credit." Andrea protested.

LaShondra was sentenced to three years in prison after pleading guilty to three counts of fraudulent use of a credit card. Judge Obenshain then split the sentence and ordered her to spend six months in jail followed by three years of probation. As part of the plea deal, she was required to pay a total of seventy two hundred dollars in restitution fees. She paid three thousand after her release and has until the end of her probation to pay the remaining amount. "In order for the case against you to be dismissed and your criminal record cleared, you must meet certain demands. If you finish paying the remaining forty two hundred within the agreed upon time frame, which is at the end of your three year probation, the case against you will be dismissed and you can have your criminal record wiped clean," her attorney informed her after the hearing. Andrea and Sterling were appalled at the outcome of the case. "After all the thievery that woman has committed, she has the gall to fess up only to attempted credit card fraud. They should lock her up and make her pay for her life wrecking crime spree." Andrea declared.

Detective Rose tried to explain what had just happened in Judge Obenshain's courtroom. "The arresting officers can only recommend charges to the prosecutor. The prosecutor is the only one responsible for actually deciding if what she's charged with is consistent with what she was arrested for. At first, Shondra pleaded not guilty. Had she gone to court and been found guilty, she could have received one to twenty years in a state correctional institution or confinement in jail for up to twelve months." Andrea shook her head in disbelief and said, "With this plea deal she managed to land, she will get out without as much as a scratch." "The D.A., Mark Justice, is well known for allowing criminals to make plea deals. I don't know if it's really because the court is so overburdened or if it's because his lazy ass would not have to deal with handling the case." Detective Beverly Rose asserted. "I can't begin to tell you how many cases that I thought should be were actually nipped in the bud by him. Judge Obenshain agrees with about fifty percent of his plea deal requests because she sees it as a way to cut through the backlog of cases that come through her courtroom," Rose elaborated.

"By all accounts she racked up approximately twelve thousand seven hundred and forty two dollars' worth of merchandise and she gets to walk. That is the biggest single load of crap I have ever seen... and I used to have to shovel out horse stables as a young boy during summer camp." Andrea couldn't resist smiling as Sterling finished his shovel story. "I understand how the system works. Andrea said. Prosecutors do not like having their calendars clogged up. Their staff ends up overworked because of the caseloads. Allowing criminals to cop a plea lightens the staff's caseload. Because plea bargains are much quicker and require less work than trials, they are also easier on the prosecutor's budget. With all the government cutbacks, D.A.s feel they will have additional time and resources for more important cases if they conclude a large number of less serious cases with plea bargains. Plea bargains are easier on the budget because they are quicker and demand less work than trials."

"Posing falsely as another person for financial gain is a criminal act that carries serious penalties. However, Ms. Jackson managed to get off by pleading to the lesser charge of attempted credit card fraud. The craziest part of all of this is that I could have been the one who actually ended up in jail if she had gone out and committed a murder or had a horrific car accident while using my name." "Yes, that is true. There's been many times that thieves never get caught. There's also been times when an identity thief commits fraud in someone else's name and the police come after the victim." Detective Beverly Rose said. The prosecutor began negotiations over LaShondra's proposed plea bargain to which both sides had agreed upon. Shondra plead guilty to lesser charges. Although

Judge Obenshain was not bound to follow the prosecutor's recommendation, she went along for the ride.

"Her plea of guilty and her consequent plea bargain resulted in a criminal conviction. Her guilt was established just as it would be after a trial and the conviction will show up on the Ms. Jackson's criminal record. She will lose her right to vote and her right to own a firearm the same as if she had gone to trial," the prosecutor continued. "The court does not condone what Ms. Jackson has done. We sincerely hope that this trial brings closure to your ordeal." Andrea did not respond because she was irate and was doing all she could not to explode.

"I came to this plea deal hearing because I wanted to see LaShondra Jackson spend time in prison for everything she put me through. Although she didn't get as much time as she deserved, I'm somewhat satisfied with the outcome because now the case is over. I now know who was responsible for turning my life upside down and I can try to move on with my life. On one hand, LaShondra freaking Jackson was able to use a false driver's license to open up numerous credit accounts in my name and buy all sorts of luxury items including Pacific Island inspired bedroom furniture, computers, large flat-screen TVs, high-end clothing and jewelry. While on the other hand, as her victim I have to deal with harassment from debt collectors, banking problems, and loan rejections." Andrea said. "Even though federal and state laws may protect victims like Ms. McNair against financial loss resulting from the theft of their identity, the worst aspect of their victimization is that their lives are disrupted. Ms. McNair has already spend many hours trying to unravel the financial mess in which her life has become entangled"

Sterling remarked to the detective. "I'm sorry that it did not go the way the both of you had hoped. At least now there will be no new accounts opened by that woman in your name. If I can be of assistance in helping you reclaim your good name as far as your credit is concerned, just give me a phone call." Detective Rose said before shaking Andrea's and Sterling's hand and saying goodbye.

Chapter 45

Lana Irwin informed LaShondra of the terms of her release from state custody. "Now that your hearing is over and you are no longer in police custody you are required to go the Adult Probation Department. Since Judge Obenshain has placed you on supervised probation and you have not had a chance to go to the Adult Probation Department, phone their office and they will give you a date and time to meet with the probation officer assigned to your case. At that meeting, your P.O. will go over the terms of probation with you. If there is anything you do not understand, ask questions because you will be held responsible for any violation of the terms of your probation." It is extremely imperative that you do not miss that appointment. It's important that you get there on time. If you run late, you should call your probation officer and let him or her know." "What does being supervised probation mean?" Shondra asked.

"Being on supervised probation means that you are required to report to a probation officer on a regular basis. You must obey all laws, make payments on court imposed retributions, participate in counseling, submit to drug tests, and do any community service ordered by the court. Commit a new crime or fail to do what the court ordered you to do and you will find yourself in violation of your probation and back in jail." Lana Irwin answered. "Shit!" LaShondra mumbled then asked. "How long do I have to do this probation thing?" Lana didn't answer that question because she was sure that Shondra heard Judge Obenshain deliver the length of time she would be on probation. Instead, she continued to recite what it meant to be on supervised probation. "Being on supervised probation also means you have to stay sober. Do not drink alcohol or use marijuana, heroin, cocaine or any other illegal drugs." "I guess that means I cannot socialize with you and your husband anymore." LaShondra said. "You can socialize with any non-felon as long as you stay clean because you will be tested for drugs and alcohol. If your test comes back dirty, you will be in violation. Smart Ass."

"I'm sorry Lana, you didn't deserve that smart remark after all you've done for me. What I should be saying is thank you so much for seeing me through this. I realize I've only known you and your husband for a short time. But even though you've known me briefly, you have been very kind to me. You didn't have to take time out from your busy lucrative law practice to represent a poor nobody like myself. Please know that I appreciate your help and I will pay you," Tears began to form in her eyes before she could finish the sentence. "Shondra, Sweetie, don't ever again refer to yourself and a poor nobody. Lana grabbed several tissues from the box of Kleenex sitting on top on her impressive chestnut finished birch and burl veneer desk, stood up from her comfortable leather executive office chair, walked up Shondra and pressed the tissues into her client's hand. She stood in front of Shondra's chair until Shondra wiped her eyes and nose. "She took LaShondra's hand and said. "Get up here. It seems like you need a hug." Shondra stood up and moved toward Lana who immediately embraced her. "I can't help it Lana, I really messed up. I don't know what I was thinking. I don't know why I thought that using Andrea McNair's identity was the right way to get things that KeKe and I needed. Worst yet, I got things that I didn't need." She started to cry again. Lana drew her closer in her arms. Feeling more comforted than she had felt in a long time, LaShondra pressed closer to Lana and let her body relax as Lana began to kiss her first softly on her damp eyelids, then her drippy nostrils and finally fully inside of her open mouth. Lana withdrew her tongue just as quickly as she had slipped it in. The salty taste of tears mixed with a little snot, something that she had never experienced, turned Shondra on. "Don't stop, Lana." She said. Lana locked eyes with Shondra then slowly moved her gaze to her lips then back to her eyes. Even though Lana saw the anticipation in LaShondra eyes, she continued to move slowly. Lana moved in so close to her she could feel both Shondra's warm breath and her heart racing. Shondra felt goosebumps as she watched Lana slowly part her lips and seductively slide across her tongue across the bright red lipstick she was wearing. Flashing back to the time she had been alone with Lana on the night of Booby's party at the Irwin's house, Shondra tilted her head and licked her own lips in anticipation.

At first, Lana's kiss was feather-light, barely grazing over Shondra's lips. The love starved felon tried hard to contain her excitement and anticipation. Holding Shondra face firmly yet gently, Lana sucked on her lips before she slipped her tongue inside her mouth. Shondra responded by embracing Lana and gently caressing her shoulders and moving her hands slowly around Lana's back. Lana's sensual tongue took complete control as she proceeded to kiss her willing partner hard and deep. After a few deep kisses, Lana turned her mouth into a soft suctioning device mimicking the way she would suck on a clitoris. She decided not to confine her kisses only to Shondra's mouth, she French kissed her chin, neck and breast. Shondra's body began to tremble as Lana knelt down and pulled her skirt up to her waistline and kissed through her panties. Oblivious to the fact that they were in her lawyer's office and Lana's young male legal aid was in an adjoining office, Shondra peeled her panties off and parted her shapely legs to reveal her wet glistening vulva. Lana teased her by softly kissing her inner thighs before sliding her tongue on Shondra's inner and outer lips. Lana licked her client's womanly entrance from bottom to top, savoring every step of the way. Shondra's breathing became spastic and her body seem to feel ten degrees warmer, almost hot to the touch. She felt muscles throughout her body including arms, legs, neck and face spasm. Lana slid her tongue along Shondra's vulva to her clitoris and along the borders of her lover's vagina. She slowly repeated the upward and downward motion of her tongue until Shondra moaned and moved her hips in sync with her rhythm. Not giving a damn if the legal aid did hear what was happening in her office, she raised Shondra's shapely buttocks off the floor and helped her encircle her long legs around her neck. Lana tossed her hair back so it would not interfere with what she was about to do with Shondra. "Come on, Baby." Shondra moaned. Shondra raised her hips higher and pulled Lana head back to the warm wet place she moved away from so that finish the job. Lana curled her long tongue and thrust it in and out of Shondra's wet, throbbing vagina mimicking intercourse. Shondra grabbed the hair that Lana had tossed back a few seconds ago, and pulled at the long blond roots. The harder Shondra tugged at her hair, the harder and faster Lana dug her magic tongue wand into Shondra's honey pot until she screamed out in ecstasy.

As Shondra put her panties back on and adjusted her clothes, Lana finished discussing what she should expect from her P.O. Your probation officer may be able to help you find another job. He or she will try to help you get on your feet but make no mistake about it your P.O. does have the authority to declare you in violation if you fail to meet certain requirements. So be sure to keep all of your appointments and if you have any problems, feel free to contact me. I'm certain that if you behave yourself, you will get this all behind you. Don't worry babe, I'll help you get your records expunged and you can go on with your life as if the crime never happened." Lana said. "What about Andrea? I messed her credit up pretty badly." Shondra said. "Don't worry about Andrea McNair, she'll bounce back sooner or later. Just worry about yourself and don't fuck with anyone else's I.D." It's been a long day, I need to get home so that I can get some rest before starting all over again in that same courtroom tomorrow. She gave Shondra one last kiss. "Can I drop you off somewhere, Sweetie?" Lana asked Shondra. "No, you've done so much for me already, I'll get a cab." As LaShondra prepared to leave the law office of Irwin, Crenshaw, Edmonds, and Yancy. The young legal aid who was hired by the firm just four months ago gave both Lana and Shondra a sly look and thought to himself. "I'll be damn, did what I think I just heard actually happen?" When the two women came out into the reception area where he worked,

Attorney Lana Irwin looks like the cat that swallowed the mouse and Client Shondra Jackson looked one hundred percent more relaxed than she looked when she first came in. I can't prove it, but I know I heard that felon moaning and groaning like someone was rocking her world, he said to himself. "Since the other associates are done for today, we can go on and lock up." Lana told the young man breaking his thoughts about what went on behind her closed office door." He quickly gathered his jacket and car keys and said "I'll See you tomorrow, Mrs. Irwin, have a good evening." "You do the same Mr. Matthews, I'll see you in the morning."

Chapter 46

$\mathcal{A}$ ndrea sat in the driver's seat of her Riviera Red Lexus GS450h while Michelle rode shotgun. Before she began driving, she adjusted the audio control. The car's twelve inch, high-resolution multimedia screen displayed an array of apps including radio stations as well as a maps and climate controls. The twelve speaker surround sound system was tuned in to Andrea's customized R&B iHeartRadio station. Andrea checked her rear view mirror LCD screen before backing her car out of her parking space. She then proceeded to drive a few city blocks before she reached the entrance to the interstate highway. Andrea got onto the ramp leading to a high speed roadway to Minneapolis. After building up her speed, she merged with the traffic already on the road, and locked her cruise control to match the flow of traffic.

The two friends had made plans to attend the grand reopening of Minneapolis Institute of Art African Galleries long before Michelle's wedding and Andrea's identity dilemma. Ten months after the news of the galleries' reopening they were on their way to view masterworks of sculpture, ceramics, metalsmithing, painting, basketry, bead, shell, and quillwork. "When we finish checking out the exhibit, we can eat at one of the three on-site cafes or we can

320

walk a couple blocks to one of the ethnic restaurants on Nicollet Ave S. or as Todd like to call it Eat Street." Michelle suggested. "Or, we could walk across the Irene Hixon Whitney pedestrian bridge into Loring Park and eat at one of the cafes or restaurants there. It's your choice. It doesn't really matter to me." She continued. Since losing her phone in the restaurant, Andrea had not initiated many lunch meetings with girlfriends or business associates. She hoped today's lunch with Michelle would revive one of her favorite things to do.

Andrea "We can decide later where we'll eat. Right now I have to get something off my chest. I am really trying to get over what the LaShondra Jackson episode did to me. After she was released I have a problem with the fact that she got off with a mere slap on the wrist. You are an attorney. Tell me how in the hell did that happen. Lady Justice must be a blind ass bitch." Michelle responded. "First of all, I work strictly will crimes against children. Most of my cases are child abuse or child neglect cases." I know that, Andrea snapped as if she was angry with all attorneys, including her best friend. I just want to know how you feel about letting someone who committed a very serious crime plea bargain their way out of a long prison sentence. Michelle answered, "To be truthful, I have never accepted a plea deal. I feel that anyone who commits a crime against a child should get what they deserve. Jesus said, 'But whoso shall offend one of these little ones which believe in me, it were better for him that a millstone were hanged about his neck, and that he were drowned in the depth of the sea.' If they are guilty they don't deserve a plea, they deserve a millstone around their neck."

Andrea used the volume control button on the steering wheel to turn down the music. She kept her eyes on the road while

321

continuing her conversation with her friend. She did not want to get off on the wrong exit. "Michelle, do you remember the day we had lunch at that downtown restaurant after shopping? I think you ordered cream of celery soup and a salad and I ordered chef salad. We sat there and talked about your wedding. I took a telephone call from Quinton while you were in the lady's room. That was the day and the place that I lost my I-phone. A woman who also had lunch there that day found it and used the information on it

"I remember eating there but I did not know that is where you lost your phone. I know that you could not locate your phone for a few days, but I had no idea that someone took it and used it the way that LaShondra Jackson did." Michelle answered. "I didn't think my phone would ever be stolen because I tried to be cognizant of its use and behavior. I tried not to call attention to the phone or create an opportunity for someone to steal it by leaving it behind. I wouldn't even think about allowing someone I didn't know to borrow it. I thought I did a good job protecting my phone from being lost or stolen." Andrea said as she glanced at the highway exits and made a mental note that the Hennepin Avenue-Lyndale Avenue exit where she needed to get off was two exits ahead.

"As soon I got that I-Phone, I locked it by setting a password that I thought was pretty hard to guess," she pointed out as she took her hands off the steering wheel and began using hand gestures to make her point. "Look girlfriend I know that the collision avoidance system in this car scans the road ahead for obstacles and will sound an alarm, boost sensitivity to your brakes, and tighten the damn seat belts in order to reduce the effects of a collision. However, I do not want to be a crash dummy in this bitch when and if it does all that. When you communicate with your hands while you drive on the interstate scares me shitless. I get what you are saying. Keep your hands glued to the steering wheel." Michelle admonished her. Andrea looked at her passenger who was visibly a bit apprehensive about her driving ten miles over the speed limit with her hands off of the steering wheel. "Sorry if I shook your cautious behind up. I'll drive like my seventy-five year old grandma until we get there." They both laughed. "Andrea, if you needed to know a password before your phone could be used, how did LaShondra Jackson manage to use it? How often did you change the password?" "That's just it. I erased my password that day with the intention of adding a new one but I was distracted by a long drawn out call from my company. After I hung up, I attended to some company related business and completely forgot about putting in a new password." Andrea answered. Michelle shook her head and looked out passenger window the traffic in the next lane.

"Too bad. That whole thing may have been avoided if the password was activated. I recall that you attempted to recover your phone on your own with the app you installed that was capable of remotely tracking a smartphone." Andrea answered as she switched lanes in anticipation of getting off at her exit. "Yes, that same app was supposed to lock and erase my smartphone. I specifically added that app because in the event my phone was stolen or lost, my personal information would be protected." "But when you activated the app, it tracked the phone to a lake," Michelle looked at Andrea and waited for a response. "That's true. After I tracked it to a lake, I just assumed that someone found the phone and skipped it across the lake like someone would skip a rock across water." "If you had an app that would erase sensitive information, why didn't you erase it or wipe it out?" "I didn't worry too much about my photos, videos, or contacts because I had a backup copy on a USB drive."

"I reported it as lost and it was replaced because it was insured. T-Mobile put a hold on my account so that if anyone found it and tried to use it, I would not be responsible for any charges incurred during the time it was not in my possession. It's amazing that a criminal mind would think to use information from a phone to do the things LaShondra Jackson did. I wish I could have walked up on her using one of those cards in a store. I would have had no reservations about whipping her ass right then and there." Andrea said and accelerated in order to get in the lane she needed to be in.

"One last thing before I let go of this conversation. I went through a twelve step program for I.D. theft victims. It was probably more strenuous than a twelve step program for alcoholics. Step One, I notified creditors and the bank affected. Step Two. I implemented fraud alerts. Step Three, I checked all three credit reports. Quinton walked me through step four which involved contacting the FTC. He also helped me with the next step that called for sending creditors my I.D. theft report. The sixth step required me to change all my account passwords. You see where I'm coming from Michelle. Do I need to go on to the rest of the steps I took? Such as freezing my credit, calling Social Security fraud hotline, getting a new driver license." Michelle was sorry that Andrea went through that ordeal, but she was now tired of Andrea's whining and felt as if she was part of a captive audience. "I hope the ride back will not be as gloomy. Hell, I should have driven my own car and met her at the museum," she thought.

Andrea drove Ninety-Four east and took the Hennepin/ Lyndale exit. Then, when Hennepin and Lyndale avenues divided, Andrea continued on Lyndale Avenue South to Twenty-Fourth Street. "I think I should turn left and proceed to Third Avenue South then turn right." She finally brought the Lexus to a stop in the art center's parking ramp but she was in no hurry to get out of the car. She sat in her car staring blankly before finally she began to sob. "Don't cry honey, none of what happened was your fault. Don't beat yourself up over losing that damn phone. Hell, if it was going to happen to you, it was going to happen. If it was in the cards for you to be ripped off, you were going to be ripped off. Someone could have hacked into your computer or scanned one of your credit cards after you made a purchase. Look at what some of those people who recently shopped at Target are going through. That Target shit happened at a level that was way beyond what LaShondra was capable of. You don't have to go through any more twelve step programs so quit worrying about it. I guess it's easy for me to say, I didn't go through it. I am just so glad that they finally caught up with the person who charged all those items in your name and she has gone to trial. Maybe now you can put this all behind you." Andrea dried her eye with a tissue, sucked up her emotions and applied a fresh coat of lipstick before opening the driver's side door and exiting the Lexus. "Let's bounce." She said.

As the two walked toward the museum's Third Street entrance Andrea turned toward her friend and said. "Michelle, I didn't invite you to go to the art exhibit with me just to burden you with my problems. I wanted to have a day out with my best friend. Enough about me already," she said while simultaneously entwining her arm around Michelle's arm. "How's married life treating you?" Happy to change the conversation, Michelle laughed and replied "It is hard to believe that my marvelous wedding is over. The guests have gone their separate ways, Todd's grooms have returned their tuxes, and my bridesmaids have closeted their gowns. My beautiful wedding gown has been dry cleaned and now it's stored away until we have children. After we have children, I'll have my aunt who loves to sew cut the train off and make it into christening gowns."

Michelle thought MIA was a wonderful place to spend a day just walking around and taking in the art. An art lover can stay there for three or four hours and not see everything in the massive building. She was amazed that the museum with its wide range of art from all over the world spanning centuries did not require an entrance charge. She and Andrea usually put a five or ten dollars in the donation box at the entrance even though there was really no pressure to do so. "You know as much as we come to MIA to browse the collections, we should really consider becoming members." Andrea said. "You're right. I'm going to fill out the online membership form and send in the fee one day this week." Michelle answered.

A few minutes, later the two were inside of the beautiful lobby of MIA's vast world class museum. Andrea looked up at the magnificent Chihuly glass sculpture of a sun that hung from the ceiling enter and smiled. "This museum reminds me of the Museum of Fine Arts in Boston, and the Metropolitan Museum of Art in NYC. It is such a huge building that it takes a few days to truly see and enjoy in full." Michelle suggested that they go to the information desk and rent audio tour headsets which would allow them to learn more about the artwork as they browsed around at their own pace. In addition to the audio tour guide, they each picked up a self-guided tour leaflet that described the museum's most popular, interesting or unusual African art items.

Andrea and Michelle took the stairway to the second floor headed towards room two-fifty to view the display of African art and artifacts. Michelle was particularly interested in the assorted masks. Many of which were made of wood, although a wide variety of other elements, such as light stone, copper, bronze, and different types of fabric were also used. Some of the masks were painted with ochre or other natural colorants. Ornamental items which included horns, teeth, sea shells, seeds, egg shell, and feathers were applied to the many of them. Animal hair or straws were sometime used for a mask's hair or beard.

"People who wore these ritual masks ideally lost their human identity and turned into the spirits represented by the masks themselves. Imagine, some person actually wore this mask as part of a costume to hide their human identity and transform into a medium through which ancestral spirits spoke with their descendants?" A light skinned woman dressed in a brightly colored African kente fabric lapa and matching gele told two pre-teen girls who were also dressed in African attire. The two beautiful young girls, who bore a striking physical resemblance to the woman, studied the masks intently for a few moments before moving on to view a different mask. "What's this one Mama?" The younger girl asked, "This is a rare Luba mask. It is one of only two known in the world." The mother responded then added. "It is a dramatic dance mask known as a "Firespitter" from Cote d'Ivoire,"

Michelle looked at the same mask and listened as the voice coming through her Audio Tour said "They wore the masks and danced as a part of most traditional African weddings, funerals, initiation rites, and other ceremonies. Most of these mask were found in Nigerian cultures such as those of the Yoruba and Edo peoples where some of the most complex rituals were performed."

Andrea moved close to a nineteenth century pigmented wooden and kaolin mask by an artist named Yombe. She paused and listened the Audio Tour description of the mask as she examined it in detail. "The filed upper teeth and black headdress indicate that we're looking at a high-ranking woman of Yombe society. Because this highly realistic mask shows her as an ancestor, her face is painted white, the color of the supernatural. When worn by a male dancer during ritual ceremonies, the spirit of the deceased woman would appear from the otherworld to bring fertility, appeasement, and wellbeing to the living." The Audio Tour voice said. "Fascinating! Andrea remarked as if the audio tour headphones could hear her.

Together the two women walked around the room two of the three rooms dedicated to African art. They paused occasionally to admire a ceramic portrait head from the ancient civilization of Ife, a thousand-year-old wooden horse-and-rider from Djenne, a cast bronze leopard and a carved ivory tusk from the eighteenth-century Kingdom of Benin. The two friends were fascinated by works from across the African continent and areas of the African Diaspora. "Can you believe that some of these objects date back from 2500 BCE in Ancient Egypt? Andrea said in amazement."

Andrea and Michelle split up and each explored the remaining room of African culture individually. They took their own time viewing the art pieces which included textiles, ceremonial blades, ceramics, gourds, musical instruments, jewelry and religious sculptures all organized into distinct thematic groupings throughout the galleries. They savored the various functional art, leadership, and spiritual themes. In each of the three rooms, museum visitors sat on benches equipped with iPads and connected with the history and the stories behind the art on display. Each iPads was loaded with photos, detailed descriptions of the art pieces, and video interviews which explained the stories behind the art, and the people and cultures who crafted them also. Michelle tried out an eighty-two-inch touch-screen wall that displayed an interactive map of Africa in the 254 gallery. She touched icons which allowed her to pull up and manipulate large images of the museum's collection, and read up on Africa's vast history, varied cultures and mixing pot of religions.

After about an hour and a half of browsing African arts and artifacts in rooms 250, 254, and 255, the comrades were ready to leave the museum in favor of a bite to eat. "Before we call it an afternoon, let's get something from one of the restaurants on Eat Street." Michelle suggested. "Sound like a good idea to me. All that walking has made me as hungry as a bear." Andrea laughed. The two exited MIA and headed back to the East Twenty-Fourth Street and Third Avenue South intersection to the parking ramp where Andrea left her car.

Chapter 47

Booby and Frieda arrived at LaShondra's condo armed with a total of six large corrugated storage boxes. "Thanks for bringing the boxes and offering to help me pack my things." She told them. "That's what friends do." Frieda said. "Me and Booby hate seeing you get evicted from this lovely condo, but we are happy to have you and KeKe stay with us until you can find another place to live." "Are you sure it's okay?" She asked. "I don't want to be an imposition on you two lovebirds." Shondra teased. "Girlfriend, don't even go there. You know damn well that me and Frieda are just the best of friends who share an apartment. She has her room, I have mine. She has her romantic interest, I have mine." Frieda chirped in "Shondra, you know we like men. Ms. Booby is a lovely person and everything but I go for the Denzel Washington type while she goes for the George Cloony type. You catch my drift?" "I know that living with you two queens is going to be quite an adventure." Shondra quipped.

"But back to being serious, my probation officer gave me the names of two or three housing programs that could possibly help me get an apartment. I plan to contact each and every one of them and ask for help relocating after I get settled at your apartment."

330

"Does your P.O. know that you are going move in with me and Booby until you find another place?" ""Yes I informed him and he said as long as you two don't have felony convictions because can't be around or associate with any felons." Did I hear you correctly? You can't be around or associate with any felons? Well, can you hang around or associate with your own damn self, Shondra because the only felon around here is you, LaShondra Jackson, Andrea McNair, or whatever the hell your name is." Booby said in his best Madea voice. "Ease up on her, Booby. Can't you see she is just trying to abide by the rules of her probation? They do tell parolees and probatees to stay away from felons so that they will stay out of trouble with the law and not commit more felonees." Frieda rhymed in sing song fashion. She then gave Shondra a reassuring hug and said. "Girl, you will get an apartment in no time. Single mothers are always the first ones to get a subsidized place." Booby packed pots, pans, and cooking utensils into one of the large box and kept quiet while focusing on the job at hand, getting as many items into one box as she could.

"Yes, Frieda, you're absolutely correct, and based on my income, I qualify for Hennepin County Childcare Assistance. The city will provide childcare for KeKe while I look for a job, work, and even attend school. I just hate to be on the government dole. I've always worked to take care of myself and KeKe." Booby looked at Frieda, pulled his chin in toward his shoulder, and pressed his lips together before giving Shondra a side eye. "Don't be giving me no damn side eye. I may have used Andrea's identity to get a few things for the past few months." She corrected herself and said. "Okay, alright it may have more like a little over a year, but

I took care of KeKe for years before I became an identify cheat." Frieda cleared her throat rather loudly. "You two buttholes think this shit is funny. The court ordered that I pay restitution and I had to sell, pawn, or return almost everything I had in order to make the first payment." "Why didn't you get Big Daddy to pay it for you since he put up my bail money?" Frieda asked trying to act like she was NeNe Leakes and Shondra was Kim, both characters on The Housewives of Atlanta. "I don't want to keep asking Danny Larson for financial help. I think very highly of him and I want a lasting relationship with him. I'm afraid that if I keep dragging him into my financial mess instead of finding my own way out, he will soon say sayonara to me." I have to dig my own self out of the deep doo doo that I've stepped into. Like I said, I care about Danny and I want him to be there for me after I pay for my crime." Shondra said in a serious tone.

Frieda brainstormed, "You could try Elim Transitional Housing. It's located on Northeast Central Ave. They offer rental subsidies that help residents who are unable to afford market rate rents. They also help you with application fees and damage deposit. They helped my aunt last summer. I had almost forgotten about that. If I'm not mistaken, that programs also provides a little financial assistance if you are facing eviction due to non-payment of rent. I don't know if it covers getting kicked out for illegally getting an apartment in someone else's name like you did. I do know that you must have minor children to be eligible and thanks to Little Miss KeKe you do meet that criteria." "I was damn sure facing eviction because the apartment was in someone else's name." Shondra admitted. "Would that someone's name also be Andrea McNair?

Damn Shondra! You had more balls that both Frieda and I ever had to do some shit like that." "I would never in a million years have the moxie to try to get an apartment or condo in someone else's name." "Booby, this is no time for you to make jokes! You've heard the saying "If you can't be part of the solution, don't be part of the problem! So stop poking fun at Shondra and be part of the solution!" Frieda said in her best Cora voice. "Eighteen months ago, I would not have thought about doing it myself, Booby. I'm not blaming Eric for my criminal behavior. But I do believe that if he hadn't been such a lying, cheating, physically abusive son of a bitch, perhaps my life I wouldn't have taken such a turn for the worst. The most I ever did was try to be a good mother to KeKe and a good woman to him." Shondra sobbed. "We know Shondra, we know. That M.F. caused some sort of short circuit to go off in your brain which forced you to try to get away from him." Frieda said as she rubbed Shondra's shoulder. "You need to hook up with one of those programs that offer counseling and support to victims of spousal abuse. They may be able to hook you up with everything you need to get back on track including free therapy so that you won't fall in love with another shit-head like Eric. The three friends packed the boxes into both the trunk and the back seat of Booby's hoopty. "That's all we can get in here now. We will come back for the other boxes after we drop these off at my place." She told her as the headed to Shondra and KeKe's temporary home.

"Booby, now that my car has been repossessed, how I am going to be able to search for a job or go on interviews, or get back and forth to work when I do find a job." "You mean to tell me that the company that financed the car would not let you just transfer that

333

Ford Fusion into your name? After all, you did make payments on time." Bobby commented in disbelief. "Girlfriend, the car was in my name, but when Ford Financing found out that I was using an alias as a cosigner, for the loan, they took the car back and threatened to press charges. "You can go to the Salvation Army. Frieda said "They offers bus passes to people who are starting a brand new job but you must call and make appointment so that they can determine your eligibility. I think you have to be referred by authorized agency such as social services or the court. Give them a call to learn all the specifics." Shondra nodded indicating that she would follow up on the suggestion. Determined to dig herself out of the hole that she had gotten herself into, Shondra jotted down 'Salvation Army' for bus tickets in a spiral notebook that she used to remind her of all the appointments she had to keep. After they delivered the boxes to a rented storage unit, the threesome picked up KeKe from her babysitter's house and had dinner at Ruby Tuesday before settling in for the night. The next day was Saturday. Everyone was in the mood for a movie so they took KeKe to see the animated film Cloudy with a Chance of Meatballs.

On Sunday, around eleven a.m., KeKe woke LaShondra up to report that it was raining. "Auntie Booby said we can't go to Sunday school today like she promised because it's too wet out there. Auntie Frieda said that this Sunday, we will bake cookies, play games, and read books instead." "That's fine, Baby. Let Mommy get a little more sleep and I'll join you guys in about an hour or so." Frieda and Booby decided to each do an individual project with KeKe. Frieda showed the little girl how to bake colorful rainbow cookies. First, they made butter cookie dough, shaped them into heart shapes.

Then, they mixed icing sugar with enough orange juice to make a thick, runny icing. Finally, they dipped one side of each cookie half into the icing and then into colorful sprinkles before putting the cute cookies on a wire rack to dry. Later, a little after 1PM when Shondra finally got out of bed that day Booby and KeKe were making cute little origami finger puppets. "Mommy look at what Auntie Booby showed me how to make. KeKe and Booby held up their paper puppet clad fingers to reveal bears, cats, and dogs that they had produced. "We made this one for you, it's a fox. Auntie said we can have a puppet show later on." "Ke, baby, come on and help me throw away all this scrap paper and put away these scissors." Booby told KeKe as they handed the puppets to LaShondra who examined them and told them that they had done a terrific job. "Tonight, Instead of telling you a story before bedtime, we will have puppet show." "Yay!" Booby cheered expressing excitement and approval.

When Monday rolled around, Shondra met with Rev. Matthew Garrett Christian Restoration's Executive Director. He explained the program to her. "We can offer you a temporary resident. We generally charge rent, but we have access to assistance from Hennepin County. You can stay at our facility for up to twenty-four months and if you can handle monthly payments, we also help you buy or rent your own house." "That's good to know, but I've arranged to move in with two friends until I can get a permanent apartment for me and my child." Shondra said. "Praise the Lord for that." Our program also have a faith-based employment program which prepares or grooms our clients for the workforce and a new life in the community. We do require that you participate in group

335

activities some of which include counseling and mentoring. You must also agree to attend a local church." He asserted. "Well, I guess it would not hurt to join a group counseling in order to vent, and it is a good idea to get a mentor who can help me reach the point where I want to get to." She said. "What about church?" He asked. "What about church? I may attend but I can't guarantee that I will join." "Fair enough he laughed. Fair enough. Where would any of us be without the Good Lord? I know you prayed while you were in jail." "Indeed I did. I promised God that I would turn my life around and that is exactly what I intend to do. I am going to pay off those debts that I got in Andrea McNair's name, clear my record, finish getting my bachelor's degree in math, be a model parent for my daughter and make my parents proud of me again."

Later that day, Shondra kept an appointment with Offender Workforce Development, an organization designed to improve the employability of people like herself who have a criminal history. She had learned from her probation officer that O.W.D. worked with the Minnesota Department of Rehabilitation and Correction to prepare offenders for employment and the job search process. She learned that they developed collaborative partnerships across the state and offered training, education, and technical assistance to community action organizations. She also learned about One-Stops, job developers, and other state agencies that worked with second chance job seekers. The O.W.D. employment specialist assigned to Shondra suggested various job training opportunities. Before leaving, she visited the program's computer lab and checked out the jobs they had listed online. She scrolled up and down O.W.D. job-seekers' web page for almost an hour. Automotive specialist technician, brick mason, cement mason, carpentry, electrician, glazier, insulation worker, marble repair technician, marble setter, and painter were some of the job listed. Shondra was not interested in any of the manual labor jobs listed. Although her first attempts at finding a job were not fruitful, she made up her mind that she would have a job within three weeks because she was anxious to get the past behind her. She vowed to go to at least three or four employment agencies a week until she found a job.

The following three weeks, consisted of the same routine for Shondra. Each week, she visited her probation officer as scheduled. When he asked her if she was searching for a job, she showed him copies of all the applications that she had submitted. She showed him proof of registration with temporary employment agencies. He gave her trite advice that she had heard at the job placement programs repeatedly. "Dress in proper attire, don't be nervous, maintain eye contact, have a positive attitude..." At the end of each visit she thanked him and headed to her next destination, a visit with Reverend Garrett and the Christian Coalition.

Reverend Garrett was pleased that Shondra was visiting his office at least once a week and participating the activities that the organization sponsored. And although he had only known her for three weeks, he agreed to be a personal reference should she need one for a job application. Matthew Garrett asked her if she was still living with Frieda and Booby. "I don't have anywhere else to stay. I don't have a job or money to move out on my own." She sighed. "Most landlords or real estate agents do a standard background checks almost each time I apply for a lease." "I'm not surprised. But don't feel too bad because it's just about impossible to find affordable housing even without a criminal record. You may end up staying with your friends for some time." "Reverend, what is really criminal is how the community continues to punish ex-felons. I've filled out over forty job applications. I've had to answer questions about my criminal history on each and every one of them. So many potential employers will automatically reject people with criminal backgrounds." Shondra said in a frustrated tone of voice. "You may have to endure being rejected or turned away many times before you are hired. Just keep the faith and take one day at a time. Whatever you do, do not lie on the application. If you do you risk a background check that will not only expose the lie, but will also interfere with the new positive and law-abiding lifestyle you are trying to establish. You won't have to go through that after you get off of probation and your attorney Lana Irwin gets your rights and record restored. I heard that she's a real good attorney." He tried to assure her. "You are right about that, she is good, real good." Shondra said as she thought about the last time she visited Lana in her office. She made a mental note to try to make an appointment with her. She cut her visit with Reverend Garrett short forgoing her usual group counseling session in order to spend a little more time at the OWD office where she would look for employment.

After a quick bite to eat at a nearby McDonalds, she made her way to the Offender Workforce Development Center. At the center she brushed up on interview techniques, resume preparation and writing effective cover and thank-you letters. After the counseling and mock interviews were over she and several other participants checked out a list of employers who hired ex-felons. Wyndham Hotel, Zenith Electronics, W.W. Grainger, Southwest

Airlines, Delta Faucets, Hanes, Fuji Film, and LifePoint Healthcare Corp. were newly listed. Shondra jotted down the names of these companies with the intention of checking out their web page for possible employment.

LaShondra's O.W.D. counselor was in the computer lab observing and offering help to the eight people who were doing online job searches. When he approached LaShondra, he suggested that she put in an application for a switchboard operator position that was being offered by a newly listed employer. "The closest I've ever come to switchboard operating is occasionally talking to one on the phone. I've never done that type of work before. "You will operate switchboards and connect callers to the appropriate person. The company will provide paid training on how to operate PBX, private branch exchange switchboard, or voiceover Internet protocol switchboards," said the O.W.D. counselor who had already perused the new job listings long before Shondra got a look at them. "No college degree required, must have excellent communication skills and a friendly personality, and computer knowledge. Zero to two years of experience in the field or in a related area. Worker will follow instructions and pre-established guidelines to perform the functions of the job. Typically reports to a supervisor or manager." Shondra read the ad aloud. "I'll apply for that if all I have to do is handle incoming, outgoing, and interoffice calls." "You will probably have to relay messages and supply information to callers but I'm sure that will be no problem for you. The starting salary is twenty-four thousand. That should be enough to get you back on your feet so to speak." He assured her. "Well, I should get busy filling out this application. May I use your name as a reference?" She asked. "As long as you are not planning on using that switchboard to commit a crime." He smiled. "To be honest, I'm not allowed to give references because every ex-felon who comes through the door looking for a job would expect me to vouch for him or her." "Never mind, I think I have enough references. Just wish me luck." She said. "Fill out that application. Then go in for the interview and remember everything we practiced and went over during our workshops. I have a very good feeling about this job being just for you Mrs. Jackson. I feel like in a few short weeks, you will be getting a paycheck with your name on it from LifePoint Healthcare Corporations."

On Monday of week five, Shondra got a call back from Randstad which advertised itself as a world leader in matching great people with great companies. During her visit the previous week, one of their agents listened carefully to her employment needs and qualifications. Her college transcript which indicated that she was proficient in MS Word, Outlook, and Excel as well as her professional appearance and demeanor impressed the agent and he worked diligently to match her skills and qualifications to the right job and company. The references that she had managed to obtain from Lana Irwin, also worked on her behalf. "Our client, a Fortune 500 company, located right here in Minneapolis, is looking for a long-term Switchboard Operator. Training for this position will be handled on the job. You will be responsible for answering and transferring incoming calls to the appropriate parties, greeting clients who come into the office for onsite meetings, restocking office supplies, and assisting the Site Services team with various administrative projects." Shondra could barely contain herself. She wanted to pinch herself to be sure that this was really happening. "Do you have any questions?" He asked. Trying to contain her happiness, she responded with a broad smile. "When do I begin? What are my hours? Will I be paid during training?" "You should go directly to their office after you leave here to fill out you tax information and whatever other paperwork they have for you. The hours are Monday through Friday from 8:00 AM. until 5:00 PM. and yes you will be paid during training." He answered and wished her luck. She thanked him and shook his hand vigorously before giving him a bear hug. "I'm sorry, that was unprofessional. I'm just so happy you believed in me and gave me the opportunity to work for this company. I promise I won't let down, sir." "I hope that's true because they send us a monthly evaluation on your progress for the first three months of your employment and if they are not satisfied with your performance, they can and will terminate you at any time." He warned. "You don't have to worry about that, because I plan on being the best switchboard operator that company has ever had!" She assured him as she left his office.

Chapter 48

$\mathcal{Q}$uinton broke the news to Andrea three months earlier that he was being considered for a new television programs that would be aired in California. After she learned of his selection on his Facebook page, Andrea phoned Quinton and invited him to meet her at McCormick and Schmick's, their favorite watering hole in downtown Minnesota, for celebratory drinks.

Although the two were scheduled to meet for dinner later in the week, she couldn't wait that long to congratulate him. Andrea wanted to have a giant bash in his honor, but decided put it on hold until she learned his schedule and had time to plan the event. Andrea scanned the fabulous room that was reminiscent of an old country club until she spotted Quinton signaling her in his direction. She walked toward the bar stool where he sat. He stood up and pulled out a seat for her.. Andrea ordered a Gold Margarita which consisted of sauza gold & fresh lime juice. The bartended appeared to be very busy but it didn't take very long for her drink to arrive

"Congratulations on landing that reality TV. Deal. I knew you would be the best candidate for that new program." She told him. "I'm glad that you had confidence in me. For a while, I didn't think I would get the job. The competition for the new program called

A Brand New You, was fierce." He responded. "Is that the name of your TV program A Brand New You? Andrea asked." "That's the name of my show A Brand New You. He assured her. "Does that mean that you are going to get all brand new on me when you're a big shot Hollywood star?" She questioned.

"With so many plastic surgery shows like The Swan, Nip Tuck, Extreme Makeover, and Dr. 90210 already airing one would wonder what type of new plastic surgery show writers and producers could possibly come up with. Andrea told Quinton before picking a jumbo fried shrimp from an appetizer plate that he had already ordered. "I hope you are not thinking about playing the role of an egotistical, oversexed, morality-challenged, self -absorbed womanizer like Julian McMahon" "Julian McMahon, who's that?" Quinton quizzed. "Julian McMahon played to role of Dr. Christian Troy on Nip Tuck. That show was supposed to be dramatic but it only satirized plastic surgery. I'm surprised that show lasted six seasons." She answered.

Quinton took a swig of Rob Roy before responding. "I thought very carefully before I agreed to do the show. I am aware that being on this type of reality TV show would involve being exposed to everyone. Family, friends, neighbors, former school teachers, the boss, old flame, you name it. Everyone will get to peep into my world." "Is this something you can handle? You wouldn't mind if people who used to know you talk about you? They will definitely have something to say and it may not always be flattering. I don't know if I'd like to live any part of my life in a fishbowl with very little privacy." Andrea responded then asked. "What is the show's concept? "It will be about me and two other prominent doctors

343

doing everything from performing plastic surgery on someone who wants to supercharge a careers and become more competitive in the workplace facility to reattaching limbs or repairing the face of someone who had a horrific accident. The show will explore the gamut of plastic surgery. Elective surgeries will be performed in a beautiful Las Vegas plastic surgery while plastic surgery emergencies will take place in an Emergency Room of a real hospital. It's very different from my current T.V. show which focuses on Jane Doe who just wants breast augmentation or Joe Blow who wants male breast reduction. My new show will be very, very different." Quinton informed her.

"Some folk may believe that operating on people who want to get a career boost borders on being extreme, but can we really deny that physical attractiveness does sometimes impact career advancement? I keep up with the latest research done in my field and based on statistics from the American Academy of Facial Plastic and Reconstructive Surgery, approximately two thirds of its members reported that many of their male and female patients, had cosmetic surgery with the goal of remaining competitive in the workplace." Quinton informed Andrea.

"I remember a heated discussion in my grad school psychology class. The professor pointed out that a tall person was more likely to be employed than a short person who met more qualifications. He went on to point out that one who was perceived to be average weight would be chosen over a heavier person, lighter complexioned blacks were at one time considered better looking than their dark skinned sisters and brothers. Members of the class argued that it wasn't really fair. To prove his point, the professor pointed out the research that showed good-looking college graduates were more likely to get hired, and supervisors who are attractive tended to be better respected. So, I suppose in this day and age, a scalpel can make all things equal." Andrea responded.

"The first episode of our program will focus on three individuals who decide to invest in surgeries in order improve their physical appearance and make them appear more employable. One doctor will perform a hair transplant and give his patient a more youthful hairline. The other plastic surgeon, a black female, will fatten up a pair of thin lips, and give the patient higher cheek bones. I will perform a relatively new cosmetic procedure on a young Korean pop star who wants her face reshaped to give her an elfin, anime-like appearance." The procedure, informally known as V-line surgery, involves breaking and shaving the jawline to create a V-shaped face. Koreans like the V-line shape because gives the face a certain fragility, and childlike appearance." Quinton said. "I think that is some stone cold Michael Jackson shit and someone is going to end up with a fucked up face," Andrea predicted. She was now clearly a bit tipsy and feeling no pain.

"What I really want to know is, are you going to accompany me to the California for my first taping? I know it's asking a lot, but coming with me on a trip to California may be just what you need as you get over what you went through this year. I mean, the misuse of your personal information has put tremendous pressure on you and this trip could help bring some normalcy back into your life." "You know Q, you may have a point. It's time for me to move on with my life, do something exciting, and get away from Minnesota for a while anyway."

Chapter 49

*I*t was around 9 P.M. when the two lively couples arrived at the Blue Nile Ethiopian restaurant for an Ethiopian meal and to partake in the traditional custom of sharing food by eating from one giant plate. Michelle, Todd, Andrea, and Quinton had been there before and knew this visit would not be disappointing. As soon as they walked in they were greeted in Amharic, by a very friendly middle-aged woman with a warm smile. She guided them through the somewhat busy main dining room where there was a hum of chatter coming from the crowed tables. She asked them if we've ever been here before. Michelle answered right away "I've been here at least seven or eight times over the past year and the food is simply amazing."

The restaurant was decorated with traditional African musical instruments, African inspired art, a few mesobs or vibrantly patterned circular tables covered with lids, and chairs with beautiful wood carvings. Classical Ethiopian music played softly in background gave the restaurant a somewhat romantic and elegant ambiance. The attractive foursome sat in the chairs that surrounded a large four foot tall mesob. "Too bad the restaurant does not offer the small barchuma stools. We could really experience Ethiopian dining." Quinton remarked. "Negro please!" Todd responded. "Your big, tall long legged behind would not be able to get back up after you sit on one of those small eight inch high stools." They all laughed. When the server came to take their order. Quinton asked if he could get a barchuma to sit on. The server looked around the room and told him that they were all taken. "Those stools are probably for decoration, most American who eat here are not accustomed to sitting that close to the floor. After sitting on a barchuma, many become uncomfortable after about a half hour." Andrea said. There were a few East Africans, engaged in lively conversation in their native tongue, sitting on barchumas around a communal table at one end of the dining room. Several other low seats were being used by four or five young people who appeared to be in their early twenties. Andrea noticed that the diners at the table next to her ordered some Ethiopian coffee which had a wonderful, smoky aroma. The roasted coffee roasting mixed with the incense was almost intoxicating, she thought as she inhaled deeply and took in the wonderful fragrances before looking over the restaurant's menu.

"Tena Yistilign," Quinton greeted the older ethnic looking server who bought them hot towels along with hand sanitizer so the group could clean their hands before the meal. "Tadiyass" the server who was dressed in traditional Ethiopian garb of a long skirt and cotton blouse, responded informally in a thick African accent. Michelle, Todd, Quinton, and Andrea each wiped their hands in their own individual towel. Instead of discarding the towels, they all knew that they were to keep them nearby for use as napkins. "I am fascinated by the Ethiopians belief that eating from the same plate gives those who share a sense of brotherhood and builds a sense of loyalty," Andrea said to her friends. Quinton added, "They also believe that the sharing food in this manner can also be used to strengthen family ties, and resolve conflicts." The group ordered a beef, lamb, chicken, and veggie sampler. They ordered drinks and talked while they waited for the food to arrive.

After ten or fifteen minutes, the server returned and placed a very large platter containing beef alicha wot --a mild stew cooked in turmeric, garlic, and ginger sauce; lamb key wot-- a curried stew in hot chili sauce and exotic spices; doro wot--chicken, tekel gomen cabbage, carrots and potatoes simmered in a mild sauce; shiro wot-- highly seasoned ground chickpeas cooked with onions, garlic, and beriberi sauce in front of them. The various foods were decoratively arranged around the large platter which was draped with the crepe like real injera made of Teff. Their server placed two long-necked bottles of Tej, an amber-colored honey wine, two bottles of dark colored beer and two separate plates of injera on the table. Quinton thanked the server again the he tore off a piece of injera into about a three inches square and used it to swoop up a small portion and roll the food in-the same way someone would roll a huge cigarette. He held the food with his long, well-man-icured fingers for a brief minute and said, "This is an Ethiopian tradition called gursha. It is basically an act of kindness, respect, and affection." Then he directed the food towards Andrea's mouth. Todd followed his lead and said "Let me give my baby gursha also and hand-fed Michelle from the same plate. Andrea exchanged gursha with Quinton. Having visited Ethiopia several times, he told her "amesege'nallo" which means thank you in the language.

"I love this tradition" Michelle said as she exchanged gursha with her mate. They each sampled different foods by using the spongy, sour, pliable Ethiopian flat bread that came with the meal, to scoop up the various shared dishes instead of forks and knives. "How ingenious! Using injera as both an eating utensil and a surface for other foods to lie on." Ethiopians came up with the brilliant idea of using injera not only to line giant centerpiece platters but also to soak up the sauces and spices of the various dishes piled on top." Michelle and Andrea drank honey wine while Todd and Quinton had a dark Ethiopian beer called Hakim. "Some of this food is really spiiiiicccyyyy. You really have to know what you are ordering or check the menu carefully." Michelle remarked. Andrea nodded in agreement and said "You are so right." "I've ordered food here without a clue what it was, and what I've always gotten was a plate of awesomeness whether the food was spicy or mild." Todd said after tasting the gomen cabbage, carrots, and potatoes.

"Praise God for the bees that help make this honey wine. "Andrea laughed as the smiling server poured more tej. "The tej may be delicious but this dark Ethiopian beer is pretty also good." Quinton said. "However, we should get some real drinks to celebrate your new California career. Inviting us to join you for dinner here was a great way for us to get together, celebrate, and wish you all the best before you leave." Todd told Q. Michelle added, "I can't say that I like the fact that my best girl is going along with you. What will I do here without my friend?" Michelle said. "It's not forever, Michelle. I'll be back home in roughly one or two months." "Getting away and changing environments will do her a world of good. Quinton quickly cut in. We are going to celebrate not only my new television program, we are going to celebrate the end of the identity theft fiasco that Andrea had to endure." "Well, what are we waiting for, let's move on upstairs where we can have a few cocktails while we check out tonight's featured performers." Todd said after he paid for all four dinners.

The upstairs section of the Blue Nile was alive with energy. It was always best to get to the lounge area early, around ten-thirty or eleven p.m., and sit back and watch the crowd grow. The foursome were in for a night of high energy, irresistible mixed rhythms and as they walked pass the slightly lit Blue Room, Andrea got a glimpse of people enjoying themselves sitting on couches, doing hookah and having a few drinks. Soft jazz was playing in the background, as two small groups of men seated on leather couches chatted about sports and current events. Quinton, Andrea, Todd, and Michelle proceeded to the Velvet Room where there was more of a club feeling, and more people were dancing to a mixture of Reggae-Ethiopian music. This room had less seating than the first and was slightly darker, but it had a full bar and live entertainment. The two good looking, well dressed, couples sat down at the last empty table for four. The featured performer was Ethiopian reggae singer Jah Lude Awol. Jah Lude sang in Amharic a variety of melodies from his latest CD. His feel good songs infused Ethiopian music with reggae rhythms and his catchy melodies gave off good vibes and positive messages.

After dancing his way back to the table with a drink in each hand, Quinton sat down and gave one of the drinks to Andrea. He then remarked, "That last song, Inde Isachew, is an ode to all the great leaders of Ethiopia. The last time I heard him perform that song, I was in Ethiopia on two month medical mission with Operation Smile." "I downloaded Jah Lude's Yachin Neger CD to my MP3 just two weeks ago! I had no idea I would be seeing a live performance of the music tonight! He's been touring places like Europe, Japan, and Australia!" Andrea, also a fan of Amharic music, said. "Quinton took a drink of his Manhattan and said, "He'll be in the U.S. for a few weeks. His next stop is Atlanta." "Is that right?" Michelle asked. "Todd is going to be in Atlanta working on a project for two or three weeks. I suppose that would be a great time for me to take some time off of work and tag along with my hubby. "Hold up, Baby! Taking some time off to stay with me in Atlanta is not tagging along." Todd asserted before hugging Michelle and planting an affectionate kiss on her cheek. They both knew that Michelle had been toying with opening her own law office in Georgia for months and they had already planned on visiting Atlanta. Michelle smiled and winked at Todd before turning her attention to Andrea.

"Speaking of trips and vacations, I am going to miss you when you leave town, Girlfriend." Michelle said. "Do you have enough leave to stay in Los Angeles for three month?" She asked. Andrea answered. "I will not have to use my vacation days or sick days because I will telecommute while I'm in L.A. I may occasionally fly here to attend meetings and touch base with a supervisor. Much of my work will involve conference calls, videoconferencing, e-mailing financial and analytical support to my company and making sure that the company's forecasting goals are met." "Sort of like being away from the mother-ship." Todd laughed. "Andrea will be very good at it because she's self-motivated, focused, and flexible. This woman definitely possess the temperament and skills to succeed as a virtual team member." Quinton said. "It's only for a few months, I'll be back before you know it." Andrea assured her friend.

Todd said "Michelle, a lot of your interaction is digital as it is. You two stay on G-chat, Twitter, or Facebook, when you're not holding entire texting conversations. So distance will not sever your connection. You girls are two best friends who can survive anything and when you see each other again, you'll pick up right where you left off." "That's true, we do a lot of texting, and a lot of Facebook, a lot of twitter, and a lot of e-mail. The only thing we haven't done was talk to each other on Skype." Michelle laughed. "There's the solution! You two can be virtual friends. Andrea is already a virtual team for her company." Quinton laughed.

When he finished singing at least six of his song from his album, Jah Lude began to sing Fayamo, a reggae song mixed with Oromiffa. He sang a few words and then he invited members of the audience who liked the song to gather on the dance floor as his musicians played upbeat Amharic mix music with traditional Ethiopian instruments including the krar, flute, drums and mesenko. Quinton and Andrea joined the group of mostly local West African men and women who had happily gathered on the dance floor. Many of the dancers allowed their whole body to follow the multiple rhythmic patterns hypnotically swaying their heads, necks, chests and shoulders, and moving their hips while others just moved a few parts of their bodies. An East African man and woman was having fun teaching their traditional dance moves to a Caucasians couple who seemed to be having the time of their lives.

"Michelle and Todd, I know you two are not fans of smoke, but you should try to experience the art of hookah smoking and sample different flavors of shisha at least once," Quinton told his friends. The smoke will not bother you that much because the room has high ceilings." "That's okay, Todd and I will pass on the Hookah Room. You two go on and knock yourselves out," Michelle laughed. "I hope you mean that figuratively and not literally." Andrea gave her a hard look before softening up and laughing. Michelle, a non-smoker, remained in the Velvet Room and ordered a coconut Mojito. As the couple left them behind, Michelle told Todd. "You know, the whole idea of doing shisha reminds me of Alice in Wonderland. In my mind, I picture Quinton as Absalom, the caterpillar in Tim Burton's version puffing a hookah." Todd added "I read in Men's Health Magazine that The World Health Organization issued an advisory note on waterpipe tobacco smoking. The article warned that waterpipe smokers and second-hand smokers are at risks for the same kinds of disease as are caused by cigarette smoking, including cancer, heart disease, and respiratory disease. I'm surprised that Dr. Q. would even indulge in smoking."

In the Blue Room, Andrea checked out a pageful of different flavors for patrons who wanted to experience some tokes from the water pipe to choose from. It was her first time trying hookah, Quinton suggested strawberry daiquiri for her because she liked fruity-flavored drinks. After the Hookah arrived, Q. schooled Andrea on doing shisha, "You puff like you're sucking in air." Andrea gave it a try. "You got to do it hard enough that the water in the bowl moves." Q. said. She immediately did as he said. Andrea, who had never even had a cigarette or smoked anything before, got

353

woozy after four or five puffs." "Damn" she said, my head feels is as light as a feather. It feels like my brain is spinning." "Well, you better not have a drink of alcohol unless you want to amplify that effect." Quinton said as stopped blowing smoke rings long enough to down a big gulp of dark colored beer. Andrea took in another toke. "Ease up a moment, Baby." He said to Andrea and warned her. "Your throat maybe a little uncomfortable the rest of the night and in the morning, so make sure you don't have a lot of talking to do tomorrow morning." "I'm done with this, I just wanted to try it. I don't think I'm ready for the side effect of smoking whether it's a cigarette, blunt, or Hookah. I'm too pretty to let smoking fuck me up." Andrea said. "When men get wrinkles and grey hair, women think they look sexy. Women get wrinkles and grey hair men think they are old hags." She added. "You will never look like an old wrinkled grey haired hag, as long as I can get my hands on a scalpel. I promise you that shit." Quinton laughed. Andrea couldn't resist joining in on the joke. "You can feature me on your plastic surgery reality television show. It'll probably run for thirty years. You can pull back or fill in my crow's feet and wrinkles and your co-host can transplant some thick black or auburn hair plugs into my scalp in order to correct my thin grey hair." "That would be a good episode, I'll present the idea up to the producers," Quinton said. After spending nearly an half hour in the Velvet Room doing hookah, chatting, and people watching, Andrea and Quinton made their way back to the Blue Room to join Michelle and Todd who were on the dance floor doing some funky moves. Andrea and Michelle jumped in and joined them with some groovy moves of their own. They had a ball on the dance floor. Dinner and Dancing at the Blue Nile with Dr. Q. was terrific RX for Andrea. She was glad that Quinton set up the double date. Now she optimistically looked forward to spending more time with the handsome, talented, fun-loving doctor, soon to be television celebrity in LA.

Epilogue

Andrea

*A*ndrea sent certified letters to each of the three credit reporting agencies and instructed them to freeze her credit information. The credit agencies sent her a secret pin number which allowed only her to unlock her credit reports. Whenever she wanted to apply for a loan or credit card, she had to inform Experian, TransUnion, and Equifax to leave the account open so that the loan company to contact them, and then close it again. Bynum Finance Company, Best Buy, Nordstrom's, Dell Computer, Kohl and Haynes eventually absolved Andrea from the debts LaShondra incurred during her identity crime spree.

In spite of her problems with personal credit, her hopes and aspirations for the future didn't ebb. After a few months of therapy, she regained her inner strength and put forth great effort to get back a sense of control, empowerment and invulnerably. Denico Paint Corporation merged with the Polish paint company, Teknos becoming Teknos-Denico. With Denico taking second billing, Andrea's job as financial forecasting analyst took a hit

Andrea Denico's C.E.O. and C.F.O. wrote impressive job recommendations on her behalf. The C.E.O. and the C.F.O. both indicated that she had the knowledge necessary to monitor the financial status of Denico's projects, identify trends and recommend actions. They also spoke highly of her ability to provide information to management by assembling and summarizing data and making presentations of findings, analyses, and recommendations. The glowing letters from those two high profile executives was the ticket she needed to embark on a new AT and T career in Atlanta, Georgia. Andrea was elated with her new role at AT and T because she knew it could potentially be a steppingstone to higher level positions, such as director of finance, financial controller, or even chief financial officer.

Quinton

After moving to Los Angeles, Dr. Taylor soon became one of the most sought after celebrity doctors in Hollywood, making frequent appearances on television including The Today Show, The View, Access Hollywood, and even Spanish NBC Telemundo. Quinton appeared as himself in a reality television show that centered on showcasing plastic surgery extremes. The program aired successfully the first year and was picked up for another season. The extremely handsome, very popular, outgoing seemingly eligible, doctor became tabloid fodder. He was often photographed by paparazzi who were out to earn a few bucks by submitting pictures of him whenever they caught a glimpse of his social life.

On the program 'A Brand New You,' patients often went under the knife to enhance their chances of landing better-paying jobs and adoring spouses. The program occasionally showcased very unusual and sometimes controversial procedures. One such procedure involved Dr. Q. and his on screen colleagues performing surgical procedures on both male and female Korean patients whose ideal of beauty was softer, slimmer jawlines, eye lifts, and raised nose bridges. Another episode showcased the highly skilled doctor performing reconstructive plastic surgery that involved replacing a thumb that was lost in a work related accident. Without a thumb, the female patient lost her ability to carry out many different tasks, one as simple as tying your shoes. Dr. Q. removed the woman's large toe and used it as a thumb replacement. The woman was interviewed on Good Morning America along with Dr. Taylor several weeks after her amazing reconstructive surgery. After the host showed clips of Dr. Taylor attaching the toe to his patient's hand, the patient going through physical therapy, and the woman eventually tying shoe laces and braiding her long hair, they both answered a few questions. The woman demonstrated the flexibility of her thumb and explained that she did have feeling in the digit. She showed a small blister on her new thumb and laughed about an incident which involved touching a hot frying pan just a few days before that morning television appearance.

Quinton answered questions about how he restored the damaged nerves and how reconstructive surgery can help accident victims realize a better quality of life. The host praised Dr. Taylor's television show for presenting an opportunity for people to learn about the merits of reconstructive surgery and allowing viewers to experience a world outside of their own.

LaShondra
After a probationary period at her new job, LaShondra became one of the most proficient PBX switchboard operators at the high

volume call center at which she worked. She made routine restitution payments to the Minnesota Department of Correction and Rehabilitation each month usually paying more than required. Her habit of paying more toward her restitution than required enabled her to pay the debt off earlier than the court had prescribed and start a new chapter in her life. She enrolled in an online college completion program that allowed her to be at home with her daughter when she was not working.

After she satisfied her court imposed probation, Attorney Lana Irwin successfully petitioned the court to expunge her client's record. LaShondra's professional as well as personal relationship with her attorney seemingly came to an end when Lana and her husband, Lester, moved to Ohio where Lana went on to manage her father's law firm. Booby was given the opportunity to put in a bid for Lester's restaurant business since it was unlikely that he would be given a regular part on Meet the Brown's.

Michelle

Michelle Shepherd became a member of the Georgia Association of Black Women Attorneys, a volunteer organization of Black women attorneys. As an active GABWA member, she is one of the state's most powerful advocates for women and children. Last year, Michelle helped GABWA spearhead a School Daze Party that was held at Dave and Busters. That effort brought so many donations of school supplies that the organization was able to service every school in Atlanta. She also finds time in her busy schedule to act as a mentor with the Sister 2 Sister program, and regularly volunteers with faith-based organizations in her community.

As a private practitioner, Attorney Michelle Shepherd has conducted numerous jury trials throughout the State of Georgia and has represented clients in high-profile cases. Her area of expertise in family law matters, includes but is not limited to cases related to deprivation and abuse, defense of abandonment, child support enforcement, child visitation and temporary protective orders. Always working to protect the best interest of children, Michelle routinely handles numerous cases ranging from simple assault to aggravated child molestation. Some of the juvenile cases she's handled includes petty theft, burglary, and auto theft in Atlanta and the surrounding counties.

Michelle keeps her legal skills sharp by attending regular training. She participated in Cobb County Parent Attorney Seminar, Parent Attorney Training and Child, the National Association for Counsel for Children and Parent Attorney Training. She is a current member of the Georgia State Bar Association's Child Protection & Advocacy, Family Law, and General Practice and Trial Law sections.

When she is not practicing law, Michelle spends quality time with the love of her life, her husband Todd. They enjoy relaxing in their five thousand thirty three sq. ft., six bedroom, five full and one half bathroom home in the affluent Alpharetta Georgia area. Todd insisted on the large home because when he and Michelle are ready, the couple plan to bring many little Shepherds into their lives.

Terry
Terry left the country for three weeks on a business trip in China. At his request, Sandy went along as his traveling companion.

Baiwei Electric Appliance Company, one of the leading manufacturers of electric blow dryers, hair straighteners, hair curlers, hair clippers, hair brushes was the go to people for hairdressing tools. The company was located in the High-tech Industrial Park in Henggang Town, Longgang District in Shenzhen, China. Terry contracted the company to produce In2Hair titanium, tourmaline and ceramic plated flat irons with a three hundred sixty degree swivel cords in three different widths and colors. He also ordered professional gold plated and tourmaline hair tongs, and professional blow dryers. All of the products would carry his business logo and branded colors.

When he was not negotiating the manufacture and the exportation of his new trademarked hair styling tools, Terry and Sandy toured Longgang. One day, they rode the Metro to Shenzhen Cultural Center and to Longgang Museum of Hakka Culture. The following day, they went to Minsk World, a military theme park. They had a grand time at Window of the World Theme Park where they saw reproductions of some of the world's most famous attractions. While they were in China, Terry surprised Sandy with a proposal. Sandy accepted and a spring wedding is being planned.

Discussions Questions

1. A cast of five characters were introduced early on in the book. Did you find their number confusing or were you able to follow along easily?
2. What character did you especially like or dislike? How would you describe that character? Does the character remind you of someone you know?
3. Which character, in your opinion, was most intriguing?
4. Have you or someone you know experienced a credit predicament similar to Andrea's? How was it handled?
5. LaShondra impulsively committed credit card fraud in an act of anger over Eric's treatment of her. Even her best friends, Booby and Frieda, are uncomfortable with her misdeeds. What do you think of her behavior? Have you, or someone close to you, ever acted on impulse in response to a situation that was hurtful or confusing?
6. Discuss the novel's title and why you think it was chosen.
7. Do you have a friendship like that between Andrea and Michelle? Do you think their friendship is a realistic portrayal? How does a friend like this help you get through life's problems?

8. What did you think of Sterling's behavior with Andrea? Was Sterling out of line professionally?

9. What motivated LaShondra's actions at Booby's party? Do you think that her behavior that night was unusual for her?

10. Can you recall a passage or chapter that was particularly interesting to you?

11. Were you as surprised as Andrea to learn of LaShondra's punishment? Do you think the ruling was fair?

12. If you were Andrea, would you be able to forgive LaShondra? Does LaShondra deserve forgiveness?

13. Andrea McNair found her solution in leaving town. Do you think that was a good decision for her? And is Dr. Quinton Taylor a good romantic choice? Do you believe it will last?

14. Where do you suppose Andrea and Dr. Quinton Taylor will be a year from the end of the book? Five years? What will their lives look like?

15. Is the ending satisfying? Why or why not? Were you surprised by the book's conclusion or did you see it coming? What unanswered questions linger at the end of the novel?

Meet the Author

A.J. Hall earned a B.A. in Fine Arts from Norfolk State University and a M.Ed. from Old Dominion University. She taught high school art in North Carolina and in Virginia. Hall is currently working on her second novel, a sequel to Identity Rip-off which takes place in Atlanta, GA. She is a resident of Hampton Roads, Virginia.